Run to the Blue

by

P N Johnson

Burning Chair Limited, Trading As Burning Chair Publishing
61 Bridge Street, Kington HR5 3DJ

www.burningchairpublishing.com

By P N Johnson
Edited by Simon Finnie and Peter Oxley
Cover by Burning Chair Publishing

First published by Burning Chair Publishing, 2023

ISBN: 978-1-912946-32-7

Also by P N Johnson:

Killer in the Crowd

Dedicated to the amazing friends and colleagues I was
privileged to work with in radio and TV

Somewhere between Calabria and Corfu the blue really begins.
- Lawrence Durrell

1. London

"Quick! The jury's coming back, he's going down for sure!" shouted a reporter, and the familiar press pack surged towards the doors. I was standing in the shadow of the Old Bailey, the Central Criminal Court, on a grey late-April morning in London. Next to me, other reporters were hastily scribbling scripts, and cameramen and women were readying their kit for the imminent feeding frenzy of rolling news.

I looked down to check that my constant companion, my phone, was still on silent. There were three missed calls within the last two minutes: two from my best friend Jane and one, just seconds ago, from Steve, my editor, back in the newsroom. A text arrived saying I had voicemail, then another from Sven, my husband. It just read: *So sorry*. I was curious, even concerned, but there wasn't time to call him and find out what he was apologising for. I dropped the phone in my bag and rushed in with the others. Jake, my cameraman, called after me; he sounded desperate but there was no time. Without looking I waved at him and hurried back to the courtroom.

There he was, centre stage in Court Number One: the accused, standing impassively in the dock flanked by wary guards. Solid and shaven headed, his smart suit was gone, and he now wore a tracksuit which reflected his beginnings back in the clubs and pubs of London. A low tee shirt under the zipped top exposed a dragon tattoo slashed by a jagged scar, Ken 'Lucky' Lean's pretence of being a respectable businessman had fallen away, revealing a criminal chameleon in his true colours. Gone was the respectable carehome owner who'd been held high as an example, a benchmark of the best; he was about to be convicted as a fraudster who'd tricked old people out of millions, and worse, much worse, as a murderer who'd cruelly injected many of them with a needle of death.

Lean knew the game was up, and the last card he had to play was intimidation. Although I couldn't risk showing it, I was scared stiff. He leaned forward, looking every inch the hard man, radiating menace as the members of the jury filed back to their seats. Like me, the jurors were careful not to meet his gaze, as if frightened he'd turn them to stone if their eyes met, like some kind of medusa of menace, a king of crime. The king, though, was about to lose his crown and be reduced to just another criminal whose reign had come to an end. And it was largely due to me. Yes, me.

I'm a *star* reporter, or so I'm told. You may have seen me, always there on the news, interviewing prime ministers, pop stars and victims. But behind the fixed stare and the authoritative smile, I'm just Tess, the not-so-confident girl from the 1970s semi-detached house, who'd clawed her way to the top. At times I'm frightened, often unsure. Sometimes crying after the camera stops, but determined to do a great job and, here in this court, I'd done that. I'd got the story of my career. I'd managed to secretly film Ken Lean murdering one of his victims, and I'd helped to expose the staggering extent of his crimes. I shone out from the crowd, but no one crossed Ken Lean with impunity. Even from the dock, he posed a threat. A threat to me.

As I took my seat in the press gallery, he craned his neck and caught my eye. He coolly raised one hand and pointed at me, making his fist into the shape of a gun. He was making it clear that he wouldn't rest until I was dead. Gasps rang out around the room and the guards moved closer to restrain him. He knew he was going down, and we both knew why. I was compelled to stare back, outwardly unmoved but inwardly petrified. I could never have imagined the story I uncovered becoming so dangerous or so big. Just as the tension rose, my adrenalin rush stopped and I stifled a giggle as someone in the public gallery sneezed, causing Lean to scream "Shat it!" which led to a burst of laughter from the room.

The final collapse of his defence had come with the showing of a clip from my secret
filming that reduced some spectators to tears, including a few of the jurors. After seeing the irrefutable evidence, the members of the jury were dismissed to consider their verdict. It was unimaginable that it could be anything other than guilty.

"The court will rise," boomed the clerk's voice, heralding the return of the judge. As we got to our feet, I saw a familiar figure scrambling his way over bags and past my neighbours to reach me in the press box. It was Greg, a colleague from the newsroom.

"Overmanning?" I whispered, curious as to why he was there. He frowned, shook his head and handed me a note, squeezing my shoulder warmly as he did.

"Tess, I'm sorry but Steve says you're to read this. Now." I took it from him and recognised the scrawl of our boss, the editor.

Tess, it's absolutely vital you come out of court NOW! Steve.

I looked at Greg, who shrugged and smiled ruefully then took out his notebook and pen; he was the substitute sent to take my place. Confused and angry I slid out of my seat and squeezed past the other reporters. They were obviously surprised to see me leaving. One of them, the new girl from *United News*, was smirking. What did she know that I didn't? I headed towards a side door, fuming. Steve had better have a damn good reason for this.

So, as the judge walked in, I walked out. Jake was waiting for me outside the building, shaking his head and looking pained. He offered me his mobile. He looked like a teenager who'd just failed an exam and didn't want to tell his mum. I'd worked with him for five years and knew him well. Whatever this was, it must be bad. I could already hear Steve's voice coming from the phone, demanding to know where I was.

"Tess, for eff's sake, Tess, this is urgent... Talk to me! Tess Anderson. Talk to me, please. *Now!*"

I was surprised; Steve never shouted, he rarely swore, and he knew I needed to be in court right now for the most important verdict I'd ever covered. The biggest story of my life. This could lead to an award, promotion, a major documentary... The Lean story could even be made into a film. I'd waited months for this trial, and I didn't want to lose my place in history; I wanted to be there at the bitter end. I already knew what I was going to say in my report on the TV news that night. I had been working on my script since before dawn; it was almost written. I just needed the verdict, the judge's comments, the prison sentence and a few reactions. I'd helped to bring this apology for a human being to justice and I deserved to be there when he went down. I'd even taken special pains with my appearance, confident that I'd be reporting the trial verdict live on national TV as the lead story. My brown hair, expensively layered and highlighted, had been carefully blow-dried; my work clothes were simple but sharp. My shoes were new and far too tight, but that was a sacrifice I gladly made: I knew they enhanced my height and gave me an air of authority on camera. My make-up was subtle, as always: I wasn't presenting lifestyle; this was hard news. I wanted viewers concentrating on the story, not my looks.

I grabbed the phone; seconds were precious. "Boss! Can't this wait?" I pleaded. "The jury's back, the judge is about to deliver! I need to be there. Now!"

His words stopped me dead.

"I'm sorry, Tess," Steve said, "but it looks like you've hit the headlines for all the wrong reasons." As he spoke, it began drizzling, the stonework of the Old Bailey dampening by the moment—just like my mood. "I know it's not your fault... this is all down to Sven, but everyone's running it—I can't blame them; it's a hell of a good story. Political dynamite. Tess, your husband is having an affair with a leading member of the government. Look, Greg's in place now, he'll work with Jake and cover the verdict. Your background piece will run, but nothing else. You can't be the story yourself; you know that. Take a few weeks out until the dust settles. Go home now, Tess, and we'll talk later. Bye."

There's an old maxim in journalism: the story is always more important than the reporter, but as I stood there on the phone, I saw two of the Fleet Street boys taking my picture. As their cameras flashed, I felt it start: the rash on my throat that I used to get whenever I was really nervous. I even wore scarves in the early days—I hadn't for years but today it was back. No one could see me like this. My confidence was crashing. I felt sick.

Steve hung up before I could speak. I stood in disbelief, rain splashing on my forehead. Too numb for tears. One of the Fleet Street snappers got nearer, keen on a close up, trying to snatch my reactions, to capture my mood.

"Sod off!" I shouted, raising my fist.

"Woah, Anderson—bit harsh, love!" he said, snapping away. "I'm only getting a story, like you."

Jake touched my shoulder. "Cool it, Tess! They'll quote you; you know that! But, hey, I'm really sorry." He positioned himself between the photographer and me, hugging me close to hide me from the lens. Jake was a wise head on young shoulders. He could see the state I was in. "See you back at base and I'll buy you lunch."

"Thanks, Jake, but I've got to hear this verdict."

"What? Tess, don't be stupid—Steve will freak!"

"I don't care. I can't miss this!" I rushed back through the door, showing my press card to the guards. Jake was pleading with me to turn back as cameras filmed me going in. I ignored him and carried on, reaching the court as the judge was finishing his summing up. The other reporters were whispering and staring at me as I walked in, and then Lean saw me. Standing in the dock he screamed with his harsh East London voice: "DEAD BITCH WALKING!"

There was uproar. I was terrified, my husband had betrayed me, and one of London's biggest villains wanted me dead. I was in a tailspin; my life was breaking up around me. Leaving the building, I held my hand over my throat, which was now glowing red, and realised my whole body was shaking. Outside, I turned my back on the Old Bailey and walked towards Newgate Street, raising my arm to hail a cab. I was doing my best to hold it together, but my mind was whirling. How could Sven have done this? And why did it have to come out today of all days? Not only had my stupid husband betrayed me, but he'd screwed up the most important moment in my career, maybe my life. I was going to be making the news myself for something *he'd* done. Dragged across the headlines for my personal, not professional, life. How could this have happened? I wanted to strangle him. What was he playing at?

As I crossed the road, I caught a glimpse of a motorbike with a rider wearing a black helmet with a silver snake on it coming my way. I ignored it, but the bike suddenly accelerated and seemed to be heading straight for me. I sped up and just got out of its way, stepping sideways between two stationary cars. The bike skidded to a halt and did a U-turn in the road. It seemed to be revving up to come back as a taxi drew up beside me. I opened the passenger door and climbed inside as the bike shot past. "Acton," I said breathlessly to the driver. I pushed myself deep into the well-worn seat and kicked off my new, too-tight shoes. Surely that wasn't just crazy London driving? It seemed deliberate—as if he was trying to run me down. Had the vengeance of the Leans already begun?

As the taxi moved off, I turned round, staring through the rain-splattered rear window. I could see the crowd by the Old Bailey, including lovely Jake—no doubt worrying about me. I pictured the rest of the press pack hard at work, the first of the bunch rushing out. They'd be digesting the sentencing right now. Damn it, I should have been there. The new girl from *United News* would be delighted that I wasn't. Frustration and fear overpowered me. I bit down on my hand and gave a muffled scream.

"Okay, love?" asked the driver.

"Sorry, yes." The smell of cheap, chemical car freshener made me wince. "I'm fine."

"Where to in Acton?"

"Smithsen Street, please. Number fourteen. Thank you."

He didn't reply; he could tell I was in no mood to chat. I pulled out my phone and pressed Sven's number, but as the first ring tone echoed in my ear, I cancelled the call. I just couldn't find the right words to say. Could it really be true? Were all these years—our years—worthless? Anger overtook me and I threw my phone down hard on the seat. Why had he done it? Why of all people had he done it with her? And why did the story damn well have to break today? *Today!*

As we left the Old Bailey behind, the reality of what Sven had done began to sink in. Sure, I'd suspected sometimes—of course I had—every woman does. But I'd never believed it. Not Sven. He was Sven, my Sven. He was handsome, yes, and he mixed with wealthy and beautiful women, but I never really thought he'd stray, never thought he could actually do that. We were so in love; why hadn't I seen the signs? Was he corrupted by her? Somehow forced? Blackmailed? It couldn't be just lust… Surely I was enough?

"You okay back there?" I saw the driver glance at me in his mirror. I must have looked as awful as I felt.

"Sorry. Bad news," I murmured. I rubbed my eyes, trying to blank out thoughts of my spouse's secrets. It didn't matter if I ruined my make-up now; I wasn't going on camera any time soon. I needed to put Sven aside for a moment and focus on another treacherous man. If Ken 'Lucky' Lean—gangster, fraudster, murderer—really had sent that biker just now, then my life was in danger. No matter that he was currently receiving

7

his well-deserved comeuppance in the most famous criminal court in the land—a court I should have been in, to watch him being dragged from the dock by the guards and taken to a cell, hopefully for life. A man like him being locked away was no guarantee of my safety. I could still be *rubbed out* just like his other victims. What if the biker was waiting for me at home to try again? Would tonight's papers carry my death? *Tess Anderson, an award-winning TV reporter, has been found dead near her home in West London. Police say they're treating her death as suspicious and haven't ruled out a link with a news story she's been working on...*

My best friend, Jane, who worked on the Guardian newspaper, would ensure I got a decent obituary at least. I could see her sitting there, writing it—stopping to twist one of her granny's pearl drop earrings, her substitute stress balls: they helped her concentrate, she said. *Tess Anderson went into journalism as a trainee with a local radio station. After joining the BBC in 2003, she quickly established herself as a familiar face and voice on national radio and television. Tess Anderson won numerous awards, including Reporter of the Year. She was married to Sven Richardson, a well-known TV marriage guidance counsellor with a number of celebrity clients. Her editor said...*

I hoped Jane never had to write my obituary, but I often feared she might. Whenever I encounter death, it always made me miss my parents. My mum and dad would have loved to have seen my work. They'd died after a car crash, while I was still in radio and totally loved-up with Sven. I hated it when well-meaning relatives said, *"Oh, your mum and dad would have been so proud of you being on TV."* It just made their absence harder.

"It's so wonderful you've got your job with that radio station, Tess. You'll be so good at it," Mum had said when I became a trainee reporter at East Mids FM. It was a lucky break in such a crowded field. They were both so encouraging, always there. "You'll be on television one day, love, I know it." I really missed them at my wedding too. I'd so wanted them to see the man I

8

loved become my husband. I took him to see them when we first got together, swept away in our whirlwind affair. Mum was bowled over by him. "He's perfect, Tess. Promise me, if you marry him, you'll make it work. The secret of marriage is to not give up." I'd promised her I would, but who could imagine then that he'd betray me in such a public way?

The driver nosed his black cab into yet another line of stationary traffic. I looked into my bag and saw my unused notebook and pen. In an instant I'd gone from being a confident hard-nosed TV reporter to a sobbing wreck huddled in the back seat of a car. In the few hours since I'd left for work that morning, everything in my world had changed. All that had been Sven and Tess was heading into history. Our marriage was broken and the whole world knew why. With a feeling of dread, I opened the news app on my phone. No matter how awful it made me feel, I had to read the gut-wrenching reality about the scandal of the day. My husband was bedding the government's campaigner for moral values. An MP, a member of the Cabinet. One of the most powerful women in the country was there on my phone, pictured kissing my husband. I felt utterly sick.

As we approached my road, I caught a glimpse of a motorbike in the taxi's mirror. The rider was wearing a black helmet with a silver snake on it. It was *him*. He'd followed me from the court. My stomach turned over. This was unreal. I could feel myself shaking, gripping the seat.

"There's a biker following us," I said to the cabbie. "Can we change our route?"

"He can go quicker than me, love, no point. He's probably a courier, unless he's a friend of yours?"

"Not at all. He tried to run me over as I got in."

"Probably just in a hurry—they all are, kids today. Time is money, you know!"

"No, really, he did," I insisted. And as I said it, I knew it was true. The fact that he'd followed me home was all the evidence I needed. What happened outside the Old Bailey had been a deliberate attack.

"Well, I can't shake him off. If he's there when we arrive, I'll have a word. Don't worry."

But I did worry. I worried a lot.

The taxi turned into my street—normally so familiar and welcoming, but not today. Thick clouds cast a shadow over my house. My heart felt drained of love and hope. My head was full of fear. As we drew up near my two-storey terrace, the biker overtook us and drove down the road, stopping at the end. I asked the driver to wait.

Sven's dark blue Audi A4 was parked outside the house. I wondered what to do. I didn't want to meet him; I couldn't face a confrontation, not yet. I'd only fall apart or slap him hard. Two minutes later he came out of the front door, wearing one of his sharp navy suits, his silver-blond hair still as thick and glossy as the day I'd met him.

Unaware of my presence, he unlocked the driver's door of the Audi then reached for his phone. My mobile lit up in my bag. He was calling me. I let it ring until the answerphone kicked in. I waited in the cab until he'd driven away.

Once inside the house I drew the curtains in the sitting room and caught a glimpse of the biker with the distinctive black helmet with its silver snake, now parked at the end of the road, standing by his motorcycle like a hunter watching his prey. He was staring at the house, in no hurry to leave. Why didn't he go? Was he waiting to strike? My thoughts were distracted by the home phone, which suddenly started ringing. The caller ID showed *number withheld;* it was probably a newsdesk, so I ignored it. My mobile told me texts were coming in too, mostly from colleagues—no doubt sending messages of support—but I didn't want to know right now. Social media alerts were pinging and buzzing. The story was probably trending, but I didn't care. I didn't want to see.

I went into the kitchen, made some coffee and switched on the TV. There was one piece of good news at least. Ken Lean had gone down for a minimum of thirty years with no prospect of parole or early release. With any luck he'd die in jail. Nothing less than he deserved. As I walked slowly back towards the hall, I heard the presenter read from the autocue.

"... a special report by Tess Anderson will follow shortly and will show for the first time the dramatic film which helped police secure Lean's conviction. First, more on this lunchtime's breaking political story... Suzanna Heffle, minister for Family Values, has admitted having an affair with celebrity marriage expert Sven Richardson, husband of crime reporter Tess Anderson. Mrs Heffle says it won't affect her ability to carry out her job. The prime minister insists the government's new campaign won't be derailed. Mrs Heffle's husband said he and their two children were absolutely devastated..." I knew how they felt.

I could still barely take in the details, even though I'd read the press coverage on my phone. I stood in the hall, listening and half-watching though the open kitchen door. It was as if subconsciously I sought to protect myself from the reality of what was unfolding by standing in the dim hallway—the nearest equivalent to a dark secluded cave. And there it was: *her* picture on the screen, the woman who'd taken my husband. The newsreader continued to pile on the agony.

"Suzanna Heffle had only launched the Government's new *Let's Stick Together* campaign yesterday afternoon. The campaign aims to persuade couples considering a divorce to reconsider, in a bid to cut down the number of single parent families and help the housing crisis. Free counselling is offered and arbitration to keep couples together. Many of the tabloid papers are showing compromising photographs on their websites of Mrs Heffle and Mr Richardson, allegedly taken whilst she was on an official visit to Paris last month. Opposition MPs are saying—far from reducing the number of single parent families, Suzanna Heffle has created more herself—her own. They're claiming this lunchtime that government policy is in tatters and Number ten is in turmoil. More now from our Political Correspondent Nicky

Adams at Westminster. Nicky…"

I shivered, feeling more lost and alone than ever before. I walked into the sitting room, hidden from the street by the closed curtains. I briefly pulled the material aside and stretched my neck to look down the street. I could see the motorbike was still there but now closer, a few houses along on the other side of the road. He was holding a phone. The man who'd tried to run me down and had followed me from the Old Bailey was staring straight back at me.

2. Chase

I had to speak to someone, but most of my friends were Sven's too. There was only one person I needed right now: if I couldn't turn to my husband I would turn to Jane. She was my *go-to* girl in times of crisis. We'd been good friends since university. I called her mobile knowing she'd be at work at the Guardian where she was a senior sub editor. She'd obviously been expecting me to ring.

"Tess!" Her voice was like a comfort blanket.

I tried to reply but failed to find the words. Tears ran down my cheeks. *"Hi"* was all I managed.

"Oh, love, I'm so sorry. Have you spoken to Sven? I can't believe it."

"No... No I haven't. I don't want to give him the chance to hurt me any more than he already has. What can he say? *Sorry?* Oh, Jane, it's just so horrible. What have you heard?"

I sat back in my favourite chair in our comfortable sitting room with its striped wooden floor and soft blue-white walls. The room we'd spent a weekend painting only a month before, celebrating its revamp with a takeaway, a bottle of wine and sex on the settee, just as we'd done on the night we moved in ten years before. Happy days, but behind me now.

"The story sort of broke about an hour ago. I tried to call you as soon as I heard."

"I've been at the Old Bailey."

"Yes, I know. I'm sorry, we had no idea—otherwise I'd have tipped you off, you know that."

"I hadn't a clue either, but apparently wives often don't. Ironically it was Sven who taught me that, and he should know. He's the one with a PhD in Psychosexual Relationships, he's the celebrity marriage guidance counsellor—and the cheat. You know what's really upsetting me, making me feel sick?"

"No."

"We had sex at the weekend… How could he do that? Was he thinking of her?" My voice faltered. "I know how my mum felt now."

"Your dad played away? You never told me that."

"I try to forget it. Dad strayed, but Mum told me it only happened once. It was when I was six or seven. Mum forgave him; after that they were the perfect couple, I guess. But his affair wasn't all over the news like Sven's."

"Look, I'm going to work through lunch and finish early. Do you want to come round to ours, get away for a bit?"

"Yes, please, I don't want to be here on my own. There's a biker outside, he followed me from the court."

"Really? Call the police, Tess." I got up and moved the curtain. The biker wasn't there.

"No need. He's gone. For good, I hope."

"Look, I'll be home by four. Head over when you want. You can sleep over if you like, in case Sven comes home. You know, to avoid a confrontation… Unless you want to have it out with him?"

"No, I don't. I want to crawl under a stone and hide. So how did the story come out?"

"Someone tipped off the tabloids," Jane said. "They wanted it to coincide with the official launch of that new *Let's Stick Together* campaign. The usual search for a mole in Number Ten goes on. Sadly, it's too good a story when the person saying *Let's*

Stick Together sods off with someone else's husband and crashes her own marriage and his in the process. And it's worse when the person she does it with, your Sven, has a regular TV slot on relationships, I bet some of those celebrity clients of his will be less than chuffed with all this."

"I'm not so *chuffed* myself."

"I know. Sorry."

"You don't think Sven brought Heffle here do you, while I've been working late? They haven't been doing it in our bed, surely?"

"Don't think that way, love. It was probably on neutral ground, you know. Trips away. I never thought he'd do that to you, but..."

"But what?"

"Looking back, I guess there were signs..." She sounded hesitant.

"When?"

"Those Christmas parties last year. I'd never seen him dance with anyone but you—until then."

"Maybe... I've been so wrapped up in the Lean story I've stopped noticing."

"You have been head-down on this for months. But it's not your fault, Tess. None of it's your fault."

"Why *her* though?" I asked. "Why Heffle? She's horrible." I was desperate for answers.

"Who knows? Maybe it's a power thing. She's older, she's driven... she might even be prime minister one day..." Her voice trailed off. "Big hugs when I see you, yes?"

"I need all the hugs I can get right now. You'd better get on if you're finishing early. Thanks for being there."

I ended the call. It still felt unreal, as if I were a character in a film. So this was what it was like to have your marriage exposed as an empty sham.

I hugged my coffee cup in both hands and stared at the wedding photograph on the mantelpiece above the fireplace. We looked totally loved-up, confident and secure. We had the rest of our lives in front of us. I was twenty-three when I met him. I'd just moved to London to work in the radio newsroom at the BBC, fresh from my job as a trainee reporter in local radio. I first saw him standing at the bar at a gig at the Roundhouse in Camden. Jane had dragged me along to see one of her favourite bands—Restless Lovers, fronted by the gorgeous but rather posy Jason L'Amour. It was the band's *Greatest Hits* tour, one of their last after ten years at the top. I knew their songs because Jane was always listening to the Lovers while writing essays, and discussing guys we fancied. She'd just started a job at the Guardian, having worked on a local paper in Wales. We were sharing a flat. We'd taken up our old student relationship where we'd left off and we were having a ball.

Sven had caught my eye as I queued to buy drinks for Jane and myself. I had spotted his bum first, thanks to the tight, faded jeans he was wearing, with a white t-shirt that accentuated his golden tan and grey eyes. He looked as if he'd walked straight out of a TV advert. His shoulders were broad and there were real muscles in his arms and neck, not like most of the boys I'd been with before. And, as for that Nordic silver-gold hair... He turned round and asked if he could save me the trouble of queuing as he was already at the bar. I smiled and asked him to get two glasses of lager. Jane gave me a knowing grin.

There was instantly something between us. As he passed me the drinks his eyes held a playful glint. He asked if he could stand with us to watch the band as he'd come to the gig on his own. We got chatting and he told me he'd been born in Oslo; his dad was Norwegian and his mum English which accounted for his striking Scandinavian looks. His parents were both language teachers. Sven had been brought up in the UK after they moved here when he was seven. We had something in common as my dad had been a teacher too, a deputy head, and my mum had taught in a primary school. Sven explained how he'd studied Psychology and then gained a PhD in Psychosexual Relationships. It was an intriguing if rather daunting chat-up line—*I'm an expert in the psychology of sex and attraction.* He said he'd be able to tell if I fancied him, which of course I did and which of course we both knew. But then, Jane knew too. You didn't need to be an expert to recognise lust at first sight.

The gig was as good as Jane and I'd hoped it would be, and during the final encore my hand ventured sideways and found Sven's. Our fingers met for the first time—hopeful, full of promise and expectation. I didn't want to let him go and only did so for the final applause. When that faded, and the house lights came up, he asked me out for a drink, so I agreed to meet him after work the next night.

I dived in headfirst that evening. After the drink, a curry and another drink, we went back to his flat. He closed the door and turned. We stood there, poised for someone to make the first move, savouring the anticipation, wanting it to last. There aren't too many moments like this in life. This was different, this was special. You could sense the expectation and feel the chemistry in the air.

"So, the curry was good, what shall we have for dessert?" I asked finally. Sven brushed back my hair and then his finger stroked my wrist in tight little circles.

"Two can play at that!" I told him, and wantonly grabbed his other hand, closing my mouth around one finger. After that there was no going back. Neither of us spoke as we kicked off our shoes and walked to his bedroom hand in hand. Words weren't necessary; our bodies said it all. In the doorway of that tiny room, we stopped and we kissed, slowly at first, then our tongues touched and our pulses soared. Blood flowed, breathing quickened and pupils dilated. Clothes were almost torn from our bodies. Flung fast across the floor.

Afterwards we lay there in the wreckage of his bed in tangled, twisted sheets, two lust worn bodies on a journey through the night. There were no shy secrets, no regrets. We didn't want to let each other go and we only broke apart when the light of a demanding dawn forced us to face the reality of looming work.

While I was reminiscing, a text arrived from Steve. I sat up in the chair and stared at my phone.

We should talk. Fancy the Victorian pub nr Holborn tube @ 7? Steve.

I texted back. *Yes. C U then boss. T.* Was I going to be suspended? Sacked? Transferred to special events? Obituaries? Back to the Midlands?

I forced myself to keep calm. The street was empty. At three o'clock, after I'd showered and changed into non-work clothes, I got ready to head to Jane's house in Kentish Town, North London. First though, I wanted to leave a note for Sven. Even for someone who makes their living using words, it was the most difficult thing I'd ever written.

Sven. I want to ask you how and why you could you have done this to me. But I can't.

I can't talk to the one person I know who could give me an answer and help me to understand why my husband, my lover and my friend, has hurt me so much and utterly destroyed me. I don't know where to turn if I can't turn to you.

I'll never understand. Don't try to apologise or to justify it. Whatever clever psychobabble interpretation you can spin, it will never be enough to undo what you've done. It's over. Just go.

I left the house and walked towards West Acton Underground station beneath a leaden sky. The twenty-minute walk was familiar to me. So was something else. As I crossed onto the main road, I saw a motorbike. The rider wore a black helmet with the distinctive silver snake. He was crawling along, turning his head from side to side as if he were looking for someone. With a sick feeling in my stomach, I realised he was looking for me. I dodged into a garden and dropped down behind a low front wall to let him pass by, narrowly dodging a pile of dog poo. Then, changing my route, I darted up a side road and started to run.

Breathless and panting, I was soon within sight of the station with its two high brick walls bookending glass in between. As I hurried past the ticket office, the motorbike reappeared and sped up to the outside of the building. The rider watched me pass through the barrier as he hurriedly dismounted.

A Central Line train was just about to leave. I squeezed through a closing door, grabbing a strap handle and staring anxiously out of the window. There he was on the platform, just seconds too late to catch me. He thumped his fist into his hand. The train pulled out and I texted Jane.

On my way but being followed. Biker in a black helmet. Hope he doesn't know where I'm going. T xx

My pursuer must have been sent by the Leans. It was a stark reminder of the reach of the criminals I was facing. Was it wrong to have run the story and put myself at risk? People had died because of them. I owed it to those who'd been murdered to see the man who'd killed them sent to jail for the rest of his life.

"The next station is Tottenham Court Road," said the automated announcement. My cue to change. I took the Northern Line to Kentish Town, keeping a careful watch for the biker. From there it was a ten-minute walk to Jane's house. It was a huge relief that there was no sign of my pursuer on the street outside the station when I arrived. I walked along by a parade of shops, glancing behind me every few steps. As I turned into a side road, the clouds darkened still further and released a veil of drizzle.

Jane opened her front door and my pretend smile fell away. I pitched myself into her arms.

"Oh Jane." My tears fell onto her top. Her familiar smell brought comfort. I had no mother, no dad, no siblings. I was so glad to have Jane; all my other friends were Sven's friends too.

"S-Sorry…" I sobbed.

"Oh, come here," she said, hugging me like a mum. "No more mystery bikers?"

She closed the door as I told her about my anxious journey, but we soon returned to Sven and my dying marriage.

19

"So glad you're here," I said as she hugged me again, my words muffled in her neck as I buried my head.

"You've been there for me. All those mornings. The broken-hearted breakfasts when yet another overnight lover left me to face the morning alone." She smiled. But now it was my turn; although I was mourning the loss of a marriage, not a passing lover.

"But he's gone. Sven. It's over."

"What a bastard … Sorry, I don't like to badmouth your husband, but there's no other word for it. He's a complete and utter bastard."

"I want him back, but I never want to see him again. I don't understand what's gone wrong between us. I can't believe he could behave like this."

"Well, if it's any consolation he had me fooled, too. Until now I always liked him—even if he was a bit of a poser." She saw my expression. "Oh come on, we all know he was," she said with a half-smile.

"Come and see my latest treasures," she said, leading me through to her cosy back kitchen. She was obviously set on distracting me from my gloomy thoughts, but the whole room was the epitome of a happy marriage. Food cooking. Kisses on the notice board. Fresh flowers in a vase by the window.

"That's new." I forced a smile and nodded towards a framed photograph on the wall.

"You know me, I can't resist moody pictures of seaside towns. It's Southwold in Suffolk."

"Nice. You've quite a collection."

"Yeah, I kind of like to change the scenery."

"It's at times like these I'm glad Sven and I never had children. Sorry," I added, remembering she and Dave had tried to conceive.

Jane sighed. "You know what? I was going to make tea but there's an open bottle of pinot in the fridge. It's got our names on it." I watched her unscrew the lid of the wine bottle. She divided it between two large glasses.

"I've another bottle when we've finished this," she smiled, sitting down.

"Better not," I said, taking the seat opposite. "I'd only drain it and end up unconscious on the floor."

"Maybe that's what you need?"

"No, I really need to think and keep a clear head."

"So, you had no idea at all? Not a single clue that Sven was having this affair with Mrs '*Let's Stick Together Until I Collar Someone Else's Husband*' Heffle?"

"None. We'd planned that holiday to Lanzarote, the one I told you about, plus dinners with friends, all the usual stuff. But he was staying away more than he used to—apparently for conferences and seminars at various universities. Or so he said."

"Including the trip to Paris?"

"Yep, including the trip to Paris. Hence the so-called *compromising photographs* they referred to on the news, I guess."

"I've seen them online." She grimaced. "You kind of... don't want to go there."

I knew I shouldn't ask, but I had to. "How bad are they?"

The look on Jane's face told me everything I needed to know.

3. Shredded

The antique clock on the wall ticked as we sipped our wine. Jane hesitated. She looked at me with sad eyes and tugged at her earrings, a sure sign of stress, then she reached over and held my hand. She knew I needed to know the truth.

"The pictures are sickening to look at… I mean, hand in hand, kissing in a restaurant, gazing into each other's eyes. You want me to go on?"

"No. But I needed to hear that. What was he wearing?"

"Er, a blue jacket, I think."

"Oh, great! The one I bought him a few months ago? I'm so glad it helped him look nice for her. Bet he was wearing those really expensive boxers I bought him too. That's horrible."

"I don't know about the underwear, but the jacket was the one he wore here when you came to dinner on New Year's Eve, and to that party we all went to in Camden. That PR woman's do. I remember it because Dave asked if he should get one. The thing is Tess… the way I see it, Sven is kind of the least of your problems." She paused, her hand reaching for her earring. "Ken Lean's brother Chris, A.K.A. Crusher, is after you. Our crime reporter said the judge made it quite clear in his summing-up that your film was the key evidence that sent Lean down."

"I know it was."

"Yeah, but you don't know the full story, Tess. You walked out after he swore at you, but our reporter said that, when the judge sent Ken Lean to jail for thirty-odd years, his brother Crusher joined in the insults. He shouted from the public gallery, *that bitch Anderson is dead!* He had to be restrained by the police, apparently. He was shaking with anger."

I felt a chill. My mind went back to the motorcyclist.

"I've seen Crusher Lean in court, and I really wouldn't want to meet him face to face."

"Yeah, he sounds heavy duty. Not sure how he got that name but probably best we don't! Look, Tess, I've got a suggestion." She opened the second bottle and topped up my wine. "I think you need to get away. Right away. At least until everything calms down."

"Run away, you mean? No, I'm not going to do that."

"Get real Tess! Sven's affair isn't just with the au pair or a colleague. It's with a government minister, for God's sake, and that's going to get very, very messy. You're on TV, Sven's on TV, his *fuck buddy*... sorry, Mrs *Family Values*... is a member of the Cabinet and a TV talking head, so this is going to run and run, you know that. All sorts of crap is going to come out and some of the people involved are seriously nasty. I've got a very bad feeling about this."

"I'll be all right at work, I feel safe there."

"But you can't live at work! You can't sleep at work, and your work puts you in the public eye. Those gangsters will find you easily. They even found you walking to the station." Jane got up and went to the worktop to check her phone. She turned back, looking serious. "Look, my villa on Paxos is empty. Why don't you go and hide in it for a while? No one's booked it until the middle of May."

"That's kind of you but it's a bit drastic, isn't it? I'd rather be here to get my life back together."

"Tess. Seriously, given how rubbish life is for you here right now, why not swap it for the blue seas and blue skies of Greece?

No one will know you're there and you can slip back into London when you're ready."

"Won't Dave mind?" I asked.

"I've already run it by him. Besides it's my house, not my husband's. It was my parents' villa, they left it to me."

"Thanks," I said. "I'll think it over."

"But not for long, Tess."

"I'm not the sort to run away. You know that. Let me talk to my contact in the Met, DI Green. Maybe there's the Witness Protection Scheme?"

"What, change your name and hide in a small anonymous town? Tess, you haven't done all this to hide in the shadows and give up your job! Look there's a nice Englishwoman on the island, a widow, a friend of mine called Jo. She looks after the villa for me. Why don't you let me tell her you're coming?"

"Because I don't know if I am yet."

"Tess, why do you have to be so stubborn?" She stood up, shaking her head, carrying the empty bottle to the recycle bin. "Just pack a few things but be careful to throw everyone off the scent, and don't tell anyone who doesn't need to know where you're going. Nobody, okay?"

"Sorry, it's a lovely offer and you may be right." I caught sight of the clock. "I'd better go, I'm meeting my boss soon in Holborn—he wants a chat." I stood up. "I promise I'll think about Paxos."

"I hope your boss is going to run a story on his star reporter being threatened," she said. "Are you coming back later to stay the night? You're more than welcome."

"Thanks, Jane, —can I let you know when I've met Steve?"

She smiled and nodded. "Hope to see you later, then. Be careful." I picked up my bag as Jane opened the front door. I was worried about leaving the sanctity of her home. I didn't know what could be waiting for me on the streets outside, but after she'd checked the coast was clear I left and caught the tube.

Looking for my editor, I walked into the pub near Holborn

station. It was rammed with office workers and city types having an end of day drink. I quickly spotted Steve by the bar buying two glasses of wine. His floppy dark hair fell over his glasses as he bent forward and gave me a hug. His six-foot frame towered above me. I had to admit he was a real looker. He'd been a very photogenic news reader and reporter in his early days. He was a former star *News Trainee*, always tipped for the top. He'd be Head of News soon, I thought. Steve was a good boss too; he knew what it was like out there on the road, racing against deadlines, chasing elusive stories, always staying one step ahead, writing scripts in the back of a car, doing voice-overs live.

We found a corner near the stairs with a couple of tall stools to sit on. The whole place was heaving and smelled of beer and stale sweat. We had to fight to make ourselves heard above the conversations all around us, but it was at least a glimpse of normality, lives being lived without a trail of murder, mayhem and broken marriages.

"Thanks, Steve, I needed this," I said, raising my glass.

"I think I did too. It's been a crazy day, rushing around with the Lean case, and crews trying to doorstep Heffle and your husband."

"Where are they?" I asked casually, as if it didn't mean a thing to me.

"Holed up in her Westminster flat. Danny Downs and the other paps are camped outside waiting for them to emerge. We've got Clare there with the satellite truck for a live into the late bulletin." I was glad he didn't criticise me for going back into the court. If he had, I think I'd have cried.

"Sven's likely to stay with her tonight, then?"

"I would in his place," said Steve apologetically. "I don't mean sleep with the Heffle-lump, of course. God, no, nightmare! Sorry, but what does he see in her? Look, if either of them leaves they'll be the front-page picture on the tabloids tomorrow, along with Ken Lean growling through the bars of a prison van… Tess, you're not crying, are you?"

"Not so you'd notice… I mean, that's Tess-speak for 'please don't notice, boss'. I'm in shock, that's all. Thought I'd found *the one*. The ever illusive *one*. You're so lucky having Jen." He'd been with his wife for years, and they had two lovely daughters. "I just missed the signs, I guess. I'm not the first and I won't be the last."

He smiled and, ignoring my comment and another call on his phone, he changed the subject.

"Are you sure you're okay to be here? Tess, you're constantly touching that necklace."

"It's silver. My dad gave it to my mum on their anniversary a month before they both died." He picked up a shell on a beach in Cephalonia and had a replica made. It always comforted me when things got tough.

"You're missing them, aren't you?"

"How's the newsroom?" I asked, trying to hold it together.

"They all send their love. I told them I was seeing you tonight. I'm representing them all by being here. You know how popular you are Tess, and you're great at your job. You'll have mine one day, or you'll be fronting a prestigious show." It was flattering to hear, but my mind was on other things "And we don't want to lose such a valuable bit of talent, Tess. How about you lie low for a bit?"

"Steve, there's been a biker following me since I left the court."

"Is he here now?" he asked, looking around.

"No, but he was definitely looking for me earlier."

"Sure it's not just paranoia?"

I shook my head. "I wish it was. But, no. The Leans have got me in their sights."

"I've spoken to HR; they've said you can work out of Salford. I can keep you deskbound for the next few months until the heat dies down, working on that documentary we discussed." We had plans for a primetime special called *The Lean Story*. "You can have a taxi to work and back, live in an apartment nearby with secure entry. When you go on the road, we can even give you a minder."

"Thanks, boss, but I can't hide here. I know who I'm dealing with." I remembered Lean's snarling face in the dock.

"Why not talk to the police before you rush into anything? You've got a good contact, haven't you?"

"DI Ted Green, yes. But they can't have officers assigned to protect me all the time, I'm not a royal or a Cabinet member." I was clearly nowhere near as important as Heffle—certainly where my husband was concerned. I gave a grim smile. "I'll let you know. I'm still weighing it up, but a friend has offered to lend me a holiday home."

"You know, Tess, off the record I honestly think you would be safer somewhere anonymous and out of the way. I have to offer you a safe haven in Manchester and suggest police protection under my *duty of care* bollocks, but at the end of the day we both know the enormity of keeping you safe. We both know what Lean's capable of. Tess, my gut says run. It gives you time away from the marriage crap too, time to think. But I do need to know where this holiday home is though, if you do go. Deal?"

I glanced round the pub, just to make sure no one was eavesdropping. "Greece," I said. "My friend Jane's got a villa in Paxos. It's quiet and secluded. She thinks it's a good bet."

"Paxos. Never been. Sounds good. I hope it's safe," he added quietly.

"So do I, because if I do go, those bastards seem pretty damn determined to find me."

*

I'd made up my mind to go home. Although Jane had offered me a bed for the night, I wanted familiar things around me. I was pretty certain Steve was right and Sven would be staying overnight with Heffle. Steve walked with me to the tube station, and we got our respective trains, me heading west and him going east. As we parted, he looked melancholy, as if he was thinking he might never see me again. As I sat on the tube, a feeling of uncertainty and fear washed over me. Every passenger was a potential threat. Then the doors opened and a guy in leathers holding a crash helmet got on. My heart leapt—until I realised it wasn't him. The helmet was black, but there was no silver snake. I stood by the doors, constantly eyeing the emergency handle just in case. I couldn't cope. I changed my mind about going home and swapped trains to head back to Jane's. I needed to sleep and knew I would feel safer at hers. Maybe she was right, perhaps I would be safer hiding away on a Greek island.

"Coffee?" asked Jane, when she opened the door to me for the second time that day.

"Still got the rest of that other bottle of wine?" I asked.

"Afraid not... I can open another?"

"Just kidding. But if that offer of a bed is still on, I'd love to stay the night. I'll be asleep in minutes though, I'm exhausted."

"I'm not surprised. You look shattered." She gave me a sympathetic look. "Well, the bed's made up. We've got Sarah staying from tomorrow... remember her from university? She'll be here for a few days. Let's go through to the kitchen." Jane closed and locked the front door.

"Sarah Bullen, as was?"

"The same. She and I kind of kept in touch, on and off, and... well, I'll tell you later." She led me back into the kitchen again, with its homely atmosphere. "What I really want to know is: have you made a decision about Greece yet?"

"Jane, I know you're right, I'm just having trouble coming to terms with it. I've just broken the story of my life. I thought I'd be celebrating with Sven... not running away from everything."

"Hey, just stay away from the television channels and online news. Oh, but I have to say—your background report on Lean was really good. They ran it this evening. That footage of him killing poor Frank Porter—wow, so sad. You'll be up for another award for this, Tess, you deserve one."

"Thanks," I said. "It's Milly the carer I really feel for, she was so young."

Jane reached for my hand and squeezed it. "You did the right thing, Tess. Putting that bastard away. I know you're paying for it now, but… it was the right thing."

"Thanks, Jane. That means a lot."

"Hey, I almost forgot! Sven called me."

"Called you? Sven called you? What?!"

"He guessed we'd be together. He wanted to talk to you. Well, you're not answering his calls or replying to his texts or emails, are you?"

"What did you tell him?"

"That you weren't here, that you were meeting someone."

"Thanks."

Jane shrugged. "Well, it was true."

"What else did he say?"

"He just asked me to tell you to contact him. That you needed to talk."

"Really? You don't say. Perhaps he should have talked to me about this before he went with her."

Jane could see how upset I was. She filled a glass with water and handed it to me. "Here, drink this, and sod Sven."

"And sod Heffle too," I said, imagining my Sven with her right now. It was sickening. I pushed the thought from my mind and headed for the stairs. This had been the longest day of my life; if I didn't lie down soon, I'd fall down. "Usual room at the back?" I asked.

Jane nodded. "There's a towel on the bed for you. You know where everything is."

I hugged her, before climbing the stairs and falling into bed.

*

The next morning, after having breakfast with Jane and Dave, I was sitting on the tube heading home. The weather was much brighter, unlike my mood. I had a headache. I put it down to stress. I'd had another two texts and an email from Sven, plus two voicemail messages. I'd ignored and deleted them all. I was so angry and hurt that I was beyond wanting to talk to him. I constantly passed newsstands in stations and saw headlines about him and his lover, Lean and the trial. I was connected with most of the coverage on nearly all of the front pages, but this was no red-letter day for me. I felt cheated. Lean should have been the headline, not my husband and his lover. I was sure the prime minister wished that, too.

Leaving the station at West Acton, I anxiously looked around for the biker who'd stalked me the day before. Luckily, he was nowhere to be seen. I kept my head down and quickly walked home. I got to my street and was relieved to see Sven's Audi wasn't there. The only vehicle parked outside was the window cleaner's van. He was assembling a flexible pole to wash the glass. I acknowledged him and went inside. He grinned, presumably having seen the papers.

There was the usual mail and a few handwritten notes pushed through the letterbox by friends. I'd read them later. Going into the kitchen, I noticed that the back door was ajar. With a racing heart, I checked the windows. They were all locked. No one had broken in; nothing had been forced. No one but Sven and I had keys to the house. What was he doing leaving a door unlocked?

I locked it and went upstairs, pulling every curtain closed as I did. Looking through the box-room window, I could see a white van had stopped directly opposite our house on the other side of the street. I could see two men inside. They looked like hard cases: shaven-headed, burly, heavily tattooed on their arms and neck. I thought little of it until, to my horror, the familiar motorbike arrived and the man with the black helmet and its horrible silver snake, stopped by the van. My pulse rose.

The biker spoke to the men inside and pointed to my house. The motorbike then rode off, but the van stayed put. The window cleaner's pole startled me when it scraped the glass I was peering through, only centimetres from my face. I knew that he'd soon finish our windows and move on to the house next door. I went into the bedroom to get a better view. Then I saw it, and almost screamed as I took a sharp intake of breath.

Dead centre on our bed lay a single pillow. Arranged over it was my blue-striped cotton nightdress. Stuck through it, pinning it to the pillow, was an ugly jagged knife buried to the hilt. Beside this sinister display was a photograph taken through the window of a café on Farringdon Street. It showed me drinking coffee with Jake. It must have been taken the day before yesterday, when we'd snatched a break from the trial. Tied to the handle of the knife was a printed note that read: *Coming soon to a face neer you.* If I hadn't been so terrified, the bad spelling would have almost made me smile.

There was no doubt now: I had no choice, I had to go to Paxos. I ran downstairs, ready to call the police, but was momentarily distracted by something coming through the letterbox. My heart leapt—but it was only the window cleaner pushing his bill through. I grabbed the house phone and dialled 999. I told them who I was and what I thought was happening. The call handler wanted to know if anyone was in the house right now. As soon as I said *no,* I sensed my call becoming less of a priority. I was told someone would be on their way "as soon as they could". I hung up and made another call.

"Jane, they've been here."

"Who's been there? And where are you, at home?"

"Yes. Lean's thugs, and they're outside my house now, I'm sure of it. I've seen the motorbike again too. They've been here, inside."

"Are you sure?"

"Yes, very. And I'm very, very scared." My hand holding the phone was shaking. "There's a knife slashed straight through my nightie, pinning it to my pillow. There's also a photograph of me taken two days ago—they've been following me for longer than I realised, and they've made it very clear they don't play nicely."

"Tess, look, you'll have to leave for Greece, now, today. Take a photograph of the knife and anything else you find and email it to that pal of yours in the Met."

"You're right, yes." My head was spinning.

"And copy me in on it, too. Look, the most important thing now is to get out of there. I'll pick you up. I'm at Ikea in Wembley so I'm half an hour away, max. Quickly, go and pack. I won't be long. Stay strong, big hugs."

As I ended the call, an ominous knocking started on the front door. I waited to see if it would stop, but it just carried on—getting louder and louder. I knew what it might be, but I wasn't going to open it. I pulled back the curtain to see who was there and immediately heard the familiar click of a camera and blinked as the flash lit my face. The camera was wielded by Danny Downs, a well-known freelance photographer who supplied the tabloids with gossip fodder; he'd have been staking out Heffle's flat. I pulled the curtain. Downs yelled at me through the letterbox, imploring me to give him a few words. Behind him, on the other side of the road, was the white van with the two watchful men inside. I knew that while Downs was at my door, they wouldn't be.

"Come on, Tess, you must hate him, right? Your husband… You must really hate him. And what about her? *Randy cow? Marriage wrecker?* minister for *non-family values*, would you say? *Husband stealer?* Come on, Tess, give me some words." Rat-faced and scruffily dressed, Downs was armed with a digital camera and a voice recorder which he was pointing towards the door, hoping for a response. He paused momentarily and then tried again, shouting through the letterbox, knowing I'd be listening.

"I've got a shot already and you look pretty cross in it… Not your best look, darlin', behind the window, maybe a tad ugly even… Hey, let's get a nice one, shall we? Do your hair but not too much," he added, no doubt smiling at the thought of the generous payment heading his way from whichever tabloid outbid the rest. "Give us just a few words and the readers will take your side. Play to the camera, Tess, give us the betrayed-wife look: rub your eyes, make them red, maybe a few sobs… you know I'll make you look good. Come on, Anderson, you know how it works. The divorce judge will remember it when it comes to the settlement, too. Do yourself a favour, and I'll help you fleece the bastard."

I certainly did know how it worked, only too well. After all these years as a reporter in radio and television news, I knew the best and worst about my profession. This guy, Downs, was the pits. I'd seen him snatch a school photo of a murdered child from a mantelpiece when the distraught parents were distracted. I'd seen him relentlessly harass grieving widows and the relatives of crash victims. He was driven by a lust for money and the constant need to get tomorrow's front-page picture together with a good headline quote. I was going to give him nothing. He had no moral or ethical filters and, besides, anything I did say would only be twisted to fit the agenda of whichever paper bought his pictures. Danny's subjects could be turned from hero to villain at the flick of a keyboard return. Inside the dirty white van opposite, the two watchers were patiently waiting.

Downs's presence at my front door proved my fellow journalists wouldn't be making my life easy either, especially those on the weekend editions. They'd be looking for angles, searching the internet looking for pictures of me, my husband and his lover; ideally on the beach, in swimwear, topless, anything to add salacious content. They'd be asking neighbours, friends, relatives, colleagues, seeking out former partners, old boyfriends, girlfriends—anyone to give them a quote about our characters, our marriage and our relationships. They'd brutally force open the tiniest crack to make it a gaping chasm.

I shouted through the letterbox, asking Downs to give me ten minutes, hoping I could stop him from leaving and so keep Lean's thugs at bay. I went upstairs and quickly pulled my old battered blue rucksack from under the bed and began thrusting clothes into it. Then I opened the wardrobe and stared in disbelief.

4. Flight

It wasn't just my nightdress that had been ruined. My other clothes had been slashed too. There were smart suits for work, favourite dresses and skirts, things I'd worn on-screen and at parties—all torn and unwearable. It felt as if someone had cut right through me. Shaking and crying, I photographed the shredded garments with my phone then rifled through the hangers, removing anything that had escaped the blade. I supposed at least my packing would be quick.

I didn't want to leave any clues as to where I was going. I deliberately didn't take any sandals or swimwear to throw Sven off the scent of a warm destination. I knew both Sven and Lean's pals wanted to track me down. One light smart summer dress, a couple of pairs of shorts and a cotton skirt went into the rucksack; they wouldn't be missed. Sven hardly noticed what I wore anyway. Maybe that was the problem. Bet he noticed her wardrobe though. Then there was my underwear drawer. Half open, its contents spilled out on the floor. My stomach turned. I was disgusted. I left it. I'd buy new *en route*. I couldn't bear to wear something that had been touched by the intruder.

I ran downstairs with my rucksack. In the kitchen I switched on the computer. I went online and searched for a seat on a flight to Corfu later that afternoon. Luckily, I was able to buy one.

To make the deception complete, I deleted the browser history and then opened another airline's website and booked a flight to Prague, just to throw anyone off the scent. Knowing Sven would check anyway, I sent a quick email to Jane and our friends saying I was going to the Czech Republic for a few weeks and gave the details of the second flight that I'd booked but would never take.

Checking through the gap in the closed curtains, I could see that Downs was still outside, and by being so was holding the men in the van at bay. But where were the police? I called Steve in the newsroom. It was a short conversation. I reminded him to keep my real location strictly to himself. I didn't even want him to tell Jake, my closest colleague. He said he would, but something worried me. How many emails would pass between him, senior management and HR? What would be overheard in the cafés outside the building? Who would drop a hint or two on social media? I worked with journalists; they were built to uncover secrets and find people.

"Keep in touch and don't worry about work. Just come back in one piece, okay?" Steve said as I cleared the call and said goodbye. By now, Downs had realised I'd been stringing him along, and after one final burst of knocking on the door, and a shout through the letterbox, he finally gave up. Peeping through a gap in the curtains, I watched him walk back to his car. He got in, put his camera on the passenger seat and closed the door. I realised he was about to go. So did the driver of the white van opposite, which started up and began to perform a lumbering three-point turn.

I saw the empty eyes of the thickset man in the passenger seat. There was an elaborate spider's web tattoo around one of his eyes. He looked at the window, straight towards me, and nodded to the driver beside him. He had another tattoo on the side of his neck—a dragon, just like the one Ken Lean had flaunted in court. Proof of a link between them, if ever I'd needed one.

The window cleaner was now working at my neighbour's house, and I knew he'd also soon be gone, then the quiet street would be free from witnesses and the men in the van would strike. Every sense I possessed was urging me to go. I didn't dare wait for the police; they could be too late. I hurriedly grabbed my rucksack, shoulder bag, fleece top, iPad and phone. I pulled a small wad of euros from the drawer in the hall, left over from our last holiday in Italy, then I remembered the photo of Mum and Dad. It was on the table next to my bed. I dashed up the stairs and grabbed the small silver frame. I took a last look at the photograph of me receiving the Royal Television Society Award for Reporter of the Year on the wall and turned to go. I thought of my little strong box full of family mementos and documents, prized among them, my mum's wedding ring, but I had no time. I almost fell, running down the stairs and, as I opened the back door, I heard the front door being forced. I knew the chain I'd put on wouldn't hold for long. I heard a thud, followed by the sound of splintering wood. I locked the back door behind me and hurried down the garden path into the alley behind the houses.

I was desperate for Jane or the police to arrive. I could barely breathe in the panic. When I got to the road, I peered around the corner and saw the second of the two men from the van, the driver, disappearing through my front door. They weren't there just to ask for their knife back, that was for sure.

At that moment I knew it could go either way. Lean's thugs were almost on me and there was no sign of help. I squeezed my mum's necklace between my fingers and peered towards the end of the road. Then, like the cavalry arriving in the nick of time, Jane's car sped round the corner and squealed to a halt in front of me, the passenger door opening as she stopped.

"GET IN!" she screamed. I threw my stuff in the back, next to her flat-packed parcels. I fell into the passenger seat. As I swung the door to and reached for the seat belt, a man rushed out of the alley and grabbed the door handle. Jane hit the lock button just in time and he was forced to let go as we sped off, leaving him cursing and hammering on the back window as he ran after the car.

I couldn't speak. Where were the police? Why hadn't they turned up?

"Don't worry," she said. "We'll get you out of here." Good old Jane, trying to calm me down. But she looked just as anxious as I did. As we reached the end of the road, I turned my head to see a police car stopping outside my house in front of the van. It was small comfort. I doubted they'd pin anything on the men other than forced entry without a statement from me, and I couldn't risk hanging around or going back. Besides, Ken Lean had more than two footsoldiers in his army. I'd escaped for now, but the chase was on. Jane was right: I had to run—run and hide. But would anywhere be safe? Even her holiday home in Greece?

As we turned the corner I slid deeper into the passenger seat, the sun visor pulled down even though it was threatening to rain. I had my sunglasses on and must have looked like a celeb heading for rehab, which in some ways maybe I was. I switched my phone off. It wasn't long before we were on London's orbital motorway, my eyes constantly scanning the traffic, always on the alert for a motorbike with a rider wearing a black helmet with a horrible silver snake.

*

An hour or so later, we were at Lakeside in Thurrock, one of Britain's biggest shopping malls. We were swallowed up by the crowd. With my sunglasses on, I hoped no one would recognise me. I needed a few more clothes. Jane and I picked out a blue and white bikini, two tops, a thin sundress and shorts—all own-brand, anonymous, simple and light. I got some sandals and underwear. Not the quality or fit I was used to, but at least no one had rifled through them. I had no idea how long I'd be away. As we queued for the checkout, I constantly scanned the people around us. Jane insisted on paying with her card so mine couldn't be traced.

"Hey, a phone shop," Jane said excitedly, just as we neared the exit.

She bought me a basic pay-as-you-go phone, using her name and address for the details. I now had a number only she and I would know. It was only capable of making and receiving calls and texts, but it was essential. We agreed that I would call myself 'Sam' when I texted or called. It all seemed very cloak-and-dagger, but it was Jane's husband, Dave, a tech consultant for a security firm, who'd suggested it.

"I could stay, you know," I said, wavering with last minute doubts. "I was a witness in a major trial. I could go for police protection. You could run a story about the attack on me; it would frighten them off, point the finger."

"It might for a short while, but pinning everything on Lean would be hard—the raid on your wardrobe, your being chased by the biker? He's not stupid. Besides, there are others out there who'd be keen to see you attacked for helping bang up one of their own."

"But you could run the story?"

"Sure," she replied. "I think the Home Editor would go for it, with a few quotes from you. We couldn't accuse Lean of course, not without proof. His lawyers would love that. But I'll do what I can."

"Thanks, Jane."

"As for police protection, it doesn't always work," she reminded me. "Lean's already had one bent copper on his side, and there may be more. You wouldn't sleep, would you—wondering if the man in blue outside was really on Lean's payroll, waiting to put a pillow over your face. And you'd have to stop working. Become someone else. That's not my Tess."

"I guess not," I said.

"This way you get out of the country, and you can leave it to your pal DI Green to try to pin it on Lean."

I knew she was right. I couldn't stay at home now anyway, not after escaping those thugs and having my failed marriage exposed to the glare of the public spotlight. Danny Downs would certainly be back, and so would Lean's nasties.

*

Back in the car park at Lakeside, sitting in Jane's dark blue VW Polo, I took my old phone out and turned it on to check the messages. Among them was a list of missed calls and texts, mainly from Sven; I ignored them all. I had a voicemail from DI Green.

"Ms Anderson, hello, it's DI Ted Green. I've just picked up on this, you called someone to your house earlier? We need to talk; you may be in danger. Can you ring me as soon as you get this message, please? Thanks."

I *may be in danger.* You don't say. Jane was right. I didn't want to hang around to discuss the finer points of the police hiding me somewhere in England. I decided to call him later, from Greece, and switched the phone off.

*

Queuing for the slip road, we edged back into the motorway traffic and headed over the Dartford Bridge towards Gatwick Airport. I remembered the holiday flights Sven and I had taken together. Hand in hand, happy and in love. However much I tried to hold them back, tears seeped from my tightly closed eyes. Jane opened the glove box and passed me some tissues.

"It's okay to cry," she said softly.

"I'm just struggling to take it all in… How can things have gone so wrong so quickly?" I wiped my eyes. "If I were writing this as a trail for tonight's news it would be: *On the run and under threat. Top TV reporter's life in ruins after husband's affair exposed and crime boss orders her death…*"

"It's awful, I know," she said, as we turned onto the M23, heading south. "But you'll pull through, Tess. I know you will."

"Thanks, Jane. You're a real friend. I still can't believe it—Sven and her, together…" I shook my head. "I suppose a famous marriage-guidance expert knows how to cover his tracks…"

"Famous, thanks to you! The ungrateful git wouldn't even be on TV if not for you putting a word in."

"True," I said. I'd known a producer looking for a new face to present an insert in a daytime show. I'd suggested a marriage-guidance slot, fronted by Sven. He was onscreen a month later. Shortly afterwards the celeb clients came calling. We'd had to increase the mortgage to rent him a smart set of 'consulting rooms' in town. It had seemed such a positive thing at the time, his career going from strength to strength. But a horrible thought occurred to me now. By helping him into the public eye, had I ended up pushing him into Heffle's arms? The idea was unbearable. "You never know," I said. "He might've got famous anyway. He's really good at marriage guidance…"

"Yeah, apart from his own," Jane said, with a sympathetic look—but I turned away, my attention caught by the sight of a motorbike rapidly approaching in my wing mirror. The rider had a black helmet.

"Jane!" I shouted, as he drew level with us in the inside lane.

"I'm on it!" Jane said, accelerating and moving into the outer lane to put traffic between us and him. "Get down, Tess!" she yelled.

I pushed myself down in the seat, heart racing. All I could do was wait for him to draw level beside us again. But instead, the motorbike accelerated away. There was no silver snake on the helmet, this time it wasn't him. Jane looked at me and we both gave a sigh of relief.

The turn-off for the airport appeared up ahead. It couldn't have been more timely or more welcome.

*

Jane and I had got some euros at the mall, as I couldn't risk using a card in Greece. When we reached the airport, she thrust another three hundred in my hand.

"You're such a good friend," I said, hugging her as we said goodbye.

"You'll get through it. You're Tess. You're the strongest woman I know."

"I don't feel too strong right now, and I know you're worried. You've been fiddling with your granny's earring non-stop."

Breathing in her familiar smell, I didn't want to let go, but eventually had to. Jane smiled and waved as I walked into the terminal building. I had an hour and a half to spare before my flight. I had time to get through check-in and security and then tackle my shopping list of toiletries and a couple of paperbacks, though I doubted I'd be relaxed enough to read them. Once I'd purchased my essentials, I bought a herbal tea from a café—my heart was pounding too fast to want caffeine—and sat in the departure lounge, flicking through the books I'd chosen but not taking anything in. Logically, I knew I was safe here, but I couldn't help looking at every new person who entered...

At last, it was time to board. I stood clutching my passport, keeping my head down. My legs shook on the walk to the plane. I was glad to find I had an aisle seat, and, even though, I knew it was irrational—where would I escape to on a plane, after all?—I was glad I wouldn't be blocked in by anyone.

It seemed to take hours before we were finally airborne. As soon as the *Fasten Seat Belt* sign was off, I went to the loo. As I washed my hands, I studied the face looking back at me from the mirror. Was that really me? The face the viewers were used to was immaculately made up, with every hair in place. Not like this—no make-up and sleep deprived. I hardly recognised myself but, sadly, that didn't mean nobody else would. I went back to my seat and strapped myself in.

As discretely as possible, I took a quick look at my fellow passengers. My only concern was a man two rows behind on the other side of the aisle. He was reading a copy of the London evening paper. There were two stories on the front page: Sven and Heffle's affair, and Ken Lean's sentencing. My picture was there in the bottom left-hand corner. Presumably, the passenger had recognised me; whenever I looked round, he was constantly staring at me. I thought maybe I'd seen him before, but I couldn't think when or where. When you're on TV, people often think they know you; they usually smile or nod. This guy did neither. He remained stern-faced and quite still, watching me. I decided to try and relax; after all, everyone had been through security. Surely I was safe. I sat back in my chair, took a deep breath, and reluctantly found my thoughts turning to Sven instead…

Three hours later, as the aircraft was banking around the southern end of the island of Corfu, I was still trying to make sense of my new world. Yesterday had started so well, my big day, the one when all my hard work in investigating and exposing Ken Lean would finally be recognised. It was, but so was my husband's infidelity. A day later I'd turned my back on my marriage, and my home, and I was on the run. It was hard to take in.

I watched through the nearest window as the aircraft dropped down and drew level with the tops of villas on the sides of the low hills between Benitses and Corfu Town. The sun was now behind the hills and shadows were turning to dusk. Some were lit, but most were still in darkness like the villa on Paxos I was heading for.

"Cabin crew to landing, doors to automatic," boomed the pilot's voice from the speakers.

The gentle whine of a small motor and a solid click beneath our feet signalled that the wheels had locked into place. I remembered the only other time I'd been in Corfu was with Sven. We'd hired an apartment in Arillas on the north-west corner of the island some ten years ago. The resort had a fantastic sandy beach, two in fact, one right at the centre and another a little further to the north. You had to walk to it and squeeze between the sea and cliffs to get there, but the soft yellow sand was worth the effort.

The beach was *clothes optional*, and we had been confronted with naked muddy people. The cliffs had a stratum of amazing mud that dried on your skin, forming a taut layer of grey. We saw other people plastering it on, so we stopped, stripped off, and covered ourselves in it too, roaring with laughter as we did. It felt great, shrink-wrapping us as it dried.

Sven had taken a photo of me wearing nothing but the mud. I even had a grey face and grey hair sticking out everywhere. I was caked in the stuff and looked like an extra from *Doctor Who,* or a contestant in some weird game show. I thought if Danny Downs and his pals got hold of that picture now… It wasn't worth worrying about; the problem was, I knew Sven had jokingly emailed it to a few of our friends after the holiday, laughingly saying I needed to either see a dermatologist, or sue the makers of our new washing powder.

The aircraft dropped almost level with the sea, passing over the top of a little white church by the water's edge, with its red terracotta tiled roof, before the start of the asphalt runway, flanked by glowing lights. I felt the wheels bounce gently as they met the ground, and I knew I'd made my escape. I was in Greece.

I briefly glanced behind me. The stern-faced man was staring again… and then I remembered where I'd seen him, and my heart sank. Adrenalin raced through my tired veins like the tyres screeching on the runway below. It pushed my body into a state of near panic. He'd been in court. At the trial. He was in the public gallery. Sitting next to Crusher Lean!

The people in the few rows ahead of me seemed to take forever to recover their cabin bags, wedged into overhead lockers. At last, I was heading towards the exit and hurrying down the steps into the evening air. I darted in and out of the shuffling queue trying to get ahead of the man from the flight. Luckily, I just had my rucksack with my shoulder bag rammed inside, no baggage-reclaim to wait for, but neither had he—I could see him pushing through the crowds towards me. I was stuck behind three people at passport control. I switched on my new phone. It bleeped to announce the arrival of a couple of messages. The first welcoming me to Greece, the next from Jane:

Hope you arrived OK Sam! Grab a taxi from outside the airport. I've booked U a room in a small hotel in the old town: Hotel Paralia on Mantzarou. I gave your real name as they'll want to see your passport. The first boat to Paxos is the hydrofoil at 9 tomorrow from the New Port. J xx

I just replied with an *X.* No time for anything else. I felt cold. I glanced round, and the man who'd been staring at me on the flight was right behind, me staring over my shoulder, trying to read the message.

5. Rooms

I dashed to the police border control. The blue uniformed young woman scanned my passport and looked at me as I gave a small, hopeful smile. Pushing ahead, I apologised to the people in front of me and mumbled about being in a hurry. Through customs and then I was in 'Arrivals'. Drivers and holiday reps held up signs with passengers' names on, patiently waiting with a pre booked smile. I was through the open concourse and outside minutes later. I looked up behind me at the metal tubes holding up the flat roof of the terminal building; the name *'Kerkyra'*— Greek for Corfu Island—stood out in big yellow letters.

The night air smelled indefinably Greek. Diesel fumes were washed away by hints of wild thyme, jasmine and scents of pine from the surrounding countryside, breezing in on the sunset wind. I caught a glimpse of the moon cutting through the lights of the airport perimeter. It was warmer than the London I'd left. There was a hint of heat in the evening air, even though it was still only April. People hurried by; Greek, German, Swedish and English spilled out from excited mouths. The muffled roar and whining of aircraft engines announced the departure and arrival of more flights.

On the other side of the road was a row of taxis—silver Mercedes and yellow Skoda Octavia cars waiting for fares. I ran across the tarmac and climbed into the one at the front, keeping as low as I could. But as I opened the door to climb in, I knew I'd been seen. I was being watched by the man from the flight, standing outside the terminal building. He was stationary while everyone else hurried on, keen to complete their journey.

He lit a cigarette and made no attempt to conceal his interest. I showed the driver the address on the text. He nodded and we slipped away into the Corfu night.

The Hotel Paralia was nothing to look at on the outside. Brown slatted shutters on old wooden windows, and ornate white rusting metalwork surrounding small balconies. Inside, my room was clean with a tiny balcony, accessed by yellowing pine shutter doors beyond the glass windows. There was a smell of cleaning products and dust. I decided to grab a quick shower and then find some food, but I made the mistake of sitting down on the bed and quickly fell asleep.

I woke at half-past midnight, fully clothed and aching. The temperature had dropped. My mind was racing. I was unable to sleep. I got off the bed and, feeling the chill of the night air, put on my fleecy top. I headed out of the hotel, hanging my key on the hook under the number of my room. I walked along the narrow street hemmed in by three- or four-storey buildings on either side, then found my way to the wide-open Venetian boulevards of the old town. It was almost deserted, but I felt safe. There was no sign of the man from the plane.

The top of the castle was lit by an orange glow and the air smelled sweet and fresh. No London pollution here, just the fragrance of the sea, a whiff of those wild herbs and the occasional burst of exhaust as a lone scooter or taxi went past. There were empty tables outside closed tavernas and bars, the last members of staff going home. The odd receipt blew along the pavement in the growing wind. Somewhere an empty beer can was blown off an abandoned table. It rolled across the street, dinging as it came to rest against the high curb.

It was here, on this same street, that Sven and I had sat on a night out during that bliss-filled holiday in Arillas. I smiled, knowing that in these hired seats other couples had made plans and promised to love each other to eternity. Just like us. Some had lived up to those promises, and relationships had blossomed; others, like ours, had withered or been cut down by disaster or desire. Maybe one day I'd have my husband back. Could I still love him after what he'd done? It might be easier to say "yes" and forgive him, the way my mum had forgiven my dad, but the more confident Tess in front of the camera would say "no".

I felt very much alone. I was so desperate to talk to him, to walk these streets holding his hand, the hand that was now holding someone else's. I couldn't bear the thought of him in bed with her. I felt angry and utterly helpless. The one person I needed right now was in someone else's arms.

As I walked back to the hotel, lost in thoughts of the past—tears stinging my face, slapped by the drying wind—I was rudely brought back to the present. I stopped short. There was the sinister man who'd been on the aircraft, walking out of the Hotel Paralia's entrance.

I dodged into a shop doorway and flattened myself against the glass, waiting until he'd gone. As he made for the end of the street, I felt safe enough to go into the hotel lobby. I could see the night porter at his reception desk. Unopened mail was stacked by the dusty computer keyboard. There were two dirty glasses by the phone, stained with the dregs of dried beer.

"Hello," I said. "Who was that man?"

"Hello, madame," the porter replied. "Man? What man? I've been resting in the back room; I didn't see man." I didn't believe a word of it. I could see a wad of euro notes pushed into his top shirt pocket.

"Where's my key?" I asked. "I put it on the board behind the counter when I went for a walk an hour ago." He shrugged, looked around and found it lying on the end of the reception desk. Next to the key was the guest book. It was open, and my name and room number were there for anyone to see. Heading upstairs I crept along the echoing tiled corridor and cautiously opened the door to my room. I switched on the light. My rucksack was on the bed. It seemed untouched, but I had my doubts.

Someone had been in the room for sure. I looked around. The background aroma hit me. I could detect the faint smell of cigarette smoke which hadn't been there before. It wasn't the smoke from a lit cigarette, but that cold, stale, unpleasant smell that smokers radiate from their clothes and hair. Everything of value and importance was in my shoulder bag which was with me; but my old phone was hidden in my rucksack. I knew that rucksack really well; I'd owned it for years. I checked it over; the strap was done up on a different notch. The usual ones were so well worn. My fears were confirmed when I opened the top and looked inside. Everything I'd packed was there, except for my old phone. It was gone. Gone, and with it all of my contacts, call logs and messages up until I left the UK. They were now with someone else, probably the man I knew to be Crusher Lean's friend.

I grabbed my stuff and headed back to the reception desk. The night porter wasn't there. I peered into the gloom and could see him lying on a sofa in the small back room beyond, fast asleep. I crept out and, after checking both ways that I was alone, I hurried into the shadows.

I found the entrance of another small hotel on the adjacent street which I'd passed a few minutes before. The light was on. An old man was slouched in front of a TV set showing a dubbed American cop show. An unlit, half-smoked cigarette in his mouth. Old religious icons glinted on the wall. A faded yellowing photograph of a couple stared out of a wooden frame.

"*Kalispera*, good evening," I offered, walking up the short steps and through the tall but thin double doors.

"Good evening, madame. Room for one persons?" he asked, looking disinterested.

"Yes, please."

"No reservation?"

"No, sorry. Late flight, then a walk. Sorry."

He shrugged and took my passport, typing my name into an old computer on the desk. "Room three. Top of stair. Nice room. Pay in morning."

"Thank you," I said and hurried up the narrow, echoing stairs, quickly checking over my shoulder. Room three was musty but clean. Small tables housed old metal lamps on woven mats either side of the bed. A pile of tourist leaflets was unevenly stacked on a dark wood chest of drawers. Opening the windows and shutters to change the air, I put my shoulder bag and rucksack on one side of the double bed. With the door closed and locked, I left the key in the lock to stop another one being used. I lay on the bed, half-dressed, ready to run, with my bags beside me, and tried to get some sleep.

The pillows were soft, their cases freshly ironed. I touched my mum's necklace, resting on my warm skin. It was my only link to her. I was reminded of her gently stroking my hair as a little girl when I was worried or ill. I was missing her. I was missing home; I was missing Sven. I could see his beautiful grey eyes looking down at me as we made love in front of the fire just a few days ago. He'd be looking into Heffle's eyes now, and she into his.

Jane, too, walked into my memories, bringing coffee and squeezing beside me on the single bed of her student room all those years ago. Walls crowded with posters. An overflowing laundry basket. Empty bottles, glasses and a pizza box littering the floor. We'd held hands and stared at the ceiling, unavoidably listening to our friend Sarah and her boyfriend Will putting the bed through its paces in the room next door. We were always there to patch the other up and rebuild the pieces of our seemingly fragile emotions. Now I had real worries that needed much more than coffee, chocolates and a hug. As I lay there, waiting to sleep, I found myself remembering how I'd first uncovered the Lean crimes. I was beginning to wish I hadn't...

My involvement with Lean had started with a tip-off call to

the newsroom from a young woman called Milly who worked in Lean's old people's home as a care assistant. She'd been shocked and deeply upset by something she'd witnessed.

It sounded like a story, and I agreed to meet her near Cockfosters Underground station. It was about forty-five minutes on the tube for me, and close enough for her by car from where she lived in St Albans. She'd told me she'd park in the quiet lane opposite the station, next to a church, so at seven-thirty on a wet October evening I left Cockfosters station and crossed the main road to find her. Milly was there, but she wouldn't be telling me anything.

I thought she was dead when I first saw her lying on the road opposite her car. It was clear from the angle at which she lay on the ground, with one leg twisted backwards, that she'd been hit by another vehicle, and it had only just happened.

Her eyes were closed but her mouth was open, as if in a soundless scream. I called 999 and waited for the howling of the sirens.

I felt I should pull her skirt down—it had ridden up around her thighs—but I couldn't have my fingerprints, my DNA, anywhere near her body. I could see that her car door had been forced open and the contents of her bag emptied onto the pavement. There was no phone. I knew she'd had one as she'd texted me earlier to confirm our meeting.

I looked at the young woman lying on the wet tarmac. She was of mixed race, in her twenties with short dark hair. This was no accident, and the story was far bigger than I'd first thought. I called the newsroom and, just after the ambulance arrived, I was standing in the chill next to the satellite rig, with Jake on camera and the truck engineer, Nish, for company. I did a short report for the London late news. The scene was eerily lit by battery lights as the police searched the area. Paramedics had moved Milly into the ambulance with its blue lights turning. She was still alive, I was told, but unconscious.

The officer in charge of the inquiry was DI Ted Green. I'd got to know him over the years and always found him helpful. Now it was my turn to reciprocate. The day after Milly was run down, I found her mother's address and phone number. I hated making calls to family and friends. A reporter is only trying to give a full picture, but often you feel like a vulture, preying on the dead and the dying and the anguish of those who loved them. Milly's mum wanted me to find her daughter's attacker, and she was happy for me to call round to see her and learn more about her daughter and her job.

I was soon in a taxi drawing up outside what looked like a former council house in the New Greens area of St Albans. Milly's mum, Brenda, was expecting me and opened the door as I walked down the path. Police had told her it looked like a possible hit-and-run, or a mugging gone wrong, and didn't seem interested when she'd mentioned Milly's care home concerns. Milly herself was in a coma. Hooked up to tubes and monitors. It was touch-and-go.

Brenda wouldn't go on camera, but she willingly showed me into Milly's bedroom. It marked the crossover stage between a teenager and a young woman. Mingled scents from makeup, perfume and deodorants hung in the air. Old, over-used chipboard furniture lined the walls. There were drawers that had been opened and closed a million times and a dressing-table mirror surrounded by makeup, jewellery and photo frames. A champagne cork and a used glow stick sat on the windowsill along with a wrist band from a festival, a couple of teddy bears and the letters l-o-v-e carved into a piece of driftwood.

The pictures showed groups of smiling girls on trips out, in school plays, at parties, on the beach and in photo booths. Grabbed glimpses of Milly's life. The biggest photo frame was in the shape of a pink heart and displayed a picture of a happy, confident girl with dreams to fulfil—dreams that had been cruelly cut short. Next to it was a netbook. Brenda turned it on and showed me a file Milly had created, with notes on the care home and her fears about what Lean was getting away with.

51

She referred to a handwritten note from a resident named Frank Porter, which I found in an envelope lying under a red hairbrush. He seemed to have befriended Milly and asked for her help. Brenda let me take away some photographs, Milly's netbook and the note from Mr Porter. I promised to bring them back.

The next morning, I visited Frank Porter. He was in his late seventies and in very poor health, too frail to get out of bed unaided. He was sitting in a wheelchair by the window of a small but neat room, the walls painted in pastel colours, with checked curtains and an en suite bathroom. A member of staff brought us tea. I waited for them to leave before I spoke.

Frank was devastated but not surprised to hear what had happened to Milly. He was formerly Detective Constable Frank Porter and was well aware of the carehome owner's criminal activities.

"When I was in the job, we tried many times to nail Ken Lean and his brother," he told me. "Ken and Chris, known as 'Crusher', operated in the district where I was based. At that time the Leans had been small-time crooks, running dodgy used car lots before going into clubs and discos." He went on to tell me how Crusher Lean had served prison terms for actual bodily harm and assault, but nothing was ever pinned on his big brother. In Crusher's absence at *Her Majesty's Pleasure*, Ken had diversified into apparently more legitimate businesses, including acquiring this care home. Frank believed it had originally been intended as a money-laundering operation, but Lean soon found he had no shortage of would-be residents willing to pay steep fees, and there was a highly profitable side-line. Ken Lean would visit each of the residents and ask them for a sizeable donation, warning if the business went bust they'd be out on their ear. They were told the more they gave, the more secure their futures would be. He even persuaded some of the old people to change their wills and leave money to the home, to the surprise and consternation of their families.

The paperwork was carried out by a local solicitor within hours of Lean's persuasive chats. Milly had noted that residents were being given sedatives just before the solicitor saw them, so they were dopey and less aware of the figures involved. Members of staff were used as witnesses, but Milly always refused. Frank himself had turned down Lean's 'requests' for money, but after being told he might be moved to the old dilapidated North Wing he told them he'd think again.

"Some of the people who'd changed their wills to benefit Lean and the home died shortly afterwards, Miss Anderson," Frank said. "I'm convinced Ken Lean was murdering them, ably assisted by a dodgy doctor." I asked him why he hadn't told his former police colleagues; Frank said he had.

"Problem is, Ms Anderson, the person who came to see me, a local inspector, is in cahoots with the solicitor. Lean's got influence. He's got friends in Parliament. He's a big donor to the Government's party."

Frank's only living relative was a brother in New Zealand. An old friend and colleague John Donaldson, who lived fifty miles away, had been named as his next-of-kin but was an infrequent visitor due to his own ill health.

Frank agreed to let me set up some secret filming in the hope of catching Lean demanding money. I returned the next afternoon with a little box of tricks which the tech guys had given me. It was ostensibly a new laptop for Frank, who actually had no interest in computers, but which was permanently plugged into the mains and had a voice-activated recording programme linked to a built-in camera and mic. We told the staff it was so he could email his brother in New Zealand. It looked as if it was switched off as no lights showed, but it was always on standby and ready to record. I set it up on the small desk in the corner pointing at Frank's bed. I also gave him a phone so he could text me.

Frank then asked to see Lean to discuss the requests for money. About half an hour passed. At last, my phone pinged with a message from Frank saying it had gone badly. Lean had sworn at him and told him he'd regret his refusal to help.

Frank's friend John called me the next day to tell me the sad news that his friend had died. Frank had called John the day before to tell him I was a friend who'd lent him a computer and I must be given it back if anything were to happen to him. Recovering the computer, I watched the recordings. Ken Lean was seen walking into the room. He seemed affable at first and introduced Frank to another man, the solicitor, who was ready and waiting to write him a new will free of charge. The visitors soon became agitated and angry when Frank accused them of defrauding residents and killing them.

"You'd never prove anything! You're just a meddling old bill, and a dying one at that," Lean was seen to say. "You're going to regret this, Porter," sneered Lean. "We know it was you who spoke to that interfering little bitch Milly. She was planning to make a fuss in the press. Heard what happened to her, did you?"

Lean and the solicitor left, having no idea the computer had been filming the whole scene. The recording showed Lean and the doctor entering the room fifteen minutes later and insisting Frank be injected with a sedative since he was agitated. After the doctor had injected Frank with the sedative, he left. Lean returned shortly afterwards. He could clearly be seen standing by Frank holding what turned out to be a more deadly syringe.

"Die, copper," he muttered as he pushed the needle into the frail old man's arm. Lean walked out of the room without a second glance at his victim. The final recording was of Frank in that empty room, gazing towards the computer while he fought to stay awake.

"I didn't have many months to go anyway, Ms Anderson... cancer... but I hope this will finally bring Lean to book."

I had passed Milly's netbook and a copy of the film recordings to DI Ted Green. Ken Lean was arrested the next day, and seven months later the case came to trial. Conveniently for the solicitor, the building where he worked was 'robbed' hours before it was raided by the police. Paperwork relating to Lean's care homes was apparently amongst items stolen.

The doctor admitted falsifying residents' medical notes to make out they were far sicker than they actually were, to avoid postmortems. The victims had been cremated and the evidence was gone. Lean had taken hundreds of thousands of pounds and murdered a lot of people, but he had no remorse. I was pleased to see him sent to prison.

I rolled over on the hotel bed, trying—and failing—to get comfortable. Eventually, sheer exhaustion took over and I dozed off, hoping against hope that I'd wake up and find someone had re-set the timeline, editing out the last twenty-four hours of my life.

6. Paxos

"*Yassas*… Welcome, welcome," said the taxi driver waiting for me outside the Hotel Paralia. It was 8:15am. The streets were getting busy. I'd booked the cab when I arrived from the flight, but I had to return to the original hotel to pay for the room I hadn't slept in. I told the receptionist I was getting a ferry to Igoumenitsa on the mainland—just in case anyone asked after me, which I felt sure they would.

As I climbed into the taxi and leaned over to do up my seatbelt, I saw a man and a woman who looked unmistakably English going into the hotel. They could have been innocent tourists, but their arrival so early in the morning made me suspicious. The woman turned and caught a glimpse of me looking back as the taxi drove off. She touched the man's shoulder and spoke. I'd been seen.

I asked the driver to go as fast as he could, and we weaved our way through the narrow waking streets of Corfu Town. We arrived at the New Port, where people pulled bumping cases along uneven pavements and impatient lorries queued for ferries.

At the passenger entrance stood a row of ticket offices taking payments for journeys between Corfu, Igoumenitsa, Patras and Italy, plus of course Paxos, Corfu's little sister lying to the south. The bullet-shaped hydrofoil I was catching would zip me over the surface of the emerald blue sea for about an hour and a half and deliver me to Paxos for a fee of some twenty euro. From there it was a short car ride to the villa, which I'd been told was near Lakka, a postcard-pretty resort in the north of the island.

After buying my ticket, I grabbed a strong coffee in a paper mug and a croissant from a street kiosk. I also bought a hat. A cheap black cap with *I love Corfu* printed in white on the front. Totally unflattering and not what I'd usually wear, which was exactly why I bought it, hoping it would help hide me from my pursuers. I sat on one of the worn wooden bench seats, waiting for the so-called *flying dolphin* to start boarding. Traditional ferries came and went from the large concrete apron behind the ticket huts. Officials blew whistles and waved frantically, urging lorries and cars to quickly board. Late drivers sped across the open tarmac, weaving in and out of other vehicles, desperate to get to boats before their bow doors closed. Opposite, across the busy road, was a small park where life was slower. Children played and old men put the world to rights. A young mimosa tree watched over them as it fluttered in the breeze.

Something told me to buy a second ticket, one for a foot passenger to Igoumenitsa. It cost ten euro, but it could be a good distraction. I headed towards the ferry for the mainland, the smell of fuel and exhaust overpowering despite the gentle wind blowing across the sea. After a few steps, I darted behind a parked lorry and made my way back to the flying dolphin. I was sure I'd seen Crusher Lean's friend, the man from the flight, walking towards my decoy vessel. My new phone vibrated and bleeped in my shoulder bag. It was a text.

Will call in 2 from home J x

I crouched down nervously behind other people waiting for the hydrofoil—Greeks visiting relatives, backpackers on adventures, businesspeople going to work. I tried to play the tourist, cap on my head, sunglasses hiding my eyes and a fleece covering my arms. Then I saw him, the man from the flight—it was definitely him, the one I suspected of taking my old phone.

He was now walking quickly towards the Igoumenitsa ferry, smoking. He must have thought I was on it. Buying a decoy ticket had worked. I kept still and pretended to be with the backpacking couple next to me, asking them the time as the man boarded the boat.

I was relieved to see the cargo doors of the big ferry close and dark smoke belch from the exhaust pipes on the vessel's roof. It was leaving. Ropes were slipped from grey concrete bollards with yellow painted tops and the boat gently moved away from the quay. Crusher Lean's pal was now heading for the mainland.

It was late April, and the temperature was in the high teens, but sitting by the water's edge at 8:50 in the morning I could feel the chill from the sea. I was tired and emotionally wrecked, not the ideal recipe for feeling warm and content. My new mobile rang.

"How are you?" Jane asked.

"Exhausted… scared… but on my way to Paxos. I'm at the New Port in Corfu. Thanks for the hotel and, for everything. I'd still be in London if it weren't for you. I bought a ticket to Igoumenitsa as well, as a decoy. I needed to throw someone off my trail." I kept my voice as low as possible. "It's weird being alone, I keep expecting to see Jake behind me, struggling with a camera in one hand and a tripod in the other." The two of us had been on some frenetic overseas shoots together.

"It's a good job you're not in London. The coverage isn't great," Jane replied in a sombre tone.

"Oh?"

"Someone put a picture of you on Twitter, looking like an old Wild West poster: *Wanted! Dead or Alive!* It was taken down, but not before the papers had grabbed a screen shot. I got our story out, with the headline: *Police investigate death threats to reporter.* The others have picked it up and followed suit on their websites. I quoted you as saying it was a *terrifying experience* and you were believed to be *heading for a secret location in Northern Europe until your attackers had been caught*. I wrote that it was believed to be connected with the recent trial and sentencing of Ken Lean, but obviously I can't say his brother's behind it. Innocent until proved guilty, as you well know. It looks pretty obvious though."

My head was spinning. I was making the news; it wasn't good.

"What did you use for visuals?" I asked, trying to imagine the story in print.

"A publicity pic of you, and that photo you sent me—the one of the knife through your nightie on the bed. Great shot. I sent it on to your editor too. They used it as well, and they interviewed your pal DI Green. He said a number of people connected to the Lean case had been questioned. I take that to be the two they caught at your house when we left."

"Probably." The bastards who'd slashed my clothes.

"He also said you could have police protection, and they were monitoring the situation daily. And he rang me."

"He rang you?"

"Yes, he's given me his number to pass on to you and said to call him when you're back in London—or before, if you're in trouble."

"Did you say where I was?" I hoped she hadn't; I wanted anonymity.

"To him, yes. He is the police, after all."

I knew Jane was only doing what she thought best but, even so, it made me nervous; the more people who knew where I was, the more exposed I'd be. There wasn't much Inspector Green could do in Corfu—or in London, sadly—unless I wanted to hide in a cell, and even then, who knows who'd be waiting. We know Lean had one bent copper on his payroll. How many more? I wondered.

"There is one thing which might make you smile…"

"Go on, I need something." I said.

"Danny Downs was found tied up and stuck in an industrial rubbish bin. Apparently, he'd tried to get a quote and a pic of Crusher Lean. Lean clearly wasn't amused!"

"I'd like to have seen that. Poor old Downs; that's karma! Well done on the attack piece in the paper though. Thanks." I hoped it would make Lean think, but I knew it wouldn't stop him.

"No worries. It's a good story. There's also more about Sven and La Heffle in the tabloids."

"No surprises there."

"Turns out they'd been seeing each other for four months. They met when they were both guests on a TV show. And… I'm really sorry to tell you this, but…"

How much more could I take? I waited for the next revelation. "Go on."

"There's a picture of you, covered in mud."

"Oh no. On a beach? In Corfu?" My spirits fell to a new low. "I was afraid that would happen."

"Sorry to have to tell you that."

"I knew that picture would come back to haunt me." Not only had my failing marriage been exposed to the world, but now my clay-covered breasts and belly too… "That's just horrible."

"Don't worry, you can't see much really; it's thick mud, but you're clearly naked underneath. The tabloids are having a field day, as you can imagine. *Tess dumped in the mud, as her husband enjoys dirty weekends.*"

I was so relieved I was out of the country; Jane was right.

"You okay, Tess? Would you rather I hadn't told you all that?"

"No, it's better I know." All these months I'd been lied to; I wanted the truth, no matter how much it hurt. "I just feel like my whole life's falling apart."

"Well, one consolation, so is Heffle's."

"Oh?"

"She's resigned."

"Good. So she should."

"There are pictures of her leaving Number ten, and one with her husband and children on a beach—the kids' faces blurred out of course. Hey, cheer up, she looks a lot less appealing in a one-piece than you do covered in mud. One paper even wrote: *Heffle's career is shagged!*"

"I can guess that wasn't in the Guardian, then." I smiled.

"Danny Downs's shot of you through your window is on one inside page, with a line about a public hero *deserving better*. It's a bit of a stark shot—reflected light and you looking surprised. The caption reads: *TV's Tess Traumatised as Heffle Hijacks Husband.*"

"Anything about my journalism bringing Lean down?"

"The quality press, including mine, are full of the *film that trapped killer Ken*, and how your report *ended his reign of death.* Oh, yes, and *Care home killer caught on camera!* That was one red-top headline. I could go on. But the Heffle story will soon run its course, you know how news works." I hoped she'd be right, and it would be off the front pages by the next day, but somehow I doubted it.

"Any news of the Leans?" I could hear her leafing through the pages.

"There's a line here... Ken Lean beginning his sentence in Belmarsh jail, and... his brother Crusher... oh... oh, fff..."

"What?"

"*Crusher Lean was believed last night to be heading back to his holiday home near Dassia on Corfu.*"

"Corfu?" I gasped. I felt sick. I quickly looked around, worried I was being overheard or watched. People hurried by heading for ferries, pulling cases and carrying bags. "Jane... that is not good news. I had no idea he had a holiday home here; I wouldn't have come if I did!"

"Don't panic, Tess. He won't expect you to be there—the world thinks you've gone to Prague."

"I think he knows exactly where I am. I may have seen his pals going into my hotel as I left this morning."

"What?"

"Yes, and someone definitely entered my room last night when I was out. I was going to tell you; my old phone is missing. It's been stolen. I had to switch hotels in the early hours. That means if it is Lean's pal who took it, he's got my contacts, and your numbers too."

"Mine! You're kidding?"

"Unfortunately not. Look, I need to get to Paxos. The flying dolphin's begun to board." People began walking through the door and picking seats.

"Go and get it, let's talk while you walk. If the signal goes, call me back when you can. I've got this afternoon off. I collected Sarah last night and I'm spending some time with her. She needs cheering up. That seems to be my new role in life! By the way, I've asked Jo to meet you when you get to Paxos. She's lovely— does all the cleaning and meets and greets guests who rent the place. I haven't said who you are, just that you're a friend of mine called Sam and you work with me." The queue moved forwards and I got to the door.

"Thanks. Can you hear me, Jane? I'm boarding the flying dolphin now." She said she could.

"Jo will show you everything… Oh and Tess, just a head's up, don't tell her I told you, but her husband killed himself not long ago. Just so you're aware, in case she seems a bit off. You know."

"That's so horrible. Poor woman," I said as I sat down halfway along the cabin with its rows of blue seats. Although I hated Sven, the last thing I wanted was for him to kill himself. Awful. I pulled my hat down to hide my eyes. I didn't want anyone to recognise me.

As the last of the ropes were cast off, I saw the man and woman who'd gone into the hotel when I was in the taxi. They were running across the concrete apron towards us. They tried to board the dolphin but, luckily, the door had just closed. They were left watching impassively as we moved away from the quay. They'd seen me through the window, and they knew where I was going.

"SHIT!" I whispered as close to the phone as I could. "I've just seen the two people who were going into my hotel this morning—they've just missed the hydrofoil. I think they're looking for me."

"They could just be tourists?" Jane suggested. The ferry passed the tall thick walls of the castle and the old customs house as we headed south. "At least they didn't manage to board your boat. Try not to worry…. Hang on, Tess, there's something I haven't told you yet. I wasn't sure you'd want to know… and I'm not his bloody errand girl either…"

I swallowed. "Just tell me, whatever it is." What else was coming? I wondered. How many more bits of bad news was Jane going to reveal?

"Sven rang me yesterday. He was desperate to know where you were. He wants to talk to you."

"You didn't tell him, did you?"

"Oh God, no, of course not. I said I thought you'd gone to Prague and didn't know how long you were going for. I don't think he believed me, though. He sent me an email. He's sent you a copy as well, but he wanted me to read it to you."

"Really?"

"Well, he knows you'll call me if you call anyone. Do you want to know what he said?"

"Just give me the summary, not the full thing."

"Basically, he said he was going to tell you about the affair himself."

"Is that the best he can do? I'll bet they all say that."

"He says there's a chance, if you want to let him back…"

"A *chance*? A *chance* of what?" I exclaimed, unable to resist raising my voice. A one-night stand I could maybe forgive and try to forget—that wouldn't be worth sacrificing everything we had for—but a four-month affair? Four months of deceit? Four months of lies, of cheating, of… loving someone else. I noticed the passenger next to me move to another seat, uncomfortable listening to my end of the conversation. I didn't care, I was shaking with anger.

"How did his email end?"

"According to him he still loves you and hopes you can work

63

something out. Yeah, yeah… You're not going to fall for that, are you, Tess?"

Really? I thought. Funny way of showing he loves me: shagging the Heffle-lump.

"Oh, and he wants his iPad back. Apparently you left yours there and took his by mistake?'

So, I'd taken the wrong iPad. I'd been in a bit of a rush, to be fair… Apart from a few notes there was nothing on mine that I couldn't live without. "Easily done," I said. "They're identical; we bought them at the same time. He ought to be able to use mine, he knows the password. Funny he never told me his…" Why was he so insistent on getting it back, I wondered? After all, the Heffle-shaped cat was well and truly out of the bag now. He had nothing to hide anymore.

The line crackled. "Tess, you're breaking up. Call later…."

The heavy rumble of the hydrofoil's engines changed in pitch as we picked up speed and the craft rose on its sea legs hurtling over the waves. I sat back in my seat. Whiffs of diesel exhaust permeated the cabin. Soon we left Corfu behind. Ahead was the humped outline of the small, low island: our destination. As we drew closer, I could see inviting little bays along its coast, backed by wooded slopes rising inland.

Now the immediate danger seemed to be receding, I felt guilty. I should have been in the newsroom, back at my desk, working on a follow-up to Ken Lean's sentencing; looking at how many people had experienced a dreadful end at his hands. I'd managed to get a few pictures of his suspected victims and a colleague had got an interview with a relative too. I'd planned to finish the item with a piece to camera outside Belmarsh Prison, saying it was here that Lean would be waking up for the next thirty years, and where he'd probably die. Hopefully. And then, there was Sven—the thought of him with her, Mrs *Family Values,* Suzanna Heffle MP, still made me feel sick. Betrayal was what happened to others—my husband couldn't do that, he was committed, loving, faithful, wasn't he? He couldn't be seduced or tempted to stray; he'd never do that to me. But he had.

*

As we approached Paxos, the water seemed bluer and the little, low island was soaked in gentle sunshine under a cloudless sky. Olive trees and green scrub gave way to rocky outcrops. Small bays lined the coast and a thin grey road wound its way along the shoreline. The hydrofoil slowed, motoring gently to its berth on the concrete quay. Standing patiently in line were foot passengers, their bags and cases ready, waiting to board the vessel for its journey back to Corfu.

I stepped out into the welcoming sunshine. It smelt good. The sound of cicadas cut through the handful of departing taxis and cars. A lonely stray dog, white with a few black patches, walked hesitantly towards the crowd, head down, eyes expectant, obviously hopeful of finding a new owner or a meal. Across the road in a shale littered, pot holed layby, was a woman in her late sixties standing beside a dusty, white Fiat Panda. She was wearing worn, cut-off jeans and a t-shirt with a thin cardigan. Her hair was long and straggly, and what had clearly once been blonde was now a mixture of highlights and grey. She smiled when she saw me. It had to be Jo. I was relieved to be met by a friend of Jane's; I needed all the friends I could get right now.

"*Yassas*! Hello, I'm Jo and you must be Sam?"

"Yes, yes, I am. Nice to meet you, Jo," I said, shaking her sun-browned hand.

"So, you're here for a holiday?" She opened the rusting rear hatch of the Fiat, dropping my rucksack between a couple of battered gas canisters, a box of fruit and veg, packs of loo rolls and cleaning stuff: the everyday kit of the holiday home cleaner.

"Yeah, sort of," I replied. "I wanted to escape for a bit, you know." I didn't want to tell Jo about the car crash of my marriage and the threats against me.

She opened the passenger door for me. "Sorry, it's a mess."

She grinned. "It's a former hire car."

The engine misfired as she started it. Jo crunched her way into first gear. Years of holidaymakers renting the little car had obviously all but done for the synchromesh. The well-worn, nearly bald, tyres clung to the road as we picked up speed. It must have been a journey she'd made hundreds of times. She had work-worn hands, brown and rough, adorned by one ring. On her wrists were several bracelets of woven leather and cord in muted browns and oranges. She had a reassuring presence and I felt comfortable beside her. I began to relax as we headed slowly along the narrow road, passing rows of yachts and motorboats along the extended quay.

"I'll show you the main town, the capital. It's not much of a detour, it's just along here," said Jo, and turned the car and we passed a sign reading *'Gaios'*. The little town had an array of pretty Venetian waterfront buildings, including one that stood out: the red ochre-painted house of the former British Governor, a shadow of its one-time grandeur, but still cutting a dash in this near-perfect setting. Further along was the main square edged with tavernas, bars and shops; tied to the old quay were more sailing yachts and tripper boats.

It was a seductive scene: blue water, pretty boats and inviting streets. Older houses, not turned into shops, displayed multiple layers of peeling paint, revealing bare wood on shutters beneath. Flowers flourished in well-watered gardens, and elsewhere, plants clung to life in the afternoon heat, fighting for space against walls and roadside kerbs. Excited chatter drifted through the car's open windows from people in café and bars. A couple walked out of a shop with big green tins of olive oil which they seemed barely able to carry.

Then, as we turned to leave and take the road to Lakka, I saw a water taxi heading towards the quay at speed. It had two passengers on board. As it slowed to come alongside between a tripper boat and a yacht, I saw a man and a woman. It was them! The couple who'd tried to board the same flying dolphin as me.

They knew I was here. They'd come to find me.

My heart pounded; my legs were like jelly. I turned back to Jo, and she wrinkled her brow. "You okay?"

"Yes, fine." I couldn't risk telling Jo the truth—not yet. Not until I knew I could trust her. I willed the car to go faster, as the dusty road rose to follow the contours of the island.

We were soon passing little bays with stone and shingle beaches basking in the mild spring sunshine. We headed inland before making our way back towards the sea. Grey green olive trees seemed to be growing wherever they could, their leaves gently moving in the soft breeze. Jo broke the silence.

"Here for long?" she asked.

"Oh, maybe a week, possibly two. Not sure, to be honest." I made an attempt at a smile.

"Jane's great. I knew her mum and dad: lovely couple. I don't know if she's told you, but I lost my husband last year."

"Oh I'm sorry." I said trying not to drop Jane in it.

"I keep busy looking after a few villas. To be honest, I need the money. It's the contact too. I get to meet interesting people— like you." She grinned. It was actually quite calming, listening to her chatter. Then she turned to look at me. "I won't tell anyone you're here, I promise. But you're Tess Anderson, aren't you? You're all over the news—I do watch it here, you know; I get lots of English channels."

I went to speak, but she carried on.

"I understand. You need a bit of peace. I won't bother you. Here's Lakka, you're going to love it."

We drove around the back of the resort and up a narrow road to a scattered collection of villas, each set in its own generous plot. Most were simple square buildings, painted white, with orange terracotta roof tiles.

"This is Villa Bougainvillea," Jo announced as she stopped the car outside a wrought iron gate. "Do come in." It was flanked by a white wall with purple bougainvillea flowers cascading profusely over the top. Beyond was a low, square, single-storey villa with a red tiled roof. There was a small, squat chimney in one corner. It was showing signs of age—and looked as if nature was reclaiming the plot—but it was amazing, and I felt so fortunate to have been offered this pretty little escape pod where I could, hopefully, be safe.

Jane was lucky to have inherited the villa, although it was sad to have lost her mum and dad. It was a pain and loss we both shared. We'd always said we'd come out for a holiday here together—Sven and I, Dave and Jane—but, of course, time had raced ahead, and we never did. Now that Sven had done the dirty on me, it wasn't likely to happen in the future either.

"And this is the sitting room..." said Jo proudly, as she opened the door to reveal white, painted walls with a sandy-coloured tiled floor. Beyond two small sofas, and a low table standing on a blue and white rug, two tall French windows led to a beautiful patio with views down the hill to the sea less than a mile beyond. It boasted two bedrooms, both with French doors, plus a bathroom and a large kitchen. The garden was a bit of a wild shrubbery, but it was teeming with insects and bird life. The wildness helped it blend in with its surroundings.

"And here's the kitchen...." She smiled and pointed to a fruitcake sitting on a small, scrubbed wood table. "I made this for you this morning, thought it would go down well."

I thanked Jo for her kindness and insisted on paying for her petrol, and time spent picking me up, which she gladly accepted.

"Oh, yes, Jane said to tell you about the moped. It's in the shed; the little brick-built storeroom to the left, with a big Greek pot outside it, opposite the gate. It has some fuel in it, and it *will* start, even though it'll complain and make you think it won't—just persist, show it who's boss! You can walk into Lakka if you prefer, it's only about a mile, but if you have shopping it can feel a long way back up the hill, especially if it's hot."

"Thanks, I'll give it a go," I smiled.

"I've put two dozen bottles of water and some basic supplies in the cupboard, and there's some milk in the fridge. It is long life, oh, and the eggs are fresh. They're from my chickens, I have three of them."

"Jo, you're so kind."

"It's a pleasure; and anyway Jane paid for the stuff I've left. It's so nice to make a new friend too. I'm sure we're going to get on really well. By the way, if you see a rather thick-set man wandering around, that's Christos—he's the local builder and odd-job man. He's going to come in at some stage and change a washer on the bathroom tap, it drips. He's a bit of a joker, always laughing, and a bit of a flirt. Just ask him how his wife is, that usually stops him!"

From the bushes a scrawny ginger-and-white cat with half an ear missing walked slowly up to Jo, and recognising her, brushed by her legs and sat at her feet.

"Ah, meet Mr Ouzo," Jo said smiling, bending down to stroke the cat's one full ear. "He's a stray who calls round every time the villa's occupied. He knows people are soppy enough to feed him. He's quite house-trained."

Jo told me to phone her if I needed anything. She hugged me, and I watched as she got back into the rusting white Fiat and rattled off down the road.

The garden smelt of wild thyme and oregano with a hint of Jasmine. Cicadas were making contented clicking noises in the twisted, timeless olives. Silvery spider webs hung across dense evergreen bushes reflecting the sunlight as a gentle wind blew them to and fro. I stood for a moment, absorbing the fresh air and sunshine then headed inside again. In the kitchen I opened the fridge. There was a bottle with a post-it attached: *Local wine!* It was just what I needed. It looked good, maybe not as good as the wines in some of the London restaurants which Sven and I were used to, but it was cold, and it was here. I was sure it would be nice. I texted Jane:

Lovely place! Jo's great, thank you for the food and especially the wine! Any news xx?

I unpacked the clothes from my rucksack and fumbled

around the kitchen drawers for some scissors to cut the labels from my new garments. I put my tops and underwear in the bedroom drawers and hung my dress and skirts up so the creases could drop out. My phone rang. It was Jane.

"The villa's beautiful, I love it!" I said before she could speak.

"That's good," she said quietly. "I'm pleased. Enjoy it." But I could hear the worry in her voice. Something was wrong.

"I know you," I said. "What's the matter?"

"Look, it's probably me overacting, but... there was a white van opposite my house today.

"What? When?"

"When I got back from work this lunchtime." Her voice was so low I could barely hear her.

"That's bad. Why are you whispering? Are you alone?"

"No. Dave's here, but he's really worried. He's come home early to be with me. Never seen him like this. He's really down."

I took a deep breath. I could feel myself starting to panic again. "What exactly happened?" I asked.

"The van was there when I walked back from the station. It started up and drove slowly past me and parked when I went in. I just feel, sort of, uncomfortable after what happened to you. It was like they wanted me to know they were there, and they knew where I lived."

Poor Jane. I'd never forgive myself if I'd put her at risk. "Have you told the police?"

"No, there's not much to tell them. I rang Dave when I got in and he came straight home. He was more freaked out than I was, shaking and really anxious."

"I don't blame him for being worried." I told her about the couple I'd seen on the water taxi. She gave a stifled gasp and sighed. We ended the call, both on edge.

*

I put Jo's number into my phone and decided to venture into

Lakka to get a few more supplies. Jo was right, the old moped started after a bit of persuasion. A blast of grey-black smoke belched from the rusting exhaust pipe and the machine rattled and vibrated as I revved it up. Putting on one of two helmets, both of them dented and grazed, I strapped a couple of shopping bags on the rear rack and gingerly set off on the bumpy road. The landscape was beautiful, and in many ways it felt good to be here, far away from everything happening back home—the situation with Sven, the newspaper headlines. But, knowing Jane was frightened, I felt too guilty to enjoy it. I was constantly on the look-out, too, for any sign of the mysterious couple. It didn't exactly make for a relaxing journey.

I parked the moped by a row of waste bins, obeying a sign which read: '*No vehicles beyond this point*'. The small, neat back streets around the squares hid little treasures of shops, restaurants and bars. Only a few places were open as the season hadn't begun, but the shutters and windows were painted in light greens, bright blues and gleaming whites. Most of them were newly decorated and the displays behind had been refreshed and refilled ready for the summer to start. It would've felt idyllic if I'd been in the right mood to enjoy it.

I entered a shop and, as I searched the shelves crammed with packets and tins, I heard two English voices, male and female; they were speaking to the shopkeeper sitting at the till by the door. I shrank back, trying to breathe quietly.

"Have you seen this woman?" demanded the man in a London accent. His partner adjusted her large sunglasses.

"She's a friend of ours," the woman said, faking concern. "We need to find her urgently." She wasn't dressed as a tourist. Tight jeans and a thin dark top emphasised a flat stomach and taut muscles on her arms.

"Very urgently," the man added forcefully. The shopkeeper shook his head.

The woman said, "If you see her, please call this number," and gave him a card, along with a picture of me, scanned from the papers.

"It really is important; there could be a reward—money for you," said the man curtly. They both turned to leave.

Hiding behind the shelves and burying my head in the tins, pretending to read labels, I kept as still as I could until the couple had gone. I put my basket down and left without buying anything. It was them. The man and woman I'd seen in Corfu who'd followed me to Paxos.

Checking every wall and alleyway, I sat in a deserted backstreet doorway and hoped no one would notice. I hunched forward, hiding my face, clutching onto Mum's necklace. For several minutes I hardly moved, just feeling adrenalin run through my veins, my palms sweating, my pulse beating like mad. How had they found me? I couldn't understand it. Would I ever be safe again? I thought of poor Jane, going through the same thing back in London. For a moment it seemed too much to bear.

Eventually I calmed down enough to stand up and walk. I ventured towards the quayside overlooking the almost enclosed bay, its translucent bright blue water reflecting the sun. As I turned a corner, I looked anxiously over my shoulder and walked straight into a man standing behind a moored yacht.

"Hey, are you okay?" His arms caught me as I fell forwards.

"Sorry, my fault." I pulled away, feeling stupid. "Yes, I'm fine, thanks. Sorry, I'm in a hurry."

"No problem. Stay safe, yes?" He grinned and turned away. Checking the coast was clear, I headed towards the far end of the quayside and a collection of cafes. One of them, Yan's Bar, was open. The waitress smiled as I sat on a small wicker settee right by the water's edge, half hidden from view.

"*Yassas*, hello, welcome. We have drinks, food, wi-fi," said a young Greek woman as she came over with a menu, "and there's a laptop too if you want." She smiled. "I'm Maria."

"Thanks, Maria." I tried to return her smile.

"You've missed your friends," she said. "A man and woman were looking for you. They showed me your picture. You are Tess someone? They said if I saw you, I should call them."

"No!" I burst out. "Please don't call them."

She looked at me in surprise. "They said they were friends and urgently needed to find you."

"They're not my friends. Really, no, *really*. They're definitely not my friends."

I could see she'd detected the note of panic in my voice. "Okay, it's all right," she said gently. "I won't call, I promise. Do you want coffee, juice, maybe even ouzo?"

An ouzo might have calmed my nerves, but I wanted to keep a clear head. "A cappuccino, thank you."

She turned to go to the kitchen.

I called after her. "Oh, could I use the laptop please?" I'd feel more comfortable using the café's rather than Sven's iPad in my rucksack; and of course, it was almost certainly password protected.

The waitress brought the laptop over and switched it on, passing me a slip of paper with the password printed on it. Hesitantly, I punched in the code and watched it connect up. I accessed my email account.

I typed in my password and hit return. My inbox quickly filled up. There were dozens of emails, but one name cropped up again and again: *Sven*. His subject lines became more and more desperate, from: *Let's talk* to: *Tess this is important!* And: *URGENT, respond now!* But I didn't open any of them. I didn't have the energy to worry about Sven right now.

The waitress put the coffee down on my table, along with a croissant.

"The croissant is on the house," she grinned.

Staring at the sunlit sea in that idyllic bar, for a few moments I felt a million miles from London with the living car crash of my marriage and the threat from the Leans that I was trying to escape.

"So, if they weren't your friends," asked Maria, "who were they?"

"I'm not sure, but if they come again, please say I was on my way to Gaios. To get a ferry to Corfu. Please?" I implored her.

"Sure." She smiled. "Man problem?"

"*Man problem*. Yes."

"Well, Tess," said Maria, looking across the quayside. "I'm afraid it looks like your *not friends* are still in Lakka. They're heading back this way."

"No!" I said, my heart racing. I switched off the laptop and grabbed my bag. "Sorry. I have to go."

"The kitchen!" Maria said. "There's a storeroom at the back—wait there! Don't worry, I won't say anything. Yanni is cooking; just tell her Maria said it was okay. Go!"

I needed no second invitation, and, keeping low, I dodged behind the bar. Through the door, in the kitchen, a middle-aged woman was preparing a tray of baklava. I tried to smile as I walked in.

"Sorry, sorry. Maria said it's okay if I wait here?"

"*Yassas*, okay," replied the woman without looking up. The kitchen led to a storeroom as I was told it would. Inside was a battered wicker chair which I sat on. I could hear the muffled conversation outside as Maria spoke to the man and woman.

Eventually she put her head around the storeroom door.

"They've gone. Back to Gaios, I think."

"Thanks, Maria." I sighed with relief. "Did they say anything?"

"No. They asked again if I'd seen you and made me promise to tell them if you showed up. They seemed very keen to find you. They offered me money, fifty euro!"

"I'll pay you fifty euro not to tell them you've seen me," I said desperately, clutching her hand.

"It's okay… Tess, really, it's okay. Please don't be frightened. Don't worry, I said I hadn't seen you, and you don't need to pay me money. It's okay." She smiled reassuringly. I went back outside and reclaimed my seat. As I did, I saw Jo's white Panda drive along the road on the other side of the quay.

My phone rang. It was Jane, but before I could tell her about the couple she spoke.

"Have you switched on the iPad you took from your house yet?"

"No. Why?"

"I've had another call from Sven. He says he simply must have his iPad back or have it destroyed. He insists I tell you to do this. He won't believe I don't know where you are."

The iPad thing was obviously a bigger deal than I'd realized. I couldn't help feeling annoyed. As if Sven was in any position to order me around!

"Oh, and sorry." Jane sounded awkward. "I'm afraid Sarah knows you're on Paxos; she was here when Dave asked me how you were getting on in the villa. I've sworn her to secrecy."

"It's okay," I said. I could hardly be cross with Jane after everything she'd done for me. "What's happening with you? Is the van still outside?"

"It's gone, thank goodness. Hey, let me know what's on his iPad. Must go. Bye."

I opened my rucksack and pulled out the iPad I'd thought was mine, but now knew to be Sven's. It was time to see what he was worried about. I switched it on and waited.

7. Nightmare

I sat back in the wicker chair on the front at Yan's Bar and stared at my husband's iPad as it connected to the internet. It was like Pandora's Box. I wondered just what I'd discover when I opened it. Taking another sip of coffee, I hesitated—and then clicked on his email account. It didn't open, of course; I needed the password.

So how well did I know my husband? Clearly not very well when it came to fidelity, but maybe a little more when it came to his admin. The last password I knew had been the name of our rescue cat which had died after just a year, run over by a delivery van. The poor creature's name was Tiberius, and the password was *Tiberiusthecat1*. So, what was the name of that first dog he had when he was a boy? It was a chocolate Labrador called… Biff. I tried it. Nothing. I tried *Biffthedog*, but again nothing. I then typed in *Biffthedog1*. Bingo. It opened.

The page showed a list of emails in his inbox and a directory on the left-hand side

with the usual headings of Clients, House, Finance, and so on. Then I saw one labelled *SH*. I opened it, but it was empty. That seemed unusual, so I opened the *Deleted Items* folder, and there they were. A series of emails between Sven and his lover, Suzanna Heffle. I hated myself for invading his privacy, but I

RUN TO THE BLUE

hated him more for destroying mine.

I didn't want to know about their exciting new relationship, but I did read the one headed *'Holiday?!'* He'd tell me he was attending a conference in Palma, Majorca to allow them to spend *'quality time together'*. Thanks. Then I saw one which had the subject line: *'Shields Up!'* It was sent the morning the trial ended. I opened it.

Sven, the problem I told you about. I'm sure it will come out after this trial ends if we're not careful.

Between us, the solicitor in the Lean case is a big donor to our party. He paid most of mine and some of my big-name colleagues' election expenses including the PM's. Through him, some of Lean's ill-gotten gains will have found their way to us. Technically you could argue I've benefitted from the proceeds of crime. All a bit worrying! Please can you distract your soon-to-be ex-wife (I hope!), from pursuing the solicitor angle of the story? Do anything, take her on holiday, even sleep with the bitch if you have to! Luckily the solicitor's office was conveniently robbed hours before the police raided it. The PM joked that Lean was perhaps doing us a favour, saving the NHS a fortune by knocking off these old biddies and rather enterprisingly getting money from them first. Just keep your wife under control, Sven. I'll make it worth your while, you know that. Suz x And delete this NOW!"

As a journalist, this was dynamite, if not sick-making, but as a wife it was devastating. There were two more: Sven's reply and another from her to him. He had deleted them, but in his usual disorganised way he hadn't emptied the *Deleted Items* folder. I needed to get these to my newsroom and DI Green, but how and when? I needed time to think. I copied them onto the memory card in my small camera and hid it at the bottom of my rucksack. Sven was now implicated, and he could be in serious trouble for not disclosing this information. He should have sent that email straight to the police, or even me.

Switching off the iPad, I stared across the bay, thinking about what I'd read. I realised I would be in real danger just by having copies of them. I wanted to publish but the journalist in me was being overshadowed. The Leans wanted me dead. I didn't want even more enemies. Sven was still my husband, even if it now meant nothing to him. I felt very alone, confused and unsure.

I paid my bill and thanked Maria before heading back to the moped. Leaving Lakka I rode up the hill, nervously checking every corner and scanning every person I passed. I was becoming scared of my own shadow, and not without reason.

*

The day was drawing to a close. Back at the villa, I turned on the shower. It was an open, square-based affair in a corner of the bathroom. There was no curtain or surround; it was more of a wet room. There were a few gurgles and splutters and then water, hot water; the solar panels on the roof had been gently heating the tank all day and soon I was sampling the soaps and shampoos left by previous guests. As I lathered up, I tried to relax, but I couldn't help feeling vulnerable. Not only was I naked, but the noise of the falling water filled the bathroom: I couldn't hear anything from outside. I started to rinse my hair—and then suddenly froze. I heard footsteps and could sense someone else in the room. Grabbing a towel, I turned around ready to scream. There was a man by the door. I gasped. He was motionless. In a panic I looked around—there was a plastic bottle of what looked like cleaning spray. I grabbed it, my only weapon. The water was hitting my back and hair as I faced the man, the towel slowly soaking as I clutched it to my front. I raised the bottle, ready to spray.

"*Signomi! Signomi!*" His voice was apologetic, his hands raised in defence. "Sorry, hi, I'm Christos. Builder. Builder," he said, smiling. He was looking at every bit of me that he could. I felt the panic drain from me but then wondered how long he'd been there. His eyes followed my outline through the now-sodden towel.

"Can you wait until I'm finished, please?"

"Yes." But he carried on standing there, watching.

"No. Can you wait outside the bathroom. Please," I said firmly.

"Okay." He grinned. "Very nice!" I locked the door and closed the window curtains. I finished rinsing my hair as fast as I could. Not exactly a relaxing shower, knowing there was a voyeur lurking outside.

Putting on a thin dressing gown I found hanging behind the door, I left Christos to fix the dripping tap. I walked around the villa taking in the atmosphere, trying to relax in the cosiness of my escape pod in the sun despite the intrusive builder. On the wall in the hallway was a picture of Jane's parents taken in their early days, a happy couple sitting at a table in the garden outside. Nearby was a shelf of treasures—urchin shells, pink and green; small pieces of smooth, sea-washed glass, and little bits of thin, twisted olive wood, bleached white by the sunlight. There was a section of brick red pottery, possibly centuries old and no doubt dug up here on the island, perhaps even in the villa's garden.

"All fixed. Have a nice stay. Nice dressing gown! *Kalinichta!*" shouted the departing Christos as he left heading for his white van. After he'd gone, I put a couple of empty tins on the edge of the gate. They'd fall if anyone opened it, making a noise as they hit the stone path below. His surprise arrival had shaken me up: I didn't want anyone else coming in uninvited. I went back inside and locked the front door. Now I'd been traced to Paxos, it was only a matter of time before someone found me. I planned for a possible rapid escape, having left the moped just inside the gate. I packed spare clothes in my shoulder bag along with my passport and cash; I had to be ready for a quick getaway.

I made myself a simple stir-fry and got ready for bed. The softening evening light was gently showing through the open French windows with their shutters pulled back. I texted Jane. I was too tired and shaken to mention the emails I'd seen on Sven's iPad earlier. That could wait. Besides, there was a more immediate danger.

The couple were looking for me in Lakka. They came into a café I was in. I had to hide in the kitchens! I'm just hoping they're now looking at the other end of the island. How are you? Any more sightings of that van? T x.

Two hours later, as the light faded, I climbed into bed, my phone beside me. I was still wearing my pants and a t-shirt, ready for a quick escape, just in case. I wouldn't be safe here for long. I was a fugitive, on the run. The mysterious couple would catch up with me eventually. But who were they? They looked too smart, too well-dressed to be part of Lean's gang. I was also running from Crusher Lean, a man filled with hate, a man driven by revenge, a man with no moral compass or concept of remorse. I knew what he would do when he found me, but the couple—they were an unknown, and possibly even more frightening, prospect. Which of my pursuers would find me first?

I lay in bed and looked across at the open glass doors and the moon creeping across what was becoming a star-rich sky. In Greek mythology the moon goddess Selene was the *eye of the night*, watching over women. Tonight, I hoped she would watch over me. I loved the silhouettes of ancient olive trees shimmering in the gentle night wind. There was a distant owl calling with its distinctive high-pitched sonar-like sound. Feeling vulnerable, I got up and closed the wooden shutters, but I had to leave the French windows open to let in fresh air. It was just too stuffy to seal myself in. I slipped back into my lonely double bed.

Lying on the soft, clean pillow, my ears picked up the whining of a mosquito on the wing, seeking food. It wanted my blood. It landed on the headboard and, not wanting to be bitten, I reluctantly squashed it with my hand. I knew Crusher Lean would have no such hesitation in squashing me. I fell into an uneasy sleep, despite being snug under the crisp white sheets in the now cool, welcoming room.

I was dragged awake at 1am as the cans on the gate crashed

to the ground. Hitting the stone path outside, they echoed and bounced as they landed. The noise pierced the still, empty night. After a moment of silence, panic filled my mind. Grabbing my phone, I leapt out of bed. I strained my ears for the sounds of footsteps, doors being forced, or windows being broken. But the silence returned. There was nothing. Nothing—until the scratching on the shutters of my room.

Pulling on my jeans and pushing the phone into my back pocket, I hugged the contours of the walls and made my way to the shuttered windows, my feet gripping the cool stone tiles of the floor. I could hear my pulse thumping in my ears. The scratching continued as I tentatively pushed open the wooden frames just a little. It was Mr Ouzo, the stray cat that called when the villa was in use. He must have knocked the cans off. I opened the shutters and let him in. He jumped on the bed, and I ran my fingers through his manky fur as he purred. I was so relieved. Relieved, that is, until I heard a car. It was gently crawling along the road outside. It didn't sound like Jo's Panda or the builder's van. Then it stopped, and the engine was switched off.

Car doors opened. Footsteps sounded. The gate opened. One of the tin cans banged. I peered from the bedroom door and strained my eyes to see through to the window at the front of the house. There was a man, with another person behind. I couldn't see if it was a man or a woman. The cat was spooked and dived under the bed. I moved quickly and slipped out through the open French doors. I hurried barefoot, across the garden, making myself as small as I could against the oleander and tamarisk shrubs that edged the plot. Should I run or hide? They were two. I was one.

Treading on a sharp stone, I gasped and had to swallow a yell. Running was out of the question: the road was uneven, stony and rough. If they saw me, they'd catch me—they had shoes on, I didn't. The car had blocked the gate, so escape by moped was out of the question too. The outside storeroom where the moped was normally kept was at the far side of the villa, illuminated by the moonlight. Perhaps Selene was showing me the way.

Keeping as low as I could, I held my breath. The shrubs jabbed at my skin as I used their shapes to hide mine. I could hear muffled voices coming from inside the villa through the open front door. The second person was a woman—I could hear her voice. Was it the couple who'd been looking for me earlier? If it was them, then what were their orders? Who were they working for? I wasn't sure, but I knew I didn't want to find out.

Torches played around the windows on the inside as I grabbed the latch on the outhouse door. Stubbing my toe on the large pot beside it, I swallowed yet another yelp of pain. I went inside and crouched in the corner. It was dusty and full of spiders. I cringed as something ran across my foot. The smell of petrol wafting from a can was sharp and unpleasant. Hanging on the wall were a pair of rusty garden shears, my only weapon—I lifted them from their hook as quietly as possible and held them close to my chest. Was this where it would finish, where my life would end?

I was tightly clutching my phone in one hand, the shears in the other. I thought about dialling 999 but of course that wasn't the emergency number here. Stupidly, I couldn't think what it was. I rang Jo and her answerphone kicked in.

"It's Tess," I whispered. "There are intruders in the villa! Get police. Please help!" That was all I had time to say. I hung up and froze as footsteps slowly crunched the ground outside. They were heading towards the storeroom. Dropping the phone I lifted the shears and held my breath as they got closer. Then came a shuffling, the sound of grating pottery on gravel. The pot was being wedged against the door. I stood up and held the shears out in front of me. I was breathing like I'd run a race. Sweat was breaking out on my face and neck. Blood was surging through my swollen veins. I could feel my throat tighten and grow red; it began to itch. They must know I was here; they'd trapped me inside. I waited for the storeroom door to open. What was their plan, why had they locked me in? What did they want? The iPad? Had they come for that?

The footsteps moved away. Car doors closed. The engine started, and the car drove off.

What was happening? Had they trapped me here? Was I meant to die of dehydration? No, someone would come, Jo would call—but what if the plan was to come back and finish me off before I escaped? Images sprang to mind of them lighting the petrol for the moped, cremating me alive in a fireball, helplessly trapped inside. I needed to calm down and try to shift the pot, get the door open.

I was getting desperate. I'd tried in vain to push the door open and was wondering if I could break part of the roof to get out. I broke a nail, cut my finger and grazed my knuckles as I pushed, pulled and shook the door. The acrid smell of petrol was burning my nose and throat. I heard a car draw up and my pulse raced. I grabbed the shears, was this it? Were they back to kill me? No, this one was different and familiar. It was Jo's old Panda.

"JO!" I shouted from behind the door. "I'm in here! I'm in the shed, OVER HERE!" I shouted desperately, hammering my fists on the wood. Now that I knew help was on its way, I felt like I was about to faint. My whole body was shaking, and weakness overwhelmed me.

"Hang on, I'll get you out. I just need to move this pot. God it's heavy. I'll roll it over, hang on." She finally opened the door. Cold air and moonlight found me.

"Hey, are you all right?"

"NO! No, I'm not. I really thought I was going to die." I hugged her and burst into tears. "They trapped me in here. Lean has sworn to kill me so if they were his thugs then why didn't they? I was helpless. Why didn't they attack me?" I said out loud, more to myself than Jo. "It must have been the couple, the man and woman."

"Well, there's no one here now. Let's check inside the villa, shall we?" She took my hand, but I couldn't walk. My legs wouldn't respond. I felt dizzy. Fresh air pushed the stale smell of petrol from my nose. The back of my throat felt as if it had been burned by the fumes. I turned to the hedge and was sick.

"Oh, come here, Tess," said Jo, and held me as if I were a frightened child. "It's all right love, you're safe. I'm here." Together we went back into the villa. The front door was still open; Mr Ouzo the cat walked by, unconcerned by the activities in the night.

"I'll put the kettle on. Do you want me to call the police? They might not come until tomorrow though if the intruders have gone and you're unhurt. Probably not worth bothering them, really. It all looks undisturbed," she said, looking round. "There's nothing broken. It can't have been that Lean man, you helped put him in jail."

"No, it's his brother who's after me. I need to check my things." I went into my bedroom and turned on the light. Immediately I saw that Sven's iPad was missing. I'd put it under my clothes in the second drawer down. It was a nasty thought that some stranger had moved my clothes and gone through my things, but at least there was no damage and nothing else was taken—not like the first time, at home in London. That confirmed it: this wasn't Lean, this was someone after the emails. Surely the couple must be working for Heffle? Or were Heffle and Lean actually working together? At least I'd made a copy on my camera card in my bag, and they hadn't taken that. So, who'd told them where I was? I made a mental list of the people who knew I was here: Jane, her husband Dave, Steve, Sarah, Jo, DI Green and Christos, the lecherous builder. Had one of them betrayed me? I could barely believe what I was thinking.

Jo stayed until dawn and then left when everything seemed more tranquil. The moonlight had given way to grey, the night over at last. She invited me to visit her later that morning for coffee. I gladly accepted and thanked her for coming to my rescue in the middle of the night, pushing a ten euro note into her hand to pay her fuel. I wanted to thank her more and decided to take her shopping and buy her some clothes when things had calmed down, as she appeared so short of cash.

After she left, with the doors locked, I dozed until the mewing of the cat outside woke me up a few hours later. I got off the bed and went to let Mr Ouzo in. Together, he and I watched the sunlight strengthen as it bled through the slatted wooden shutters, lighting small particles of dust floating in the air.

In the daylight I felt safe but exhausted. The last few days had caught up with me and I was physically and emotionally drained. I gave the cat some milk, made a coffee and then crawled back onto the bed with a couple of headache pills. Yesterday's wine hadn't helped. I thought of what I'd be doing at work right now, had all this not happened. I'd had a meeting with Steve planned, to talk about a documentary on Ken Lean and another on Milly, the *Care Home Carer*, as she'd become known; the girl whose call had led to Ken Lean's downfall. The girl who was now in intensive care. She deserved to be recognised for what she'd done.

I finished the coffee, grabbed a slice of toast, and emptied a tin of tuna fish in an old, chipped bowl for the patiently waiting Mr Ouzo. Then I dragged myself into the shower to wake myself up, this time locking the front door first. Hanging up the towel, I got dressed in a new t-shirt and shorts. I noticed the time and remembered Jo had invited me over for coffee. I wanted to text her saying I'd be late as I'd overslept, but my phone was completely flat. Where was my charger? I couldn't find it. I couldn't call Jane either, although I desperately wanted to tell her what had happened, but I was already late. Locking the door, I picked up my shoulder bag, complete with my ever-ready escape kit, and mounted the moped. I had a little map of the island which Jo had left me with her house circled on it. There weren't that many on the narrow lane where she lived.

I rode along the twisting coast road and then inland to find Jo's house. There were a series of properties clearly occupied by ex-pats, names like Saunders, Schmidt and Wilson on nameplates by their gates. It was a roll call of retired professionals. Built on a hillside with shrubs and trees forming a backdrop, Jo's run-down home looked at peace with its surroundings, albeit in desperate need of repair. A window was broken, and the door lacked paint. She was there in the garden, cutting back overgrown oleander bushes which tumbled over the tired, low stone wall. Jo waved, smiled and, laying down her shears, she walked towards me. She was wearing a baggy t-shirt, old, torn shorts and a large, floppy, brown hat.

"Tess, you found it okay, then?"

"Yes," I said, taking off my crash helmet. "The map was perfect. Sorry I'm late, by the way. I dozed for a few hours this morning."

"I don't blame you! Are you all right now?"

"Yes, fine. I can't thank you enough for coming out last night, I'd probably still be in that storeroom if you hadn't."

"That's no problem," she smiled. I looked around.

"What a beautiful garden," I remarked.

"Oh, it's the climate—that and the soil. I just cut the occasional branch, and harvest the fruit and veg; the island does the rest."

"These bushes are oleanders, aren't they?" I said admiring the white and the red blooms on the row of plants.

"Oleanders, yes. Local shrubs with beautiful leaves. They flower from spring to autumn. Just be careful, they're poisonous."

"Hope you didn't find out the hard way!" I laughed.

Jo led me on a tour of the grounds that she obviously loved and cared for. It was such an 'English' morning. We ate in the garden, enjoying coffee and sweet, crusty dry pastries from a local bakery. She'd also made a cake. It was so nice to feel relaxed, although I did look up every time I heard a car or motorbike go by.

"So, how long have you lived here on Paxos?" I asked my host.

"A few years now. Bryn and I moved here after his coronary" We sat in silence for a moment, a range of emotions passing across Jo's face. Then she turned to me with a smile. "Would you like to see inside the house?"

"I'd love to." We both stood up. She led me past aloes and prickly pears, growing in old olive oil tins by the door.

The entrance led straight to the small sitting room. I spotted a phone charger lead running from a plug in the wall.

"Do you mind if I charge my phone, Jo?" I asked, "It's totally flat and I hate being cut off." She smiled and nodded so I plugged it in. The kitchen was simple, with stone and wooden surfaces. Two skanky-looking cats both with bits of fur missing lay together on a cushion near the open back door, lit by dappled sunlight.

"Oh, that's Pixie and Dixie," said Jo. "They were strays who found me—now they live here; just a bit of a shame they can't pay rent of course!" I smiled and looked at the jars of herbs and spices stacked on a shelf near the oven. Obviously, Jo was a keen cook. "You look a lot calmer than you did last night Tess," she continued. "Mind you, I'm not surprised—I've never heard of a robbery from a villa on the island before."

I was torn. Jo seemed so nice, it was tempting to tell her the full story, but I needed to get to know my new friend a little better first. I was missing Jane desperately. "I'm really sorry for ringing you so late," I said. "I tried to call the police, but I didn't know the local emergency number."

"It's 112. It's written on the noticeboard on the kitchen wall, but that wasn't any use while you were in the outhouse, I guess. Please don't hesitate to call me if you're worried, I'm always here; besides it's nice to have someone to talk to, even if it is at three o'clock in the morning!"

"There's an English couple who've been asking after me here on Paxos. I'm convinced it was them who broke in last night. Whoever they were they stole an iPad while I was locked in the outhouse. I'm just trying to work out how they knew where I was. Jo, you haven't spoken to any strangers, have you?"

"Me? Strangers? I've hardly spoken to anyone in the last twenty-four hours, and certainly not strangers. Besides, why would I tell strangers who was staying in which villa? I clean half a dozen properties on the island. I'd remember if anyone had asked me about you."

"Of course. Yours must be an interesting job." I smiled politely. I hoped my comment didn't come across as patronising. Cleaning villas on a beautiful island was starting to seem like a much better career path than journalism…

Jo shrugged. "I do it out of necessity, not choice, and there's very little work out of season. The people are nice though, most of the time."

An hour later I said goodbye to Jo and rode the little moped back, retracing my steps on the narrow lanes. When I got to the villa I switched on my phone; it was showing sixty percent battery. I saw three missed calls from Jane. I immediately dialled her number.

She answered on the second ring. "I've been trying to call you!"

"Sorry, my phone was drained. You sound edgy, what's happened?"

"Sven's been here."

"What?! At your house?"

"Yes, last night. He was beside himself, wanting his iPad back, he said other people were taking steps to find and retrieve it. I don't…."

"They already have," I interrupted.

"What?"

"They've 'retrieved' it." I told her of the night's events and how Jo had rescued me from the stone shed. She was horrified. "I think that proves it wasn't Lean. He'd have totally trashed the place—and me with it. He wouldn't have just locked me in the shed and left… I do think Lean's just one step behind me though. I'm expecting him or his thugs at any time. I'm sure it was one of his mob who stole my old phone from that hotel room in Corfu."

"But you think this couple—the ones who took the iPad—they're working for Heffle?" she asked.

"I think they're spooks: secret service types. Yes. I also think Lean and Heffle have a connection. Sure of it."

"Why?" asked Jane. "And what was on his iPad?"

I told her what I'd read. She was silent for a moment.

"That's pretty explosive stuff. Like, no wonder Sven wants it back. How will Heffle react when she finds out he didn't empty the deleted files folder? Can you make copies?"

"I already have," I said quietly.

"That's my Tess! Hey, do you think you'll be alright sleeping in the villa tonight? Do you want to stay with Jo? I can ask her for you."

"No. Jo's lovely but I don't feel I know her that well, and it's unfair to put her in danger too. No, I'll find a room somewhere for tonight, and then move on."

"You'll have to get a ferry to Corfu unless you can get on a tripper boat to Parga on the mainland. Otherwise, well, you could come home and ask for police protection of course."

"Hang on…" Something had just occurred to me. "Sven knows you have a villa on Paxos and that you'd probably offer it to me. I'll bet that's how Heffle knows! How her spooks knew to follow me here via Corfu."

"Yes, but how did they find you in my villa? He may know I have a villa on Paxos, but I doubt he knows which one it is. Paxos may be small, but there are a lot of properties on the island. It's not easy if you're just randomly looking for someone."

"Good point," I said. Although no doubt a woman like Heffle would have connections to call on. "How's Dave?" I asked.

"Acting strange. Stressed out. Not eating." Jane's voice was strained. "It was our anniversary yesterday."

"Oh, sorry, Jane. I completely forgot."

"Hey, my anniversary should be the last thing on your mind right now! The worrying thing is that Dave forgot it too. That's not like him. He didn't even want, you know, something fun after dinner; in fact, he didn't even want dinner. I had to cancel a reservation at the Climber, that restaurant on the High Street that he likes. You and I went there once."

"He's probably just worried, with that van having been outside. Has it been back?"

"Not that I've seen it, no. But I've been at work and so has Dave. We're trying very hard to carry on as normal, whatever that is. It isn't easy." She paused for a moment. "Look, something else has happened here which might explain a lot about last night."

"What's that?"

"Well, it's probably something and nothing but... Sarah's been talking to Will again."

"The boy she married?"

"Her soon-to-be-ex-husband, Will," replied Jane. "Yes, and she may have blabbed about you and where you've gone."

"And why is that bad?" I asked.

"Will is an accountant."

"And?"

"An accountant for a company which runs nightclubs."

"So?"

"I was interested and checked who the directors of the company were."

"Oh, don't tell me."

"Yes. One of the directors of the company is also a director of a care home run by two brothers called Lean."

"Oh, what!"

"Now I'm not saying Sarah has said something, or that Will is anything other than honest; or even that he would have passed it on to the Leans. But."

"But. It's a risk. Jane, are you fiddling with your granny's earrings?"

"Yes-s, sort of, why?"

"Because I now know you're really worried. Look, I'll go into Lakka now and try to find a room for tonight. I'll come back and pack tomorrow. I can't stay here; I don't feel safe."

Dropping the phone in my bag, I stroked the cat, which followed me outside as I closed the front door. My relaxing escape to Villa Bougainvillea was fading as quickly as the evening sun. I had to run before any more night terrors took their toll. The problem was that nightmares could happen during the day as well.

8. Caught

The friendly owner of the small hotel in Lakka found me a room. It wasn't difficult; they were all empty. Every one of them was clean, vacant and waiting, ready for the summer season to begin. I was tired and just wanted to sleep, and somewhere to sleep safely. I locked the door, had a relaxing shower—knowing that no one was watching—then slipped between the crisp white sheets on the small, well-used mattress. I missed Jane's villa a mile or so inland, but I just didn't feel safe staying there on my own anymore, not now.

At 2am I woke with a start. I was anxious. Nothing I could put my finger on, but something just wasn't right. I checked the door. It was locked. There wasn't a sound outside in the corridor. I opened the shutters and carefully peered into the alley below. Nothing, no one, but nevertheless I had a bad feeling. There was a single dark cloud obscuring the moon in an otherwise perfectly clear sky. I watched it for a moment from the balcony of the empty hotel. After a while I went back to bed, holding mum's necklace, and finally fell asleep again.

I got dressed for breakfast and walked in the early morning sunshine to Yan's Bar on the front. Sitting by the sea in the small wicker seat, I ordered a fresh orange juice, and fruit with Greek yogurt and honey. Maria, the waitress, smiled when she saw me.

"They haven't been back," she said. "The couple who were looking for you."

"I think they've gone," I replied. Gone with Sven's iPad.

As I ate my breakfast, I had to get back to the villa to grab the rest of my stuff and find my missing my phone charger. I also thought about Mr Ouzo the cat, wanting his breakfast, silly really, because when I went away he'd have to forage elsewhere until Jane's next guests arrived; he'd survived the winter, so I was sure he knew how to look after himself. Maybe he even had owners but liked to visit other people. Extra dinners always came in handy.

I went back to the moped. It was going to be a warm day and there was expectation in the air; the first charter flights were coming into Corfu, the nearest airport, and soon the holidaymakers would arrive. I rode the tired bike with its rasping engine up the hill out of Lakka and on to the villa. The smell of wild herbs had begun to find their place in the air. It was unmistakably, beautifully Greece.

One of the other villas had been opened up, and there was a hire car outside; no doubt the first of many. I braked on the corner, the first time I'd had to as I'd been steadily climbing the hill since leaving Lakka. To my horror, the brakes didn't work. I tried again. Nothing, there was no resistance. I decelerated but the moped carried on. The brakes were useless. I picked a row of the least prickly looking shrubs and aimed for them in a bid to stop. I braced myself and turned my face away to avoid the spiky branches. I bounced off the foliage and was thrown sideways. The moped toppled over and landed on top of me, trapping me beneath it.

The moped stuttered and stalled. I pulled myself out from under its frame. I had cuts and grazes and could feel a bruise forming on my leg. As I crawled out and lifted it up, I looked at the wheels. I'm no mechanic, but even I could see that the brake cables had been cut. The pain in my leg was increasing but I was relieved I hadn't been badly hurt or broken anything. The feeling of relief soon evaporated when I looked up and saw the villa. I hurried as much as the pain in my leg would let me.

The door had been smashed. It was gaping open. As I got closer, I could see splintered wood surrounding the remains of the lock. I looked inside and gasped. Furniture was tipped over. Bedclothes were thrown on the floor, the wardrobe pulled onto its side. I hesitated and slowly ventured further in. The clothes I'd left had been strewn around the bedroom. Then I realised they'd been angrily ripped as well. It was reminiscent of the damage in my bedroom at home the day I left. The phone charger, though, was on the floor.

I grabbed it and followed the trail of destruction to the kitchen. Mugs and glasses were smashed. Plates were broken and cutlery emptied out of drawers. Then I looked in the bathroom and screamed. It was horrific. There, tied from the light, hanging from the ceiling was Mr Ouzo. His poor little pink tongue poking out grotesquely from his open mouth, his last scream frozen in time. I stared at the poor creature, motionless on a piece of cord. My chest hurt, I felt weak. I sat on the floor with my back to the wall. Unable to move. I was terrified.

Written on the wall beside him in red marker pen were the words: *Your next!* The bad grammar pointed to the culprit immediately. It had to be Crusher Lean. How could even he do that to a friendly, defenceless animal? He was nothing less than a monster, leaving me in no doubt as to his plans for me. What if he'd found me here in the villa when he'd called? And when would he be back?

I couldn't leave poor Mr Ouzo there. I struggled to my feet and, with trembling hands—and tears running down my cheeks—I untied him. I hugged the poor cat as I continued crying, my tears dampening his fur as I held him in my arms. His pink tongue was still sticking out as I wrapped him in a towel and carried him into the garden. I dug a hole in the wildest part as fast as I could. It was a shallow grave, which was difficult to dig as the stones were thick and plentiful under the thin layer of topsoil. Flies gathered as I toiled to put the poor animal to rest. Stupidly, I poured a carton of milk over his grave. I knew it was pointless and crazy, but somehow it helped.

Stunned and numb, I had to get out quick. I couldn't stay in the property a minute longer. I threw my damaged clothes in the bin outside the gate. I had a few items to keep me going in my shoulder bag, my old MP3 player and a couple of other bits that had been in the washing machine when Lean had called. Luckily, he'd missed my favourite cotton dress and a short summer skirt. I photographed the chaos and walked out leaving the door hanging open with its shattered lock. I was too angry to speak, too shocked to cry anymore.

I headed down the hill. It was painful to walk, the bruises on my legs were aching and my muscles needed to rest. As I walked, I called Jo to tell her what I'd found. She invited me to stay at hers, but I declined. I then phoned Jane and told her the grim news. She gasped when she heard.

"That's just awful! Oh God, Tess I'm so sorry. I thought you'd be safe! It's all my fault. You could be dead. If he'd found you there… Horrible." Jane was crying, and her words distorting on the phone.

"It's not your fault, it's mine. I took on one of London's biggest bad guys. He was never going to let it rest. I've been so naïve."

"You have to run, Tess. Get away, now!"

"I am. There's no point in my calling the police. We know who did it, and he'll be untraceable. Long gone, unless he's lying in wait. I don't think the local cops, as good as they are, will be any match for Crusher Lean. He's evaded London's best for decades."

"Go. I'll get Jo to sort it all out and arrange for Christos to do any repairs. I'm just so glad you weren't there when Lean called. Look, get back to Lakka; leave the moped by the bins and I'll arrange for Jo to move it later."

"I can't use the moped; the brake cable's been cut and it's in the ditch where I left it. I'll have to walk."

"What? Cut! Just get off the island, Tess. Run."

*

The forty-minute walk to Lakka should have been pleasant, but it made me wince. My legs hurt; everything ached. The bruise on my leg throbbed as I went as quickly as I could. It was largely downhill and, in spite of everything, I couldn't help noticing that the little port with the bay beyond looked absolutely lovely in the fresh May sunshine. More boats were arriving. The holiday season had started.

I made my way to Yan's Bar, where I sat in my favourite place with a bottle of sparking water and a tuna salad, although I didn't feel like eating. It was the wrong thing to have ordered. I felt so sad thinking of poor Mr Ouzo; he'd loved the tuna I'd given him the day before.

"Oh, no!" Maria came over, noticing my scratches and bruises. "You're hurt! Look at your legs, your arms! Are you okay? Do you need a doctor?"

"No, thank you. I fell off the moped. I'll be fine," I said. "Is there a flying dolphin back to Corfu today?"

"Yes, every day at four o'clock."

I decided to catch it, find a different hotel in Corfu then head to the mainland the next morning. I got my money out to pay and was about to ask Maria to book me a taxi to Gaios when I saw a man climb off a motorboat and walk along the quayside. He was looking for someone. He was familiar, very familiar. He was thick set, well built, a bit overweight but a bruiser for sure. Shaven-head, dark glasses. I looked again. To my horror, I realised it was Crusher Lean—and the person he was looking for, was me.

I got up and I rushed straight into the loo. Maria looked up and nodded as if she understood. I locked the door and clutched my mum's necklace.

"The *trouble?*" she shouted after me.

"Yes!" I replied in a panic from behind the locked door. "Big trouble!" I was shaking. I could hear Lean muttering as he walked into the bar and headed straight towards the toilets; he'd seen me go in. He reached into his bag. Maria challenged him. He roughly pushed her aside. She shouted. I heard Greek voices, males, they shouted at Lean. I strained to hear, clutching Mum's necklace, my palms sweating and my legs feeling weak. I heard *'leave'* and *'police'* shouted in English. I heard other Greek voices and hoped Crusher Lean would realise he was outnumbered and back off. He shouted obscenities at me through the door as they pushed him away, manhandling him off the premises. I tentatively looked through the door.

"Hope you liked the cat!" he sneered as he walked away along the paved quayside. "Paxos is a good place to *hang* around, as you'll soon find out!"

I stood frozen with fear, listening to the Greeks shouting after him, telling him to go.

Maria told me it was safe to come out, but Lean hadn't gone far. I could see he was standing next to the motorboat, waiting, looking, staring: a man on a mission—a mission to kill me. The hatred was sweating out of him all over his over tight white tee shirt. His thick neck displayed the same dragon tattoo that I'd seen on his brother Ken in Court. His hands were shaking, his fists formed, his anger directed at me.

The Greek men went about their business now peace had returned. I stood behind Maria trying to shield myself from his angry stare. She asked if it was a marriage problem and if he was my husband. I said no. She had no idea who she was dealing with. I asked her if she could get me a taxi, fast, to Gaios so I could catch the ferry. I'd go to the police station on the harbour front and wait there until the flying dolphin left. Maria nodded and picked up the phone. The quayside was quiet. I was keeping an eye on Lean, and he was keeping an eye on me. Except that he wasn't there... I couldn't see him. A large van was driving slowly along the quay obscuring my view.

I looked around, and then there he was—he'd been walking the other side of the van, hidden from view. I grabbed my rucksack and bag and, despite the pain, I ran. I ran like I'd never run before, adrenalin overriding the signals from the nerves in my legs. I pulled chairs over as I went; Maria shouted at him, throwing down the phone. The men came out of the kitchen, but Lean was following me close behind. He pulled out a large knife from inside his bag.

I was younger and fitter than Crusher Lean but very frightened. I got a few paces ahead, but he was really close. A woman crossed in front of me, unaware of the drama unfolding. I tripped as I fell into her. I banged my head and leg on the rough stone of the quayside. Lean ran towards me. The jagged blade glinted in the morning sun.

The look on his face was one of expectant joy, but then… he fell too. Out of the corner of my eye, I saw the man I'd walked into the day before pull a hosepipe straight up in the air. It stretched from a tap on the wall, across the pavement and onto his yacht, filling its tanks with water. Pulled upwards, it acted like a trip wire. Crusher Lean had gone over, his knife landing inches from my shoulder. The point of the blade clunked as it came in contact with the ground. Stainless Sheffield steel met solid Greek stone. It could easily have been stainless Sheffield steel meeting thin, vulnerable skin.

Lean growled, grunted and swore but, as he got up, he shouted out in pain and fell forward again, his head coming to rest inches from mine. His yellow teeth were exposed by his snarling lips. He was groaning. The man from the yacht had hit the back of Lean's knees with a metal winch handle. I saw the hatred in Crusher Lean's eyes and smelt his vile breath close to my mouth. It stank of stale beer and cigarettes.

I felt my legs being pulled away and, clutching my bag and rucksack, I was hauled up like a rag doll and literally pushed onto the yacht. The man who'd rescued me started an engine and quickly undid two ropes which he pulled back into the boat. Maria had rushed to help, and she shouted at the yachtsman, "Go, Jason, go now!"

I was relieved; if Maria knew him, he must be okay. Lean staggered to his feet and lunged towards us, trying to get on the yacht too. The men from the bar, urged on by Maria, had now caught up with him and were pulling him back, yanking his hands from the vessel's stern as he got within a whisker of jumping on board.

As the yacht left the quayside, putting clear water between us and Lean, I saw him pull himself free. He threatened the bar staff with the knife and then threw it into his boat, swearing. He boarded his vessel and thumped the steering wheel, screaming in frustration. I couldn't hear him over the noise of the yacht's engine, but I could see him shouting and pointing at us, obviously furious. I turned to the man at the wheel.

"Hello again," he smiled.

"Thank you. Whoever you are. It was a really brave thing to do, but he's going to catch us; that's a power boat."

"Well, he would do," he said in a smooth American accent, "but not without these—they, er, *dropped* out of his pocket when he fell. I thought it prudent to pick them up and keep them safe." I saw a cork float on a ring and the keys which were clearly needed to start Lean's engines. Lean was thumping the wheel of his motorboat again and again, screaming threats at us. We'd slowed him down but not stopped him, by any means; now he knew I was here, he wouldn't stop.

"That was really brave of you." I was shaking but relieved.

"I like helping the underdog. *Remember the Alamo* and all that." He smiled, blue eyes highlighted by tanned skin.

As we motored away, a police car arrived on the quayside. Two officers got out and Lean was pointed out by the men from Yan's Bar. I doubted they'd be able to detain him for long.

I watched the man who'd saved me pull up the mainsail of the yacht as we headed out to sea. He was in his forties, slim, tanned, good looking and pretty well preserved. He wore expensive sunglasses. A sailing cap was pulled down over what looked like an almost shaved head. There was also something about him, something hauntingly familiar.

"I'm Jason," he said. "Jason Howard. Welcome aboard."

"Thanks, Jason, I'm…" I hesitated. "Sam… Sam … Swinton."

"You don't seem so sure, Sam Swinton."

"Sorry… I'm a bit shaken. I'm so grateful for your help; he's a pretty nasty guy."

"No kidding. Really? I kind of guessed that. He didn't seem to be in the mood to discuss your differences over a latte or a lager. So why is he after you? Don't tell me if it's personal."

"Maybe later," I said.

"Well, he seems pretty pissed off. That knife was a bit scary too. Are you okay?"

"Yes. These cuts are from falling off a moped earlier, and my tripping up just then. The knife didn't get me. Hey, I really can't thank you enough for pulling me onto your boat and getting me away from Lakka. If you hadn't…"

"It's all right. Really. Did you know your leg's bleeding? Quite badly. I've a first aid kit below."

"No, I'm fine, really." Now that I'd made my escape from Crusher Lean—even if it was only temporary—I had time to feel slightly self-conscious about this handsome stranger looking at my legs.

"Here," he said, handing me a piece of kitchen roll. "You need to stop the bleeding."

"Thank you." I wiped off the worst of the blood and pressed the kitchen roll against the wound.

"Look, I'm taking us to Parga on the mainland. It's eleven miles away; we should be there in a couple of hours with this wind. I'll put the auto pilot on in a bit and show you round the boat; it won't take long. I've got a t-shirt you can wear too—there's blood on yours."

"Thanks, that's kind, but I've got a few things in my bags.

Although, actually, I don't have that many—most of my clothes were ripped to shreds by that guy last night." He raised his eyebrows, and I found myself adding, "Luckily, I wasn't in them at the time. I've been expecting to make a dash for it at some point." I wanted to trust him, but I wasn't sure who he was; although right now the idea of getting away from Paxos and Crusher Lean appealed, a lot.

"We just have to avoid a reef up ahead, it's pretty dangerous." Jason said as we left the bay behind and carefully steered the yacht around it. We were heading into open water which was hundreds of metres deep. I was well out of my depth in more ways than one, and it was vital that I kept my wits about me. Yes, he'd rescued me from being stabbed or killed by Crusher Lean, but what were his real motives in putting himself in danger? After all, he too would now be on Lean's hit list. Wouldn't he?

"There, the auto pilot's on. Now, Sam Swinton, I have a big question for you, and one I need an answer to, and an answer to right now."

"Okay?"

"Is it tea, coffee or something stronger to drink?"

I laughed and settled on coffee. It was too early for alcohol; besides, I wasn't sure how I'd feel being on a sailing boat for the first time. The gentle motion, the sound of the waves all around us and the warm wind were liberating, and every minute was getting me further away from Crusher Lean.

"Come and have a look round the boat." He smiled and I followed him down the small steps to the cabin below.

"This little cubby hole is the bathroom," he said, opening the door, "the toilet's quite easy to use, look." He pointed to a pump handle. "You'll find a clean towel in the locker here under the sink. "I've got new soap and lots of stuff other people have left behind," he said, gesturing to a shelf full of half-used products, such as shampoos, soaps and creams. "Help yourself to anything."

"Other people? Do you often rescue people being chased by

101

crazed killers?"

"Nope, you're a first in that respect. I just have the occasional guest, usually old pals from the past."

While Jason put the kettle on and popped his head through the hatch to check outside, I washed my cuts and swapped my top for another one from my rucksack. The yacht was lighter inside than I was expecting; it was neat, tidy, and clearly an expensive boat, and one he'd looked after. There was a small cabin at the back, a large open central area with a small kitchen section to one side, and the bathroom to the other. At the front was another V-shaped cabin mirroring the shape of the bow of the boat. That was where Jason slept. It looked very inviting and romantic. My mind drifted and for a second I imagined myself climbing onto the bed with this knight in shining armour. But was it all just too good to be true? I'd escaped a madman but was I insane going off to sea with a stranger? Could I actually be putting myself in more danger?

"You okay?" he asked, handing me a mug. "Let's go back topside."

"Thanks. Is there a Mrs Jason or anyone else, hidden away somewhere on the boat?" I asked as we sat down in the cockpit.

"Nope, not here, or in fact not anywhere now. As you can see, the boat's empty; just you and me."

"Sorry, I didn't mean to pry."

"No problem. There was a Mrs Jason, but not anymore. How about you? Is there a Mr Sam?"

"Yes, well… my husband, but he's now… well he's now with someone else."

"Oh?"

"Yes. I only found out a few days ago, so it's all a bit fresh and raw right now."

"I'm sorry to hear that. So, we're both two heart-wrecks passing by, hey?"

Heart-wreck was a pretty good description for how I felt right then. I thought I'd better change the subject before I burst into tears.

"Are you on holiday?" I asked.

"Nope. Unless you consider living here part time to be a permanent holiday." He laughed.

"Do you work? If you don't mind me asking."

"Not anymore." He looked down, his expression hard to read. There it was again, that flash of recognition—he was so familiar, but I couldn't work it out. I'd interviewed so many people over the years; maybe he just looked like one of them.

"What did you do to retire so young?"

"Oh, nothing serious."

"Hey, look, I've met people from the weirdest jobs and strangest lives. It won't faze me, unless you're a murderer or a terrorist; besides, I can keep secrets."

"Hey, see those birds?" he said, as if he hadn't heard me. Graceful, large-winged birds swooped low over the waves ahead of us. "They're Mediterranean Shearwaters. We may see dolphins if we're lucky too." The change of subject was an obvious cue to back off. Apparently Jason was just as uneasy discussing his previous career as I'd felt discussing Sven." He put his coffee cup down beside mine on the white fibreglass cockpit seat. I tried to smile, but my cuts and bruises were beginning to throb and, on top of everything else, I suddenly realised I'd left the bar without paying. I hoped Maria would understand; after all, it's not every day you're chased away from your lunch by a knife-wielding killer. I made a mental note to make sure I paid them when I went back, which I knew I would do; I just didn't know when.

"I was hoping to catch the flying dolphin from Gaios to Corfu."

"Is that what you want? I think Parga would be safer as it's on the mainland, unless you're aiming to fly out?"

"No, I'm not going back to the UK yet. I'm safer here, I think, although maybe not if the last half an hour's anything to go by. Okay, Parga is fine, thank you."

"Great. Okay, the wind's just right. I'll get the sails up; you just enjoy the ride."

I sat back and looked ahead at the open sea and the mountains on the mainland opposite. The man who'd saved me from Crusher Lean was pulling out the front sail and looking at the instruments on the white metal pillar in front of the wheel. Digital displays showed numbers and symbols which meant very little to me. Jason switched off the engine and there was just the sound of the wind and the waves; the sails flexed as they filled with wind, and the boat speeded up. The sound of the wind and the water under the bow of the boat were beautiful. There were no other sounds to pollute the scene. Jason took his seat, turning off the auto pilot and taking the wheel.

"Are you sure you're all right?" he asked.

"Yes, thanks," I replied.

"Really? I'm not sure you are. There's a madman with a knife back there on the quayside who was trying to kill you, or didn't you notice?"

"Just a bit. It's lovely, your yacht. So, do you live on it, here in Greece?"

"Yes, well I have done for a few years on and off. I have a house in the UK too."

"The UK? But you're American, right?"

"Yes, and yes. I was actually born in England. Long story." I was hoping he'd tell me more, but only silence followed.

"Do they have flying dolphin ferries in Parga?" I asked after a few minutes.

"No, it's a taxi or bus to Igoumenitsa if you want to get to Corfu, but hey, forget flying dolphins—there are real dolphins over there, look! Two of them, swimming together. Maybe a good omen."

"Oh, wow, yes!" It was the first time I'd seen dolphins that close. I watched the sleek grey creatures leap out from under the water in formation, and then glide in and under the waves in front of us before heading off out of sight.

The gentle movement of the boat was hypnotic. We were

travelling at about six miles an hour; all I could hear was the lapping of the water, as the yacht sliced through the waves, and could feel the warm wind as it went into the sails. I wanted to feel safe, but I was still unsure.

I went for my phone to call Jane, but the signal had gone. No network, no service. No one that I trusted knew what had happened to me, where I was or where I was going. I wasn't even sure myself. I was heading out on the open sea on my own with a complete stranger. Why was he helping me? Could I trust him? And just who the hell was Jason Howard anyway? Something was nagging me. Where had I seen him before?

9. Parga

"Are you awake? Sorry, but this is worth seeing." Jason roused me from my sleep.

"Is it?" I yawned as I crawled back into consciousness. My leg ached as I sat up and swung myself round to see Parga getting bigger in front of us. It was an impressive sight. I couldn't say the same for my leg though—the cuts were raised and angry, ringed with dried blood, and the bruises were almost black and getting darker by the hour. The yacht's sails were down and the engine was on; a gentle thudding echoed around the boat, a far cry from the earlier whooshing of the wind and the lapping of the waves.

There was a large castle ahead with the town to the right of it. Jason turned the yacht and we headed towards a long sandy beach to the left of the fortress. I could see people; I was almost back in civilisation. He hadn't attacked me or turned me over to Crusher Lean or to Heffle's spooks; so far, so good, I supposed.

"Voltos beach," said Jason. "It's a kilometre long and in the summer it'll be full of sunbeds and water sports. The weather's quiet, so I think we'll anchor here for the night, off the beach. Don't worry, there's no tide to speak of, and it's sand below us. We're quite safe, I promise."

"How do we get ashore?" I asked.

"See that lump on the deck at the front of the boat? It's a

dinghy. I either launch that or we wait for a taxi."

"Taxi?"

"Yeah, a water taxi."

"Do we have to book it?"

"No," he laughed. "Wait and see." We slowed down. Jason gently turned the boat so its nose was into the wind and pressed a button on the side of the cockpit. The noise of the anchor chain dropping rumbled from the bow. We gently motored backwards until I felt a small jolt.

"That's it; the anchor has dug itself into the sand below. We're going nowhere. Well not until I pull it up again." I was in awe of his skills.

Jason busied himself inside the yacht whilst I took in the view. I pulled my phone from my bag, checked I had a signal, and went to the very front of the boat, out of earshot, to call Jane.

"Hi. It's me," I said quietly.

"Tess! How are you?" Jane asked. "I've been really worried. I've been trying your number for ages. Where've you been?"

"I ran away to sea."

"Oh? Really? Are you on a ferry? Are you all right?"

"No. I'm on a yacht, and yes, I'm fine."

"A yacht? What...what's happened?" she asked hesitantly.

"Crusher Lean found me," I said, looking over my shoulder to check Jason wasn't listening.

"No! Where?"

"In Lakka, a couple of hours ago. He attacked me with a bloody knife—well, it would have been bloody, had I not had a knight in shining armour to rescue me."

"Oh?"

"He's called Jason, he lives on a yacht. A bit mysterious but he's nice—American, and... also quite cute. He seems... I don't know, just... familiar... Anyway, he tripped Lean up with a hosepipe."

"No!"

107

"Yep. Crusher Lean went over just as I fell. I collided with some random person who got in the way. Jason pulled me onto his boat before Lean could have another go at me. He actually nicked Lean's boat keys which were sticking out of his pocket so he couldn't follow us! Hero, hey? Well, it was a good job because Lean has a motorboat which would have overtaken us in minutes. I'm on a small sailing yacht. Nice though."

"Hell, that sounds kind of scary."

"I've got a few cuts and bruises but, apart from that, I'm all good, thanks to Jason. I'm on the mainland now, in that place you suggested: Parga. Are you all right? No more white van sightings?"

"Yeah, I'm fine, no sign of the van or the biker, so far. Dave's still anxious though."

"Well, it's good they've not been back," I said. "Sorry to hear about Dave." He'd always seemed so sorted recently, unfazed by anything; this wasn't like him these days. "Do you think he'll be all right?"

"I'm sure he will. Eventually." She sighed. "At least the calls from Sven, demanding I get you to return his iPad, have stopped."

"I'm not surprised. He's got it back now; or rather his lover Suzanna has."

"I spoke to your police pal DI Green about ten minutes ago."

"You called to tell him about Sven's iPad?" I asked.

"No. He called me, to get a message to you. He's heard from an informer that Crusher Lean's put the word out to his pals living in Greece to find you. Apparently, he's got his chums scouring the area around Corfu and the mainland to track you down; you, and wait for it, you and a man on a yacht. Of course I said you weren't with a man on a yacht. I hadn't spoken to you then and I didn't know you'd even left Paxos, but it all makes sense now."

"Did you tell him about the white van outside your house?"

"I did, yes," Jane replied. "But if you speak to Dave, don't tell him."

"Why not?" I asked.

"He's really het up. I can't understand it. I should be the worried one. Oh, I've spoken to Jo and she's sorting out the villa, she's already cleaned it up. She's pretty upset about poor Mr Ouzo though."

"So am I. It was horrible. I'll pay you for her time, and a new door," I said. "I'm really sorry you've had all this hassle." I was feeling really guilty for the trouble I'd caused.

"Hey, it's not a problem. Don't worry about it."

"No, Jane, I will pay for it. Any chance you could get back to DI Green and tell him where I am and how Crusher Lean nearly got me? Can you give him this number? I think he should have it. I'd do it but I'm low on credit."

"Sure, of course. At least Crusher Lean didn't get you. Oh, I miss you, Tess."

"I miss you too. I even miss my cheating, lying husband."

"Really! After what he's done? Oh, Sarah sends her love. She's just got out of the car."

*

As I walked back to the cockpit, a small speedboat sped past, sending waves of wash into the side of the yacht. I lost my footing and, grabbing the mast to stop myself falling, I nearly dropped my phone over the side. My shoulder bag fell from the cockpit seat where I'd left it, spilling its contents across the floor. Jason popped his head out of the cabin.

"You okay? Sorry. Idiots."

"I'm fine. I was just caught off guard," I replied.

"Here, I'll help." Jason began putting the stuff back in my shoulder bag. He picked up my passport which had fallen open at my picture.

"Looks like you've got someone else's passport, Sam Swinton."

I didn't know what to say. I just stood there, hopefully not looking quite as guilty as I felt.

"I'm not stupid," he said. "I read the papers. Your picture's all over them."

"Mm," was all I could muster.

"It's a shame you didn't think you could tell me your real name."

"I'm on the run, Jason—if that's your real name? Sorry. It was kind of you to rescue me. Yes, I'm that TV reporter who investigated the killings and fraud at a care home. I set up secret filming and caught Mr Big, the home's owner, red-handed. He's now serving thirty years in prison. The man who attacked me is his brother."

"Thanks for the update, but it's not necessary." It was his turn to look a bit guilty. "I recognised you when I saw you running along the quayside. That's why I rescued you."

"Why didn't you say?"

He shrugged. "You weren't ready to tell me. I do understand, you know. Why you lied. Some strange guy picks you up on his yacht—you weren't to know if you could trust me."

"Sorry."

"Sorry for what? I'd have done the same in your shoes. Anyway, it's nice to meet the real you. And I really am called Jason." He smiled reassuringly, but I somehow knew he was hiding a secret too. I just couldn't work out what it was.

*

The daylight was fading. The ancient castle was suddenly lit up by orange floodlights as the town behind it came to life. Parga was waking up.

"Jason, I'm getting hungry. Can we go ashore? I'm buying, it's the least I can do. I can find a room as well."

"Yes to the food; but no to you getting a room, unless you insist. You're really not imposing. I'm enjoying your company, Tess, and don't worry, I'm not hitting on you—I just get lonely.

It's nice to have a guest on the boat. There's the back cabin you can sleep in, I'm in the front. There's a clean towel and clean sheets in there. Besides, I can show you a few out- of-the-way bays and coves where I know you'll be safe, just until the heat dies down. Yes?"

"Well, if you're absolutely sure, then thank you; but what about going ashore?"

"Taxi. It'll be here in half an hour. Believe me!"

I went below; the little cabin seemed safe and cosy. There was hot water in the bathroom which was good as my hair was stiff with salt. I cleaned and put plasters on the cuts on my legs. I had one skirt and a nice top left, along with my new sandals. It would have to do. With my fleece wrapped around my shoulders I went back on deck. Jason was waving to an approaching boat. His sailing cap had gone, as had the shades. His eyes were a piercing blue, and his hair was sparse. But there was something I couldn't work out. Somehow, I knew him. But how? As the water taxi came closer, I heard Greek music, the sort of music you get in seafront tavernas. Driving the boat was a Greek man of almost indeterminate age with a very big moustache and a large brown hat. He was smiling broadly. Flags of various holiday companies flew along the taxi's length.

"See!" said Jason laughing. "Taxi's here!" I shook my head and smiled. Only in Greece, I thought. Gently, the approaching boat expertly pulled alongside Jason's yacht, which I discovered was called Sea Biscuit, and we climbed aboard. We were dropped at the main town quay with instructions to be back by half past ten. I followed Jason along the front with its rows of brightly coloured, inviting tavernas, and then up the narrow, cobbled back streets to find little shops selling everything from jewellery to shoes, t-shirts to honey. I grabbed a few essentials and topped up my phone credit. The scent of leather belts, olive oil soaps and herbs wrapped my senses in comforting smells.

At the end of the seafront, we went up some steps to a second-floor restaurant with simple wooden seating. We took in the view at a table overlooking the street and the sea. I felt very anonymous, hidden and safe. Candles flickered on the table, lighting baskets of crusty, fresh bread next to small bottles of golden olive oil.

"Are you on holiday? Honeymoon?" asked the waiter, taking our orders.

"Oh no," I spluttered, embarrassed.

Jason smiled. "We're just friends, on a little escape. I'll have the Briam please."

"Briam?" I asked.

"Kind of slow roast Mediterranean veg. Tomato-heavy but nice," he replied. "Rubbish if you hate tomatoes." He grinned.

"Love them! Sounds good. I'll have the same please."

"Alpha beer for me and wine for the lady?" Jason looked at me.

"Glass of white please," I replied, smiling at the waiter. "Have you been here before, Jason?"

"Yes. I love the view." I glanced down onto the street below, the bustle of early season holidaymakers pouring over menus and looking at shops. "It's heaving mid-summer."

"I'll bet," I replied, "it's beautiful. That smell in the air, what is it?"

"Roasting corn on the cob from street sellers below, mixed with the smell of the herbs growing wild on the hillsides... and the scent of love."

"Sorry?" I said, taken aback.

"That couple down there. See them? He's proposing to her, look—there's a ring box in his left hand behind his back, and she's going to be all coy, and then she'll throw her arms around him." We watched the scene play out just as Jason predicted. "You see!"

"Oh... so sweet. So, tell me about your wife." From the look that appeared on Jason's face, my question was as unwelcome as a stomach bug on a camping trip.

"So, the reporter's looking for a story, huh?"

"Jason, I'm not at work."

"Reporters are *always* at work!" he snapped. "I've learnt that the hard way. Got drunk with one in Berlin once."

"Trust me, even if it's just once. I trusted *you* today."

"Okay... well, she's a model, and she was attracted by... well, by my life, I guess."

"A life you won't tell me about?"

"Lindy, or 'Eve' as she was known, Eve Eversson, hated it when my so-called work stopped. She... oh, I can't say all this now. Sorry, another time, anyway here's our food." The approaching waiter grinned and placed plates in front of us.

"So..." I tried to continue the conversation, but he jumped in.

"Hey, you see the castle? Well, there's another castle up on that far hill, over to the north; it's all lit up and looks innocent enough today."

"Jason," I interrupted, "I'm sorry, I shouldn't have asked about your wife."

"It's okay," he mumbled, but I knew it wasn't.

"So, this castle then, is it famous?" I asked, giving in to Jason's obvious attempt to change the subject.

"Infamous. It was built by Ali Pasha; he invaded here, a real butcher. He tortured and enslaved the local women. Many of them gathered on the cliffs, before holding hands and dancing over the edge to be killed on the rocks below."

"Wow, that's awful. Horrible."

"It was called the *Death Dance,* and it was seen as a welcome escape. At least those days are over, thankfully. People don't dance over cliff tops any longer."

*

The taxi took us back to the yacht bobbing at anchor as a slight swell rode into the bay. Going below we shut out the night. Jason was in the front cabin; I was at the back in the small one. I looked up through a thin window at the distant ruins of Ali Pasha's castle on the hill, and thought about those poor women, leaping to their deaths to escape a tyrant. Was that what would happen to me? Would death be the only way out of this nightmare? I shivered and drew the thin cream curtains.

*

The next morning, I woke to the sounds of Jason on deck. For a moment I thought it was Sven. I'd been dreaming of him, and the good times we'd had. I poked my head out of the companion way and squinted as the bright sunlight hit me. Jason was putting the rubber dinghy into the water. I climbed out of the cabin to see his tanned brown back rising from his blue shorts and bare feet set against the backdrop of the sea and the white fibreglass of the decks. He turned and smiled.

"Breakfast ashore?" I asked.

"Yes, and I have a suggestion for you."

"Go on," I said, intrigued.

"You need a disguise. Why not have your hair cut short and dyed?"

"Er… actually, Jason… that's… that's the most sensible thing a strange man has ever said to me."

We pulled the little rubber craft with its outboard motor out of the water and on to the fine, yellow sand. There was an open-fronted café behind the beach. Jason asked the waiter if there was a hairdresser in the town. He recommended a German woman called Helga and drew a map on a napkin to show us where she was.

Walking up the steps from the beach to the town, I suddenly had cold feet. The thought of my hair being cut worried me. I didn't want it short and dyed. I wanted to be me—but I also knew that was silly. If Crusher Lean recognised me, he'd kill me. What choice did I have? The Tess I knew would have to hide behind the Tess that Lean didn't know.

*

An hour later, Helga's scissors tore into my helpless hair; it quickly fell to the salon floor, making little piles around my feet. After the chopping came the colouring. I wasn't used to this; it felt unnatural. I looked at my reflection in the mirror. The conversation was difficult as Helga rattled on in poor English about her Greek husband and his taxi business. It didn't take her experienced hands long to turn my familiar, collar-length auburn hair to a sharp, cropped blonde. As I left the hairdressers feeling like a stranger, I took advantage of a small boutique I spied close by. I needed more clothes. There wasn't much I fancied inside but a few t-shirts, shorts and underwear were welcome. What did Jason's wife wear, I wondered? Being a model, she'd probably look good in anything, even my trashy choices. I found a couple of tops that made me feel vaguely feminine and headed back, unsure of my new hair.

I found Jason in a cafe on the way back to the beach. He ordered me a coffee and smiled approvingly.

"Know the voice, can't place the face." He laughed. "You look really good. Different, but good." I wasn't convinced and doubted that he was either. But if it put Crusher off the scent, it was worth it.

I noticed two missed calls from Steve in the newsroom. When Jason went to the loo, I grabbed the chance to call him back.

"Tess Anderson, my favourite reporter! How are you? I've been worried," Steve said.

"Hi, Steve, so have I."

"You're in Parga, aren't you?"

"How do you know that, boss?"

"The same way everyone else does. It's in the papers. You were recognised and photographed in the town last night. Someone saw you walking by some shops. It's all over social media too."

"What?"

"'Fraid so. *On the run in the sun,* and *TV's Tess hides in Greece* are two headlines."

"Oh, I don't believe it. Great."

"Not only that, some joker's sent flowers to the newsroom."

"Oh?"

"White lilies, funeral flowers, with *'RIP Tess Anderson'* on a card." Steve's voice was solemn.

"How nice. Very nearly appropriate too."

"How so?" asked Steve.

"Crusher Lean found me yesterday. I only just got away from him. He had a knife."

"God! Really? Are you okay?"

"Yes, luckily."

"Look, come back, we can put you up somewhere safe. You can work out of Manchester…"

"Thanks, but not yet, I just can't. Steve…" I paused. "There are other forces at work here too. I may have a story for you soon. I've seen some emails; I can't discuss them now, but they're dynamite. The guys at the political unit at Millbank will be very busy if it gets out. More later. Meanwhile, I have no computer and only a basic, not very smart, phone, so can you do me a favour, please?"

"Sure—these emails interest me though."

"They will do. But in the meantime can you find out anything you can about a model called Eve Eversson? Real name Lindy." I felt a bit low for going behind Jason's back, but we were alone together in the middle of the ocean, and it was clear there was something more here than Jason was telling me. "I know you're really busy but…"

"Tess, no worries. Eversson, got it. Any reason why?"

"I'll tell you later, but any info would be welcomed, boss." I could see Jason on his way back from the loo. "Sorry, got to go, talk later. Bye, Steve."

Jason looked quizzically at me.

"My boss, sorry—quick work catch-up. Oh fff…. Keep very

quiet and look down," I said as two men walked in and sat on a table behind me. One of them was the mystery man from the flight, the one who'd entered my hotel room in Corfu and caught the ferry to the mainland when I went to Paxos. I buried my head in my shoulder bag and made sure they could only see the back of my head. Then one of them spoke. His smoke-scarred, east London accent shook me.

"I'll call him in a mo. You get the beers, mate, it's your shout your stingy bastard." As his pal called the waiter over, he was on the phone and said two words which made me shiver.

"Hello, Crusher. No sign of her yet, guv, but it's only time. We know she's here somewhere. Dead bitch walking."

I grabbed a pen from my shoulder bag and hurriedly scrawled on a napkin in front of me: *'DON'T CALL ME TESS! LET'S GO, NOW!'* Jason looked at me. I screwed up my face, pleading with my eyes. Then the penny dropped as he listened in to the conversation behind us.

"Yeah, we looked in Plataria first thing as well, and Bonehead Bill's going on to Preveza soon, but there's no sign of that Anderson, or her new boyfriend. We'll find 'em though. There's a few yachts here to check out when we've had a beer. She can't get far."

Jason put money on the table to pay for the coffees and grabbed my hand.

"Stacey," he said. "We've got to get to the hotel. It's the last few days of our honeymoon and we're back Stateside soon honey. Let's hit the pool. Can't wait to see you in that bikini!"

I didn't reply. I just grabbed my bag and we left, hoping the men were looking for an auburn-haired Tess on the run, not a spiky-haired *American* blonde Stacey on 'honeymoon'.

As I got up from the table, he put his hand in mine. I made sure I didn't turn towards the men and tried to bury my head in Jason's shoulder like I was madly in love with him. The new hair they wouldn't recognise, but the face they would. With my pulse racing I tried to stay calm as we walked towards the beach to get back to the boat.

For the first time I realised I was holding another man's hand, our fingers gently moving together. Jason was really attractive; his eyes were reassuring and warm, pulling me in like a welcoming smile. He hadn't shaved for two days and was looking the part: the tanned, mysterious stranger who'd sailed to my rescue out of the sun. Our pace quickened and we broke into a jog on the way back to the dinghy, desperate to get away before the two men found the yacht they were looking for. Ours.

Sea Biscuit headed out of Parga under motor. I called Jane while I still had a phone signal. I sat at the front of the yacht whilst Jason stood in the cockpit, his hands on the wheel. Jane answered quickly.

"Hello, it's your friend lost at sea with a mysterious American sailor," I said.

"Tess! Everyone knows you're in Parga! You need to get out quick."

"I know. I've just seen Crusher Lean's pals. I've got a new look."

"Really?"

"I'm a victim of Helga the hairdresser."

"Who?"

"Local stylist. Jason's idea."

"Ohh… I'm sure it's fine."

"Don't say *fine,* anything but *fine. Fine* is what men say when they don't really like something you're wearing, but don't want you to go and change again because you're already late and they've been ready for hours."

Jane chuckled. "What's it like, then, the new hairstyle?"

"Er, blonde, spiky, post-punk."

"To be honest, Tess, you'd look good with any style, you've got that sort of face. Jason sounds interesting, what do you know about him?"

"Very little, except that he has an ex, but no one current it seems. He does look familiar though. There's just something, I'm not sure what."

"Send me a pic?"

"I can't from this phone. Anything from Sven? Is he alright?"

"Tess, you sound concerned for him." My silence spoke volumes. "You can't want him back surely?" She sounded exasperated.

"I dreamt I'd woken up with him this morning. It was all back as we were, everything was back to normal, and I have to say, it felt good."

"Oh, come on, girl, where's my feisty Tess? Remember what he's done."

"I know, I know. But there's still a lot of me in Tess and Sven."

"Right now, there's a lot of Sven in Suzanna Heffle."

"Jane, don't! Maybe he'll get this out of his system, and we can press the reset button. Tess-and-Sven version two." It was Jane's turn to be quiet. "Was it my fault?" I asked. "Should I have tried harder?"

"Harder at what?" she roared. "I like Sven, always have, he's fun, good looking, and, well, sorry, I hate to say it, but he's obviously damn good at hiding affairs too."

There wasn't much I could say to that. I decided to move to a different topic. "Jane, could you look into someone for me? A model called Eve Eversson." It might be a while before Steve got round to it and, anyway, two heads would be better than one.

"What do you want to know?"

"If she's still alive would be good for starters. Jason's her former husband. He seems like a decent bloke, but we're miles from anywhere and all alone. There's something he's hiding from me; I know there is. It's freaking me out."

"Sure. I'll look her up, but don't panic. If he was one of Lean's lot, you'd know by now."

"Maybe, but Heffle's got contacts too. Sorry, the signal's going, I'd bett..." The line went dead.

"Where are we going, Skipper?" I asked Jason as I re-joined him in the cockpit.

"Two Rock Bay."

"What's at Two Rock Bay?

"Oh, you'll soon find out." Jason gripped the wheel.

10. Two Rock Bay

About ten miles south of Parga, guarded by two large rocks, is a small, isolated bay named after them. Jason told me it was a cosy little spot for yachts to find shelter in. It was also a peaceful hideaway, unpolluted and unspoiled by lights or people. There were no other boats when we slowly nosed in under motor. We were alone. Light brown rocks with sparse scrub dropped down into shallow, bright blue water. From the shore, the sound of cicadas clicking drifted out to us as we slowed down. The sky seemed endless and blue, and the heat radiating from the land was reaching out to me with its warm embrace.

Jason let *Sea Biscuit's* anchor fall into the water and go to the bottom. I felt the now familiar little tug as it bit into the sea floor, and we stopped. The boat swung around as she settled and lay with her nose to the direction of the wind. The sea was calm and the temperature was rising; it was a classic Greek, blue water day.

It seemed as if we were the only humans for miles; there was nothing but the sound of ripples, insects and birds. It was utterly beautiful.

"We'll have lunch in a while," Jason smiled, his brown skin almost shining in the sun. "First though," he said, "I'm going to have a swim; now, you can go inside, sit up the front or whatever, but I swim naked. It's what happens here so please don't read anything into it. Join me if you like."

"Um, sure," I said hesitantly. "I might sit for a while. You go ahead." Apart from Sven, no man had seen me naked for years. And my body could hardly compare to a model's.

Jason threw two swimming towels on the seats and walked to the back of the boat. Opening a locker, he pulled out a mask and snorkel, then started undoing his shorts. I turned my head and looked at the rocks towards the front of the yacht until I heard a splash.

"Wow! It's really good in here," said a voice from the water as Jason pulled the mask over his face and put the snorkel in his mouth.

I moved to the back of the boat and watched Jason swimming towards the shore, his brown back and bum looking taut and strong under the clear, gentle ripples. I could see to the bottom. The seabed was sandy and there were long, pointed, thin-armed starfish on the sand below.

"I'm going towards the rocks," he shouted, pulling the snorkel from his lips. "I want to see if I can spot a conger eel, I saw one here last year." He put the snorkel back in his mouth, pushing his head under the surface. The sun was warm, the sea looked inviting, and I felt an unstoppable urge to join him skinny-dipping.

Why was I missing this opportunity, I thought? If I was living on borrowed time, I ought to be taking every chance to enjoy myself. Besides, my cuts would benefit from a saltwater bath, or so I told myself. Hesitantly I undid my things but, still feeling vulnerable, I climbed down the ladder at the back of the boat and got into the water in my bra and pants.

I allowed the water to slowly slide up my body, drawing me under. It felt good. Warm. I looked round and Jason had swum up beside me. Lifting his head out of the water, he pulled off the mask and took the snorkel out of his mouth. Grabbing a breath and shaking his head, he grinned.

"Lovely, isn't it!"

"This is special," I said. "Very special".

"Sure is." He was special too, I thought, and I wondered what he thought of me; this dishevelled, cut-and-bruised runaway with a god-awful haircut.

"Jason, I look worse than I've ever looked in my life."

"You look okay to me, Tess Anderson. Even in wet underwear, which you ought to know has gone totally see through, in case you were trying to be modest." He grinned like a naughty schoolboy and tilted his head to one side. I knew I'd seen that expression before, but where? I laughed and took my things off under the water, throwing them onto the deck.

We ate lunch off our laps dressed in towels. Jason found me an old straw hat left by another visitor; he said I looked very cute as it sat at an angle on my head.

"So, Jason, just how long do I have to be on this boat with you before you tell me who you were, slash, *are*—or what you do, slash *did*?"

"Once a journalist, always a journalist, huh? Oh, I picked up a couple of *spanakopitas* while you were having your hair done, you know? Spinach pies, for supper later." He was obviously determined to avoid talking about his past.

"I love those; I used to eat them with Sven when we holidayed at Arillas in Corfu." I didn't know why I was telling him that. It felt weird, discussing Sven when I'd just been swimming naked with another man.

"Sven," Jason said. "That's your husband, isn't it?

"Supposedly, but you'd hardly know it," I scoffed. "He's more interested in his government-minister girlfriend than his wife and marriage. Or *ex*-minister, I should say." At least I could salvage some comfort from her fall from grace. "Although the way these things work, she'll be back in another department soon for sure."

"Sounds likely, but it's so wrong." He said and turned to look at the rocks, lifting a beer bottle to his mouth. That side view

123

of his face with the bottle stirred my memory even more. There was also a hint of familiarity in his voice despite the accent. Had I met him before? Interviewed him? Seen him on a programme? It was baffling.

*

An hour later I took the remnants of lunch down into the cabin. After getting dressed, I washed up. I saw my old MP3 player and was suddenly desperate to be reunited with some of my favourite music. It was my refuge and my medicine, although I hadn't listened to any of it for ages. My phone had been charging but I still had just one bar of signal. I took the player and the phone up on deck and walked to the front of the yacht. Two bars flicked on the meter, and then it rang, but stopped. It was Jane. I tried to call her back, but I had *no network* showing. The phone dinged as if a text had come in, but it didn't show up in messages. She must have been getting anxious as I'd said I'd call. Then a *missed call* showed from another number, Steve's. They were both trying to tell me something. Urgently.

The phone refused to connect; maybe it was the wind or the direction the boat was facing. I kept looking at the thin black unit trying to connect me with the no doubt grim reality that was waiting for me, but of course it made no difference. There was nothing I could do for now. I'd just have to be patient until I had a proper signal. I picked up my MP3 player and flicked through the tracks. I might as well listen to something in the meantime. Try to relax.

I was about to put my earbuds in when Jason spoke. "I'm more than happy to listen to your music as well. We can put it through the boat's music system if you want."

"If you're sure," I said, and moments later one of my favourite songs was playing.

Jason knew who it was immediately. "Springsteen. Nice. Saw him."

I shuffled through to a series of tracks by other artists, all of which Jason recognised. He was obviously as into music as I was. I put on a playlist of more gentle tracks and began to relax. The sun was beating down; we were miles from Lean, Sven and work. We were hidden in a small bay behind giant guardian rocks. I curled up in the cockpit on a cushion with my now dry, borrowed swimming towel as a pillow and drifted off.

The phone ringing pulled me back from my doze. The boat had changed direction because the wind had shifted, and the signal must have improved. Coming to, I grabbed it, but it stopped. Then a text came through saying I had voicemail. I dialled, but the call failed to connect. The missed call was from Jane. It was so frustrating. Jason went below and came back a few minutes later with a glass of clear liquid and slices of fresh lemon which he'd picked up from under a tree near the beach in Parga while I was having my hair cut.

"Fancy a gin and tonic? It is after six; you've been asleep for a bit. Or you could join me in a beer?"

"Wow, is it really that late? Er, yes thanks. Gin is good." I needed some more familiar songs. I flipped through my MP3 and stopped at one of Jane's favourite bands.

"I'll probably cry if I play this," I said. "It reminds me of Jane, my best friend, who was always playing this at university. We saw this band the night I met Sven. Jane had a thing about the singer. I thought he was a bit of a poser myself. All that hair and those skin-tight white jeans." My voice stumbled as I began to shed tears, thinking back to carefree times.

"I don't mind if you cry," Jason said gently. "Crying can be good. Who is it?"

"Oh, you'll know them when you hear them; they were pretty big in the nineties and early 2000s." I pressed the key and the music started. "It's Restless Lovers."

Before I could tell him the song title, he interrupted, a big grin on his face. "*Our Weekend, Our Affair*. It was their biggest hit."

125

"Yes, I think it was. Jane loves it…. Yeah, it's not bad. Were you ever a fan?"

"Not personally, but my ex-wife was. She had a thing about the singer, too. Despite him being a …poser." He looked away. I found myself singing along. The tears flowed as I knew they would. All my mixed-up feelings for Sven—that I'd done my best to bury in the last few days—rose instantly to the surface. I hated him for betraying me, but I couldn't deny I still loved him too. I'd planned to spend my entire life with him, and I thought he had with me too; we'd committed to that, together, forever. I couldn't just un-love him after all these years, after so much had happened between us. Jason was looking away into the distance. Was he thinking of his ex too? Had I triggered some memory for him with this song as well?

My phone chose that moment to kick into life again. I wiped my eyes and read the text that had finally come through. It was from Jane: *Did you get my voice mail? Wow really can't believe it! Had to pinch myself :)*

I looked at my phone and, seeing I now had three bars, I dialled voicemail and listened. "*You have two new messages,*" the robotic voice told me. The music was still playing, with all its powerful memories of Jane, Sven, and our early days. I stopped the MP3 player so I could concentrate on the messages.

"*Message one, received at 14:26 pm…*"

"Tess, I tried to get you. It's Steve. Eve Eversson is alive and well, and now living with a member of The West Way—they're a boyband, but you probably know that. Hope you're okay. Cheers, bye."

"*Message two received at 14:46 pm…*"

"Oh my god!" For a moment all I could hear was Jane screaming down the phone. "Your mystery man… Oh my god, you're not going to believe this…Tess… He's Jason L'Amour! From Restless Lovers! My favourite band! Tess you're with a real rock star! Well in my eyes anyway. Despite the white trousers!"

I stared at him. Of course! The side view with the beer—

it was like the album cover I'd seen of him holding a mic. Of course it was him; why hadn't I noticed before? The hair, it must have been the hair. My heart pumped faster; I'd been swimming naked with Jane's musical hero.

"Jason, please tell me, that song I just played…"

"*Our Weekend, Our Affair?*"

"You're going to tell me you wrote it aren't you. You're—fuck—you're Jason L'Amour, aren't you?"

"Guilty." He smiled. I had the sense he was secretly pleased.

"What the f… Why the hell didn't you tell me?" Then I went red. "Oh god, sorry, the *poser* bit, oh…you weren't that bad, I mean, …they all were in those days."

Jason grinned. Sighed, shrugged, and shook his head slowly. "You're right, guilty again! I was a poser, but it went with the territory back then. Hey. These days I'm just Jason. Jason on his yacht. Okay? I'm no longer Jason L'Amour, I'm Jason Howard. That's my real name by the way. I don't do the sparkly shirts and the big hair—good job really as I don't have any these days." He ruffled what was left of it. "And you'll be glad to know the white jeans went years ago, along with those bloody shoes. Please, Tess, seriously, don't do the *what was it like, tell me some stories, who did you meet et cetera.*"

I sat there staring, trying to take it in. This guy had been Jane's favourite singer—still was, really.

"I'm going red. Sorry. It's a bit of a shock."

"Don't worry; that'll be the sun burn."

"I'm relieved, actually. At least I know you're not a criminal, or trying to kill me." I laughed. "And don't worry, I'm not starstruck. I've interviewed bigger stars than you, mate!"

He laughed too. "Glad to hear it."

"It was just a shock, that's all. And yours really is good music. Thanks to Jane, it got us through our finals, and my parents' deaths. I promise I won't act like a star-struck teenager. Not even if you want me to. Jane would if she were here for sure, but not me."

"Good. I just want you to be yourself."

"And I want you to be you," I said, but the smile on my face just wouldn't fade. If only Jane were here.

*

The evening was spreading pink tentacles across the sky to the west; the night would soon surround us. The cicadas would cease their clicking, and the sunset wind would bring a gentle chill. I looked at Jason but, before I could speak, he jumped in.

"So you wanted to know about Lindy—or Eve, as she called herself. The truth is she left me. Because the band asked me to reform, and I said no."

"Really?"

"Fact is, she loved the parties, the glamour and the gigs. She lived for it, it helped her career as a model, and she just loved being surrounded by music people. *The Brits* and the other award ceremonies were just heaven for her; being photographed and *seen* with the right people. When I stepped away from it, she just couldn't live without it. So, rather than leave it, she left me."

"So, she found someone else in music?"

"She ran off with Jeremy, or—as he calls himself—Strugger, from The West Way. He has a load of tattoos, a fake scar, and a very strong, totally put-on Essex accent. Did you know he actually went to a very exclusive public school? Strugger is an act. Whereas Lindy's the opposite. She pretends she's cultured, but she's, well, okay, I'm not knocking her—that would be unfair— but let's just say she's not all she seems. She's a bit fake—some bits of her in particular. I should know, I paid for them." He gave a shrug and a brief laugh.

"Can I ask just one question?"

"Let me guess. Was *Our Weekend, Our Affair* based on an affair I had with Hollywood actress Julia Trim? ...Yes, it was."

"I already knew that."

"Oh. You really *were* a fan."

128

"No, sadly I followed celeb gossip for work. The question I was going to ask was—why did you bust up the band?"

Jason opened another bottle of alpha beer. Lifting the little bottle to his lips he took a mouthful then looked at me. "Truth is, after three albums and seven hits, I'd run out of material."

"Really?"

"That, and the fact I'd spent ten years writing, touring and gigging. I needed to get out and chill for a bit. The rest of the guys still want to reform. So does my agent, Baz. He's brilliant. Always getting old bands back together. He reckons we'd sell out a reunion tour and our old label wants to issue our greatest hits remastered, or a new album."

"Will you?" I said, leaning forward and pouring more tonic into my gin.

"The jury's still out. Did you know there's even a Restless Lovers tribute band? Stressless Lovers, they call themselves. Sneaked in and saw them once. The singer does me better than I do! Not such a poser though!"

"Oh stop it!" I laughed. "I'm sure that's not true. You were good. Unless you're telling me Jane and I have crap taste?"

He laughed.

"Do you miss it?" I asked.

"Yes, of course. There's a real buzz walking out on stage, and when they're clapping, stamping and shouting for an encore... what's not to like?"

*

The sky was clear and the stars were bright as we sat down to eat spanakopita off our laps on the front of Sea Biscuit. I felt lost. It was weird, but the person I most wanted to tell about Jason was Sven. I wanted to tell him I'd met Jason L'Amour, but Sven and Tess were now just a memory, like Jason and Lindy. Hopeless victims of another failed marriage.

"Thank you," I said.

"For what?" he asked.

"For this. All this beauty. The bay, the sea, the smells, the sky. I'd never have seen this if it weren't for you. And what a shipmate you turn out to be. A posy old pop star! Oh … it's unreal."

"And you're one of the best, award-winning TV reporters on the planet. I'm pretty awestruck actually, Tess," he said, lightly punching my shoulder.

I put my empty plate down and flicked through the MP3. Jason fetched a bottle of wine and poured two glasses. I drank one and swayed under the stars of Two Rock Bay, watched only by Jason and the moon. With the magic of the night and the music, I could let myself dream that one day I might be able to fall in love again.

"Hey, don't fall over. Let me hold you," said Jason, putting down his wine, his brown arms going to my shoulders. We swayed together and, in that moment, I looked into Jason's hypnotic blue eyes and glimpsed a future I wasn't supposed to have. The wine and gin hitting home and the music seducing me, I pushed my mouth forward and let my lips just touch his. His grip tightened and his body moved closer. Then my phone rang. It was Jane, from her home phone.

"Sorry," I muttered, Jason smiled and turned down the music. I answered but only caught a fragment of what she said as the signal came and went.

"Tess. I've be… attac… Tess… vital…" Then the signal went altogether. My phone was useless. Jason rushed to get his from the cabin below but, as he pushed it into my hands, I realised it had no signal either. As I held my phone to the sky, hoping to pick up a signal from anywhere, I heard the rumble of an engine. I froze as the shape of a hull edged into the bay.

"Tess, relax," said Jason. "It's just another yacht."

An anchor chain rattled into the water and a French voice drifted across the night. "*Salut! Bonne soir. Ca va?*"

I had no idea what had happened to Jane or how she was. There were more missed calls from her mobile, three of them, all in the last hour, but none had got through. What was she trying to tell me?

"Jason, is there any way we can get a better signal?"

"Only by moving to a different area. This is pretty damn remote, no transmitters for miles. Sorry." So, it would have to wait until morning when we moved out of the bay. The magic had gone, and the moment was ruined. I went to bed, and as I closed the door of my cabin and got under the sheet, I imagined a dozen different versions of Jane's messages and calls. None of them ended well.

At 4:15 I woke and could hear Jason on deck. I quickly dressed and went to see what was happening. He was standing in the cockpit, watching quietly. The French boat was leaving. He saw me looking anxiously up at him from the cabin below and gave me a reassuring smile.

"It's okay," he said quietly. "It's just our neighbours. Early start."

This level of anxiety couldn't be sustained. It was draining both of us. I climbed back into bed to wait for the dawn, and noticed my phone had yet another missed call from Jane's mobile.

11. Breaking News

Despite trying, I just couldn't sleep any more. I checked my phone again and again. Still no signal. My mind was racing with thoughts about Jane. I went back up into the cockpit. It was barely light and Jason was already in the water, a grey shape swimming around the yacht. I wondered if last night might have ended differently had it not been for the phone call.

"Morning, fugitive!" he shouted when he saw me leaning over the guardrail. I waved and managed a smile.

"Coffee?" I offered.

"Let's get going first," he replied, climbing up the ladder and grabbing his towel. "I want to get somewhere you can get a signal and move on in case your friend Crusher Lean comes looking. We'll have breakfast soon, Greek style. There's yogurt and fruit in the fridge and honey in the cupboard."

As the morning sun began to rise over the mainland, we were heading out of Two Rock Bay leaving the starfish in peace. It was a place I'd never forget, and I promised myself that one day I'd be back, either with Jason, or perhaps even with Sven. The phones were still out of signal. I was desperate to contact Jane. My head was racing with the possibilities of what had happened.

We passed Parga, and Jason pointed out a cliff where the *death dance* was said to have taken place all those years ago. Holding my phone and constantly checking for any sign of a signal, I looked across the water. I could make out the low misty shape of Paxos, some twelve miles to the west. I wondered how Jane's villa and Jo were, and where Crusher Lean was right now. Then my phone suddenly rang. It was Jane, from her home phone.

"Jane, what's happened?" I said. "I've had no signal."

"Tess, my mobile's been stolen. I was mugged, attacked in the street near work. I'm all right—just shaken and angry. I tried to tell you last night, but you obviously couldn't hear me."

"Stolen? But I had four missed calls from you overnight."

"Seriously? Well, they weren't from me. Someone grabbed my bag with my phone in it."

"When did it happen?"

"Yesterday evening. I was on the late shift. I left the building for a quick walk to clear my head—about 7:30. A motorbike rider nearly ran into me. At the same time, a man walking the other way grabbed me, asking if I was all right and holding my arms. The biker got hold of my bag and helped the other man pull it off me. He rode off one way, and the pedestrian ran off in the other direction."

"Ow... That's awful. The rider, did he have a black helmet with a silver snake on it?"

"I don't think so. I'm not sure."

"Still, it must have been Lean's thugs. It was planned."

"Yes, I think it was. To be honest, Tess, I think my phone was stolen to order."

"Why, though? What were they after?"

"Your new number. I can't think of any other reason. They only took my phone."

"I thought they got your bag?"

"No, the biker stopped at the end of the street. After taking the phone out, he dropped the bag on the ground where I could see. It was a very neat operation. Two burly looking white guys."

"Well, at least you got the bag back," I said. "And you're okay, that's the main thing. I've been worried about you. Have you

133

told the police?"

"Yes, I've got a crime number."

"Hey, could you tell DI Green? If you think it's connected with me, he ought to know." Although I doubted there was anything much he could do.

"Of course," she said. "I've got a new phone; I'll text you the number. Are you on the move again?"

"Yes, we're just north of Parga. Heading for somewhere called Mourtos."

"Oh, I know it. Nice place. I need a hug, Tess."

"Me too. Please take care. Bye."

Poor Jane must have been so shaken; it sounded like a horrible experience. I told Jason what had happened. Then, ten minutes later my phone rang again. I jumped when I saw Jane's old number on the screen. I instinctively answered but I had a real dread that the person who'd stolen Jane's phone was on the other end, and I was right. I put it on speaker.

"We know where you are, Anderson. You and lover boy. Enjoy your last few days on *Sea Business*. You're both going to swing like that pussy ca—"

I hit the red button. So, Jane was right. Her phone had been stolen just so Lean's thugs could get at me. The good thing was they hadn't got the name of Jason's boat right, although that was little comfort. I blocked the number. That hideous voice would haunt me for the rest of the day.

"So, he thinks we're *Sea Business*, not Sea Biscuit," Jason said thoughtfully. "That's one good thing, at least."

"How come?" I asked

"Lots of boats have similar names, and there is a boat called *Sea Business* I've seen recently in Lakka. Maybe that's why. Easy mistake to make."

"Jason, I feel really bad, because as long as I'm onboard with you, then you're in danger too."

"I think I can handle it. We could go south, go through the Lefkas canal and down into the southern Ionian. There are so many bays and islands to hide in, Crusher Lean could spend years and never find us."

"Well, it's kind of you to offer, but you've got a life of your own to lead. And I'm not sure if I can stay that long myself. I've got to decide if I'm going for a divorce. I own half a house in London. Plus, I've got a job which won't be kept open for ever…"

"It wouldn't take that long. I'm pretty free, but I do need to fly home soon for a couple of weeks. Later we could move on to Athens, Cyprus. Sea Biscuit is capable of even crossing the Atlantic."

"We can't just turn up in Long Island without a visa."

"I can. I've an American passport. Dual nationality, remember?"

"Which parent?"

"My dad. He was an American flyer, a pilot at a base in Suffolk called Bentwaters. It's closed now. He and my mum met on the coast where she grew up. He got posted back to the States, but it didn't work out. They got divorced."

"That's sad."

"Yes, it wasn't great. She and I moved back to Suffolk when I was twelve. I visited my dad most summers and switched accents to feel at home with him, but I perfected the English one in Suffolk. So I'm half American and half English. The wild half of both, I always think!"

"You're full of surprises. Why didn't that come out when you were L'Amour?"

"In those days reporters just wanted to know about my clothes, cars and girls."

"Well, this reporter's more concerned about keeping herself, you and Jane alive right now."

"You could always fly home from Athens? For now, shall we press on to Mourtos and get water and supplies?"

"Okay, but…"

"Hey, sorry to interrupt, can you pass me the binoculars,

135

please? They're on the chart table."

"Sure." I handed them to him. "Any reason?"

Jason peered through them. "I don't want to worry you, but there's a power boat heading flat out towards Parga from Paxos."

"You think it's Crusher Lean?"

"Well, there are a lot of power boats out here but not that many this time of the year and, let me look, yes, it's an old Fairline. That's what Crusher Lean had on the quay in Lakka. There's a red ensign flying too, so it's British registered."

"Can he see us?"

"Only if he's looking, and at that speed I doubt it. Besides, he's in open sea and very obvious. We're close inshore so we'll blend into the cliffs and background more easily. We don't have sails up either, so we're a low profile. He's about three miles off us."

"That's a fair way away."

"Not really, I'm afraid. He's travelling at about twenty miles an hour, so he could be here in ten or fifteen minutes. He's going to get pretty close to us."

Adrenalin started to pump through me. I squinted across the horizon to where Jason was looking but couldn't see anything clearly. "What can we do?" I asked, clutching his arm.

"I have a little plan," said Jason.

"What?"

"Let's see if it's him. He thinks we're called *Sea Business*, doesn't he? Let me try something."

"Please be careful…"

"Don't worry." Jason reached into the cabin and picked up the radio handset.

He stretched it up on its cable and spoke into the microphone. "This is sailing yacht *Sea Business, Sea Business, Sea Business,* requesting a radio check. Receiving over?"

"Jason, he'll find us!"

"No, he can't trace where we're calling from, he just knows we're within line of sight—but we could be anywhere in this area, twenty or thirty-plus miles away or more. He'd need tracking equipment to trace our position."

After a few seconds, the speaker burst into life. It was the chilling voice of Crusher Lean. I went cold and shrank in my skin. The mere sound of his rough, grating tones sent me into a tailspin of dread.

"*Sea Business, Sea Business, Sea Business*, this is motor yacht *Rosie Cheeks* receiving you loud and clear. Er, where are you, *Sea Business?*"

"Just passing Corfu Town, making for Gouvia Marina," Jason said into the microphone. Thanks, *Rosie Cheeks. Sea Business* out." The radio went silent.

"Will he take the bait?"

"He already has, look!" Jason pointed out to sea. "He's changed direction—he's turning northeast to go up the Corfu channel. Looks like he's going to Gouvia; it's a big marina north of Corfu Town."

"Oh, well done, Jason. So cool." I sat back, relieved. Once again, thanks to Jason, the danger was over. But for how long?

*

A few hours later, my phone rang. It was 8:30, and we were motoring through a narrow gap between the islands near Mourtos and over a submerged sand bar. It was Jane, on her office number.

"You were right about your phone," I said. "I've had a call—"

"Tess. Breaking news. Ken Lean's critically ill."

"What?" I recoiled in shock.

"He was attacked in prison last night. Word is, he's dying".

"What! really? what happened?"

"Don't know, but we've heard from a prison officer that he was found unconscious after a so-called *altercation* with two other inmates."

"Seriously?"

"Yep. I checked with the prison service press office, and they confirmed he was in hospital under police guard. But they wouldn't say anything more, except that an investigation was underway and his family had been informed."

"I wonder if it's old scores being settled? Relatives of those he killed? Revenge?"

"Could be anything. I'll keep my ear to the ground. I guess this means that Crusher Lean will come back to the UK to see him."

"Let's hope so. He was motoring towards us a couple of hours ago."

"Bloody hell, that's not good."

"No, but Jason pulled a blinder and put him off the scent."

"He's the gift that keeps on giving, that man. Is it worth you asking your pals in your newsroom about Ken Lean? They might have more on it."

"Will do," I said. "Thanks Jane, keep in touch." I rang Steve. He answered almost straightaway.

"Hi, *top TV reporter Tess Anderson*, as you were described in the papers. Did you get my message about the model you wanted me to find out about?"

"Yes, thanks, it's all good. Have you heard about Ken Lean?"

"I certainly have. Word from the ward is, he won't make it. We've got a friendly medic there who tells us he's being kept alive on life support until Crusher flies in. He's due in about… er… hang on, I've got it here… 17:55 UK time at… Gatwick. There's a sister coming over from Canada too. She won't be here until tomorrow morning…. 7am Heathrow."

"Wow, good intel. So, they won't switch off his life support until the rest of the family's been, then?"

"That's what we've heard, yes. I've got Clare working on it; she's on to the police press office at the moment. I've got your favourite camera op, Jake, heading to the hospital to get comings and goings. There are a few old names from London's underworld past showing up with flowers, but they won't let

138

them in. It's family only; also, it might have been someone from Ken Lean's past who arranged the attack. Pity you're not here to pull this one together, Tess." I felt the same. It was my story and my turf; I knew I should be there reporting on it.

"You know what, I could be there, boss." I'd had enough. I couldn't run forever; maybe this was a chance to end it in London, where the police were on top of the case. "Maybe I could help set a trap for Crusher Lean?"

"Go on."

"Well, if Crusher Lean's seeing his brother in hospital, and Ken Lean dies some time tomorrow after the sister's been, the family won't be after me for a few days, will they? There'll be a funeral to arrange and maybe a few scores to settle. Perhaps even bigger scores than the one they want to settle with me," I said.

"That's madness, Tess, I couldn't be part of that."

"He's going to catch me sometime; he nearly did this morning. I'd rather him catch me with armed police at my side."

"As your editor it would be great to have you on it, you're our Lean expert after all. But as your friend…"

"Is there another flight apart from the one Lean's on? I could be on it and do a live into tonight's bulletins from outside the hospital." My mind was back in work mode, considering the options, working out how I'd cover the story. "It would show Crusher Lean I was very much around, and if he's in the hospital with the cops outside the room then I'm pretty safe."

"Do you promise me you'll call the police and ask for protection?" I promised I would, and Steve sounded as excited as I felt.

"If you can you make Corfu airport by… let me see, I'll just open up the travel site… flights... yep, there's one at 15:15 Corfu time. It gets into Luton at 17:10. Tight, but do-able. I'll get the transport assistant to book the flight and arrange a car to meet you. Are you sure you can do this?"

Jason was watching quizzically; I whispered to him that I'd explain everything in a minute. "Have I ever let you down?" I asked Steve. "If we're going to do this, I'll need someone to cut together twenty seconds of old Ken Lean pics, his first court appearance and a few old stills just in case, although I hope to do a straight piece to camera from outside the hospital. Also, can you send me five facts about his time inside; length of days served so far; a quick reminder of a couple of other big names serving time in Belmarsh prison at the moment, and the total number of inmates there, please?" I could hear Steve typing. "Oh, and the hospital ward we think he's on, plus the name of his sister. Which hospital is it?"

"Royal London. Okay, will do, Tess. It'll be good to see you on screen again."

"If Jake's my camera, tell him I want two cappuccinos and one of those lovely cheesy croissants, can't work without one! He'll know. Oh, and one very strange request—don't laugh, but can you find me a Tess Anderson wig?"

"What?"

"I had all my hair cut off and now look like a member of an eighties punk band. I wanted to be in disguise, but if I'm going on screen, I want to look like me. Plus, I'll need my disguise again afterwards, so I don't want to give the game away! I'm not coming back to work full time, Steve, not yet anyway, I'm just coming for this job—and to try and catch Crusher Lean. If that's all right with you?"

"Of course. No one knows the Lean story like you do."

"And the wig? I can't do the live piece to camera without it."

"Anything else?" he said. "Fake tattoo? False moustache and beard?"

I laughed. "Just the wig. And a hotel room—I don't think it's a good idea to go home. Not with Lean's mob after me and, besides, I don't want to run into Sven or his new woman either, thanks." I glanced at Jason and gave him a smile. He was looking concerned, hearing just my side of the conversation.

"Sure," Steve said.

"Cheers, boss, really appreciated. It'll be great to get back on the grid, even if it's just for an hour or two." I put down my phone and turned to Jason. We were approaching a quayside and he was about to start sorting out ropes to tie the boat up.

"Jason, er, sorry, any chance…?"

"Probably yes, but can I ask, *any chance* of what?"

"Not stopping here."

"Any reason?"

"I need to get to Corfu airport by 14:00. I've a plane to catch."

12. Fade to Black

We were heading to Petriti, a small port near the bottom of Corfu. Jason was confident we'd get there in time for me to get a taxi to the airport. There was no sign of Crusher's boat; by now he'd be in the marina at Corfu, just a few miles from the airport.

I'd explained what had happened. Jason offered to come with me to London, but I declined; I told him I was leaving my recent clothes purchases behind, if it was okay. I'd just take my shoulder bag in my rucksack as cabin luggage. I didn't need much, as I always kept a set of work clothes at work; you never knew if you were going to be called in or have to stay overnight and just carry on in the morning.

As we made our way to Petriti, I called Jane and told her I was coming back and would be working with Jake. She was delighted and insisted on meeting up. I suggested the following lunchtime, outside the café in Kensington Gardens, near the Boardwalk. It was close to the tube station, busy, anonymous and there were plenty of little benches where we could chat. I also called DI Green.

"Miss Anderson! Good to hear you're okay. You're playing cat and mouse with Crusher Lean I hear? A bit of a dangerous game, that."

"Very. Look, there's a chance to catch him trying to get me. I'm happy to be bait."

"This doesn't sound good."

"I'm on my way to London, to report on Lean Senior's demise. I'll be outside the hospital tonight with my cameraman colleague, Jake, for a live inject into the national news. I think Crusher will try to attack me."

"He's going to be tied up at his brother's bedside, besides we've got officers outside the hospital room, and we'll have one next to your outside broadcast truck. I doubt he'll risk that. I think he'll be too upset over his brother. We hear it's only a matter of time before they switch off the life support."

"Yes, but I don't trust Crusher Lean."

"Nor do I. Talk soon."

*

Arriving in Petriti, Jason dropped the anchor and then reversed close to the high sea wall. He left me to pack while he went to a taverna at the end of the quay. He soon returned and told me a taxi would be there at one o'clock. It was 12:10, so we'd have time for lunch.

My battered blue rucksack with its faded leather straps sat on the bed in the back cabin of the boat. It seemed almost my entire, and very wanting, wardrobe was either stuffed in it or hanging out of its open pockets and flaps. It had been with me on stories to trouble spots all over Europe and the world. How appropriate that it was now with me in a trouble spot of my very own. So, what did I really need for this one-night trip?

I packed my notebook and pens, the tools of my trade, old-fashioned but reliable—the battery never goes flat on a biro. Then the photo of Mum and Dad, looking so happy, the one I'd taken the summer that they died. Plus, Mum's necklace of course; it seemed even more important to me now. I checked my phone, money, cards, keys, and lastly my passport. I looked at its bent, creased, over-thumbed pages which told stories of long, often anxious airport queues at countries where journalists weren't welcome, and where it was often a case of *would I get in?* Or *would I get out again?* There just was one thing I wanted to do. I grabbed a black pen and turned to *Emergencies* on the last page. I changed the details of my next of kin. I wrote Jane's name instead of Sven's. I wanted her to be the first to know if I was found floating face down, bloated and bruised in the Thames.

I left the rest of my stuff on the bed, grabbed the straps of my shoulder bag and stuffed it in my blue rucksack ready to leave the yacht, sunglasses on my head. There was still one last thing. My hand had its own piece of baggage which I always carried but wondered if I still should. My wedding ring. No. I just couldn't take it off. Despite everything, I still wanted Sven with me. I knew Jane would be cross with me, but against my better judgement I wanted to ring Sven. He'd been a complete and utter shit. But he was *my* complete and utter shit. As I stood there, my dream came back to me—the one about us getting back together. I remembered how good it had felt. How everything had been fine again… just the way it always used to be… Before I knew what I was doing, I'd picked up my phone and was dialling Sven's number.

"Hello, it's me," I said when he answered after four rings.

"Tess. Err, sorry, one moment."

"Sven? You're with her, aren't you?" I could hear his hand over the phone.

"I'd love to talk, but I can't talk now," he whispered. "I'll call you later." I could hear her in the background, telling him to end the call.

"Don't bother, Sven. Don't bother!" I hung up, annoyed with myself as much as him, and fell onto the bed. It had been good to hear his voice, but knowing they were in the same room together had opened my wounds even more. Why had she picked *my* husband to steal? Why not someone else's? And who was I kidding? Dreams weren't real life. *This* was real life: me on the run from Crusher Lean while my husband cosied up with his lover. Tears started to fall, but I wiped them away and stood up. I was Tess Anderson, and I had a job to do. That was all that mattered right now.

*

Jason and I ate a classic Greek omelette with chips, and big fat local tomatoes, in the taverna at the end of Petriti quay. As we ate, he looked deep in thought. It was going to be a wrench leaving him and Sea Biscuit but, after all, I was only borrowing his boat, and only borrowing him. It was a temporary friendship, nothing more. Wasn't it?

"Tess," he said suddenly, "you keep mentioning Jake. Good friend, or something more?" Was this a hint of jealousy?

"Jake's my favourite camera op," I said as the waiter brought the bill. "We've worked together on so many stories—going on police raids against gun runners in Spain, secret filming in dangerous places, crashing out in the last remaining hotel room together after missing a flight home."

"You must be close."

"We are. You don't work that much with someone without getting close. Jake's lovely. But he married his boyfriend last year so, yeah, platonic, if that's what you were asking."

Jason smiled. "He sounds like a lovely guy. I'd like to meet him. Hey, the taxi's here," he said, and we both stood up as a dark Mercedes came to a halt outside.

Saying goodbye was awkward. We hugged, probably for too long. Then he kissed me. Properly kissed me. I felt myself slip further into his arms, pressing against his chest. He smelt good, felt good, it all seemed so natural. We'd shared scary moments; he'd saved my life and shown me some fantastic places. The night in Two Rock Bay could have ended so differently, I wished it had but I hoped to be back. I waved as I left him outside the Taverna at the bottom of the hill and the taxi took me inland.

The plan was for me to meet him at a yacht marina underneath Corfu castle the next night. Plans, though, could change.

*

As the plane went through the thick layer of cloud on our descent, water droplets started hitting the windows. The landing lights of Luton's runway illuminated the relentless rain; a stark reminder that I was back in Britain. Luckily, among my clothes at work was a plain mac and a news-branded umbrella if I needed them.

Soon I was out of the airport in the taxi Steve had sent, heading past the sprawling buildings of the Vauxhall vehicles factory. The car smelt of cheap air freshener. Beside me on the seat was the box with my Tess wig inside. Then we were into the traffic and on the way to London. I kept a watchful eye for a motorbike. After a few miles I felt sure that we weren't being followed and I read the script I'd written in my notebook during the flight. Old-school style, not tonight the laptop- or iPad- emailed script; this was pen and paper. The rain continued and I was missing the Greek climate, feeling distinctly chilly in my Corfu clothing. The air outside was different too, no smells of jasmine, thyme and other wild herbs, this air had a strong flavour of fumes. I rang DI Green.

"Hi, Tess. You're in the UK now?"

"Yes, I've just landed."

"Look, we'd love to lock up Crusher Lean, of course," said the DI, "but as far as my boss is aware he hasn't committed any offence here that we've evidence of, or that we can pin on him. I know your friend Jane had her phone stolen, and I know your house was entered, but unfortunately we can't prove it was ordered by him. Nor can I get an operation authorised to try and trap him in some way with you as bait, I'm afraid. The top brass won't sanction it. They think he'll be too tied up with his brother dying."

"How about my being attacked in Paxos? I have witnesses."

146

"That's for the Greek police to request his arrest, but if we detain him, we could question him while they investigate. Are the witnesses solid?"

"A waitress and… a former pop star." It seemed the best way to describe him.

"Hmmm. Look, where are you staying?"

"Russell Square, the Boston. I'll text you the room number when I check in but that'll be late tonight. I know Crusher will be with his brother until they switch off the life support, but that won't be until the sister arrives early tomorrow."

"You're well informed."

"I'm a reporter."

"And a good one. Without you, Lean Senior would never have been convicted. So, what are your plans?"

"I'm on my way to the newsroom, then to do that live report into the late news from outside the hospital. Then I'll be at the Boston."

"I can't advise the live report. Putting yourself in the public eye is the last thing you should do right now. It's crazy."

"I have to. I need to prove to Crusher Lean I won't be beaten or scared into not doing my job." I'd been running for too long; it was time for Tess to take control of her life again.

"Okay, well, your choice. We'll have someone tail Crusher Lean when he leaves the hospital, he's due there later. We can't really arrest him on what you say while he's at his brother's bedside, unless the Greeks say it's urgent."

"I haven't reported it to them, but they were called to Lakka when he tried to stab me on the quay. Maria from Yan's Bar called them, so they'll have a record."

"Okay. I'll talk to him when he leaves the hospital, tell him we know he assaulted you in Greece. You'd better give me the details later." I watched the traffic pass us as the taxi headed for central London. "As I said earlier, I'll have someone outside the hospital by your vehicle when you do your report, and there'll be officers at your hotel when you arrive. If Lean turns up there, we'll nab

147

him. That's the best I can do. We can meet in the morning. I've got to go now; I'm tied up in a stake-out in Battersea."

The taxi slowed as we met traffic heading into London. "Sounds good," I said. "I know you're being held back by your bosses. Let's hope they're right about Crusher being wrapped up with the family tragedy, but thanks for what you're doing. Let's keep in touch." I ended the call and re-read my script as we went through familiar streets heading for the newsroom.

*

Leaving the taxi, with my wig in place, the sky cleared. I walked through the revolving glass doors at work and smiled at the receptionist. My pass worked. The inner doors opened, and it was good to be back. I walked down into the newsroom, where scores of journalists, producers and other staff beavered away, servicing news bulletins and current affairs programmes around the clock. News is a job that never sleeps, that never stops.

"Hello, stranger." Steve grinned, looking up.

"Hi, boss, and thanks for the wig," I whispered. He stood up and hugged me.

"Hey, guys, Tess is back, but only for tonight. Mum's the word, okay?" I was treated to a round of applause and a stream of handshakes, hugs and pats on the back. I got a bit tearful and used the excuse of needing the loo to rush off.

I dug out the spare clothes from my locker and soon it was as if nothing had changed. I hadn't worn any makeup in Greece at all and, as I walked into make-up I looked into the mirror. I realised I had a nice tan. Being on Jason's boat had had a few positives. It felt good as I sat down and let the makeup artist take care of my face. I was beginning to feel like a reporter again. TV's Tess Anderson had returned. I felt a sudden burst of strength. I could do this; I could really do this. I was safe, surrounded by friends and colleagues. I just hoped no one would attack Jason and Sea Biscuit while I was away. He seemed so vulnerable on that small yacht in such a big sea. I knew it was ridiculous, given that he'd saved me from Crusher Lean, but it felt as if I needed to be there to protect him, rather than the other way round.

Walking back into the newsroom, wearing black work trousers and a white top under a thin pullover, it was as if I'd grown a couple of centimetres; and it wasn't just the spare pair of work heels I'd got out of my locker either. Hell, they pinched, after the bare feet and sandals of Greece.

Steve was at his desk, ending a call, as I walked over.

"Jake's near the hospital with the satellite truck, he's expecting you, there's a car waiting outside. If you log in, you can see the piece which will go before you. It's already cut. There's a link written in the running order for the ten o'clock." He stopped and sat back, his hand touching his chin as he looked at me. "Tess. Are you really up to this? You don't have to do it. You know that, don't you? Clare's standing by to go on instead if you want?"

"Thanks, Steve, but I wouldn't have offered unless I could deliver. You know me better than that. It's been a really rough week or so and it isn't over yet, as they say, but look, I feel good about doing this. I'll be ready for a run-through in half an hour, okay?"

"Great, I'll tell the bulletin producer, go for it. We'll have a chat about it all tomorrow after the morning meeting, all right?"

I walked out of the newsroom towards a waiting car, grabbing a sandwich from the café en route. I was soon off to the location, my earpiece in hand. I was dropped by the hospital and saw Jake waving frantically and grinning as I got out of the car.

"Yay! Hey, buddy. I've heard of some weak excuses to get a few days off work, but this is so damn lame!"

"Good to see you, Jake, how's it been?"

"It's been okay, but not the same. I've missed you. Cuddle?" We collided in a big bear hug.

"I've missed you too, Jake, it's been a real panic. I've had Lean's brother after me, and, well, I'll tell you after we've done the lives. So, down to work. Who's on the truck?"

"Nish, he's just getting a couple of coffees, including one for you—cappuccino as always. When I knew you were on your way back, I was so excited. I've been in Manchester covering a medical conference with Rhea and I was a bit miffed to have been called back to London, but when I was told you were coming, I was just proper pleased. Just like old times."

"Well, it's a one-off for a while, Jake. I'm going to ground again after this. I just wanted to cover the story; it seems so right for me to do it. It also puts two fingers up at Crusher Lean, showing I'm still here, especially when he thinks I'm hiding in Paxos."

"Is that why a copper asked if I was expecting you to turn up? He's over there." I looked round to see a young, uniformed officer between us and the hospital entrance. The usual traffic passed, and the air was heavy with fumes. The starry Greek night had been replaced by the dull orange glow of street-lit London.

"Happy, Tess? Okay, let's do a white balance, then and a sound check as soon as Nish's back, and then we'll offer the studio an inject whenever they want. Welcome back to the joys of rolling news."

"Ready when you are. Pass me the battery pack and radio mic when you can, thanks."

"Sure, so what's the word on Lean senior, then?" Jake asked, pulling the mic kit from his bag.

"I got the latest condition check as I arrived. There's no change—well, there won't be until they switch off his life support. He's unconscious at the moment and he won't be coming round, or so I understand. Do you know if Crusher is in there? Ward four, isn't it? The Adult Critical Care Unit," I said, clipping the battery and transmitter pack to the back of my trousers.

"I think he is, yes. There are a few cops coming and going too, keeping an eye on things. I was just told by the cop watching over us that it's close family only by his bed. I got a nod when I asked if 'close family' included Crusher."

I nodded and clipped the small microphone to my top. The police presence was reassuring. Nish turned up with a tray of coffee as I pushed the transparent pink plastic earpiece into my right ear and dropped the cable down the back of my top, pulling it out by my waist and plugging it into the little transmitter clipped to the back of my trousers. I could hear talkback from the studio control gallery, and they could speak to me. We checked sound and vision.

"Tess, this is Priti in the gallery, nice to see you back." Priti was the studio PA. "No time for a run-through but can you just give us your opening words, please?"

"Hi, Priti, hi, everyone. It'll be: *Here outside the Royal London Hospital* et cetera. Okay? So, you're coming to me off the back of a short package on the assault and Ken Lean's time inside, and then you want a twenty-five second *upsum* from me with one question and answer as planned, and then a standard throwback to studio?"

"That's it, Tess, we're coming to you in three minutes. Standby, Truck, Jake, Nish."

The seconds ticked by. I smiled at Jake who gave me a thumbs up. The red light on the front of the camera pierced through the street-lit gloom of the night as traffic drove along the road beside us. I stared into the black lens, as I'd done so many times before, and listened to the words of the reporter on the item before me. She was telling the story of Ken Lean's imprisonment, assault and hospitalization. Cutting through it, the director's voice told the newsreader it was them next, to link to me live from the hospital.

Priti said, "Standby, Hospital truck, coming to Tess in ten, nine…"

"Tighten up a bit, Jake," the Director added, "let's see Tess a bit closer please. Come on, we've missed her! That's it, thank you, great."

"Three, two, one, and cue Tess," said Priti, and I went straight into reporter mode. I nodded earnestly as the newsreader finished the link to me and paused for two seconds before speaking.

"Yes, here at the Royal London Hospital close family are believed to be at the bedside. His brother, sixty-year-old Crusher Lean, is thought to have arrived late this afternoon from his holiday home on Corfu to join Ken Lean and his wife, Denise." Oh, how I wanted to add, *Where he's been trying to kill me*, but of course I couldn't. I continued to speculate as to what would be happening in the hospital room.

The newsreader then asked me the pre-arranged question I'd given him. "So, do we know any more tonight about the alleged assault which led to Ken Lean being in hospital?"

The director cut back to me.

"Very little. The Prison Service described it as an *incident*, which took place early this morning, involving two other inmates. There's speculation tonight that it was a revenge attack of some sort for Lean's care home crimes. One thing is certain— it's going to be a long night for the Lean family here..." But I never finished my sentence or said my pre-planned last words of: *"Back to you in the studio"*. I heard a tyre screech somewhere behind me. As I concentrated on my words, and fixed my stare at the black glass of the camera lens in front of me, there was a scream in my ear from Priti in the gallery: "TESS... CAR... MOVE!"

I saw Jake rush out from behind the camera, a look of panic in his eyes. As if in slow motion, I watched his arms fly up towards me. He pushed me violently sideways, away from the road. I stumbled. My feet lost contact with the ground, and I fell. The officer nearby rushed towards me.

I was terrified. I couldn't think. I tried to stand up but was forced back by a whoosh of air and the loud screaming of an engine. Grey metal passing centimetres from my face. The car stopped. It stopped because it had hit Jake. Hit his camera. Hit the back of the satellite truck.

I lay there in disbelief. Stunned. Shocked. I was shaking, my mouth wouldn't work. My earpiece had fallen out. I could hear panicked voices coming from it. They sounded miles away. I tried to scream but nothing came. My voice was frozen in fear. I was aware of people around me. I somehow got back control of my body and tried to stand up. I fell forwards and rolled onto my bottom. I was grabbed by the young police officer. I struggled to sit up; my shoulder was touching the car's front right tyre. I could smell hot rubber.

Jake was lying in front of me. I grabbed him and tried to lift him. He was half under the car. I slid myself under his back. I lifted his arms and shoulders onto my thighs. I stroked his head. Confused and shocked, I felt my senses trying to tell me a million things, like *get out quick*. But I couldn't. I found my voice and I just screamed like I was in the biggest nightmare in history. To me, I was.

Through the ringing in my ears and the haze in my head, I was aware of Nish shouting for help. The policeman grabbed the door handle of the car. He pulled the driver out with angry words. I heard handcuffs click around wrists. Two nurses finishing their shifts rushed over. In amongst the noise and hustle, I refused to release my grip on Jake. I cradled his head and felt his blood soak into my trousers. It was warm. It spread across my thighs. It was unreal. I tried to stop it, putting my hand over the wound, but it was pumping out. Nish had called 999, but a doctor from the hospital was already on the scene. An ambulance was pulling up.

I held Jake's hand and said it would be okay, but it wasn't. I begged him to stay with me, but he didn't. I told him to look at me, but he couldn't. I let my tears fall onto his lips, but they wouldn't open. I bent forward and kissed him as voices tried to persuade me to let them pull me away. There was a growing sense of panic as the smell of petrol filled the air; it was dripping from under the bonnet of the car. A hissing sound came from the engine. The blue lights of a fire engine strobed in front of me, forcing me to close my eyes. A young doctor put her hand on my shoulder.

"He's gone. I'm so sorry. He's dead. We need to get you to

153

safety and checked over. You're in shock. You need to come and sit in the ambulance." When I didn't respond, her voice became more urgent. "Please let go of him. He's not coming back, and we need to move now. We're all in danger with this petrol leak."

I heard fire fighters arrive beside me. I still refused to let Jake go.

"He's coming with me," I sobbed. "I'm not leaving him."

But calmly, and with tenderness and concern, I was lifted up and pulled away.

Numb, and unable to lose my look of panic, I cried as I was helped to my feet and supported under each arm. I took one last look at Jake, my fallen comrade. I called to him to come back. Someone stroked my hand. My trousers were clinging to my legs with his congealing blood, gluing the material to my thighs. I was led, helped and half-carried to the ambulance where I was laid on a stretcher bed as I started to shake. I was shivering, weak, dizzy, sick. I felt for my earpiece, my notebook, my bag. The sound of the car and the impact were repeating themselves over and over again in my memory. Jake had died instead of me but for Crusher Lean it was just a setback. I knew he wouldn't give up until I was dead too.

I sat in the ambulance while they checked it was only Jake's blood and not mine covering my legs. I could stand. I had bruising and shock, but I'd escaped unhurt, thanks to Jake's sacrifice. I just couldn't stop crying. Jake's face and voice were in my head. All the great times. The filming, the laughs, the pressures, the deadlines, the hair-raising drives across foreign lands, getting to locations and back to catch a plane. Running after him with his tripod and trying to keep up. Sharing bags of chips and sleeping on the floors of ferries and sharing cheap hotels. Laughing about colleagues, and him teasing me when I forgot my lines. His impressions of Steve and my pretending to be his sister, his wife, his mum. All those memories fading away and no more to be made. Our shoot was over. He'd faded to black. Jake was gone.

*

I was told I needed to stay in hospital for observation, but I refused: I needed to get back to Greece. Besides, if I could be attacked while an officer stood a hundred metres away, how could I be sure I'd be safe in hospital?

A doctor had given me sedatives. In my hotel room, I filled a glass with water and swallowed one. I noticed my rucksack leaning on a chair; someone had kindly sent it over from the newsroom so I'd have my Corfu clothes. I fell asleep crying, and when I woke up, I woke up crying. My pillow was wet with tears, my trousers were stained with Jake's blood, and my memory was seeded with future nightmares. I'd taken painkillers as well as the sedative. The sensible thing would have been to stay alert, but how could I be concerned about my own life when saving me had cost Jake his? Besides, there was an armed officer outside my door and another in the hotel reception. DI Green's superiors now realised Crusher Lean was serious. I reached out, my wanting hand spreading across the vacant sheet, wishing I wasn't alone, but the bed was empty, cold and unforgiving. I kept the curtains open and a side light on as the darkness was too damning. I was guilty. It was my fault Jake was dead.

13. Suffolk

Dawn was painful. After a few minutes, the numbness in my legs began to ease, unlike the numbness in my heart. With two police officers following discreetly behind me, I left the hotel on Russell Square and walked to the newsroom. I tried to blend in with the crowd, one of thousands beginning their working day, except that my working days could never be the same again. Inside, it felt like the whole building was in mourning. Steve put his arm around my shoulder and took me into a meeting room.

"It was my decision to let you do it Tess; it's my responsibility, not yours. I should never have agreed." Tears still stained my cheeks and were never far away. I must have looked terrible. I hadn't put any make up on. I was just numb. Steve passed me a coffee. I hugged the cup.

"Ken Lean's life support was switched off at 9 15 this morning. He's dead. Go back to Corfu and rest; really rest. Hopefully this is over now. There's a car for you for the rest of the day and it will take you to get your flight. It's Gatwick you're flying from, yes?" I nodded. "Okay, so go now and call me when you can. We can talk properly later, when you've had a chance to recover."

As I walked past my colleagues, the chatter stopped. Everyone half-smiled in sympathy, some gently touching my arm or whispering a few words of comfort and support as I walked out. The banks of monitors and screens continued to display the constant traffic of moving images coming in and out of the building, feeding the ever-hungry beast that was rolling news. I saw our bulletin going out. A shot of Jake and then me flashed up on the screens. For a moment all eyes turned away from the monitors and focused on me. There was a real sense of loss. Jake would never walk through the doors again. We'd all lost his infectious smile and an enthusiasm few could match. But at least they could get back to work; they didn't have to carry the haunting image of his last smile like I would, forever.

DI Ted Green was waiting for me in reception.

"Tess, so sorry about your cameraman. We had no idea. I did say it wasn't sensible to put yourself at risk, but at least you're safe. We've got the driver, and we will get Crusher Lean, I promise."

"For Jake."

"For everyone. But yes, for Jake. When are you going back to Greece?"

"Soon. Later today. I'm in a car provided by work; it'll be one of the regular drivers. I'll be okay."

"We'll be around at a distance, but don't hesitate to call me."

*

I decided to go back to my home. With Jake dead, my own life felt less valid, and bumping into Sven seemed less of a worry. It was still my home, after all. I hoped it would be empty. I wanted to check my mail and grab some more clothes, the few that hadn't been slashed, to take back to Corfu. I texted Jane saying I was desperate to see her later; I needed a hug from my best friend. I also needed a hug from Jason. I knew I couldn't hug Sven or Jake. I texted Jason to tell him what had happened. He messaged back, sad and shocked, and assured me he'd be waiting at the airport. He ended his text with an 'X'. It was only a small gesture but a very important one. I needed all the 'X's I could get.

As the car drew up outside, my house looked just as it had

when I'd left it—except that the front door was closed and not smashed open, as it had been the day I was chased off in Jane's car. I asked the driver to wait. What I took to be an unmarked police car drew up nearby; I was pleased to see it. I didn't want to be alone in case a motorbike or white van raced up behind me. I went in, the street sounds fading as I closed the door. A new sound took over. The radio.

There was a pair of court shoes in the hallway. They weren't mine. Next to them stood a woman's leather work bag. Through the open kitchen door I could see the person who owned the bag and shoes. She was making coffee, with my coffee machine: the one Sven had bought me for Christmas two years ago. She stood there in an off-white silk dressing gown, oblivious to my presence. Was this what she had seduced my husband in? He'd fallen for *that*? I was both surprised and sad. She was wearing my moccasin slippers with the backs squashed down. She couldn't even be bothered to put them on properly. The radio news was playing, telling the story of how a cameraman had been killed whilst saving reporter Tess Anderson from what was believed to have been a hit and run attempt on her life, and how numerous witnesses claimed the car had deliberately tried to run the reporter over. Suzanna Heffle laughed loudly, her grating House of Commons voice bleating: "Ha! Give that driver a medal, pity he didn't get her."

I fought to keep sane and rational. I so nearly lost it. I wanted to scream and grab her hair—I imagined yanking it backwards, smashing her head on the counter. But I froze. My anger seethed inside. Suzanna Heffle jolted, then slowly turned and saw me. Her mouth opened and she screamed, putting her hands up to protect her face, presumably convinced I was about to attack her. I stood there scowling, my fists clenched and my jaw locked. My breathing was fast, my throat tight. Then, as if in slow motion, she dropped the coffee pot. It fell, smashing on the floor, near-boiling brown liquid and broken glass spreading across the tiles. She was whimpering, waiting for the blows which never came.

Footsteps thundered down the stairs. Sven had heard the crash. I stood motionless, like an injured wild animal waiting to strike. I wanted her to feel the fear I'd experienced when Crusher Lean attacked me.

"You fucking bitch," I said quietly, surprised at my choice of language. She was obviously surprised too, and stepped back. "My lovely colleague Jake was murdered last night, and you just laugh about it?" She didn't reply; she couldn't. I heard a noise behind me, and Sven, my unfaithful, back-stabbing apology for a husband, rushed in.

"Tess, please, no. Calm down!"

I swung round and he stepped back. Heffle rushed behind him, shaking, her hands around his waist, putting him between us so he'd take any blows.

"She attacked me Sven, she broke the coffee pot. Call the police! She attacked me. She spat at me," Heffle bleated.

"What? Okay, yes, please call the cops and I'll call Danny Downs," I said. "I spat at you? Then my DNA will be on you, and if it isn't, then you're lying to the police. I wonder how many times you've done that, minister?" I pulled off my wedding ring and threw it at Sven. He raised his hand to bat it away. It hit the tiles with a ding and bounced across the room, disappearing under the fridge.

I grabbed the phone from its stand and thrust it towards her. "Call the police, then. Go on, or better still open the door: they're outside protecting me. Do it, and just watch as I send those emails that were on my husband's iPad straight to Fleet Street and my editor."

"But," said Heffle, turning to Sven, "the iPad was recovered, I saw it? The emails had been deleted."

"But the deleted folder hadn't been emptied, so they were still there. And thanks for confirming it was you who arranged for the villa to be broken into and the iPad stolen. I'll be reporting you for false imprisonment. I was locked in a garden shed for half the night and scared witless." I was shaking with anger.

"Tess, we need to behave like adults here," said Sven holding up his open right hand.

"Really. Behave like adults? My workmate was killed last night," I screamed at them. "He died saving my life. Your pathetic little tart here says the man who killed him should *get a medal*. How do you think I might respond to that? You're a psychologist, think about it. So go on then, get me arrested and let me recount that phrase in court. The papers will love it."

Sven swallowed hard.

"I meant..." Heffle spluttered from behind my husband. "I meant it as a joke."

"I have a better joke, but you might not find this funny," I said, raising my hand as she cowered. "Don't worry," I growled, "I wouldn't waste my energy. You are pathetic. Both of you. You deserve each other." I lowered my arm.

I went into the sitting room and picked up our wedding photo, which had always had pride of place on the mantelpiece. I took it back into the hall, calmly placed it in the middle of the wooden floor and smashed it with my heel, the full force of my anger powering my foot. The glass had no chance. It splintered with a dull crack, its fragments spilling from the frame. The picture of two happy people, broken.

Leaving, I slammed the front door. I wasn't proud of my little scene, but I was pleased I'd contained my anger. Once out of sight of the house, I burst into tears. I could barely walk to the car; I just wanted to collapse. I was swirling with emotion. It was my house, my bed and my husband—not hers. I sobbed into a quickly sodden tissue. Back in the car, shaking all over, I apologised to the driver and called Jane, trying to sound as normal as possible as I recalled the encounter in the kitchen. We agreed to meet as planned for lunch at twelve, at the café in Kensington Palace Gardens. I called Jason but he didn't answer; his phone was off. I just wept into his answerphone and told him what had happened.

At the café, Jane brought two cups of Earl Grey tea and a pair of baguettes stuffed with cheese and salad. This was no time to consider the calories; it was comfort I needed. We sat on a fading painted bench near the café. People walked past, people without fear. I noticed a young man I took to be a police officer sitting on a similar bench nearby. When he noticed me watching, he gave a slight nod. Jane moved closer, bits of grated cheese dropping to the ground to the delight of the waiting pigeons daring each other to swoop and grab.

"Tess, you must be shattered. I'm so sorry about Jake. At least Ken-not-so-lucky-now-Lean is dead. So, no doubt about a divorce then? Having seen Heffle with Sven close up."

"She was there, Jane, there in my kitchen, in my slippers, using my coffee machine and using my husband. I was verging on the psychotic. I so nearly hit her. Oh, I'm just imploding. I've lost everything." I laid the baguette on my lap and held my head in my hands.

"No, you haven't lost everything," Jane said. "You've still got me, you've got your job and you've got a stunning man waiting for you in Greece. After the last twelve hours, you're actually doing okay. You were nearly killed last night, and your best work friend was. Most people would be sedated all day today. I'd have done far worse had I seen Heffle in my kitchen with Dave. In time it'll get easier. It's kind of how it works."

"It doesn't always." I looked up at her. "I miss my mum and dad as much now as when I lost them. It's like everything's changing, nothing's the same. I just feel lost."

"I know, but you're strong. You'll survive and come through it even stronger than you already are," she said, putting her arm around my shoulder.

"My heart's a wreck."

"You'll be rescued. Jason's throwing you a lifeline, you've just got to be brave enough to take it. It'll happen. Now what time's

161

your flight?"

"Six, from Gatwick."

"Is Jason waiting for you?"

"He's meeting me at Corfu airport. He's really sweet."

"Hey, about that, Tess. You're within a kiss of landing Jason L'Amour! Dream or what?"

"Well, actually…"

"What? You haven't kissed him already, have you?"

"I might have done…" I said coyly.

"Oh my god! Details, I need details…!" She dropped a piece of tomato from her baguette as she jumped with excitement.

"Yeah, on the boat in Two Rock Bay and when I left for the airport."

"I'm impressed!"

"He's so nice, Jane. But I'm in no state to risk being hurt again. I think it would destroy me."

Jane gave me a sympathetic look and squeezed my hand. "Do stay at the villa again. There's no one booked in until the week after next."

"Thanks. But so long as Jason's okay with it, I think I feel safer on *Sea Biscuit*."

*

After leaving Jane, I went to get yet another phone sim card. The one I had was compromised; Crusher Lean had the number. I wanted a better phone too; the one Jane had bought me on the way to Gatwick was simple and limited. I was followed at a distance by my cop minder, and I was glad he was there. I went to Paddington Green police station to give a formal statement about the night's attack. The DI was waiting for me. The car driver who'd killed Jake was in custody. The chances of proving that Crusher Lean had forced him to do it were slim, but he might weaken. Ted Green told me Ken Lean's funeral would be early next week, and he'd heard that Crusher Lean was thinking of going to Canada with his sister to help her grieve. That gave me a sense of relief; I needed space to breathe although I wasn't sure Crusher wouldn't have one of his thugs trailing me. Ted Green told me they'd be picking Crusher Lean up to question him about the night's events, but I knew he was likely to just walk away.

At Gatwick, I headed to the check-in and caught sight of a screen showing TV news. There were pictures of the Royal London Hospital with a strapline running underneath reading: *Care Home Killer Ken dies after prison attack.* The pictures changed to shots of the car which killed Jake, and the strapline became: *Police charge driver after car kills cameraman.*

I texted Jason to give him my new number and tell him my flight was on schedule, but worryingly he didn't reply. Hopefully it was just a poor signal on *Sea Biscuit.*

*

The rain had started when I'd arrived at Gatwick, which made the prospect of a warm Greek sun even more appealing. As I walked to the stairs leading to security and departures, someone called my name, and stopped me just before I went through.

"Tess!" I recognised the voice, but it was in the wrong place. I turned and saw Jason. Sailing cap on, wrap-around shades over his eyes, and tanned skin under a tight white t-shirt and jeans. I rushed towards him and he opened his arms.

"Jason? W-what the hell are you doing here?"

"Nice to see you too!" he laughed.

"Sorry, it's lovely to see you—I'm just surprised."

"I just caught you. Another minute and you'd have gone through. I just couldn't bear to be away from you after what happened last night. I have a plan. You need to rest, and not be on edge and worrying about one of Crusher Lean or Heffle's mob finding us, so why don't we go to my house in Suffolk? No one will know we're there unless you tell them, and yes, you will have your own room. If that's what you want, of course."

I wasn't entirely sure what I wanted, with respect to sleeping arrangements. But the house sounded a good plan. Everyone expected me to fly out, so staying in England might just work.

"Thanks, Jason, that sounds nice. I'll let you know about the room later."

Ten minutes later we were in a hire car heading up the M23 towards the M25 and then north. I sat low in the passenger seat, my bag and wig in the back. Jason listened tenderly while I tearfully relived Jake's death and my confrontation with Suzanna Heffle and Sven. We passed under the Dartford tunnel and were soon on the A12 heading north.

Passing through busy Essex, we left Chelmsford and Colchester behind and were soon in Suffolk, closing on Ipswich. Jason turned off near Dedham.

"So," I said, "this is where pop stars go to retire, is it?"

"You'd be surprised how many of us there are hiding away in dusty old houses down country lanes like this." We passed through idyllic little villages and hamlets with ancient pink or white houses nestling in a landscape that looked as if it hadn't changed much for centuries. Our destination was a village named Polington.

"Not far now," said Jason as we weaved our way along tiny, hedge-lined lanes. We turned into an open five-barred gate, stopping in the grounds of an old, white-painted timber-framed farmhouse. A single light shone above the front door, a dim beacon in a darkening night.

"1705, I'm told it was built," he said proudly, and put a reassuring hand on my knee. I couldn't help thinking that literally no one but Jason knew where I was. If I had any lingering doubts about whether or not I could trust him, I realised I'd soon know for sure, one way or the other.

As he opened the heavy-planked wooden door, I was met with a soft smell of mustiness, and then the heavy scent of old smoke from an inglenook fireplace. The room had a low ceiling, with big, hefty beams of light oak, chamfered at the ends. Tasteful, simple furnishings and soft, pastel-painted walls completed the scene. Just looking at the fireplace made me feel warm. The blacked bricks behind the big iron grate told of centuries of flames offering comfort and safety. The kitchen was a classic farmhouse style, straight out of a country living magazine. A large Aga took pride of place at one end, edged by bespoke wooden units and worktops inset with tiles. An old wooden wall clock showed 3:45; no battery or chip in it, just an old-fashioned mechanism, stranded in time.

"This is beautiful," I said, nodding my approval.

Jason took his coat off. "It's cost me a fortune—the house, not just the kitchen. Mainly because I had to buy my ex out after our divorce, but it's all mine now. Sorry it's a bit musty, I usually get Irene in the village to open it up for me—she keeps an eye on things while I'm away—but there wasn't time, and I wasn't certain you'd want to come."

"Don't you miss it, this beautiful house, being away on *Sea Biscuit* so much?"

"I do miss my home, but then I miss *Sea Biscuit* as well. She's my other home. I love the life out there. Sorry, but I don't have any food in, apart from some long-life milk and frozen bread. But I can book a table at the village pub if you fancy it? Otherwise, I can fetch a takeaway, they don't tend to deliver out here."

"I'd prefer to eat in, if it's okay. I don't want to be near people at the moment. Is that all right?"

"Of course. I'll be about an hour. Lock the door while I'm gone and explore the place. The back-door key is on a hook by the Aga. What can I get you to eat? I've got a few options here." He opened a drawer and pulled out some menus from Indian, Chinese and pizza restaurants. "Take a look while I turn on the boiler. We'll need some hot water, and a bit of background heat would be good, the place feels kind of damp."

"Jason. You're sweet. Thank you. I'll have a veggie curry of some sort and…"

"Yes?"

"And is there a washing machine I could use?"

"Of course. Help yourself. It's round the corner in the utility room, there's a downstairs toilet there as well. Just make yourself at home." He smiled, then left and I listened as he drove off into the thickening night.

I felt very alone. No one else knew I was here. I was struck by the total silence of the place. There were no close neighbours. The nearest house was a small field away, further along the road. I put my clothes in the washing machine, wrapped a kitchen towel around me and went upstairs in search of a dressing gown. It was spooky. The old, wide, deep-brown floorboards creaked and groaned as they felt the pressure of my presence. The landing was long and dim. The lights took a while to brighten, and while they warmed up, I was able to imagine all sorts of horrors waiting for me in the dim-lit corners, like Crusher Lean leaping out from behind a closed door with a knife or a gun.

The rooms were neat and clean and, once I got used to the quiet, the house had a warm cosy feeling, reassuringly peaceful. I found a couple of dressing gowns hanging on the back of what I realised was Jason's bedroom door; I picked the one that smelt of him and hoped he wouldn't mind. I looked around his bedroom, not daring to go further in. The double bed was covered in a woven Greek blanket. Dried flowers hung from the walls. There was a large-framed photograph of Restless Lovers in action on stage with Jason at the front leaning forward holding a mic. This gave me the strong impression that he missed those days. What looked like an expensive oil painting hung from the sidewall, and an art nouveau sculpture, a bronze of a naked woman dancing, stood on a plinth near the window. On the back of a chest of drawers was an award, a glass guitar with *Restless Lovers, Winner, Best Band Awards 1998* engraved across the neck. I smiled and backed out, not wanting to pry. Would I find a photograph of Lindy if I looked? I wasn't sure.

The house was long and thin, just one room deep with the upper rooms off a single landing running its length. Exploring the ground floor, I walked from the sitting room to the dining room, and then through to a further space leading off it. It was a small room, and clearly a shrine to Restless Lovers. There were gold discs in cases and posters for gigs on the walls. A row of guitars was lined up at the far end. Next to them were a sound system, a mic stand, and a microphone plugged into an amplifier. There were photographs of Jason and the band on stage, and one with him and his ex-wife Lindy-*call-me-Eve*-Eversson. She really was a looker. I knew I'd feel inadequate if the clothes were ever shed at the foot of the bed. A clothes rack displayed Jason L'Amour's old stage clothes, covered in long clear plastic bags. I recognised a deep blue suit he'd worn on a video and a black leather jacket from one of their album covers. And there they were, the damn white jeans. It made me smile. I put my hand under the plastic and touched them, shaking my head.

The other side of the sitting room was the kitchen. I walked through it and ventured outside. The garden was mainly shrubs and trees but there was a patio with a well and a pond. Originally the house would have had a thatched roof, but now dark red pantiles kept out the rain.

Sitting at the far end of the pond on the branch of a bush staring at me was a white barn owl. It watched me but remained perfectly still. Thick rain clouds passed overhead, briefly uncovering the moon, the owl standing out against the dark foliage behind. I peered into its big eyes, mesmerised as the fleeting moonlight momentarily illuminated this beautiful bird. It stared, blinked and flew off with a whoosh of its slow, graceful wings.

"No, don't go," I whispered, finding my thoughts turning back to Jake's death. If I hadn't been so *gung-ho* about being back on screen, gloating over Ken Lean's death and challenging Crusher Lean to have a go at me, he'd still be here. This time the night before, we'd been laughing together and waiting to go on air. Now he was dead. How could I ever live with that?

Thinking about Jake my tears started, and were soon joined by large raindrops as the clouds overhead opened and the rain began to fall. I heard a noise and turned to see Jason by the back door looking at me. I ran to him and cried like a baby, suddenly aware of my nakedness beneath his flimsy open dressing gown, bare foot outside his back door on that wet Suffolk night.

When I'd calmed down, we had our takeaway in the kitchen. The only sound was the wall clock which Jason had wound back to life. Its ticking merged into the gentle trickle of rain on the glass.

"I guess you'll sleep better on your own. You've been through such a rubbish twenty-four hours, Tess," said Jason kindly, his hand reaching over the table and squeezing mine. I smiled, nodded and squeezed back.

I actually slept well, helped by two glasses of wine which I drank sitting in the deep, comfy, burgundy armchairs in Jason's sitting room with a growing sense of exhaustion. The bedroom was small but nicely decorated. The walls were a crisscross of small wooden beams with white painted plaster between. Old lace lavender bags hung from a nail along with a bunch of yellow helichrysums, flowers known as *everlastings* as they dried so well. The rain had gone, and the old ill-fitting leaded window was open. I switched on the light by my bed and a moth was drawn in from outside, attracted by the glowing bulb. As I fell asleep, I remembered I had to send my new number to Jane from the sim I'd bought earlier. I'd leave it until the morning, as I didn't want to risk waking her up; besides, she needed time out from my troubles. I also realised I'd forgotten to tell DI Green the number as well. As I drifted off, through the open window, I heard the owl.

At 3am I sat bolt upright in bed. I'd had a nightmare. Jake had come to say goodbye; he was in the field behind the house. It was foggy. He walked out of the mist as I watched through the window. He waved and then turned to walk away forever.

He was holding hands with someone I knew. She was waving goodbye too. It was Jane.

14. Target

The next morning, under a leaden sky, we walked to the village pub for breakfast. It was at a crossroads opposite the church. A scattering of houses fanned out along the four roads beyond it. The original part of the Griffin Inn seemed small compared to the modern restaurant extension which had grown from its gable end. Presumably, like many, it had become a gastro pub to survive. The large car park behind it, once a meadow, was testament to the number of customers which now visited. As I walked in, its attractions were obvious. There was a cosy, old-world atmosphere with low-beamed ceilings and large open fireplaces.

The Griffin was almost empty when we arrived, but the manager told us she was expecting a few guests from the neighbouring Airbnb to drop in soon. Breakfast wasn't the Greek yogurt and honey under a blue sky that I'd become used to in recent days, but it was a decent scrambled eggs on toast and they produced a good smoothie too. The coffee that followed made up for the gloomy sky.

With the expected rain holding off, Jason and I took a detour on the walk back to his house, following a waymarked footpath around the village, passing old barns and pink-coloured houses with black timber frames. Many of these former land workers' cottages and simple farmhouses were now prime property, reflected in the value of the cars parked outside. As we walked across fields and through dappled woodland, we were both lost in our own little worlds. The scenery was a good distraction from the haunting dream I'd had of Jane which kept coming back into my thoughts. At least Jason had passed the *safe* test: he was the only person who knew where I was, and no one had come for me in the night.

We walked along ancient green lanes lined with hawthorn hedges between centuries-old oaks. Checking my phone had a signal, I texted Jane.

Hi, didn't want to disturb you earlier, but it's me with that new number I said I was getting. Talk soon. T xx

My phone rang straight away. It was Jane, and the beauty and tranquillity of the morning was soon to be shattered.

"Tess, hi, I've been waiting to hear from you. Are you back in Greece?"

"No, I'm in Suffolk, at Jason's house."

"Oh? In his bed?"

"No! You're a bad girl!" I laughed.

"I thought you were going back to Paxos last night."

"Last minute change of plan."

"I've just popped out to get a paper," Jane said. "Look, I'm nearly at my front door. Can I call back in a…" She went quiet.

"Jane?"

"Sorry, I can barely hear you. There's a motorbike revving like hell behind me."

"JANE!" I shouted but she couldn't hear me. "JANE! Does the rider have a black helmet with a silver snake on it?"

"Sorry, Tess, yes—shit, he's mounting the pavement!"

"JANE!" I heard a crack, followed by the sound of a motorbike engine driving away. I shouted again, fearing the worst, remembering my dream. After a few long anxious seconds, Jane's voice came back.

"Tess, it's okay. Except my phone screen's broken. I got into the doorway just in time; that eff-ing idiot almost hit me. Is he the one that tried to get you?"

"Probably, if he's wearing a black crash helmet with that snake emblem, and rode at you, yes. That wasn't an accident. That was a warning. Are you sure you're all right?"

"Just a bit shaken."

"I'm so sorry, Jane. This is all my fault."

"He could have killed me!" She started crying as the shock took hold.

"Has he gone?" I wanted to cry too. I thought back to my dream last night—I couldn't lose Jane as well as Jake. I just couldn't.

"Yes, but I'm not hanging around out here in case he comes back. I'm going in."

"Call the police, Jane. Call Ted Green now! I'll go, call me when you've spoken to him." I ended the call. Jason could sense my fear and shock.

"Trouble?" he asked, moving forwards and gently holding my shoulders.

"Jason, Jane's been attacked. I no longer care if they kill me, but I worry they'll kill Jane… kill you… kill everyone I care about, just for helping me."

I suddenly had an overwhelming urge to be sick. I quickly turned my head and stepped away from him as I threw up down the tree trunk and onto the path. I was panicking and my breathing sounded like a diver desperate for air.

It took several minutes for Jason to calm me down. He put his arms around me and stroked my hair. He was such a comforting presence. My panic began to subside at last, and I said I felt well enough to walk back to the house. Jason held my hand the whole way.

"Look, I don't want to freak you out," he said, as we walked down the drive together, "but if he threatened Jane, then your other friends may be in danger too." As we went inside, he put his keys on a cupboard. "Is there anyone you need to warn? Your editor, maybe? Your husband…?"

As much as I hated the idea of contacting Sven, I knew Jason was right. In spite of everything he was still my husband. Would Crusher go after him, too? I couldn't risk it. I wouldn't forgive myself if anything happened to him because of me. Reluctantly, I called Sven's mobile.

"Hello?" he answered.

"Sven, it's me."

"Tess! New number: that's why I haven't been able to reach you. We need to talk about these emails you might have seen."

"Just listen," I interrupted, "I just want to tell you one thing and one thing only. Someone's tried to run Jane over. The police are on to it, but I think it's Crusher Lean's doing, unless it's linked to your damn lover."

"What! Suzanna would never hurt Jane."

"Maybe you don't know her as well as you think you do, Sven. You need to be careful. There's no guarantee Crusher Lean won't send his minions after you as well. Although it's less likely, of course, because—like the rest of the world—he knows you've cheated on me and dumped me."

"Tess, you must hear this. In the kitchen during your little outburst, you said you'd copied those emails. You must get rid of them; it's bigger than you can imagine. You'll be in danger while they exist."

"Oh, in danger, me? You don't say. That's unusual. I've got a manic mobster trying to kill me. He's already killed Jake, now he's after my best friend, and you're telling me your lover's pals are still after me too? Is there some dark department in a basement in Whitehall planning to take me out?" Before he could answer, I angrily hit the *end call* button.

My head was a whirl. Muttering darkly, I walked out into Jason's garden and sat on an old wooden chair. I still had the emails; they were clearly causing Heffle and Sven a lot of angst. I had to decide what to do with them. I called Ted Green to tell him my new number, but I had to leave a voicemail asking him to call me. Waiting for him to get back was like watching a drip forming on a tap. Everything seemed to be in slow motion until the call finally came.

"Tess, it's Ted Green. I'm assuming you're calling about your friend Jane. I've just spoken to her; we've got someone going over there now. We picked up Crusher Lean earlier this morning. He was at his brother's house with Ken's widow. Does Crusher think you're in England or Greece?"

"I really don't know. I was heading to Gatwick yesterday afternoon to fly back to Corfu, a few people knew that, but it was a last-minute decision to stay here. I'm with a friend in Polington, Suffolk."

"Yes, I know. I had you followed from Gatwick."

"What?"

"For your own safety. The house is registered to a Jason Howard, a dual British-American national. He's as pure as snow. He's never even had a parking ticket."

"You checked him out?"

"We had to. You're a valuable witness and you've been threatened. Can you imagine what your Rottweiler-like chums in your newsroom would say if you were found dead under our noses? That's why we had a car at the end of the road all night, in case Crusher's mob had followed you, but it looks like they think you're in Greece."

"Why do you say that?"

"I fed Crusher Lean a lie that you'd been attacked in London yesterday evening. He seemed surprised; clearly thought you'd gone back to Greece. I'm holding him as long as I can. We're putting pressure on the driver of the car that killed your colleague. Can you tell us your plans?"

"I'm staying here in Polington."

"You'll be safe there; I'll keep the car outside."

"So, you know I'm with Jason Howard. He's helping me." Just then, Jason wandered out with two mugs of coffee and, on hearing his name, gave me a quizzical look as he sat on the wall of the old well. I ended the call and told Jason about the car outside. He seemed relieved. Knowing there were police nearby was reassuring and helped me to relax. We sat in silence for a little while, just enjoying the garden.

Jason smiled and pointed to a female blackbird flying into a large shrub carrying twigs. I could see why this beautiful garden was a perfect place to make a nest. It seemed a shame that this stunning house wasn't home to a family. It was perfect for children.

"How old is that well?" I asked Jason.

"As old as the house, probably. Want to make a wish?" He smiled.

"Is it deep?" I asked, standing up and moving towards it to look inside, its low, thin red-brick wall rising out of the flagstones which surrounded it.

"It sounds deep when you drop something in it, that's for sure." He pulled a fifty-pence piece from his pocket and handed it to me. "Make a wish, Tess. But don't tell me what it is, or it won't come true." I smiled, took the coin and gently dropped it into the well. There was a muffled splash as the coin carrying my dreams broke the surface below. I screwed up my eyes and made a wish.

Jason went to find the unmarked police car to say hello. He didn't want to be mistaken for an intruder if he went outside at night. I asked him if I could use his laptop to transfer the emails from the data card in my camera to a memory stick. I needed a back-up. Even if it put me in danger, I knew I'd have to expose these emails; it was just a matter of when. I hid it above the door inside an outbuilding, the old washhouse behind the house. When Jason walked in, I stood in front of him, blocking his way.

"Jason. I have to ask you something." He looked at me, obviously wondering where this was going. "Do you really want me to come back to Greece with you?"

"Yes, I do. If you want to."

"Even if it puts you and *Sea Biscuit* in danger?"

"Yes." He didn't hesitate.

"But even if Crusher Lean's charged and held on remand, he can still get his friends in Greece to attack us—and then there's Heffle and her private spooks. They're still out there."

"But having you on *Sea Biscuit* with me is fun. Don't you get it, Tess? I want to protect you. It's the American in me; we Yanks like beating the odds—or at least trying. *Remember the Alamo*, and all that." He smiled and squeezed my hand. "Keeping you safe may be dangerous," he whispered, moving closer, "but you're worth it." He hugged me; it felt good.

"I think I want to go back tomorrow," I said. "Even if they keep Crusher in custody, he still has his mob, and that biker is still out there on the streets. I think Greece might be safer than England right now."

"I'm happy to go back to Greece tomorrow, but on one important condition." He grinned.

"Oh?" I asked. "And that is?"

"I need to do some laundry." He laughed. I put a couple of things in too and Jason lent me some track suit bottoms and an old late '90s Restless Lovers tour hoody. They were baggy and worn but comforting. The hoody smelt of him, and I liked it. It brought back memories as I sank into it.

"Do you still play your guitar?" I asked.

"If that's really *will you play your guitar*, then I might after we've eaten."

It was dark and, after clearing away from a simple pasta supper, Jason suggested we went to his Restless Lovers room. The curtains were closed throughout the house and the doors locked and bolted. There was a cold wind blowing outside, rattling the windows. Rain came and went, hitting the glass, making a tinny sound, a far cry from the early summer of Greece. We passed through the sitting room with its tasteful lamps and simple wall lights giving off a reassuring glow. I followed Jason into the far room and watched as he turned a switch. Low-wattage lamps threw a soft light around us, illuminating the old band posters staring out from the walls, a young Jason frozen in time, a snapshot of his extended youth.

Jason bent down and turned on a bank of switches at the bottom of the wall. He nodded towards a small settee, and I sat down. A couple of black amplifiers and speaker stacks glowed with little red lights. I watched Jane's music hero from the past pick up a blue Fender Stratocaster from the row of guitars against the back wall. Selecting a plectrum from a dish on top of a speaker cabinet, he plugged a lead from the guitar into the amplifier. There was a hum as the jack plug was pushed home and then silence, until his right hand brushed the strings.

I could only assume he'd already tuned it, knowing I'd ask, and knowing he'd agree to let me hear him perform at least one of his beautiful songs with their romantic lyrics that had meant so much to my best friend. I sat there watching Jason L'Amour, the one-time pin-up on her bedroom wall, standing there in front of me, his guitar in hand waiting to perform. I wished Jane was with me to see it, but this was a special show, for me alone.

"So, what do you want to hear? Go on, you choose."

"I'm honoured. I guess one of my favourites is the second track from your first album. Jane used to sing it in the kitchen, drove me mad at times but it grew. It's *Thanks, Janine*.

"Ha, really? I'd never have guessed that. I haven't played that song for literally years. Hope I can still remember it." He played a few chords as if trying to recall the song. "Okay, here it is, just for you. *Thanks, Janine.*"

The familiar chords rang out and, as a stripped-down version of an old favourite echoed around the room, my brain filled in the missing bass, drums, keys and other guitar parts. Soon my eyes were closed and my head was swaying as his familiar voice, as absorbing as ever, sang this bittersweet song telling the story of a long-lost love. It had such hauntingly beautiful words:

Do you remember the day after the party, the day we started our affair,

The day you said you loved me, in the days we used to care.

The summer night you kissed me, before we grew apart.
That winter day you left me, that day you broke my heart.

I joined in the chorus and sang along with the last verse. It took me back to long nights writing essays and Jane coming in with mugs of tea or cheap supermarket wine. As the last chord faded, we both looked at each other. Sadly, my moment of magic was interrupted. My phone rang.

"I'll leave it," I said, but it rang again. It was Ted Green.

"Sorry, Jason, much as I don't want to, I have to get this. Sorry." He nodded and put down his guitar.

"Another time, don't worry." He smiled reassuringly as I answered the call.

"It's DI Green. I've some good news." This sounded hopeful. I was eager to hear more.

"How did questioning Crusher Lean go?"

"Started badly, the usual smart defence lawyer putting up as many obstacles as he could. We've been going through the mobiles Crusher used and tracking the calls. We've got proof he asked the white van and its drivers to stake out both your and Jane's houses. But we can't substantiate any connection to the black-helmeted biker, I'm afraid. Crusher maintains adamantly that he knows nothing about him. You know I might just believe that."

"That's a shame. Who could he be then, our mysterious rider?"

"It's certainly an unknown right now. But there is some good news. We've had a major breakthrough."

"Really?"

"Yes, the driver of the car which killed your colleague has finally coughed that it was Crusher Lean who ordered him to do it."

"Brilliant! Well done." Relief surged through me. I put a thumbs-up to Jason.

"So, we're charging Crusher Lean with conspiracy to murder. He'll be held on remand. Other charges to follow, I hope. We're having to give the car driver a new identity, of course. I don't think he'll last five minutes in prison if we don't. He's been charged with manslaughter and attempted murder."

"That's a good result."

"And it's officially DCI Ted Green now by the way. I've been acting Detective Chief Inspector for a while, but it's been confirmed."

"Congratulations. Well done! You've always been a good cop."

"I hope so. Thank you. Between us, the paperwork we've recovered from Crusher Lean's house is getting interesting. I've only skimmed some of it, but there could be something in it— something that goes beyond all of this. But that's for another day."

"Hey, let me know. Top reporter here, remember? Always keen for a story." But Ted Green didn't laugh, and when he spoke again he sounded a bit uneasy.

"So, we'll process Crusher but we're taking him to attend his brother's funeral next week."

"Really? Is that wise?"

"Well, it's a hard request to refuse but we will be with him, even during the actual service. I'll be sending officers along and he'll be handcuffed to a prison guard.

"Thanks." It was a massive relief to know that they'd got him and could prove he'd arranged Jake's death. "Do you need me again at the moment?" I asked.

"No, we have your statement. I've got your new number. What are your plans?"

"I'm going back to Greece tomorrow. I need to take stock and chill for a bit. Is this really going to be over now, do you think?"

"That's hard to tell. I hope so. Crusher will be in custody, held on remand until his trial and then locked up for a good stretch. But who knows? I can't guarantee he can't get instructions out through his brief for someone to have another go at you, or to have a go at Jane, for that matter, or even your friend in Greece. He's a very dangerous man. Let's just hope we can keep him occupied for a while."

I stared at my phone after ending the call. So Crusher was in custody and was facing a long spell inside, but clearly his determination to get me wasn't going away. I told Jason and called Jane to give her the good news. Jason and I sat on the big burgundy chairs sharing a bottle of Greek wine. It reminded me of sunny days and warm nights in Greece and made me realise how chilly England was. Jason lit the fire for comfort. The logs had been cut from a tree brought down in Jason's garden a year ago by storms. I watched the glowing flames dance as they consumed them; thin wispy lines of grey twisted and turned as they rose up the chimney, its crumbling bricks scarred with centuries of fires.

"Do you mind if I stay up?" I asked when Jason said he was turning in. "I had such bad nightmares in bed last night that I'd rather curl up by the fire for a while."

"You can sleep wherever you want to, Tess." He smiled and gently touched my shoulder.

"A big part of me would like to sleep with you, Jason," I said, looking up at him. I suddenly felt I couldn't let him go without saying something. "But I'm so lost at the moment, I'm just not sure. This chair is good for now."

He nodded and smiled.

"Sleep well, Tess. You know where I am if you need me."

He put some more wood on the fire and went upstairs. I pulled a blanket over me and dozed off, wrapped in his old band hoody.

15. Mongonissi

The next day, after an uneventful journey, we were back in Corfu under a bright blue sky and a warm breeze. *Sea Biscuit* was raring to go; her sails were full, and the wind was keen to push us south.

"Six knots and a lovely north-westerly force four, just what we need," said Jason. As I handed him a mug of coffee and took my place at his side in the cockpit, the wind on my neck reminded me how short my hair really was, but at least it didn't need brushing. The wig was below deck. I'd kept it on long-term loan so I could become TV's Tess Anderson whenever I returned to the UK, but why would I want to? Standing next to Jason surrounded by all this beauty, it seemed a dream life. What more did I need?

Paxos came into view after we left the bottom of Corfu and were overtaken by the flying dolphin. We followed in its wake as it raced in front of us, heading for the island's capital. A few hours later, Jason carefully picked our way over the sand bar at the far end of Gaios; we'd stopped on the town's quay to get some supplies and take in the fabulous sea front with its popular cafés, shops and people. It was a beautiful sight, the sort that always brings a smile. Soon we were in open water, leaving the bright and breezy little port behind. We travelled south for another half a mile or so and then turned into an opening between low cliffs.

"Mongonissi," Jason announced as we nosed into an almost enclosed bay with a café

and a taverna at one end, behind a thin but inviting beach. Jason asked me to drop the anchor, and then reversed the yacht up to the concrete quay, where we tied up to two large metal rings. Minutes later, we were sitting in the taverna drinking coffee and eating olives whilst using their wi-fi. We'd picked a table close to the beach, where shallow, gentle waves lapped gritty sand. Behind us, low terraces rose to the taverna building, with the white-painted trunks of olive trees looking almost luminous in the setting sun. A handful of yachts were bobbing at anchor in the bay and everywhere there were smiling faces.

Jason was deep in conversation with other yachties, discussing some port or other, so I rang Steve.

"Hey! Are you back in Paxos?" He sounded pleased to hear my voice.

"Sure am boss, and it's just so lovely."

"And safe, I hope. How's the weather?"

"Wonderful. Can't think of much to drag me back to rainy London. Ever."

"That's a shame. What about winning Reporter of the Year for the second time?"

"That's unlikely. It's got the name of the new girl at United News all over it."

"Well, I hear it's more than possible it might go to a certain Ms. Anderson again." A stream of boats arrived in the bay, a holiday flotilla. There was lots of movement as yachts were tied to the quay in a line. Steve started to dig. "What about this stuff concerning your husband's lover you mentioned earlier? I got the impression there might be an even bigger story brewing."

"Mm, there may be."

"We did some sniffing. Our security correspondent had a whisper from a contact in MI5 and, although it's nothing to do with them, word is, some former agents who now offer some sort of freelance operation had retrieved an iPad with some sensitive data on it."

"That would be them."

"Okay, but do you have copies of this *sensitive information*?"

"Who's listening to this call, Steve?"

"Just me."

"I might have, despite the best efforts of these freelance spooks. I'm still thinking what to do with it though."

"I'm intrigued by these emails Tess. And why aren't you letting us have them? You're still on the payroll, last time I looked."

"I'll let you know later, Steve; I'll decide soon, I promise."

"What's holding you back, Tess?"

"My safety, for one. And, well, Sven might be arrested and even sent to prison for withholding evidence. I'll make even more enemies if this explodes the way I think it will. More than just the Leans or these spooks. You don't take down a government without risk. I could endanger Jason as well as myself. You too."

"Are you serious? Is it that big?"

"Could be, yes."

"Wow. Well, Tess, think of who and what you are."

"I don't need reminding, boss. But I nearly died. I cost Jake his life, and nearly my friend Jane's too. One of Crusher Lean's crew tried to run her down. I'm not sure how much more danger and death I can bring to others. Or cope with myself."

*

We stayed at our table in the taverna as evening became night and coffee cups and beer bottles stacked up, the result of our continued purchases to rent this spectacular little spot. We ate there too. There was no incentive to move anywhere. The sailing flotilla was safely tied up around *Sea Biscuit* on the quay, and the excited chatter of holidaymakers filled the air.

In groups and couples they arrived to sit at a series of tables pushed together for a shared meal. Lights flickered around the taverna as candles burned in jars, while coloured bulbs hung from cables strung between trees and across the front of the bar. The temperature dropped and the sky darkened as white-shirted waiters rushed back and forth carrying plates, bottles and glasses. As the meal progressed and dessert was served, the flotilla members enjoyed a performance of traditional Greek music and dancing put on by the Taverna staff.

I left Jason chatting to other diners on an adjacent table and slipped back to the boat to sleep. I felt I needed a whole month's sleep. I lay under a thin blanket listening to the strains of Greek music, which was followed by an eclectic dance mix peppered with old favourites which had clearly got the holiday makers excited.

I woke about two o'clock. There was silence, just the lapping of gentle waves at the rear of *Sea Biscuit* below my little bed. I looked through the open cabin door, just centimetres from my head. At the front of the boat, I could make out the low shape of Jason asleep in his bed. I curled up and felt secure.

In the morning I decided to walk over and see Jo. Her house was about a mile and a half from where we were tied up. I wanted to tell her I was back in Greece and to thank her for sorting out Jane's villa. I called to make sure she'd be there and, although she offered to come and pick me up, I fancied a walk. I hadn't been that way on foot before, and the little lanes flanked by old stone walls were a revelation. Lichens and mosses grew in every crack where moisture could hide. Small lizards scurried away as I approached, disturbing them as they basked in the sun.

The walls might have been unchanged for centuries. I felt like I was walking in the footsteps of the ancients, even the gods. Pan had died on Paxos after all, or so it was said. While I visited Jo, Jason was going to walk into Gaios to look for some engine oil. We'd agreed to meet up again mid-afternoon at the taverna by the quay in Mongonissi. I felt sure she would have cake and buns waiting for me, so I knew I wouldn't starve.

"Hi, Tess!" she shouted enthusiastically as she saw me approaching. She was wearing an old, battered straw hat which looked as if it had been found in a bin. Her cut-off shorts looked even more tatty, and her top was a long way past its best. She was trimming the oleander bushes poking through the rusting railings on the white brick wall near the gate. Jo was smiling, a battered pair of shears in her hands. Her two cats sauntered by and nonchalantly wandered down the road as I gave her a big hug.

"You're making a good job of that," I smiled encouragingly.

"Trying to," she replied, sighing. "These shears are blunt and very old, but I can't afford new ones. Everything like that is so expensive here, and I rarely go to Corfu. A chap down the road was throwing them out so I took them on. Needs must!"

"Absolutely, why not. Good recycling," I said sympathetically.

"Well, it's lovely to see you, Tess. Thanks for phoning the other day to warn me," I'd called Jo from the ferry terminal in Corfu to tell her about a possible threat from Crusher Lean, "but I don't see why I would be in danger? I'm not involved with London gangsters. But at least you're safe, that's good, and you're here! I'm glad you got out of England okay. I've got a cake in the oven especially; it's almost ready."

"Jo," I said. I needed her to understand the gravity of the situation we still faced. It wasn't over yet. "There is a chance Crusher Lean could have a go at you, to get at me. He has friends in Greece and, although he's in police custody in London, we all still need to be careful. I'd hate anything to happen to you."

"Well, after your poor cameraman was killed, I can understand your worries. Oh, Tess, that must have been horrible. Just awful. So frightening too," she said kindly, slipping her arm around me. "I hope those memories will fade in time."

"In many ways I hope they don't. I want to hold on to Jake's last moments forever."

"I understand," she said. "Are you in the villa again?"

"No, I'm staying on Jason's boat." Jo looked up and sniffed.

"Oh, the oven! Quick, it'll be ruined if I don't get it out. Come on, let's rescue the cake!"

We were soon in the garden again, sitting on old painted metal chairs by a three-legged metal table; a missing fourth leg had been replaced by olive wood to prop it up. As the cake cooled, Jo poured tea. I watched a small brown lizard scurry up the wall and disappear under a creeper. I told Jo some more, but not all, of what had happened in the last few days.

"So is Jane's villa back in a presentable state again?" I asked.

"Oh yes, the first guests arrive in a couple of weeks. They hire it most years for a fortnight, they love it here. Linda and Des from Derby, a lovely couple. So, did you see your husband while you were in London as well?"

"Yes, we had a bit of a row."

"Oh?"

"I found him and his lover in my kitchen, in our house; they'd been sleeping in our bed."

"Do you hate her? His lover?"

"Hate's a strong word; not sure I hate anyone. Let's just say she and Sven are not my favourite people right now."

Jo smiled and looked at the oleanders she'd been cutting as they waved in the wind.

"You're a better person than me, Tess. I've never had any problem hating people who've done me wrong!" She moved the cake plate towards her and picked up a knife. "But on to more important topics. How big a slice do you want?"

*

At five-to-five I was sitting in the taverna back on the quay in Mongonissi nursing an iced coffee when I saw Jason hurrying along the path on the other side of the small bay. He ran round to join me, putting a two-litre plastic oil container and a hessian bag of food down beside my seat.

"In a hurry?" I asked, smiling. "Coffee?"

"Phew, I'm unfit!"

"What?! I've just watched you running around the bay with

186

that oil can; that's fit!"

"We need to get back onboard, there's a storm coming. It's already raining near Gaios and heading this way—you can see it moving towards us from the top of the hill back there." I wasn't surprised as I'd seen dark clouds building over the mountains on the mainland earlier while making my way back from Jo's house. The wind was bringing them our way and rain was about to hit. You could smell it. Heavy rain, really heavy rain, and it was about to be unleashed onto our little bit of the island.

Getting back to the boat, we snuggled down in *Sea Biscuit* with the hatches closed, listening to the wind howling in the rigging outside. Soon the deluge began. It pelted down. Even if we'd wanted to leave, we couldn't go out in that. We cooked pasta and pesto on the boat and listened to music.

*

It was a hot night. We couldn't have the hatches open as the rain was so strong. The yacht was so airless that we stripped down to t-shirts and pants. The two small fans in the cabin were unable to cool us in the brooding heat.

"Cards?" suggested Jason.

"Sure, what do you want to play? And don't say strip poker because it will be a short game!" I laughed.

"Ha. Okay, something simple. Pontoon?"

"You'll have to remind me how to play though, it's been a while." I watched Jason shuffle the pack. "Wow, that rain, it really is something."

"Yes, it is. It'll blow out tomorrow night I think, but probably not before." Jason dealt the cards and then paused. "So do you want to get back with Sven?" he asked.

"Oh, wow. That's a bit of tough one. I feel torn. On one hand he cheated on me, he doesn't deserve me, he's not worth all those years we spent together... and, well add the rest, I guess. But then—was it my fault? Was I naïve, should I have seen it

187

coming? She's obviously offering him something I'm not, or something I can't. Maybe I was too job-centric?"

"More job-centric than a cabinet minister? That seems hard to believe."

"What about your wife?" I asked. "Did you know she'd gone off with that boy-band singer straight away or did she cheat on you too?

"Lindy? Oh yes, she announced it. She told me she wanted to be enjoying the backstage parties again, the *green room groove* as she called it. She couldn't live without it, and when he made a play for her, she told me she was, in her words, *ripe for an affair*, and she clearly was."

"Ouch," I said.

"She went off to a gig where his band was playing. She lied at the door and said I was coming later, and she was my *plus one,* just so she could get onto the guest list, and then she went to some backstage party with him afterwards. I was sent photos by a couple of pals saying she was all over him, asking if I wanted them to say anything to her. I said no, let her go: if that's what she wants, it's her choice. I didn't own her. We were married by choice, not obligation."

"That was very grown-up of you."

"I was hardly going to go round there and thump him, was I? Thumping's not my style; I don't do the caveman bit."

"No, the white trousers are a giveaway there!"

"They can be very intimidating white trousers." He laughed.

"Apparently I don't do thumping neither. When it came to it, I couldn't actually hit Heffle or Sven. I got pretty close to it though."

"Well, there is one thing I did that was childish..."

"Go on, confess!" I grinned.

"I did tell someone I knew, who worked on a paper, that she'd once done a shoot for a haemorrhoid commercial in Denmark. Thanks to me, a still of the advert appeared in the papers with the caption *Eve Eversson's a pain in the bum, says husband L'Amour.*"

"Ha, I'll forgive you that. Well done: better than my outburst."

We finished a half-hearted game of cards and called it a day. The wind was howling and the rain bucketing down. I lay on my bed in the small rear cabin with its low roof and single thin window above me being washed by the storm. The water slapped at the bottom of the boat beneath my bed. I was low and lonely. The boat was quiet, but I knew Jason was still awake.

"Jason…" I called out through the half open door.

"Yes?"

"Please don't take this the wrong way."

"Take what the wrong way?"

"Is there room in your bed?"

"Room for?"

"A friend who needs a cuddle."

"Always, if it's you."

I climbed out of my bed, clutching my pillow, and made my way to his. "This feels weird," I said, lifting the sheet and climbing in beside him. "Lying next to a man who isn't Sven." I pulled the sheet over me and snuggled into the pillow.

"It's been a long time since I shared a bed too, Tess."

"Sometimes I just feel so alone."

"You've no family?" he asked.

"Not really; not since my parents were killed."

"It must have been awful," said Jason softly as I snuggled closer, our bodies touching.

"It was a few weeks before my wedding."

"How did they die? Don't tell me if you'd rather not," he said, tenderly touching my arm.

"Car crash, drunk driver. Dad was killed outright. Mum was critically injured and died a few days later. The driver got a few years. He's out by now, probably drinking and driving again."

"That's hard to accept, for sure."

We lay there in his bed in the front cabin. It smelt reassuringly of him. It was comforting. Our thighs were touching. His hand reached out and found mine. We both lay on our backs and looked up at the hatch above our heads to watch big drops of rain hitting the glass lid. They spread out, forming bigger and bigger drops, before running off to the edges of the glass. The boat tugged at her mooring lines as the wind pushed and the waves formed around us. They were choppy, and constantly bashed into the white fiberglass of the hull. Inside we were snug, safe and dry. *Sea Biscuit* was looking after us, and I felt she somehow always would.

"Would you ever go back with Lindy? I asked.

"Nope, never, that ship sailed long ago. She was never in love with Jason Howard. She was in love with Jason L'Amour. And his white trousers," he laughed. "It could have been anyone for her, so long as they'd charted and had their faces and names on album covers. So long as they were chased and desired by screaming fans and she could hold them up and say *he's mine*. She was on the front cover of the third and final album. Do you know it?"

"Sure, I've seen it. Jane has them all. She bought a copy of that for me once: birthday present. Oh, so that's her. It's hard to tell with all those effects on it, but the girl in the yellow bikini?"

"The same. It's how we met, at the shoot for the album cover."

"I always wondered, where did the name Jason L'Amour come from?"

"Our first agent. He said I needed a new name. I was, in his words, a pretty boy and we should exploit it. He certainly exploited us. We were teenagers when we started—naive, innocent and swept away by success."

"It must have been unreal, being really famous. I've had a taste of it, being on TV—people recognise me, they call my name out in a friendly way. People seem to think that all TV people hang around together at some giant, never-ending party."

"Yup, fans think musicians do that too."

"It's a crazy world; at least we have a bit of anonymity here, me with my short hair!"

"And me without much of it these days!" He laughed. "Shall
190

we sleep?" he asked.

"Only if we can dream nice dreams." I smiled as I rolled over, facing away from him.

"I dream, Tess," he said softly.

"What do you dream of, Jason?"

"That would be telling. Goodnight, Tess."

*

The rain thundered down and the wind tugged harder at *Sea Biscuit's* ropes. I felt the whole boat shudder. Mugs rattled in the sink, and we moved up and down as the waves grew bigger and hit the hull. Did I dream of Jason? Of course, but Sven was somehow there too, the man I felt I was supposed to be with. Falling asleep, I'd felt secure with Jason so close, but the feeling didn't last: I woke up at 3a.m. screaming. In my dream I'd replayed the events of the attack on my live broadcast and Jane being nearly run down by the manic biker. It hadn't ended well. So much for nice dreams. But Jason was quick to bring me back, stroking my hair and squeezing my hand.

"Tess, you're okay, you're on *Sea Biscuit* and you're safe. You're with me, no one's got you, and no one's going to hurt you." He held me tight, his voice reassuring.

"Sorry, I just…"

"You'll have lots of these nightmares. Just remember, you won. Crusher Lean lost and he's in custody, and his brother Ken is dead. It's okay."

He was right, I had won, but the war wasn't over, and Crusher knew it. He wasn't going to just go away.

16. Emerald Bay

At nine the next morning, forgetting the time difference, I slipped out of bed and rang Jane who sounded unsurprisingly bleary at what was 7am in the UK. After my nightmare, I wanted to check she and Dave were okay. They were worried but otherwise fine, she said. The police were keeping a car outside. While we talked, I heard Dave beside her, his voice sounding panicked.

"You all right?" I asked. "Dave sounds on edge."

"Yes, he is, I'll just head downstairs, it'll be easier to talk. There's a police car outside, so they're sort of keeping an eye on me."

"Dave's obviously not as reassured by that as you are?"

I heard her closing a door, then she said in a whisper, "No. I don't know what's wrong with him. He's like a frightened child scared of the bogeyman."

"Yeah, well, Crusher Lean is quite some bogeyman."

*

An hour later, the rain had all but gone although the wind was still blowing. I checked the weather app on Jason's phone lying on the table. It was predicting the winds would still be strong for a while. I went to make some tea.

"Yes, please, tea would be great," said a sleepy voice from under the sheet. He'd heard the gas being lit. I'd noticed Jason always seem to be half-awake and always alert, listening for sounds on the boat.

"On its way," I laughed.

"That was nice, last night," he said as I put his favourite mug on the shelf beside him. "Just being there, together." He was right, it was more than all right, it was nice, natural.

"Yes, it was. Thank you."

"I didn't do much." He yawned.

"You were there, Jason. That was more than enough," I said, sipping my tea, "I'm going to have to go into Gaios to get some more phone credit, top-up cards, and I need a walk anyway. I feel I've been cooped up here for days—nice as it is, don't get me wrong, and with such wonderful company of course—but I need some air. I'll get some bread and stuff for lunch too."

Jason sat up in bed and opened the front hatch above him.

"Sounds good. The rain's stopped; let's eat in the Taverna tonight. I think the flotilla's going today so it should be quiet there later."

"Sure, that would be nice."

"It's nice to have you here, Tess." He reached out, touching my arm. I smiled warmly.

*

My walk into Gaios was accompanied by an overwhelming smell of fresh aromatic herbs washed by the rain. There was a damp warmth, which was rare on Paxos. The well-watered ground seemed to ooze new life, and I was sure I could almost see leaves growing in the moist, humid air after the storm. A small tortoise emerged from the scrub. It was moving slowly towards me, the first one I'd seen in the wild. I stopped to watch as it stuck out its neck and seemed to smell the air. It was a memorable sight. I stood and watched its light, yellowy-brown shell as it lumbered along the side of the road before heading back into the undergrowth. I carried on into Gaios. The narrow road dropping down to the sea on my right, whilst villas came into view, dotted along the inland side to the left. Square, grey stones formed their walls, topped by shallow, red-tiled roofs. Intricate, immaculately built garden walls with automatic metal gates gave them a grand appeal, despite most of the houses being small. I doubted few of them were full time homes.

As I arrived back carrying two bigger-than-planned bags of shopping, Jason walked from the yacht along the path around the small bay to meet me. We dropped the food off in the boat then went to the taverna for coffee.

"I'll just check the news feeds," I said, looking at my phone as Jason went to the counter to order two cappuccinos. It was the day of Ken 'Lucky' Lean's funeral. There was a report from my colleague Clare standing outside the crematorium. Three police cars and a prison van were queueing to get in. There were a lot of mourners, lots of stocky men in identical black coats. The crowd seemed antagonised by the presence of the police who they clearly blamed for Lean's death. There were conspiracy theories emerging that the so-called *fight* in the prison was some sort of police-inspired execution. I shuddered. Then a picture of me popped up in Clare's report, and a clip of my secret filming which had taken Lean down. I'd seen enough and turned it off.

"Problem?" asked Jason, sitting down and taking off his sunglasses.

"I hope not, I'm just worried. I hope Ted Green isn't underestimating Crusher Lean."

"Hey, we're here in the sun, and he's there in handcuffs. Enjoy our day and forget his." Jason smiled reassuringly, but I couldn't, it went around me head as I drank my coffee.

I wandered down to the little beach in front of the taverna and sat on a white flat stone on the sand. Unable to resist I checked my phone again. I was still just in range of the taverna wi-fi. I looked at the news feed. The funeral was underway and there was a shot of Crusher Lean walking between two guards into the crematorium. He was still too close for me, even two thousand miles away. Jason came and joined me, finding another stone nearby and putting it next to mine. He sat beside me and persuaded me to turn my phone off again. After watching a boat motor in and anchor in the middle of the bay, we walked to the end of the headland and looked out to Anti Paxos, the little off-shoot island a couple of miles to the south. It looked so peaceful and alluring in the sun.

The taverna was all but empty all day, and that evening we went back to our now-usual table. We were almost their only customers and were served quickly. A few new boats had arrived but, with the flotilla having moved on and the recent bad weather, there were very few yachts about. The night was peaceful, pretty and dangerously romantic. Some familiar favourites drifted out from the music system including one of Jason's, and he leaned across.

"Do you fancy a little dance?" he asked.

"Why not? That would be nice." But just as I stood up, my phone rang.

"Tess, it's DCI Green. I know it's getting late over there but I had to call."

"Hi, Ted, no problem. Is something wrong?"

"I'm not sure how to tell you this…"

"Why? What's happened? Is Jane okay?" I grabbed the back of the chair; my thoughts were all Jane. Jason sensed my anxiety and stood behind me putting his hands on my shoulders, rubbing them gently.

"As far as I know she's fine. I've still got a car outside her house."

"So, what's the problem?"

I heard him draw a breath. "Lean's disappeared."

"What?! How? You had officers with him at the funeral!"

"We did. Lean's a clever bastard."

"Oh, wow, you mean you've only just realised that? Sorry

195

I'm... just frustrated."

"So are we. We agreed only the prison guards would go into the actual service. The police officers stood outside. It was very tense, Tess. The mourners were turning ugly. I admit we'd lowered our guard a little—Crusher's solicitor said he was considering a guilty plea if we dropped the money-laundering charges against his sister. That decision's well above my pay grade, but we did agree to give him and his sister some space inside the crematorium at the request of the priest doing the service."

"Go on," I said, finding it hard to believe what I was hearing. Jason and I exchanged looks of bewilderment as I shook my head from side to side.

"Between us, Tess—and this isn't for your newsdesk—he somehow persuaded, threatened, or paid the guards to undo the handcuffs so he could be one of the pallbearers carrying his brother's coffin into the crematorium."

"Sorry, can you speak up, Ted?" The music in the taverna had got louder. I wandered down to the little beach, Jason following close behind.

"In hindsight," the DCI explained, "it was clearly planned because the mourners all stood between the police and the undertaker's hearse, and as the coffin was taken out, Crusher joined five other men wearing identical black coats, hats and sunglasses to carry it into the building. A couple of the mourners—women—started getting angry with the police officers, claiming they were intimidating them. A scuffle broke out and, by the time order was restored, the coffin was inside the crematorium and the undertaker's hearse was being driven off. The driver, we later learned, had switched places with Crusher Lean."

"I don't believe this, Ted."

"No, I understand." I could hear the frustration in his voice. "We didn't notice until the service ended. The person we thought was Crusher was crying on his sister's shoulder throughout, but he was just another of Crusher's men, and he laughed when we apprehended him."

"So where is he? Where's Crusher now?"

"Your guess, Tess?"

"I can't guess where he is now, but I can guess where he wants to be—half a metre from me. Right here. Oh, come on, Ted, you actually lost him? Seriously!"

"You're not the only one who thinks we're stupid; the Commissioner wants a full report by morning. We've also got a pile of complaints for harassment by various Lean relatives who claim our officers were heavy handed. Your pal Danny Downs was in amongst them; he'd been invited to be there just in case there was trouble. They'd planned all this very well."

This was so difficult to take in. All that police work wasted. And there I was thinking it might all soon be over. "Have you found the hearse?" I asked.

"Yes, we tracked it on motorway cameras and found it abandoned at a private flying club in Kent. A Cessna light aircraft took off from there and landed at Nantes in central France this evening. French police will find him, Tess."

"Don't bank on it. You said it yourself: he's a clever bastard."

"Not clever enough to have stopped us from arresting his gang. Most of which were the other pallbearers."

"But he's escaped! From right under your noses!"

"Tess. Can you confirm where you are right now?"

"Mongonissi. It's a small port on the southern tip of Paxos."

"I've alerted Greek police and I have a direct line to their HQ in Corfu, so I'll be keeping a watch."

"I hope so Ted, I really do. From what I hear there are only a couple of officers here on Paxos. If he caught them unawares, Crusher would make mincemeat of them."

*

I no longer felt in the mood for dancing, so we went back to *Sea Biscuit*. Crusher Lean was looming large in my thoughts. The next morning, after a mostly sleepless night, I made coffee and decided to ring Steve. Jason and I had shared a bed again, but even his comforting presence hadn't been enough to settle me down. Whenever I'd fallen asleep, I'd seen Crusher Lean's face…

"You've heard about Crusher?" I asked my boss.

"Oh, just a bit. Lead story here as you might expect. Red-faced cops lose Lean. An embarrassing headline for the Met. Fancy doing a piece to camera in Corfu with a local camera crew for us? Speculating on his whereabouts?"

"What, just as he leaps out behind me and sticks a ten-inch blade into my neck?"

"I was only joking," he said.

But I wasn't so sure—and I knew Crusher wouldn't be joking if he found me. Steve was worried about me, I knew, but he couldn't quite keep the excitement out of his voice. I remembered feeling that way myself—the thrill of a really big story. I rang off, promising to keep in touch, and dialled Jane's number. I wanted to hear her voice, but the conversation only left me more depressed. She'd been given sleeping pills and signed off work for three weeks because of stress. Dave was still in a state about it all. I felt awful. They were in the middle of all this, in danger and suffering because of my mess, while I was hiding here in Greece.

Half an hour later, we'd filled *Sea Biscuit's* water tanks and coiled up the hosepipe, which was back in the cockpit locker. With the engine running, Jason untied the mooring ropes holding the boat to the quay. I operated the windlass control to pull up the anchor as he pushed the engine lever slowly forward, and *Sea Biscuit's* propeller pushed her gently along. Having something physical to focus on had helped calm my troubled mind.

"Where to, Skipper?" I asked.

"Anti Paxos, the little island we looked across at yesterday. I'm going to show you Emerald Bay. It's the most beautiful blue water you'll find in these parts, and you really should see it. Tripper boats bring people here from Parga and even further away, it's that good."

In spite of everything, it was great to be on the water and on the move once more. We had the sails up, the wind on our faces and the sun on our skin. My scars and cuts were still there but my hair was beginning to grow. I was with a wonderful caring man and desperate to enjoy life again. I knew I was still in danger, but I was determined to snatch moments of enjoyment when I could. Crusher could threaten my life at any time, but while I still had a life left, I was going to make the most of it.

We dropped the anchor in Emerald Bay and watched the tripper boats come and go. Some were small replica *pirate ships* and others were just big open boats, but they were all packed with tourists. Each one had the same routine. They'd stop, drop anchor, and people—mostly the younger ones—would jump into the water, screaming with delight. After a while some would gingerly approach a small, wobbly jetty and drop a boarding plank down for their passengers to go ashore, attracted by shack-like cafés and bars on the almost white sand beach. Music played from each of the boats' sound systems; it was a hectic jumble of happy trippers. As evening fell, the last of the tourist boats left and along with just two other yachts, we had the big bay to ourselves.

"There's no real wind predicted," said Jason, "and what there is, is coming from the south-west, so we're protected in here. Safe to stay the night."

We swam, sat, talked, listened, and just generally enjoyed that magical place. Cicadas clicked ashore, and the smells of wild thyme and rosemary drifted across the almost still water. Apart from waving to the nearest boat, which still seemed a long way away, we had no contact with anyone else.

*

As light faded, the bleating goats came down for an evening drink from freshwater springs bubbling up around the edge of the bay. The white rocks and small cliffs backing the water were disappearing into the shadows as night approached.

"If a dance is still on offer, now would be good," I said, as Jason brought two glasses of local wine up from below.

"That could be arranged." He grinned, and soon a few of my favourite songs were drifting around us. We danced on the deck until a slow love song broke through my defences, and I threw my arms around him.

"Do I kiss you again, Tess?"

"I'd like nothing more, but not yet. I'm scared, Jason."

"Scared of Crusher? I'm not surprised."

"Yes, but also scared of something else. Scared of going further, because I might fall in love." He brushed my cheek, but the mood was broken by the sound of a text arriving on my phone.

"I'm beginning to think that thing is conspiring against us," he said. The text was from Sven. I read it with a pounding heart:

Tess, are you OK? I heard about Crusher Lean escaping and I'm sure you'll be worrying he's after you. I'm worried too. We may be apart right now, but I just wanted you to know I still love you. I always will.

I stood holding the phone, just staring at it. If Sven still loved me, what did that mean? Did it mean he loved me in a fond-memories sort of way, or a getting-back-together way? Or was Sven—the relationships expert—just playing mind games, keeping me dangling in case things didn't pan out with Heffle the way he wanted them to?

I looked up and saw Jason. His face was concerned.

"Are you okay?" He asked.

"It's Sven."

"Oh. What's he done now?"

"He's been nice to me."

Jason frowned. "And that's a problem because…?"

"Because it makes it harder for me to hate him."

"Do you need to hate him?" Jason asked gently.

200

"I'd rather hate him than love him."

"Oh," Jason said. He frowned again, and then turned away. I assumed he was giving me some space, or else just thinking his own thoughts. I knew I should reach out to him, reassure him, but I couldn't make myself do it. I was totally torn. When Crusher was finally caught again and put in prison, and Heffle released her grip on Sven—if she ever did—would Jason and these beautiful islands be just a memory? Could I re-make my life with Sven? I looked for the moon, but she had no advice to give. There was a strange cloud formation high up and, as a brief burst of wind found us, I felt a chill.

*

Sea Biscuit kept us safe overnight. Again, we shared his bed. It was comforting—although Jason was just a little cooler than he'd been the night before—but I couldn't get Sven out of my mind. Or Crusher Lean. Morning brought an early swim before the first tripper boats belted into the bay. We jumped in naked; it was a stunning feeling of freedom and excitement, both of us washing away the bad taste left behind by Sven's text the night before. Like kids, we laughed and splashed before getting out. After showering on the back of the boat to get the salt off, we snuggled into big towels and ate breakfast. My phone rang, bringing me back to reality with a bang.

"Morning, Tess. DCI Ted Green."

"Hi," I said, pushing my breakfast aside. I'd suddenly lost my appetite. "Why does my pulse race whenever you call?"

"Sorry, Tess. I've got some good news as well as bad this time. We've picked up the last of the Leans' network."

"Including the mystery biker?"

"Unfortunately not. But your friend Sarah Bullen's husband Will is in the clear—unless anything else comes up."

"Really?"

"Yes. He was the bean counter for a company with links to

the Leans, but it looks like it was unconnected with the pair's criminal activities. It was the one legitimate business they had. I don't think your pal Sarah actually told him anything. I get the impression their relationship has broken down to the extent that they're only talking to each other through solicitors."

That was one worry sorted, at least. "So, who's the mole?"

"Not sure. But I'm really sorry to have to tell you—"

"What?" I leapt in, somehow knowing what I was about to hear.

"Crusher Lean is in Greece."

"You're kidding me! He really couldn't be intercepted on the way?"

"Sadly, no, and I'm not kidding. The Cessna plane was impounded in Nantes. The pilot is under arrest there for aiding a fugitive. He's highly miffed because not only did Crusher Lean not pay him a promised five thousand pounds in cash to fly him from Kent, but he also stole his wallet! Once a crook and all that. So, it looks like Crusher used a fake ID to hire a car in Nantes. That vehicle was found outside the ferry terminal in Ancona, Italy. The fake ID was used by a foot passenger catching the ferry to Corfu."

"Oh, come on!" I said, raising my voice. "He's Crusher Lean, an overweight sixty-year-old London thug, not James Bond!"

Jason abandoned his own breakfast too and went below after giving my hand a sympathetic squeeze; I could hear him talking to another yacht on the radio.

Ted Green tried to offer some wafer-thin reassurances. "The Greek authorities are searching for him but, as you know, there's a lot of bays and islands around there. I would think it's a safe bet that he's after you, Tess. I wish I could do more to help."

"Thanks for the warning."

"Look, my phone is always on, and I've a direct line to the Corfiot cops, the police on Corfu, so call me if you see him— and, Tess, please be careful. You're not just a star witness, you're a star yourself. My wife says if anything happens to you and you're not on the news anymore it'll be my fault, and she's right."

"Careful is my watchword these days. That and *paranoia*. I just need to know who's betraying me, Ted."

"That makes two of us. Talk soon."

Jason came back up to the cockpit and we sat in silence. The sunny setting of this beautiful bay was losing its appeal with the prospect of a mad Crusher Lean appearing on the horizon at any moment, desperate for my blood.

"Let's move soon," said Jason, having heard my side of my call. "We're sitting ducks here if he shows up in that Fairline motorboat of his. We can't outrun him. Sorry, but we really can't."

"Someone must have told him I was back on Paxos. He's been one step behind me this whole time—he couldn't have got so close to me without inside info."

"At least you know it wasn't me. Or I hope you do!"

If it was Jason, of course, I'd have been attacked in Suffolk. "I do. It took me a while, but… I really do trust you now."

"That means a lot. So, who do you think it is?"

"Well, Sarah and her husband Will are in the clear, but I bet someone has told Lean I'm back on Paxos."

"But who?"

"I'm not sure." I counted them off on my fingers. "There's Steve, my editor. Jane and her husband Dave. Jo, who looks after the villa I stayed in…" But I couldn't believe that any of those four would betray me. "Maybe Steve's told someone at work…"

"You asked him not to."

"Yes, but he may have mentioned it in a news meeting, so theoretically it could be a leak from work. There's one other unthinkable scenario."

"Which is?"

"Is Ted Green on the take?"

"No. I can't believe that," Jason said immediately. "He knew we were at my house in Suffolk, he even got a local police car to sit outside all night to protect you. Besides, he'd hardly call to warn you Crusher Lean was back on Corfu, would he?"

"No, but if he's talking about the case at home then his wife might have said something."

"Hmm, have you suggested this to him?"

"Not yet, no. Not without evidence. What if Heffle's paid Green to inform on me?"

"A bent DCI or his wife feeding Heffle doesn't bear thinking about," said Jason, blowing out his cheeks. "Okay, we need to leave. Let's get dressed."

"I agree, so where are we heading?" I asked, clearing up the breakfast things.

"Well, there's still a bit of a southerly blowing. It's going to pick up later, and then should switch round to a north-westerly. So, if we go now, we'll be okay; the wind will blow us north to Lakka. After that, when it changes, we'll travel overnight. We'll be much harder to find in the dark."

"Do we have to go back to Lakka?"

"Yes. If we head away from Paxos now, we'll stand out: a single yacht in a big sea. Crusher's boat is fast, and he can search a wide area. If we're caught out alone at sea, we're stuffed. It's much better to leave Paxos in the dark. I've arranged to cruise back to Lakka in company."

"Sorry?"

"While you were on the phone. I spoke to Ben, the skipper of a flotilla I know. They're having a swim stop in the next bay just around those rocks. They're heading for Lakka shortly. I've asked them to call us on the radio, on channel eleven, when they leave. I thought we'd shadow and hide among them. We'll be one of fifteen similar-sized yachts, so if Crusher does come looking, he may not spot us that easily."

"Clever idea, but isn't Lakka the first place he'll look for us?"

"I doubt it: it's also the first place the police will search. We can moor among the flotilla boats out in the bay. The skipper will lend me one of their flags, so we'll look as if we're part of their group."

"But what about tomorrow?"

"Tomorrow we'll be in Preveza by first light. My plan is to leave Lakka after dark at about ten o'clock tonight when the wind will have changed. We'll sail south-east to a sweet little town called Vonitsa on the mainland. We'll be able to hide on the quay for a few days. I don't think Crusher will come looking for us that far south. Hopefully by then the Greek police will have caught him. I doubt he'll come to Lakka either: he knows the Greeks will be on the look-out for him there. He'd be mad to risk it."

"But Jason—he *is* mad. Totally and utterly mad."

17. The Reef

An hour later the radio burst into life as the flotilla skipper called us up as planned. Soon the anchor chain was rattling its way out of the water into the locker at the front of the boat, a few pieces of dark green and brown sea grass falling back to the surface as they fell from the fast-moving chain. The flotilla boats passed the entrance to Emerald Bay, and we slipped between them, staying close to the lead boat. Ben brought his vessel close to us and threw Jason a flag which he hauled up the rigging. Travelling in convoy was fun as the boats raced along, their genoa sails filling up with the warm, helpful wind. I was looking forward to eventually heading south, away from Paxos and the seemingly ever-present menace of Crusher Lean.

As we passed Gaios the wind turned, and front sails were joined by main sails as the breeze caught the yachts sideways on. Soon we were entering the beautiful blue bay at Lakka. Jason dropped *Sea Biscuit's* sails and we motored in with the flotilla yachts. The wind was now starting to turn and come from the north; soon we hoped it would continue and come from the north-west, ready to push us south to safety.

On the radio, Jason thanked the flotilla skipper for his company and we slowed down, waiting for our turn to anchor. As we slowly motored into Lakka Bay, following the flotilla, we were overtaken by a Fairline Targa motor yacht like Crusher's. I looked at the man behind the wheel as he looked at me. As our eyes met, my heart lurched. My nightmares collided in one massive panic. Gripping the wheel, with gritted teeth and an angry stare, was Crusher Lean himself. The snarling dragon tattoo was unmistakable. He'd found me.

"JASON! It's HIM!" I screamed.

"Hold on, Tess, we're going about." Jason turned up the motor and swung the wheel over to one side. *Sea Biscuit* turned around to face the way we'd just come. "We'll get the sails up as soon as we're out of the bay, Tess. Help me get ready to pull the main halyard when I say."

"He's turning! He'll catch us. He can outrun us, you said so yourself!"

"Hang on. Pass me the handheld radio." Jason called the skipper of the flotilla just ahead of us.

"Ben. Jason. Horrible ask, I know, but please slow this bastard in the Fairline down, PLEASE!"

The flotilla boats which hadn't yet anchored turned under motor almost as one; their sails were down, forming an almost solid line of boats blocking Crusher's path. He hooted his horn and shouted angrily at them to get out of his way. The skipper shouted back, saying it was a training flotilla and they were all novices. Crusher was forced to stop dead in the water. It gave us a chance to get to sea and pull our sails up as the flotilla began to circle him, much to his annoyance. Sadly, it didn't buy us much time, and Crusher, cursing loudly, soon barged his way through the friendly flotilla.

"Sorry, Jason, I did all I could," said the skipper on the radio.

"Cheers, Ben, I owe you one. *Sea Biscuit* out," said Jason.

Feeling desperate, I called DCI Green. "Ted, Tess. Crusher is behind us! We're just leaving Lakka on Paxos in Jason's yacht. Crusher's in a motorboat, a fast one. Tell the local police. *Please!*"

"On to it now!" he replied.

We had both sails up and the engine on full. We were

ploughing through the waves, heading south as fast as we could, but we were no match for Lean's motorboat, which could travel at five times our speed. It was only a matter of time before he was on us. I looked around for something to defend us with.

"There's a grab bag under the chart table with flares inside. Tess, please, quick!"

I went below and fetched the bag. The flares were yellowy-orange with red ends. One was fat and round.

"Pull the cord on a thin one and point it upwards, now."

I did. I felt a whoosh as what seemed like a firework took off from within the plastic casing in my hand.

"That's a rocket parachute flare; it'll take forty seconds to fall to the sea. Hopefully the cops will see it. There's another, set that off as well."

I did, and watched it roar upwards.

Lean was just coming out of the entrance to Lakka, close behind us. Jason picked up the radio mic.

"Mayday, mayday, mayday, sailing yacht *Sea Biscuit*, *Sea Biscuit*, *Sea Biscuit*. Mayday, mayday, mayday. We are being pursued by a dangerous criminal. We are half a mile out of Lakka on Paxos, heading south-east at six knots. Two people on board. Mayday, mayday mayday."

"Too little too late, you're DEAD!" crackled a voice on the radio. It was Crusher. "Death comes to those who wait, and I've waited too long to kill you, Tess Anderson. You can't run and you can't hide. I've got you at last, you filthy bitch."

I looked at Jason and thought how brave he was, putting his life and his boat in danger for a woman he hardly knew. This situation had always been likely if not inevitable. I'd known Crusher would catch me one day. I'd escaped too many times and my luck was running out. I reached for my mum's necklace, gripping it tight.

"He's gaining!" I shouted, desperate to do anything to help.

"Grab that fat orange flare. Hold it near the back of the boat and get ready to pull the tab. It's a smoke flare."

A voice came over the radio: "*Sea Biscuit, Sea Biscuit, Sea Biscuit*, this is the Hellenic Coastguard. We are heading towards you. *Motor Yacht Rosy Cheeks*, Mr Crusher, stop your pursuit now. There is a warrant for your arrest. We have armed police with us. Stop now."

Crusher replied, "Stuff your warrant up your *baklava*, you twats, you won't stop me now. I'll get Anderson first!"

Jason replied to the coastguard: "*Sea Biscuit*. Message received, Hellenic Coastguard, *efharisto*, thank you. *Sea Biscuit* listening on sixteen."

He looked at me and smiled. "Hey, Tess, another time, another life, we could... Maybe, things might..." But his words were cut short, as we saw Crusher getting even closer.

"JASON, he's nearly here! What are we going to do?"

"Hold on, Tess. Hold that big fat flare. Pull the tab on it... NOW!"

I did, just as Jason threw the wheel over hard to the left and *Sea Biscuit* obeyed. The radio came to life again. It was Crusher taunting us.

"Ha! You can't outrun me, you fuckin' numpties. You're going to die, both of you. I only wish it was more slowly. At least I'll see your faces when I pull the trigger."

The thick orange smoke poured from the flare right in the path of Crusher, who was now holding a gun: a revolver.

"What are you doing? You're going to tip us over!" I yelled, bracing myself against Jason's legs as I held the flare high. There was a crack as a bullet whizzed by above my head. It hit the mast and bounced off with a loud metallic *ting*, leaving a dent.

"Shi-t, hang o-n!" shouted Jason, and the boat swung back. I fell sideways, dropping the flare over the back of the boat. It hit the water but floated and continued releasing smoke. Crusher Lean went straight into it as another bullet came our way and hit the side of the yacht's hull.

There was a loud, horrible noise. The noise of fibreglass hitting rock. The engines on Crusher's boat roared to a high pitch, whining across the water. I was sure I heard a short sharp muffled scream above the noise.

"Oh yes! YES!" screamed Jason. "Tess! Remember the first time we left Lakka?" He was shaking and grinning. "Remember we had to turn because there's a reef out here? Well, Crusher's just tried to go right go over it!"

"Has he hit it?" I was shaking too. I felt sick.

"He's only gone and rammed it! Flat out! He's smacked straight into it! Oh, you beautiful little lump of jagged rock, thank you! Thank you!" Jason slowed the yacht down. He pulled the rope, allowing the sails to fall to the deck and we looked back at Crusher's boat, or what was left of it. But where was Crusher Lean?

The smoke was clearing and Crusher's wrecked motorboat was sitting, half out of the water, resting on the reef. The front of the vessel was smashed and there, lying over its broken windscreen looking ghostly in the haze of drifting orange smoke, was Crusher Lean. He rolled off into the water, banging his head on the wreckage as he slipped into the waves.

"Jason, we must get him out, he's still alive!" I screamed.

"But he just tried to kill us, Tess. Wouldn't we be doing the world a favour if we just left him there?"

"Yes, but then we'd be no better than he is. Much as I hate it," I said through gritted teeth, "we have to save him."

"You're right, sorry," said Jason, pulling a life ring from the rear metal work of the cockpit. Lean opened his eyes.

"I'll kill you basta—" he spluttered as his head slipped under the waves.

"Quick!" I shouted. Jason climbed overboard and tied a rope under Crusher Lean's arms.

"Tie it around that winch, Tess, and turn the handle."

I did, but the weight was too much. Jason climbed up beside me and started to winch the rope, and Lean, towards the boat. With his head and shoulders above the water, Lean looked pathetic, like a beached shark, still showing its teeth but unable to bite. I couldn't help thinking we were just delaying another attack on us but, however hideous he was, I couldn't let him die.

The Greek coastguard roared up and came alongside us, their wake making *Sea Biscuit* bounce up and down. Jason and I stood in silence, stunned and dazed. As the Greek police's boat came up behind us, strong arms pulled Lean out of the water.

"Mr Lean," said a sergeant, standing over the soggy villain. "What was this about our *baklava*?"

"S'pose you're going to send me back to London to face the law?" he said holding his head.

"After we've had the medics look at you, but London may be some time away."

"Oh that's good," Crusher said.

"Not really, Mr Lean," replied the Greek cop. "You may be spending a few years inside a Greek prison first. Attempted murder, failing to stop for the police, oh, and there was quite a lot of cocaine in your house on Corfu as well."

"Shit, you cops are the same the world over. Utter bast… aahhh…" he doubled up, "….my bloody tooth's come out."

The coastguard suggested we follow them into Gaios. They offered us a tow, but Jason declined, and we thanked them for their help. We wanted to be as far from Lean as we could.

Neither of us spoke as we motored behind them. I took Jason's hand and squeezed it tight, thinking how different things might have been. As we entered the harbour, I phoned DCI Green. I could barely hit last-number redial, I was shaking so much.

"Lean's in custody…" I said into the phone.

"Yes, I've heard. They've just called me. He's on his way to a nice cell in the sun, I hear, then we can have him back and press our own charges, too. I hear your friend Jason is quite a yachtsman, getting away like that. They relayed the radio talk to me. They called me so I could hear it all, including Crusher Lean's comments. Well, it saves us arresting him here."

"I know it's good news, Ted, but I can't take it in just yet. Sorry, I'm still too shaken. Dodging death is beginning to be a habit. I'd like to give it up, to be honest."

"Well, hopefully now the Leans are out of the way, your life can return to normal."

"I hope so too." Of course, there was still the matter of Heffle and her spooks. But I'd worry about that later. Crusher Lean was in custody, and that was all that really mattered right now.

*

An hour later, we were in the small Port Police station in Gaios. We gave a statement to the officers who'd come to our aid: two men and a woman in smart dark uniforms with guns by their sides. They were friendly and helpful. They offered us medical attention, but we declined. It was just shock, and nothing that a few weeks of rest and recuperation wouldn't cure. Our passports were checked and returned.

Ten minutes later we were sitting at a café in the square. I texted Jane two words. *Crusher arrested!* There, bathed in sunshine, we had cold beers and sat in silence, staring at the small dish of nuts and crisps that had been put in front of us by an attentive waiter. Neither of us could eat. Around us, people weaved between the tavernas, each with as many tables out as possible, making maximum use of every metre of space. Next to our beers a small glass vase displayed a single bloom. It was a world away from what we'd just been through, but our moment of quiet reflection was interrupted as my phone rang. It was Jane.

"Is he really off the streets?" I could hear the emotion in her voice. "Is it really all over?"

"I was just about to call you. Yes. He's off the streets, and off the water." I went on to tell Jane what had happened.

"Pity the bastard didn't die. But I guess you were right to save him. At least my ear can recover now."

"Ear?" I asked.

"I've been fiddling with my gran's earring so much, it's really sore."

I almost managed to laugh. "Well, maybe the Greek gods were smiling on us. Hey, I tell you something, this guy sitting next to me can certainly handle a boat." I looked at Jason, sitting calmly in his designer shades and blue sailing cap. He glanced up and smiled.

"Aw, shucks Tess." He gave me a coy grin.

"Tess," said Jane. "How many times does this guy have to save your life before you realise he loves you?"

I looked at Jason and just coughed. "So…"

"Look, Tess, I'm flying out tomorrow to the villa now for sure. I need a break and with Crusher dead I think it's safe. It'll do me good and there's a week before the next guests arrive. Besides, I kind of need to thank Jo for sorting out the mess from the break-in earlier. Can you stay there with me? Jason too, if he wants? Can't wait to see him."

"It'll be nice to join you in the villa. I'll ask Jason if he wants to come. When are you arriving?"

"Not sure: I haven't booked yet, but I'll let you know. Depends on flights. Look, go and stay there tonight if you want and wait for me. I'll tell Jo. Do you still have a key?"

"Yes, I do, it's in my bag—somewhere. Oh, Jane, Sarah's soon to be ex-husband Will is in the clear. There's nothing to suggest he was the mole. Sarah's adamant she didn't tell him anything either. DCI Green has been through the texts and emails supplied by Lean's phone providers."

"So, the mole is still out there," said Jane.

"Seems that way." I'd been thinking about it since getting back to Greece. There were one or two gaps in their knowledge, whoever they were. They didn't know I was in Suffolk at Jason's house. They didn't know which hotel I was staying at in London—the night of the live news attack—so it wasn't someone at work. They didn't know we were in Two Rock Bay either. "See you tomorrow. Let me know when you're arriving." I ended the call.

"Jason," I said, finishing my beer, "you may have gathered

that Jane's coming to the island tomorrow. She's invited us both to stay in her villa with her. Fancy coming along? I'd like you to meet her."

"That's kind of her," he said, emptying his beer glass, "but I think you two need a bit of girl-time together. I want to sort *Sea Biscuit* out as well; I need to check there's no damage—like bullet holes in the fibreglass. But I'll stay in Lakka, and I won't go until you want me to, okay?"

"Yes. If you're sure?" I knew I'd miss Jason there beside me, but it would be good to have some time with Jane like we used to.

"So long as you promise you won't leave Paxos without saying goodbye to me. No sneaking off in the night. Promise?"

"I promise, Jason. Besides, you can't leave without meeting Jane." I grinned and offered him my hand. He shook it like we were completing a sale.

"Deal, then." He laughed.

*

I realised I was still a journalist, so I called my editor. "Breaking news! Crusher Lean is in police custody. I can't send you much as I'm in a bar with just my phone, but if you want I can dictate a few lines for you."

"Wow! Tess. Are you sure?"

"Positive. One hundred percent."

"Good source then?"

"Me."

"You?"

"Put it this way—I've seen him surrounded by cops. The police will confirm it when you call them."

I heard an intake of breath and then Steve said, "Okay, let me have it, I'm poised and ready to type—fingers on the keyboard."

"Here goes." I said switching into work mode, dictating the story. "*Crusher Lean, who's wanted by the police in connection*

214

with the death of a TV cameraman and other offences, has been arrested. Lean, was caught by police after being hurt in a boating accident off the island of Paxos near Corfu in Greece. It's reported that his motorboat hit a reef whilst travelling at high speed. He was being pursued by the Greek coastguard at the time. No one else was injured.

"Crusher Lean is the brother of Ken Lean, who died in hospital recently while serving a thirty-year prison sentence. He'd been convicted of multiple murder and defrauding the residents of a care home, which he owned, out of millions of pounds... You can fill in the rest, Steve. Cheers." I heard him typing the last words.

"Thanks, Tess. Now what about these emails you mentioned?"

"I'll get back to you on that. I promise. I just fear if I release them, I'll never be safe again. Can you... just give me a few days to get over this?"

"Okay."

"Look, Steve, strictly between us, Crusher Lean was trying to kill me when he hit a reef. He was chasing me—I was in the yacht, and he actually fired a gun at me." I felt my pulse rise as I recalled the events. "I actually saved his life, but I really don't want that broadcast though, okay?"

"Wow, that was another close one. So you're a hero too. Hey, when you're ready to do the definitive documentary on the Lean brothers we can hopefully include that? Even a reconstruction?"

"With an actor, not with me, thanks. I couldn't live through that again." Typical Steve, always looking for ways to get the most out of a story.

"No worries. Hey, glad you're all right and Crusher's finally out of the way. Take care and call again when you can. We all miss you; you know that. It's not the same here without our Tess."

"Cheers, boss, that's appreciated. I miss you guys too. Please send my love to everyone in the newsroom."

I ended the call. Jason was paying the bill and getting ready to go back to the boat.

"Want a lift back to Lakka?" he smiled.

"Love one."

"Tess, can we have just one more night together on *Sea Biscuit*?"

"Tonight?"

"Yes. We could go to Lakka. I love it there. There's a great little restaurant I know. My treat."

"Go on then." I smiled. How could I refuse?

*

We untied the boat and motored gently against the wind up to Lakka, passing the scene of Crusher's arrest. The wreck of his boat was being towed to Corfu. I wondered who'd have mourned him had he died? I'd learned from my research that Crusher Lean wasn't married. He had been once, but she'd died from so-called 'accidental gas poisoning' in her new house just a week after she left him. Like anyone really believed that had been an accident.

Jason nosed the yacht into the entrance to the bay. We spotted a boat leaving the quay and slipped into its place. I left Jason tidying his yacht and went to Yan's Bar where Crusher Lean had found me. I owed them for the lunch I'd had to run away from while being chased by a crazed man with a knife. I thanked Maria. She was pleased to see me.

"So, you have a nice date tonight with the man who saved your life, again!" She smiled, nodding towards Jason, who was refilling *Sea Biscuit* with fresh water from the hose pipe on the quayside, the very one he'd use to trip Crusher up while he was chasing me.

"Oh, it's not a date, Maria," I smiled, embarrassed.

"But you can't let a man like that sail out of your life. There's a big moon tonight, a big omen, yes?" She grinned. I brushed it off, feeling myself blush. She sniggered and pushed my shoulder playfully just as Jason walked over to join us. He looked gorgeous striding along the quay with his sun-browned arms and legs set off by a clean white t-shirt and stone-coloured shorts. Maybe Maria was right—I'd be making a huge mistake letting him sail out of my life. But now Crusher was in custody and I was safe, what was keeping him with me?

18. Lovers' Bay

I used one of the showers that the shops and tavernas hire out to yachties. This one was upstairs, in an unrented apartment, and for five euro it was pure luxury. I felt the hot water washing away the fear of Crusher Lean and the angst and agony of knowing he was always one step behind, spending his waking days planning my death. It was such a feeling of relief and release.

I shampooed my short hair and realised I could grow it out now. I wouldn't need the wig; I no longer needed a disguise. Already the roots were showing but I didn't care; I would soon go back to my normal colour. I'd be me; I'd be Tess. I enjoyed shaving my legs, cutting my nails and using what seemed like a litre of creams. Meanwhile Jason was buying Ben the flotilla skipper a beer or two for helping us earlier.

I got back to the yacht to find Jason had also showered and was unusually wearing a shirt and jeans rather than t-shirt and shorts. I put on my best dress, the only dress I had, and we stepped off the boat together and out into the streets of Lakka. We looked the perfect couple. We could have been on holiday or honeymoon and, right then, both scenarios had their attractions. In amongst the brightly-lit shops on the streets leading back from the quayside, was a clothes and trinkets shop. Jason insisted on going in. He picked out and bought me a top. It was white cotton, embroidered in bright colours. Indian-looking, a bit hippy.

"I've only got a black bra or a blue bikini top Jason, it'll show right through this. It's really nice of you to buy it for me though."

"It's to be worn without a bra, Tess."

I felt a blush spread through my cheeks.

We walked through the streets and Jason led me to the little restaurant in the former garden of a house. It was exquisite; we were the only customers there. We sat half-sheltered by an olive tree, its branches lit by deep blue fairy lights. There were only ten tables; it was intimate and special. High walls surrounded the dining area. Old pots and urns were leaning against the sides, some painted white, whilst others were that magical Greek blue, the colour of the sea and the sky. Candles and low lights completed the scene. The gentle evening sounds of Lakka's streets were kept out by the walls of the garden. The food was perfect; we had *Briam* again; it was as good as the one we'd enjoyed in Parga. So much had happened since that first night with Jason after he'd rescued me from the quayside just a few hundred metres from the taverna we were in. Sweet honey desserts followed.

"You look stunning, Tess," said Jason, the low glow and candlelight dancing in his eyes.

"Thank you. You don't look bad yourself. For an ageing posy pop star that is." I grinned.

"Posy yes, but not so much of the ageing." He laughed. "A toast?" he lifted his wine glass.

"We ought to celebrate the arrest of Crusher Lean," I said. "Sad though it is."

"Sad?"

"Sad because he brought us together, and now he's going to spend a long time in jail." I looked up and our eyes met. "So now we have to resume our lives and, I guess, we have to go our separate ways. Don't we?"

"Hmm," said Jason thoughtfully, pouring Prosecco. "Here's

to us, then, and the capture of Crusher Lean. The world is certainly a safer and better place, now he's no longer at large."

"And here's to doing the right thing, even though it stinks," I said. "Hmm, remind me again why we saved the bastard?"

"We saved him because we're decent people, Tess, you and I, and he's scum, and he'll have many years inside a cell to reflect on that."

We emptied the bottle and the waiter brought us a local liqueur, which was on the house. The bill soon arrived. It was sad to leave the little cocoon of the garden taverna, but we wandered back to the boat through the gently-lit streets, flanked by white walls and inviting shop windows. I was relaxed for the first time in ages. I reached out and took his hand. He squeezed my fingers gently. It was so good, but I felt a little sad as I knew Sven would have loved this place.

Jason suggested we slip *Sea Biscuit's* mooring lines and take the yacht out into the bay. Being early season, the almost enclosed stretch of water was nearly empty, apart from Ben's flotilla which was moored at anchor close to the town.

The moon was bright on that fabulously warm night. Jason pulled up the anchor and I took in the mooring lines, stowing them neatly in the locker under the side seat of the cockpit. I was now quite used to being his 'crew'. It was like we were slipping away furtively for a night in the bay. It was all so different from the last time I'd left Lakka in his yacht; this time I was doing it on my terms.

We motored out slowly, the rumble of the propeller under the water leaving little ripples of wake behind us. Jason headed for the far corner of the bay, by the tall white cliffs. Sprinkled on top of them was a sporadic row of luxury villas, all but one unlit and waiting patiently for their summers to begin. Jason slowed the engine and *Sea Biscuit* drifted gently.

"This is a good spot," he said. "The water's always warm here; I think there's a spring somewhere beneath us."

"The water's warm? Are we swimming, then?"

"Think so. Come on."

"Hey, I'm too tired to even get undressed, and I'm a bit squiffy with all that wine. I doubt I can take my things off."

"I'm sure I can help. Only as a friend, of course."

I shook my head, grinning. He tried to look innocent but laughed. He started undressing and soon he stood naked in front of me. I let my eyes briefly run over his taut body.

"Well, I'm not hanging around," he said. "Want to come in?"

"It seems a shame not to. I guess there aren't many nights like these."

"No, there aren't," he replied. "A beautiful night, a lovely moon, warm water beneath us, a cosy yacht to sleep in and wonderful company. Coming in?"

"Okay," I whispered and undid my dress. I stood back as it fell to the cockpit floor. I stepped out of it, standing in my underwear. "As a friend?" I asked.

"You choose," he replied, smiling warmly.

With the tenderness of a friend, but with the passion of a lover, Jason touched my shoulder as I stood under the moon in the yacht. I unclipped my bra. Slipping it off I laid it on the seat. His eyes fixed on mine, and I smiled. I was soon naked too, and silently he took my hand and led me to the ladder at the back of the boat. He was right. The water was warm.

"Beat you to the anchor chain!" he grinned, swimming away from me. I swam the other way around the boat, and we met where the anchor chain went into the water.

"Five laps of the boat?" he suggested.

"Five! Well, let's try two," I said and pushed my way through the water. We went opposite ways around the yacht, giggling as we passed each other. After the second full circuit I grabbed the ladder on the back of the boat and pulled myself out of the water, the liquid running down my body, dripping from me as I hauled myself into the cockpit. Jason followed me.

He put his arms either side of my hips. I put mine around his shoulders. Smiling, I glanced up at the moon.

"Hi, Selene," I said.

"Selene?" he asked.

"Ancient Greek moon goddess, sort of thing," I mumbled.

"Is she a happy Greek moon goddess, sort of thing?" he asked.

"I think so. I know I am, are you?"

"Happier than I can remember being for a long time, Tess."

"I won't jump in and swim away if you kiss me."

"Why's that?" he asked, his face moving closer.

"Because the night belongs to lovers, as Patti Smith once sang." There was a pause. I remembered a pause like this on my first night with Sven, but I didn't want Sven in my head right now; I wanted Jason. Sven was probably in bed with Heffle. I shouldn't have had any guilt, but I did. Just a little.

We moved towards each other. Our mouths met. Warm, soft, anticipating. His grip tightened; my skin tingled with his touch. He hugged me closer. Soon we were lying on a cushion on the cockpit seat. The nearest boat was hundreds of metres away; there were no prying eyes.

"Are we friends tonight," he asked. "Or lovers?" His eyes sparkled.

"I think you know the answer to that, Jason," I said. "There's just one thing…"

"What's that?" he asked.

"I want to make love to Jason Howard, not Jason L'Amour."

"And I want to make love to Tess the bedraggled run-away, not *TV's Tess Anderson*, the star reporter… And don't you dare say *now back to the studio* at the end!"

I burst out laughing as his lips found mine.

It was the first time a man other than my husband had touched me in years. I felt a streak of guilt flash through my brain, but it was chased away by a bolt of anger. I was cross, angry with myself for having felt guilty at all. Sven had been to bed with Suzanna Heffle countless times, probably more than he had with me in the last year. Was I so wrong to enjoy one night with someone else? Not just anyone else either, but the man who'd devoted the last few days of his life to me; the man who could have easily lost his own life today saving mine.

I felt a warmth creep over me. Safe in the arms of the man who'd saved me from Crusher Lean. I kissed him as I ran my fingers along his body. My heartbeat quickened under the watchful moon as his hands gently caressed me.

"What took you so long, Jason?" I asked, smiling lovingly into his eyes. The gentle waves glistened around us, lit by the moon.

"Not wanting to hurt you. I've wanted to do this since the day we met."

"We've shared a bed a few times."

"Yep, and that was really tough, you being so close, but I didn't want to put pressure on you. You had so much to cope with, a madman trying to kill you and a husband you still have feelings for. I don't want to split you up for good; that's your decision, not mine. I'd rather have you as a friend if I can't have you as a lover."

"Tonight you can have me as both."

"I want to make this moment last," he said.

"It will linger forever, whatever happens and wherever we drift. We both have baggage but what once seemed wrong now seems right. I can't promise it'll be more than just this night, but I'll always hold a place for you, somewhere."

"We're just two heart-wrecks rescuing each other in the night."

"Love me, Jason. Tonight there's just us, us and the moon, and she doesn't mind."

"Please don't regret this tomorrow, Tess."

"I'm a big girl. I can face the morning, whatever it brings and however I feel. Even if we never touch again we'll always have this moment, this night. Kiss me again, we could have both died today, kiss me like it's our last ever kiss."

The moon lit us as the boat swayed in the all-embracing sea. *Thanks, Selene,* I whispered as we lay down together on that perfect Paxos night.

*

As the dawn broke, we woke up and just held hands. I kissed his cheek. He squeezed my knee.

"Hey you," I whispered.

"You okay?" he asked, gently taking my hand.

"More than okay. You?"

"Yeah."

I smiled. We both knew how special last night had been.

I got out of his bed and walked to the back of the yacht, then climbed into the welcoming water warmed by the sun. Jason soon joined me. I watched his taut body in the calm of the bay. I'd actually slept with him, with Jason L'Amour, the Restless Lover himself, and what a lover. I needed to tell Jane, who would be beside herself when she found out.

After a swim, we waited until there was space on the quay and motored in, tying *Sea Biscuit* near the spot where Jason had rescued me not very long ago. We didn't speak much, both feeling a little awkward after the night's excess. A text arrived on my phone from Sven.

Just reading about Crusher Lean's arrest. That's my girl, bet you had a big part in it, so pleased you're OK and finally safe from that monster. S xx

The flash of guilt I'd felt last night returned, more intensely. Whatever he'd done, Sven was still my husband, and breaking our vows was a big deal to me—if not to him. But why was he suddenly sending these texts? Was he making a play to come back? Had he dumped Heffle? I started to type a reply and then changed my mind. I had nothing to say.

Later, I went to meet Jane from the *flying dolphin* as it came into Gaios. I'd got a taxi waiting, even though I knew Jo would have picked her up had I asked. I needed Jane to myself for a while, not least because I knew she'd have lots of questions about my night with 'Jason L'Amour'. It would have been headline news for our twenty-something selves. It would still make a story somewhere in the press even today. I could see the headlines now: *TV's Tess finds L'Amour in Greek love boat!*

When Jane saw me waiting on the quayside, she almost ran from the hydrofoil. Dropping her bag, we hugged like long-lost sisters and allowed ourselves an excited squeal. The last time we'd been together was in London the morning after Jake's death. Now the Leans' reign of fear was over, we could almost return to normality, except I had the emails and a decision to make. If I released them, normality might never return.

I'd been back to the villa earlier with shopping and to check it was okay. The garden hummed with life—insects, birds and flowers. I looked at the brick storeroom where I'd sought shelter and been locked in. It seemed so unthreatening now. Jo had done a good job, as I'd known she would. It was immaculate and clean; and, thanks to Christos the leering builder, it was also repaired and freshly painted, all ready for the summer. As I paid the taxi waiting by the gate, we saw something that made us both smile. There was a stray cat sitting by the door, hoping for some attention.

"Mr Ouzo Two?" I laughed.

"Ahh, well. So long as she or he knows they'll only get fed if there's someone here that's stupid or soft enough to feed them... Looking after a moggy is not part of the rental agreement."

"Maybe we should call it *Boutari* after the lovely local wine?"

"That wine gets better." She laughed.

"What, in time?"

"No, usually after the second or third bottle!"

"That's good, then, because there are four of them in the fridge," I said, picking up her bags and carrying them in.

I took the same room I'd slept in on the night of the iPad theft, the only night I'd stayed there. I did look around to make sure I wasn't missing something unexpected or unpleasant, but the atmosphere of anxiety had gone. The villa now seemed peaceful and welcoming, as if nothing horrible had ever happened within its walls, although I would never forget what I'd seen that day in the bathroom.

We cooked together and ate outside, with citronella candles burning to try and keep away the mosquitos: they wanted their dinner too.

"So," said Jane, quizzically, as she put down her knife and fork and picked up her glass of wine. "What's happened with you and Jason? Tell all."

"We had a nice dinner out last night..."

"You've gone and slept with him, haven't you?" she said accusingly, grinning widely. "I know that look. It's the classic Tess Anderson morning-after smile, the *I've had a shag, and I'm desperate to tell all* smile."

"Well... I have been a bit of a bad girl." I couldn't help giggling, like a teenager after a first date.

"Knew it! Tell." She smiled expectantly, turning to face me full-on and grabbing my arm.

"Well, if you must know..." I pretended to sigh. "We had amazing, passionate, brilliant, unforgettable sex on the boat."

"Knew it!"

"Oh, Jane, it was in the most romantic setting—Lakka Bay under the moon. It was perfect. Well, except that the lever which makes the engine go fast or slow was sticking into my side."

"Could have been worse! Was it wonderful? Was it rock and roll, sleeping with a star?"

"He was just Jason, and I was just me." I paused. "I just don't know if it will happen again."

"Why not?"

"Because it was so perfect, I don't see how it could be repeated. It was a one-off."

"Don't be silly; you know it doesn't work that way. When you fall in love with someone, it just gets better... Do you think you could fall in love with Jason?"

"I think I'm halfway there already." I reached for my wine.

"But…" I needed to tell someone, and who better than Jane? "I'm feeling guilty."

Her eyes widened. "Guilty? What for?"

"I know I shouldn't, after what Sven's done, but I somehow feel I've sunk to his depths…"

"Tess, *after what he's done* is the crucial phrase. For God's sake, Sven dumped you. He's been shagging Heffle for months. One night is all you've had! One night!"

"I know, I know. We did have a few kisses before I returned to London and I've been thinking about Jason for longer than one night, though… Is that bad?"

"Are you kidding?" Jane rolled her eyes. "I would've jumped him my first night on board. You've been very restrained, under the circumstances. Seriously, Tess, don't beat yourself up."

"I have to admit, it was special. The boat, the moon, the two of us. It just seemed… so natural, so real."

"Hollywood sex."

"Sort of."

"Well, I sort of reckon Jason's in love with you."

"You haven't even met him!"

"And that needs to change; I'm not having some stranger bed my friend without my say-so—not even Jason L'Amour! When can I meet him?"

"Tomorrow morning? We'll go and find him on the quay."

"I'll look forward to it. More wine?"

"Well, I've already had two glasses, but why not?"

Jane poured the wine. She looked at me and could obviously tell I was churning things over in my mind. "You need to relax," she ordered.

"I can't relax," I said firmly. "Not until this email business is resolved."

"Resolve it then. Either give them to someone—me for my newspaper, or Steve for TV and radio—or delete all reference to them and move on. Simple as that."

"Problem is, Jane, you know if I release them it could cause a massive scandal, criminal proceedings, and look what happened last time I did that. Besides, Sven could be in the frame too, as an accessory maybe? Can I do that to him after I've cheated on him with Jason?"

"*You've* cheated on *him*? What?! Er, excuse me, he played away first—big time—and exposing criminals is part of your job, Tess."

"Yeah, but… This could even bring down the government! Do I want more enemies who are even more dangerous than the Leans? I'm not strong enough to run forever. I've already lost Jake and you're very precious to me, Jane, I can't risk losing you."

She smiled and took my hand in hers. "Ohh, I know. Except that the spooks who took Sven's iPad from this very villa—and locked you in the outhouse—didn't actually hurt you, did they? Hardly the quintessential James Bond bad guys, were they? You weren't found riddled with bullets on the drive, were you? Once it's out there, those two will be locking the stable door after the horse has bolted. They'll be looking after their own backsides rather than trying to kick yours."

"Maybe you're right."

"Come on. You're a journalist, you've got the story of the year, you're never going to sit on it, are you? Get real."

"I'm not sure," I said looking down, uncertain.

"Have you heard from Sven at all?" Jane asked.

"Yes, this morning."

"And?"

"He was glad I was safe and Crusher was out of the way, but there was a flash of the old Sven there, with kisses too."

"Hmmm. Shall we check your emails? I have my laptop in my bag, and we can soon turn the wi-fi on."

"Okay, I guess I should," I replied.

I watched as Jane's netbook burst into life. The screen lit up and found the wi-fi. Jane entered the password and went online. She passed it over to me and I accessed my email account. There were some more from colleagues at work and one from Sven which brought me down to earth with a bump. It said: *'Our Divorce.'* Two words without compromise. I opened it. *'Tess, do you want a divorce? If so, we can do it amicably without the expense of solicitors. We have no children, and our assets can just be split fifty/fifty. I have the forms and I can fill them out. If you want to go ahead with this, I think we should meet. Suzanna and I can be in Paxos within forty-eight hours. Can we meet like adults in a public place on the island to sign the papers? That way it's a clean break for both of us. Please let me know. Sven.'*

No kisses, and so different from the text he'd sent me earlier. Did he write this himself or was he told to write it? Was Heffle that much in control of Sven?

"Jane," I said cautiously. "Sven and the Heffle-lump want to meet me here on Paxos to go through our divorce, if I want one."

"When?"

"Within forty-eight hours if I say yes."

"No mention of the emails?" she asked.

"None."

"Mm. Okay. They seem very keen to travel all this way for a signature on some DIY divorce papers which you could post or sign when you go back to London. It would certainly clarify things and bring this all to a close, though, if you met them and hammered it out. You either divorce Sven or you don't. It would help you decide about Jason and your future. Let's face it, there's no way you'd take Sven back, is there? After everything that's happened. Surely the only way is forwards, Tess."

"Okay. I'll say yes to a meeting." I could always just keep my copy of the papers and think about it. "So... when and where?"

"Well, if they're coming here there's a hydrofoil twice a day, to and from Corfu, so mid-morning, I guess. As to where, what about Yan's Bar, the one you like on the quayside? I can be there too, and Jason might be happy to come along as well if you want back up."

"No. I don't want to involve Jason; that's not fair on him. You'd be welcome as a witness though; after all there'll be two of them and I need support too."

"Sure, no worries. Oh, Dave is coming out; he doesn't like leaving me alone after what happened. I said I'd be with you, but he wants to come to the island. He's off work anyway."

"Off work?"

"Depression. He's been signed off by the doctor. I'm really worried about him, Tess. It's not like him."

"Why didn't he fly out with you today?"

"He has a doctor's appointment and a meeting with his boss."

"Shit, sorry, and there was me going on about Jason and Sven. You've got your own stuff to deal with."

"Hey, I wanted to hear about it. Your night of passion with Jason L'Amour! A man like Jason doesn't come along every day."

"That's what you said about Sven when I met him."

"And I was right. But sadly, Sven has become a different man."

"Or maybe I became a different woman. Maybe Heffle offered him something more akin to what I used to be?"

"Tess! She's a dull, boring politician. You were NEVER like that. Stop making excuses for him. Got it! These damn mosquitoes are persistent, that's the second one I've killed on my arm."

"Well done. One less to bite us." I stood up, yawning. "I think it's time for bed. I'll reply to Sven in the morning."

*

I lay in the bed I'd slept in the first night I stayed at the villa, when Jake and Mr Ouzo were still alive. The night I was locked in the outhouse. I turned off the light, but I couldn't sleep. The room held bad memories for me. I heard Jane in the adjacent bedroom. Getting out of bed, I walked into the hallway and opened the door to her room. She was in bed and facing the window, her back to me. I crept up and lay on the sheet beside her.

"Hello. I thought you might do that. I was just waiting for

the patter of your feet," whispered Jane softly. "It's all right. I'm glad you're here."

"Are you sure? I woke up last night, I'd been screaming in my dream, and there's no guarantee I won't have a nightmare again tonight."

"Well, that's even more reason for me to be here. We can both fight off each other's demons in the dark and scream together."

It was nice to know Jane was beside me, and I did sleep better knowing I wasn't alone. I was missing Jason more than I'd thought, but I was also missing Sven more than I'd thought I would too. It was partly familiarity and routine—knowing someone so well. But then, did I actually know Sven that well? I was so mixed up. His email had got me thinking. Did I really want a divorce? I drifted in and out of an uneasy sleep. The emails were haunting me, and who was the mole who'd nearly got me killed?

The only Greeks who knew where I was on the island were Christos the builder and Maria the waitress in Yan's Bar. There was Jo of course, and what about Sarah? Her husband was in the clear, but was she? And Dave, Jane's husband? Plus Steve, oh God, and of course DCI Green. No. Surely not him. But what about his wife? I knew Jason was in the clear; he'd saved my life. He couldn't be working for Crusher Lean, but could he be working for Heffle? No, he could easily have stolen or destroyed my memory card... The thoughts went round and round in my head. All questions, no answers. The only thing I knew for sure was that *someone* was betraying me.

19. Feelings

It was 10:30 in the morning. Jane and I had spent the last forty-five minutes walking down the hill from the villa into Lakka. She'd kindly bought me a pretty little light blue and grey cotton summer dress, perfect for Paxos. It went well with my sandals—but not so well with my fading scars. It was just nice to be in different clothes, though. I'd texted Jason to warn him we were coming and, as we approached the quayside, we saw him sitting in the sun, in the cockpit of *Sea Biscuit*, looking every bit the faded rock star.

He was wearing a tight white t-shirt which hugged the curves of his slender body and showed off his tan. He had on a new pair of shorts I hadn't seen before; they were a deep faded blue and clearly expensive. They gripped his shapely legs. The sunglasses were secured with a bright blue strap seemingly gluing them to his closely cropped remaining hair. He saw us and took off his glasses, smiling with those welcoming blue eyes. I heard Jane mutter under her breath.

"Tess, he's kind of hot."

"Down, Jane," I whispered through my smile. "The hair's gone."

"So what? The rest hasn't! And you've actually slept with him. Nice bum too."

"Jane, shut it!" I laughed, nudging her in the ribs with my elbow.

"Morning, Jason," I smiled.

"Hey, you." He stood up and gave me a hug. He was more than a friend, but not quite a lover. There was a little distance between the man I held today and the man I'd made love to in Lakka Bay.

"You look refreshed," he said.

"Oh, you mean I looked haggard and worn before?" I laughed. "Jason, this is Jane."

"Good to meet you, Jason, I've heard so much about you. Tess has probably told you we listened to your music all the time at university. I had your poster on my wall," she said, a bit too enthusiastically.

"Hi, Jane, good to meet you too.' He gestured to the boat. 'This is *Sea Biscuit*: she's been Tess's escape pod."

"Wow, so this is the boat that beat Crusher Lean," said Jane, shaking her head. "Now I really am starstruck!"

Jason shrugged. "He was just so obsessed with chasing us and killing Tess that he forgot the basics. The reef is clearly marked, he had a chart, he was just totally single-minded, and seeing us in front assumed we would all miss it."

"Jason's being modest," I said. "It was his brilliant seamanship that got us away from the reef in the nick of time. We must have been so close."

"Too close, actually," Jason jumped in. "If I'd turned just a second or two later, we'd have hit it too. He hit it at full speed going much faster than us, which was nearly fatal."

"Well, it was a great result," said Jane. "You're safe and he's in a police cell. Let's go to Yan's Bar. My treat. Come on, we'll have a late breakfast."

*

We sat at my favourite table by the sea. A two-seater wicker chair and a single were arranged in a semi-circle, giving an uninterrupted view of the bay. We watched boats come and go. The three of us ate the usual yogurt, honey and fruit breakfast with fresh orange juice and cappuccinos. We paid, and then Jason made his excuses. He went off for a walk to the lighthouse on the hill above the little resort. Jane waited until he'd started up the path and then grabbed my hand.

"Tess. Listen. As my mum would have said: *he's a keeper!* Come on, stop pretending, you're both so obviously fond of each other, he's lovely, and he really is the actual Jason L'Amour, for God's sake! Wow, er… excuse me but, wow! Plus, you've had an amazing shag!"

"Okay, calm down. Yes, all of that's true. But it wasn't a *shag* Jane: it was making love."

"Yeah, yeah, what-ever." She gave my shoulder a playful push. "You say potato and I say *potarto*. And what's with that American accent, so cute!"

"The accent's real. He's half American, but I think you're forgetting something—I'm married to Sven."

Jane frowned. "I think Sven's the one who's forgotten that."

I thought back to that day in the Registry Office all those years ago. I'd married Sven because I really loved him. We'd made a commitment, for better or worse. "We always said we'd forgive an indiscretion…"

"Indiscretion! Oh, Tess, you drive me to distraction. Shagging Suzanna what's-her-pants, the Heffle-lump, for four months is more than an *indiscretion*. It's not a drunken grope at a party, for God's sake."

"But what if he wants me back and it's only Heffle that's pushing him to get a divorce? And Jason's lovely, yes, a real dream in so many ways. But if he wanted me, where would I live? I can't commute to central London from Suffolk every day."

"What's it like? His house."

"Oh, absolutely lovely, real *Homes & Gardens* stuff—low ceilings, beams, white-rendered outside, big garden, fabulous kitchen, inglenook fireplaces, the lot. There's even a wishing well in the garden."

"Wishing well?"

"It's really just an old drinking water well, but I made a wish in it."

"What did you wish for?"

"I can't say, or it won't come true."

"Nor will this fairy tale ending with Jason unless you let it."

"But am I just on the rebound? And can I really trust another man? Can I trust any man after what Sven has done?"

"I think I'd trust Jason," Jane said sagely.

"Can I use your laptop to reply to Sven's email?"

"Sure, go ahead." She pulled her netbook from her bag.

'Hi Sven,' I wrote, while Jane went to the bar to order more coffee. *'Thanks for your email. I've been too angry and too preoccupied with staying alive to get back to you before now, and seeing you and her in our kitchen when I'd just lost a friend who died saving my life was too much.*

'I'm not sure if I want a divorce or not, I need more time. If you are staying with Heffle then clearly there's no point in our being married. Also, I've met someone else. I'm very uncertain right now.

'If you want to come to Greece then I'll meet you, although I don't know what my decision will be. If we decide to go ahead, we can file for divorce without delay. If we are doing that, then the sooner the better, so we can both get on with our lives. I'm happy with a 50/50 split. If you're coming out tomorrow, can you please bring my mum's wedding ring from my strong box in the sitting room cupboard. Meet me at Yan's Bar, Lakka, Paxos. Tomorrow at 11:00 if that works. Let me know, I'll text you my new number. Tess.'

I had to see Sven again to make a decision. It was make or break. I needed to know if I really did still love him and if I should fight to keep him, or if I should move on forever and try to make a go of it with Jason. I knew I couldn't lead him on until I'd decided whether I was through with Sven; it wasn't fair on either of us. I re-read the email, pressed send and then closed the laptop. I wanted Mum's ring. I needed her near me right now and her ring was really important to me. What would Mum have said about Sven? She always wanted me to stand by him, like she did with Dad. Dad, though, hadn't dragged her marriage through the papers and shagged a damn politician.

Jane came back with more coffee.

"Hey, fancy a little detour on our way back?" I asked, lifting the white cup. "I need to clear my head."

"Sure," said Jane, "we can walk to the end of the road on the other side of the bay, there's a ruined house there that's worth a look. It's for sale; you never know, you might want to buy it. One day."

Maria cleared the table as we got up to leave. A text arrived. It was from Sven.

'Got your email Tess. Sorry things are the way they are, I didn't want it to be like this. Still love you. S x'

*

As Jane and I returned from our walk and reached her villa, we saw Jo's car parked outside. She was watering the garden. She greeted Jane like an old friend.

"You should have called," she said, smiling. "I'd have picked you up from the ferry." She turned to me. "I hear you narrowly escaped a high-speed chase by a mad criminal."

"News travels fast," I said. "Was all that in the news? I didn't mention I was being chased by him when he crashed his boat."

"No, the local police told me. I heard there'd been a boat wreck and I wanted to make sure it wasn't you. I'm so glad you're okay."

"We all are," Jane said. "Listen, Jo. Tess's husband is coming here tomorrow. They need to talk."

"Oh?" said Jo quizzically. "It's a long way to come for a talk."

"Well, big decisions to make, a bit of a crossroads for both of them."

"Oh, I see."

"How's Christos, still checking the paintwork by peering through open windows and doors at my guests?" Jane asked sarcastically.

"He doesn't change," said Jo, shaking her head.

"Hah. No excuse. He should. Hey, Jo, do you want to stay and eat with us?" asked Jane.

"Thanks for the offer but I need to get back; the cats need feeding and the chickens too. Besides, I've got another villa to clean. Come over and see me soon though, won't you? Have a nice evening."

*

At eleven o'clock the next morning, Jane and I were in Yan's Bar sitting by the water's edge. We could see *Sea Biscuit* still tied to the quay, but there was no sign of Jason. I texted him to ask if he was all right. He replied, saying he was around if I needed him. He'd gone for a long walk at first light, but he'd be back by the time Sven and Heffle arrived.

They were right on time.

"Hey look, they're here. Play nice," said Jane, holding her hand firmly over mine. I looked across and saw them. It was the first time I'd seen Sven since that time in our kitchen, the morning after that dreadful night outside the hospital when everything had changed. He was in light chinos with a smart ironed white checked shirt, one that I'd bought him. She was wearing a dark grey patterned summer dress, smart enough to show she was a powerful woman.

They made a nice couple. She was confident, he was attractive, and I was jealous. It didn't seem right seeing him with another woman, knowing they were together, and he and I weren't. Memories of Arillas and other holidays came flooding back. The sun, the smell, the scenery. It should have been us together in this romantic place, not him and her.

"Hello, Tess. Hi, Jane," said Sven. "Do you mind if we join you?"

"Sven, Suzanna, it would be a bit silly to come all this way not to. Help yourself." I did my best to sound polite. My voice was shaky and strained. They sat down as I waved to Maria, who smiled and walked over. I scanned for signs of recognition between them and Maria, but there were none. I was being totally paranoid. Maria was beyond suspicion, surely?

"Nice flight?" asked Jane politely.

"Yes, thank you," Heffle said, putting her bag by her side.

"Tess, I've brought you something." Sven reached into his pocket and retrieved a ring box. "It's your mother's wedding ring, as requested." I let out a little moan of recognition as I took it. I touched his hand as he put the small red box into mine. I opened it and touched the metal circle which connected me to Mum. As I did it, I remembered Sven putting a ring on my finger and me one on his. I felt a sadness and a longing deep inside.

"Thanks, Sven. You know this means a lot."

Jane looked at me as if to say, *he's done that to weaken you, to make you feel indebted.* If so, it had worked.

"I know it does. I've got your little strong box. It's quite safe."

"What do you mean you've got it? It should be in the house where I left it."

"It's at Suzanna's apartment. I moved it to keep it secure in case Lean's lot came looking for it. It was Suzanna's idea."

"I bet it was her idea." I could feel my pulse racing. "That box is mine. It has nothing to do with you, Sven, and certainly nothing to do with her. It's got my personal family stuff inside. You need to put it back in the house as soon as you get home. Okay?" I glanced at Suzanna, who had a thin satisfied smile on her face.

"So, here are the divorce papers," he said, ignoring my demands. So where was the man who'd been texting me saying he still loved me? Sven was acting like a businessman executing a deal. "It can be pretty simple if everyone agrees. I've filled it all in; all you have to do is check and sign it, and get Jane or someone here to witness it. I'll deal with it as soon as I get back to the UK."

"Yes," added Heffle. "These things are better done and dusted as soon as possible. Clean break, fresh start and all that."

"So, you've started divorce proceedings with your husband, have you, Suzanna?" It came out more aggressively than I'd intended.

"No, not yet. It's more complicated, there are children involved. You couldn't have children, could you, Tess?" Her smile was sarcastic. My heart was pounding. That had been a joint decision: Sven's and mine. Maria brought a tray of drinks, and sensing the growing tension, hurried away.

"It's not that I couldn't, Suzanna." This was harder than I'd expected. It was taking a lot of self-control not to lash out at her and throw her off the decking into the sea.

"Suzanna wants to ask you something," said Sven, interrupting.

"Oh really?" I sighed. "I couldn't possibly guess what."

"The emails," she said. "Do you have copies?"

"Yes, I do. Despite the best efforts of your friends."

"I don't know what you mean." I could see she was exercising a fair amount of self-control too. "They're personal and they could be misinterpreted and cause a lot of upset."

"I bet they could."

"Yes, Tess, but they were a joke and are totally untrue. If they were published, I'd simply say you made them up."

"I'm sure you would, but then emails are traceable from the day, time and place they were sent. You must know that. Why would you make that up, Suzanna? Make up something so outrageous which connected you with a major criminal? After all, that dodgy solicitor claims to be a friend of yours, and the PM's, and someone who contributes handsomely to your election campaign funds too. You knew Lean was extracting money from vulnerable people. Did you know he was killing them too?" I said, leaning forwards in my best, accusatory reporter style.

"Don't be ridiculous," she snapped.

Sven looked uncomfortable. "I think we should try to keep calm," he offered, weakly.

"Do you deny it?" I pushed her angrily.

"No, really, let's keep calm." Sven said it more assertively this time, but he was quickly shut down.

"Keep out of it, Sven!" shouted Suzanna Heffle. Just who was this woman telling my husband what to do?

"Is this how you want to be treated, Sven?" I asked him. "Is this what you really want?"

"Sven knows what he wants," she snarled.

"Hey, you keep out of it; I'm talking to my husband."

"There's more to this than you think," she barked. "It's your job to be sensible and responsible, and not to meddle in things that are out of your league." Heffle spoke sternly, as if I was an errant pupil standing before the Head.

"Perhaps a court should decide if you knowingly took his blood money and whether you were helping to cover things up? Out of my league? I play in the biggest league, Suzanna."

"Look," said Heffle, raising her voice as I realised this was the real reason they'd come all the way to Greece to see me. "I need an assurance that you will destroy the last copies. If you do, I'll ensure you're not bothered again, and you'll get not only half, but the total value of your house. I will also cover Sven's portion immediately—once you sign the divorce papers, that is."

"And if not, there'll be more black ops from freelance spooks?"

"Er, no."

"So, you admit they were working for you?"

"I'm admitting nothing. This isn't some game, Tess Anderson, it's very serious. You'd be wise to remember that." I looked at Jane, who was furious. She was shaking. I wished Jason were there. He was standing on the quay, discreetly keeping his distance.

"I'm a reporter, Mrs Heffle. I can't be bought, bribed or

blackmailed."

"You should think very carefully about all of the consequences of declining this very generous offer. Meet us here tomorrow at 9:15 to give us your decision. Remember, the whole of the value of your and Sven's property in exchange for an assurance on the emails and a divorce from Sven. Oh, and that strong box of course. No emails, no strong box."

Heffle stood up, grabbing her bag.

"Sven, we must go," she instructed my husband, who smiled weakly and obeyed. "Tomorrow, then. Here at 9.15 for your answer. It had better be the right one."

"Bye, Tess," said Sven uncomfortably.

I watched them leave. Neither of them looked back. They walked along the quayside and passed Christos the builder who raised a hand as if to wave.

"That's Christos. Does he know them?" I asked.

"Maybe he's just being friendly," said Jane, but I couldn't help wondering. My paranoia was alive and well.

Seeing they'd gone, Jason walked over from the quayside to join us.

"Did that go well?" he asked.

"No. It went badly. I'm bloody angry," said Jane. "What a way to treat Tess."

I was deep in thought.

"Basically, I have to agree to a divorce, agree to never pass on the emails—and probably sign something agreeing I'll never mention or discuss the matter again," I told him. "If I do that, I get the total value of our London house, plus my strong box which they're holding hostage."

"Shows how desperate she is to stop those emails," Jason said, sitting down beside me and squeezing my hand.

"And if I don't, I get more black ops, and more enemies."

"Except," said Jane, "once those emails are in the public domain there'll be no need for anyone to try and destroy them. Heffle and her pals will be firefighting to limit the damage.

241

Also…" She grinned, picking up a little voice recorder from beside her bag.

"Also?" I asked.

"I've just recorded that conversation. Shall I send it to your friend DCI Green? She implied she'd send in her spooks again. That's threatening behaviour, isn't it?" She smiled proudly.

"Well done, ever the reporter—even though you're deskbound!" It was times like this that I couldn't believe how lucky I was to have Jane on my side. "But I just don't know if I can cope with any more excitement. A quiet life is appealing."

"A *quiet life*? You're a dark horse!"

"It's a good offer though, and I do want that strong box; I worry I might not see it again if I don't play nicely. A quiet life has its appeal," I reflected. "Putting it all behind me… including my failed marriage."

"So, when do you give them your answer?" Jason asked.

"They're coming back tomorrow, at 9:15."

"I saw them this morning on my walk," he said. "They were in a car with a woman. A white Fiat Panda."

"Fiat Panda?" asked Jane, surprised. "That sounds like Jo's car. What did the woman look like?"

"Blondish grey hair," Jason said. "Quite slim. Late fifties, sixties?"

"That's Jo," I said looking at Jane. What the hell were Sven and Heffle doing in Jo's car? My phone rang.

"Hi, Tess." It was Steve. "Just a couple of things. Your hubby's pal, Suzanna Heffle?"

"What about her?" I asked.

"Word has it, she's got a way back into the Cabinet. There are whispers she's getting a Home Office job: junior minister to start with, but she could become the new Home Secretary. It'll be announced in a reshuffle in time for the party conference later in the year."

"So, you're saying Heffle will be in charge of MI5?" I felt sick at the thought.

"What I'm saying is, this would be a very good time to release those emails if they relate to her in any way," Steve said. "If you're going to release them, of course. I wish you'd tell me what they say, Tess. Maybe I could help you decide what to do."

"Steve, give me twenty-four hours."

"To release them?"

"To give you a decision."

He sighed. "You're a tough nut to crack, Tess. Okay, look, call me day or night, my phone will be on."

"Don't hold your breath, boss. No promises either way."

"It's your call, Tess. But don't let exhaustion cloud your judgement. Or sentimentality."

"I hear you, boss. Anything else?"

"Afraid so." His tone changed. "It was Jake's funeral today, Tess." My heart sank. I should have been there.

"I went along with Nish and Clare. We made it very clear you'd have been there if you could."

"Did it go okay?" I asked quietly.

"As well as these things can. Local crematorium, humanist service. Lots of mourners, he was a popular guy. Jake's parents had a big photo on his coffin of you and him at the Reporter of the Year Award. That was so good of you to call him up on stage with you that night."

"Without Jake my reports wouldn't have been half as good. I'm going to miss him so much. In so many ways."

"We all will. Clare said some words on our behalf." Tears started to fall as Steve described the service; how devastated Jake's parents were; the beautiful eulogy his dad had read. "You okay, Tess?"

"I will be," I said, and felt Jason squeeze my hand again, "it's just a bit much at the moment. I'll call you in twenty-four hours, okay?"

"What's happened?" Jane asked.

"Jake's funeral was today."

She hugged me as I buried my head in her shoulder. We were

sitting in the sun, surrounded by happy people, beauty, warmth. Life. Why did Jake's have to end like that? It was so unfair. A tripper boat hooted as it swept into the bay and came to tie up on the quay.

"So, if it was Sven and Heffle in Jo's car, what were they doing?" I asked. Jason shrugged.

"If it was them," Jane said uncertainly.

"Look guys," I said, standing up. "I've got some thinking to do. I just need to walk for a bit. Clear my head."

"There's a nice walk behind the bay, up to the old lighthouse I told you about the other day," said Jason. "I'll take you there if you want."

"Thanks," I told him. "But I need to go alone. I need to think this out myself. I know you're both about if I need advice, but I have to work a few things through."

Jason drew a little map on a paper napkin, and I set off with my bag and a bottle of water. The climb up the hill was refreshing. I was surrounded by the smells of wild herbs and the sound of the cicadas. The scrub-littered path wound its way upwards. I stopped and picked a few wildflowers. After twenty minutes, I reached the white painted lighthouse on the top of the hill. I laid my small bunch of flowers in a pretty spot for Jake. It was peaceful.

Ringed by a low, off-white wall, the lighthouse braved the winds and all the weather could throw at it for three-hundred-and-sixty-five days of the year. Its guiding light warned sailors of the rocks on the north end of Paxos. I needed a guiding light myself right now. I stared at the seemingly endless sea, Corfu beyond and the mainland to the east. To the west lay Italy, some seventy-odd miles away. Leaning on that wall I realised the enormity of the decisions I had to make. Did I give Heffle what she wanted and ensure a quiet life, with or without Jason? Would Jason want me? He'd risked his life for me, protected me and cared for me, but could he love again? Would he want me? Had I put him off? Could I ever be with him and forget Sven, when it was Jason's music that had brought Sven and me together in the first place? Did I give Steve the emails and plunge myself into the abyss again and dump Sven in the shit, too? Was there any hope of saving me and Sven? No. He'd made his own bed and now he needed to lie in it—I couldn't protect him anymore, and he didn't deserve me. But then would Jason just think he was a booby prize, as I hadn't gone for him straight away? I agonised for a long time, until a pair of shearwaters skimmed the sea below and it became clear where my heart really lay.

20. Decisions

I got back from my walk to find Jane on the phone to Jo. She had the speaker on so I could listen.

"Hey, Jo, just calling to ask if you'd like to join us for dinner tonight? My treat. Tess has some really hard decisions to make, and it'll take her mind off it for a bit. Besides, I owe you for all the help with the Villa. I really don't know how I'd cope without you."

"Oh, that's kind," I heard Jo say. "I'd like that; you know I can't afford restaurants these days. Where were you thinking?"

"Lakka. The one in the small square, the place I took you to last year. Near the bakery? Is 7:30 all right?"

Jo said that was fine and Jane ended the call.

"What are you up to, Jane?"

"I thought it would kind of help take your mind of it all a little, and lesson the tension between you and Jason."

"Tension?" I pulled back a chair and sat beside her.

"You haven't noticed? He's hurt, hurt because he's offered you what you need and you're dithering. Tess, I've no idea why you're dithering over this! He's bloody brilliant."

"Jane, I'm so churned up. I know he's amazing, but...my head's all over the place."

"Yeah? And just remember who you're being offered here, he's

Jason L'Amour for eff's sake!"

*

At 7:30 Jane, Jason and I sat at a four-seater table with a white printed tablecloth. On it was a map of the island, held to the table by four metal clips. Fresh bread lay on a paper serviette in a basket in the middle. There were bottles of olive oil and vinegar next to it in a thin wire tray with handles at either end. It was a scene replicated in hundreds of restaurants across Greece.

Jo arrived. "Sorry I'm late, had to feed Pixie and Dixie, the cats." She looked across the table. "You must be Jason." She smiled, offering him her hand.

"Good to meet you, Jo. You're the hero who sorted the villa after it was trashed, I hear."

"Oh, that's nothing. It was a pleasure. Well, Christos did the hard work. I just did the cleaning up afterwards. That sounded like a close thing though, the boat chase with that madman. If you ask me, it's a good job he's no longer around." She sat down, putting a paper napkin over her lap. It was clear she was wearing what was probably her one and only decent dress and was keen to preserve it.

We ordered, ate, and made conversation about Paxos, villas and the people who hire them. Jane brought up the subject of Heffle.

"Tess and I had a slightly uncomfortable meeting today." She was looking at Jo. "With Sven, her husband, and his lover, Suzanna Heffle. Have you met them?"

"Don't think so. I've heard about them, of course."

"Jason thinks he saw them in your car earlier today." I watched Jo's reaction carefully.

"My car?" She recoiled.

"Yes," Jason said. "About nine-ish. I was on a walk, inland. A white Fiat Panda."

"Oh, that was just a couple I gave a lift to. Wow, was that

them?" Her eyes widened. "I was cleaning a villa over that way and saw them walking, so I offered them a lift. I dropped them outside Lakka. So that's who they were."

I was relieved. It seemed that Jo was just being her usual helpful self. She was the sort who'd give anyone a lift, even if it meant going out of her way. I must be getting paranoid, I realised, if I was even suspecting the cleaner. The same woman who'd rescued me from being locked in the shed.

"They were pleasant enough to me," Jo said. "If I'd known who they were…" She gave me a sympathetic look. "I take it they weren't so pleasant to you?"

"Sven wants a divorce," I said. "And Heffle wants me to destroy some emails."

"Oh?"

"I'm not going into details, but they'd be very damaging for her if they got released."

"Why would they get released?" Jo asked.

"Because Tess is a journalist and it's her job to expose corruption!" Jane said. Her face was a little flushed—whether from the wine or the conversation, I wasn't sure.

"But I'm torn," I said. "I know in my heart it's the right thing to do—but if I publish them, it could put me in danger—well, it could put all of us in danger, actually. Even you, Jo."

"Well, I always go for an easy life," Jo said, with a shrug. "The path of least resistance. Also, if they're not yours it's sort of stealing, isn't it?"

"Well, exposing the truth in the public interest isn't stealing, but I understand your thoughts on an easy life. I could certainly do with one of those for a bit." I sighed. "Well, we already know what Jane thinks on the issue—" I grinned at her. "That means you have the casting vote, Jason."

I turned to look at him. He was frowning. "I can't tell you what to do, Tess. It's got to be your decision. But I can tell you one thing—don't worry about me being in danger. Just do what's right for you."

"Thanks, Jason. If only I knew what that was!" I sighed again. "I can't deny a quiet life is very tempting. I could even buy that empty villa on the edge of Lakka and live here in the sun…"

"Well, if you need a cleaner, you know where I am!" Jo laughed. "But maybe don't ask Christos to mend the shower; not until after you've used it! Right, then." She rubbed her hands together. As she'd said, it was obviously a rare treat for Jo to have a meal like this. "Are we having coffee? I wouldn't mind some before I drive back."

Jason signalled to the waiter. After taking our order he produced some free drinks—a local speciality, a strong-tasting liqueur—which we sipped while waiting for coffee.

"Tess," Jo said, reaching over to touch my arm. "Were you serious about buying a place here?"

"Who knows," I said. "It's a beautiful area…"

"Why don't you come for dinner tomorrow? I've got loads of advice for you, if you want it—villas in Greece could be my specialist subject if I ever went on *Mastermind*!" She laughed. "And I've been thinking I'd love to get to know you better."

"I'd like that," I said. "Thanks, Jo." I could hardly believe I'd been ready to think she was working with Heffle: it seemed ridiculous now. I caught Jason's eye.

"Tomorrow?" he said, "I was going to invite you to sail around the north of the island, to watch the sunset, it may be your last trip on *Sea Biscuit*."

"Oh, Jason, sorry, that would be lovely." I turned to Jo. "Another time?"

Jane sipped her liqueur. "I'm sure Jo can make room for Jason." While Jason and Jo exchanged a glance, Jane gave me a wink. "If you've already planned to spend the evening together…"

"Oh… um…" Poor Jo looked embarrassed. I kicked Jane's ankle under the table. "Don't feel obliged, Jo. I think Jane's had a bit too much wine…"

"No, no," Jo said, "I can make room for Jason, of course I can." She still seemed hesitant, but she smiled anyway. I made a mental note to have words with Jane later. "About six? I was thinking we'd go to the Tripitos Arch; it's the island's best feature. I'd love to show it to you, Tess. And you, of course, Jason!" She grinned. "We'll do it as a posh picnic, with a cake of course. We can celebrate the arrest of that nasty Lean man."

"The Tripitos Arch really is stunning," Jane chipped in. "It's literally an arch over the sea. I'd invite myself too if it wasn't for Dave arriving."

The waiter brought our coffees. I thanked Jo again for the invitation and told her I'd book a taxi. The idea of buying a place here was probably just a pipe dream, but maybe talking to Jo about it would help me make up my mind about everything.

As we left the restaurant, I said goodnight to Jason. I could see he was disappointed—no doubt he'd been hoping I'd share his bed—but my meeting with Sven and Heffle hadn't exactly left me in a romantic mood. Maybe there'd be other nights, I hoped. He walked away towards the boat without looking back as Jane and I waited for a taxi to take us to the villa.

I fell into an uneasy sleep and woke about an hour before dawn, desperate for the loo. I couldn't go back to sleep and stayed out of bed. I walked to the front door. Opening it I found Mrs Boutari, the new cat, waiting to get in. I almost tripped over her. She scuttled away towards the kitchen. I pulled on my fleece top and wandered around the garden, replaying snippets of the day's conversations. There was the sonar-like blip of the little owl again, distant but still there. The olive trees swayed in the breeze, their distinctive shapes a unique feature of the night. The moon was dipping to the west. The fine fingers of grey were beginning to throw the first faint light of dawn onto the mainland mountains to the east. I heard a rustle behind me and threw myself around rapidly, expecting the worst, waiting for something horrible to happen. I shouted out, but a hand touched my lips.

"Shhh, it's just me." Jane had woken up and come to find me. "I think someone's staying in the villa next door. Let's go inside, I don't want to wake them up. Sounds travel at night and it's really late, or really early," she said quietly.

"Sorry," I whispered back. "I'm still pretty jumpy."

"I'm not surprised; you're allowed to be jumpy. I am too." In the kitchen, Jane put the kettle on. There was no sign of Mrs Boutari.

"You know what," I said. "There's one person whose opinion I haven't asked for about these emails." Jane looked at me sideways, raising her eyebrows as she filled two cups.

"But you can't ask him, can you?" she said. "If you mean Jake."

I nodded.

"I think we both know what he'd say. All of your colleagues would say it too." I looked into Jane's eyes. We shared a defiant smile. "You're a crime reporter," she said. "You've even got the awards to prove it! Think how proud your mum and dad would be, to know you were breaking the biggest story of the year."

I held my mum's necklace and turned to look out the window. The moon was bright overhead. Jane was right; I knew she was right. "Okay," I said.

"*Okay?*" Jane's voice was tentative. "Does that mean what I think it means?"

I turned back to her, still holding Mum's necklace. "It means I'm not hiding anymore. I'm not going to let them scare me. I'm doing this for Jake and Milly. I can't let them down."

"Yay!" Jane squeezed my arm. "I knew you'd see sense!"

"Can I borrow your laptop?" I needed to do this now, before I could change my mind.

"Of course," Jane said. "I'll turn the wi-fi on."

I went into the sitting room and grabbed my mobile. Scrolling down to Steve's number, I hit the call button. A few rings later, a sleepy voice answered.

"Hello?"

"Sorry to wake you, boss. It's Tess. About those emails."

"What time is it?" he mumbled. Then my words seemed to

251

register: "Emails, did you say?" He was suddenly alert.

"They'll be with you. As soon as."

"Wow, really?"

"We're just firing up the wi-fi in my friend's villa. I'm going to let her give them to *The Guardian* too; but I'll give us a head start. I will have to send them to DCI Green, just to let you know. There are links to crimes in these emails and I can't withhold evidence." I was speaking so fast I was stumbling over the words. My heart was pounding. Was I definitely doing the right thing? Could I really live with the consequences? It wasn't just everything I was giving up—my peace of mind, my safety, the chance of a new life here in Greece—but what I was doing to Sven. This could cause him huge problems. He could face charges—or even go to prison. But he'd made his choices. I had to make mine, and I had to be on the side of what was right.

"Wow, Tess, that's worth being woken up for! Clare is duty overnight reporter and Ash is the duty editor. I'll call them both. Can you send them to the newsdesk as well as to me, please?"

"Will do. Listen, this is important, Steve: can we hold off running the story until 7:30 your time?" I'd slipped straight back into reporter mode; it was almost as if I'd never been away. "I'll get Jane to ask her desk to hold it until after our story hits the air."

"Of course. What made you decide in the end?"

"Jake would have wanted me to," I said. "And I don't like being blackmailed either. I'm a reporter."

"Not just a reporter, Tess—as far as I'm concerned, you're the best reporter on British television. Well done, Tess. Thank you."

"Thanks, boss." I hung up the call and turned to Jane. "Wow." I took a sharp intake of breath, blowing it out slowly. "I think we're really doing this! Do you want to send them to your newsdesk too?"

"Are you kidding? Yes! Look, I heard what you said to your editor; I'll tell them to wait until your mob put them out before we do. Here, the laptop's online, ready to go. Where's the memory card?"

"Base of my bag. I sewed it in before we left Jason's house in Suffolk. You'll need to cut the stitching to get it out. There's another stick back at his house, for emergencies. I put it in the outhouse above the door lintel, in case anything happened to me."

While Jane retrieved the memory card, I texted DCI Green. I told him I was forwarding him three emails which he urgently needed to read. I told him they'd gone to my newsdesk. I texted Jason:

'Stand by for fireworks. I'm sending the emails! T x'

His reply was immediate. *'I'd been awake wondering. Proud of you! X'*

Jane and I watched as the emails appeared in the sent folder, and then came the *'ding, ding'* of received receipts landing. After more tea and a bit of sober reflection I looked at my watch and told Jane to forward them to her colleagues in London. One broadcaster and one quality newspaper. Bingo. They all went.

"It's done now, Jane," I said. "No going back."

"It's the right decision," she said.

I agreed. But I knew the consequences would be enormous.

*

A few hours later, Jane and I walked down the hill into Lakka to find Jason. He was up and waiting, sitting in the cockpit of *Sea Biscuit* safely tied to the quay. He left the yacht and ran to meet us, throwing his arms around me.

"Well done, Tess, I'm so proud of you!" He kissed me then dropped back, presumably thinking he'd overstepped the mark. We hadn't spoken about *us* or what we'd shared since our night together.

"Thanks. I appreciate the vote of confidence. I just have to deal with the fall out."

"I'm there if you need me."

"Come on," said Jane. "Yan's cafe will be open soon. Let's grab our favourite seats; there'll be fresh yogurt and honey. Our guests won't be here until 9.15, so we've got time for breakfast."

*

At ten-to-nine, as we'd just finished eating, my phone rang.

"Hello, DCI Green. You got my text."

"It woke me up, but it was well worth it. The emails are quite a revelation, Tess, thank you. They're being looked at by senior officers; warrants are being prepared as we speak, to search a number of premises—including the one your husband is staying in at the moment, Suzanna Heffle's flat in Westminster. Between us, MI5 are helping trace a couple of their former agents too."

"Ted, re: those two, my friend Jane has a recording she'll email you." To think Heffle could have become Home Secretary too. "I'll ask Jane to send it to you now. One more thing, can I beg a favour?"

"Go on."

"If you're able, there's a small, red metal strongbox in Heffle's flat. It's mine. Heffle's holding it hostage, blackmailing me not to release these emails. It contains family death and marriage certificates and stuff like that. Any chance it could be taken into *protective custody* for me?" That would finally finish Sven, I thought, but I was beginning to feel less guilty about condemning him.

"Well, if you can prove it's yours, and it's not evidential, then yes. I think Mrs Heffle will have enough to worry about, if these emails and that recording turn out to be what they appear. It hasn't hit the headlines yet."

"It'll break soon. I asked for a 7.30 embargo your time, 9.30 here. My husband and Heffle are here on the island. I'm meeting them at 9.15."

"I can't advise you meeting them, Tess. Heffle could react in any number of ways. You're putting yourself in danger." As the

DCI spoke, I had a sense of déjà vu. "But you're going to ignore me, aren't you?"

"Afraid so, Ted. Sorry."

He sighed. "Where are you meeting them?"

"At Yan's Bar in Lakka. I've got Jane with me, and Jason's close by. I want to surprise her."

"I think she'll be surprised, all right, as will some people in the corridors of power. This has gone all the way to the top. I've seen the Cabinet Secretary entering the building already this morning. Well done, Tess. Good luck!"

I hung up. It was five-to-nine Greek time, and five-to-seven in the UK, when Jason walked back to *Sea Biscuit*, leaving Jane and me to meet Sven and Heffle alone.

*

I watched them as their sea taxi swept in and drew up alongside the quay. Heffle was talking to the boatman while Sven picked up her bag. He helped her ashore and then kissed her, although she barely responded. How would I feel if he kissed me now? Kissed me like he used to. I looked beyond them to *Sea Biscuit* and Jason, standing in the cockpit checking the sail cover. Jane gently touched my arm.

"It's okay, Tess, I'm here with you," she said quietly. I watched them walk towards us. Heffle sat down and nodded to Sven to sit beside her. He obeyed like a lapdog. She was obviously in no mood for pleasantries.

"So, Tess, do I take it we have an agreement?"

"I don't know where you got that from, Suzanna?"

"Oh," she stumbled. "I assumed you'd see sense and agree to our offer. It seems perfectly fair and generous to me."

"I gave it a lot of thought, Suzanna—"

"Before you answer, I have something else to put into the pot. You like this island, yes?"

"Why?"

"You like your friend's villa?"

"Are you going to threaten to burn it down?"

"Don't be ridiculous. Of course not. I will buy you one, a villa, here on the island. You can stay and enjoy a relaxing quiet life in the sun, out of harm's way. I'll even pay a local builder to check it over for you."

"Wow, Suzanna, that's a very generous offer. Which builder is that? He's not called Christos by any chance?"

"It is a generous offer," she said, ignoring my question. "Far more generous than I need to be. A nice gift." Hmm, well I had a very nice gift for her and my ex.

"She's right, Tess," Sven added. "Please consider it carefully."

"Well, since you've asked so nicely… Okay, let me think about it." I watched the clock go round to 9.20. 7.20 back home. My heart was racing and my need to smile almost overwhelmed me. I went to the loo and asked Maria to turn on the big TV screen above the bar and switch it to my station's news output. I retook my seat. It was 9.29. Heffle was impatient.

"Tess, we need an answer. I have a water taxi booked for ten, on the quay over there. We've got a flight to make. I have meetings in London."

"Okay, Mrs Heffle-lump, architect of the Government's *Let's Stay Together* campaign. Except you two won't be staying together as they don't have mixed cells in Belmarsh prison."

"What the hell…?" she demanded, thumping her hand on the table. Coffee spilled over the edges of our cups. I almost felt sorry for Sven; this woman clearly had a temper. I didn't doubt he'd felt the brunt of it a few times recently too. Now it was my turn.

"Suzanna, I won't be bought, I won't be blackmailed, and I won't be bullied. The truth and the public interest are paramount: it's my job."

"Be very careful, you sanctimonious little shit. You're dealing with a very powerful woman here," she was trembling with rage. "And one who might soon have more power than you could ever imagine."

At that moment, Maria turned up the sound on the TV set.

"Really?" I grinned. We all looked round. Heffle's mouth fell open as the newsreader's words sank in.

"First, breaking news. There are allegations this morning that a former government minister may be linked to crime baron Ken Lean and the killings at a care home. The prime minister is said to have ordered an immediate inquiry. The police are carrying out a number of raids this morning, including one at the home of the former minister, MP Suzanna Heffle..."

"A *sanctimonious little shit* I may be, Suzanna. But I'm a sanctimonious shit who can do her job without fear or favour. Oh, and we recorded what you said yesterday. The recording is with the police now. You're dealing with two very *powerful* women here: we're journalists, and we expose the truth."

"And this conversation is being recorded now as well," Jane grinned, waving her voice recorder which she'd been holding just out of sight.

"Damn you!" shouted Heffle. Standing up, she threw her coffee over me. The shock of it hitting my chest and bare arms was replaced by a sense of relief as it was cooler than I'd feared. She bent forwards screwing up her face and raising her fist. Jane leapt up and grabbed her arm.

Sven held his lover back: "Suzanna! STOP! Please, that man on the yacht over there is taking photos, and a police car's just drawn up on the quayside."

Jason waved his phone in his hand. Heffle turned to him and stuck her finger up. His phone camera caught it perfectly.

"Oh, yes please, Jason," Jane shouted across to him. "Our picture desk would like that. Eat your heart out, Danny Downs!" Jane raised a clenched fist in the air in glee.

Sven pulled Suzanna to her feet, muttering about the water taxi, just as two police officers walked up to the table. I dabbed the wet coffee from my top with a serviette.

"Mrs Suzanna Heffle. We have an international arrest warrant for you from police in London. You must come with us."

"What?" Heffle was aghast. "Do you know who I am?"

"Of course we know who you are, that's why we are arresting you. You will be flown to London when a British police officer comes to collect you. Until then you are in our custody."

Heffle's mouth fell open.

"Not bad for a sanctimonious little what's-it!" Jane giggled. "Well done, Tess."

"I think that was DCI Green, not me." I sat back in my coffee-stained top as Heffle and Sven were driven off in the police car. His eyes were pleading with me through the window of the vehicle as it bounced along the stone quayside and up the dusty street.

Jane ordered drinks and we watched as the story unfolded on TV. By lunchtime the strap line running underneath the pictures was: *Suzanna Heffle arrested in Greece. Likely to be flown to London for questioning today.* By mid-afternoon it was: *Prime minister denies links to Lean.* Texts rolled in from Steve, conveying congratulations from the Head of News. Maria didn't quite understand everything that was happening, but she kept us supplied with a steady flow of coffee, which soon became ouzo and prosecco.

21. The Tripitos Arch

After returning to the villa, I showered and changed into a top without coffee stains, then Jason and I took a taxi to Jo's house. We'd discussed postponing our plans with Jo, but we knew Jane and Dave needed time together and, after all, it was good to be doing something normal, like having dinner with a friend—something Jo didn't seem to have many of. It felt mean to cancel, especially after she'd been so accommodating about inviting Jason too. She was waiting by the gate and came straight out to meet us.

"So glad you've come. I was worried you'd cancel—you've had a busy day, I understand." Jo seemed a little on edge. With her obvious money worries, I hoped it wasn't too much for her—providing a picnic for three instead of two.

"We have," I said, "but it's all over now. Both Lean and Heffle are out of the way, and we can finally relax. All of us—you as well, Jo."

The taxi performed a tight three-point-turn in the narrow road and drove off as we walked into the garden.

"That would be nice. I get so few visitors…" We followed her inside the house. "I just wish the place wasn't in such a state, but it all costs so much…" She was scratching her wrist; it looked sore.

"Are you all right, Jo?" I asked. "You seem tense."

"Just a few things on my mind, that's all."

"If you'd rather not go out, we're happy to eat here, Jo. Your garden's so lovely." I smiled, taking in the heavy scent.

"No, no, it's all ready. I'm looking forward to showing you the arch. You're going to love it. The views are absolutely stunning."

"I've seen it from the sea, of course," Jason said. "It's impressive! Very high too."

"Let's get in the car; we'll go and watch the sunset. It's a very romantic place. I'll grab the food bag; there's salad, cake and wine! I make the wine myself from things in my garden, can't wait for you to try it and see what you think. I'm sure it'll be great for a celebration." Jo was fussing around like she was running a school trip.

"It all sounds delicious, thank you." I gave her a smile. "We've bought a bottle too; shall we bring it along?"

"Oh no, mine will be more than enough. Besides, Jason's going to have enough to carry, the food bag is quite heavy."

We were soon driving down the lane in her beaten-up Panda, the rear suspension providing little comfort as we bounced around on the back seat. About a mile later we parked by a metal fence.

"Such a lovely evening," Jo said. "It's not far now, just along this path. Do be careful, it's quite dangerous in places. It's the crumbling stones and the mosses that grow in the shady bits that are the problem."

In single file we made our way along the path, which began to descend towards the Arch as it slowly came into view. It was impressive, if not a little worrying. A thin stretch of rock led from the cliffs, with a deep drop either side, leading to the thicker rock formation jutting out into the sea.

"Gosh, Jo, that thin strip, the top of the arch, it looks dangerous."

"It is, but don't worry, it's wider than it looks from here. This path is worrying though, especially the last part as it descends quite quickly. You may need to hold onto the rocks on the sides as you go down the final bit. It's a long way if you fall."

As she spoke my foot dislodged a small piece of stone which bounced and rolled downwards, seeming to jump from rock to rock as it disappeared down the cliff edge and out of sight. This path was treacherous, and not to be attempted after a few drinks for sure. It was probably a good job we'd only got one bottle of wine with us.

We made our way to the famous arch. Deep blue grey waves were crashing on the rocks below. Jo led the way; I followed, and then came Jason, carrying the food bag.

"Isn't this beautiful!" announced Jo as she lay a blanket on the thin tufts of grass which covered the small area of rock. We were alone among all of this dramatic scenery.

"Sure is," said Jason, lying down to catch the last fading rays of sunlight. I looked towards Anti Paxos a couple of miles beyond. The last of the day's tripper boats motored past, heading back to Gaios. The bright white cliffs shone in the setting sun. It was nice to finally relax; the Leans were finished and Heffle arrested. Maybe it really was all over, at last.

"So," said Jo. "A toast." She pulled a bottle from the food bag. "My homemade wine," she said proudly, pouring it into two of the three plastic glasses.

"Aren't you joining us?" I asked.

"I'd better not, I'm driving. I've made a cordial too; I'll have some of that. But you two enjoy the wine—you deserve a celebration after everything you've been through! Cheers!" She passed us a glass each as Jason sat up smiling. I sipped mine slowly. I'd got a headache from the stress of the day, so I didn't want much. It didn't taste too good either. Jason knocked his straight back, perhaps he was being polite.

"Steady on," I teased him. "We don't know how strong this is!"

His blue eyes twinkled. "I trust you not to take advantage of me if I get a little tipsy." He grinned.

The look we exchanged made me suddenly wish that he and I

were here alone—Jo was right; it was a romantic spot. But if not for Jo, I reminded myself, we wouldn't be here at all. She'd gone to so much trouble on our behalf. I turned to her and smiled. The whole point of this trip, after all, was to get to know her better, not to flirt with Jason. "The wine's lovely," I said politely. "You'll have to tell us how you make it."

"I'll write it down for you," Jo said. "When we get back to mine."

We sat for a while, enjoying the beautiful view, the silence and big open sky beyond. Pulling a quiche from the food bag, Jo proudly announced it was another of her homemade delights.

"Too many ingredients to tell you about," she said, "but all wholesome and natural and all from my own little garden. Eggs from my own chickens too. I'm sure you'll love it! I so rarely get to bake for other people these days."

"It looks very nice," I said encouragingly.

"Full of garden favourites!" said Jo excitedly. She was very animated but still seemed on edge. Was she just worried we wouldn't enjoy her food and wine? I noticed she kept looking back along the path.

"Are you expecting someone else?" I asked, taking a piece of quiche in my fingers, wondering why it wasn't being served with the salad she'd mentioned, which I could see was still in the food bag inside a plastic box.

"No, why do you ask?"

"Because you keep looking back the way we came," I said.

"Oh no, I just thought I saw Christos."

"The builder?"

"Yes, he often comes here."

"What, this late?"

"He's an odd one, that man." Jo laughed.

"I hope you have a torch for the way back," Jason said. "It'll be tricky on that path."

"Oh yes, but once you know the way it's easy." Jo grinned. "More wine? Here you are, let's fill those glasses." I tried to decline but Jo was insistent. In the end I accepted a top-up, so as not to offend her.

I struggled with the quiche too; it was dense, with intense flavours, some nice and recognisable while others were a little odd. The pastry was fine, but something felt wrong. I noticed Jason was nibbling at his piece too; he didn't seem to be enjoying it that much either. Jo didn't seem to be eating at all.

"You not having some, Jo?" I asked, swallowing another mouthful of quiche.

"Oh, I'll have some soon, I'm just not that hungry. I had a snack earlier while I was cooking. It's a fault of mine, I'm always snacking."

The evening was not what I'd expected. We'd been invited for dinner but were being fed pieces of quiche and homemade wine on a lump of rock overhanging the sea. It was turning into one of the weirdest dinner parties I'd ever been to. Definitely an anecdote for future meals with friends.

"It'll soon be sunset," Jo announced. "Can you smell the air changing? The scents of the plants at night are so different. Some flowers close up and other release their smell. I find it fascinating."

"What sort of wine is this, Jo?" Jason asked. "It's pretty strong, that's for sure." He was beginning to slur his words. "I'm not usually like this after just two glasses." I glanced over and saw that he looked asleep, totally out of it. I lay back too; my arms felt weak. Jason was lying flat on his back, his eyes closed.

"Yes, Jo, it's really strong, what exactly is in it?" I asked.

"Oleander."

"Oleander! Jo, that—that's poisonous, isn't it?"

"Oh yes. Quite poisonous. Yes, I've poisoned you, Tess. Both of you."

"You've what?" I spluttered, trying to sit up but unable to move my arms.

"I've poisoned you. Just like I poisoned my husband, Bryn. He drank the same oleander wine you're drinking now."

"Why?" I was finding it hard to see, and couldn't focus very well on Jo.

"So I could push him over the edge. Over the edge of the arch, right here, on a night

quite similar to this. I told the police he'd committed suicide, you know, jumped off the edge, and the darlings believed me."

"Jo," I said, struggling to speak as I fought an overwhelming urge to sleep. "Why? Why did you poison your husband? And why have you poisoned us?"

"My Bryn left us penniless. Gambling debts. We were struggling so badly, and everything I earned from cleaning he gambled away. He just spent it. He'd pushed me too far, so I pushed him, over the edge."

"But—"

"He hit the rocks and was killed outright. Just like you will be, both of you. A tragic suicide they'll think."

"Why would..." It was hard to speak. "Why would Jason and I do that?"

"Because you couldn't stand it, Tess, knowing your husband wanted a divorce, and because you couldn't live with yourself after sending those hateful emails." I felt for my phone in my pocket while Jo carried on.

"And Jason couldn't bear to live without you. He'd saved your life when Crusher Lean chased you, and as you wanted to die, the pair of you made a lovers' suicide pact. You both died together. Ahhh, how romantic!" She laughed.

I managed to pull my phone out and hold it near my leg. I glanced down and pressed the shortcut dial for DCI Green and left my phone open on the ground, hoping Jo hadn't seen.

"So you've... brought us to the Tripitos Arch on Paxos..." I struggled to get the words out, hoping they would be picked up by the phone. "And you're going to... throw us... over the edge and... kill us, Jo?"

"I'm sorry, Tess. But thanks to Bryn's gambling I'm utterly broke, you see. Every day's a struggle. I'm not like you or Jason—

I'm not rich, I'm not a former pop star or a well-paid journalist. I can barely afford to eat. That couple who were looking for you—well, they found me. They heard I managed villas and they asked about you. They offered to pay me for information. Paid well. Do you think I really do all that awful cleaning for fun? I hate it! I hate the people, I hate the mess they leave. I hate it all. When I was in England, *I* had a cleaner, and now I am one!"

"But, Jo…" I pinched my arm to stay awake. "They didn't… pay you to kill us? Did they?"

"*They* didn't, no. But Suzanna Heffle did. When I gave her and your husband a lift. You see, she knew who I was. Oh, your husband wasn't part of it, don't worry—but she promised me 40,000 euro if you had an accident. 40,000 euro. Tess, that's life changing for me. She couldn't have you testify against her in court. I'm so sorry but I couldn't say no, could I? It's a shame because I'm sure you're both lovely people, but it's too much money for me to refuse. I know you understand."

"But Heffle's been… arrested." I could barely make my lips move anymore. Jo leaned closer, listening. "How can she pay you now?"

"I had a call this afternoon, from London. Someone told me I must go ahead. Half of the money had already been put in my bank account. The rest would follow when your death was confirmed."

"You told Lean's lot where I was too?" I asked. I was just about clinging on to consciousness.

"No, that wasn't me, you must have a Judas in your midst."

My eyes felt heavier and heavier; the ground seemed to get softer, and my senses were sending unexpected and uncoordinated signals to my brain. My fingers and toes felt numb, and I wanted to be sick.

"You'll… you'll…"

"What, I'll never get away with it? Oh, I think I will. I did with Bryn, and I will with you." I tried to grab hold of something, anything, but my fingers wouldn't respond. "I'll tell Jane you left my house very depressed. We had a picnic but you two stayed on. That's the last I saw of you both. She'll tell the police, and the coastguard will come looking and find your bodies in the morning. Unless of course you drift on the currents, and then you'll be spotted by a passing boat, maybe in a day or so. You get very bloated, floating around dead. Bryn certainly did. Hardly recognised him."

I saw Jason trying to move and reach out to me. Jo stood up and grabbed my hands.

"Come along, Tess, time for your jump. We'll do the old *death dance* like they did on the mainland opposite all those years ago. It only takes a few seconds to hit the rocks, and then it's all over. Bryn didn't even scream. The waves will soon wash away the blood. So come along, be a good girl." She pulled me to my feet and twisted me round. She was surprisingly strong for someone so slight. She was clearly determined to kill us.

The background slurred into a blur and I lost focus; I couldn't see. My sense of direction was gone. I felt sick. I couldn't find my balance, but I sensed I was getting closer to the edge. I could feel the sea rising up, soft droplets of spray from the crashing waves hitting the rocks below.

I saw the moon had started to rise. I remembered my first night on Paxos, then I thought of my parents: how had they felt when they knew they were about to die, or had they never known? I thought of Jake cradled in my arms, his head on my thighs, bleeding and unconscious. I thought of Jane, I thought of Sven, and then I thought of Jason and our brilliant, beautiful night in Lakka, making love under the moon, the same moon that was about to watch me die.

I could hear the wind and feel my breathing slowing down. Then I felt a jolt and I fell, but I didn't fall into air. I fell onto the hard short grass on the top of the arch. I looked round and saw Jason; he'd grabbed Jo's foot and was pulling her over. She lost her balance.

Struggling to stay awake and fighting the poison, he wrestled with her and together

they rolled towards the edge. I heard her screaming at him; her fists hit his back, but he wouldn't let go. He rolled, pushed and crawled with her towards the edge.

"Jason!" I managed to shout. But I don't think he heard. He looked at me and spoke just two, strained words.

"Love you."

Then, as if in a dream, I was losing consciousness. My head fell back, heavy. My muscles wouldn't work. The last thing I saw was Jason and Jo rolling over the edge of the Tripitos Arch.

As I lost consciousness, I heard a thin distant voice coming from my phone. It was DCI Green.

"TESS,

"TESS,

"TESS!"

22. Waking

Jason. Where was Jason? I was dreaming of him and those precious hours we'd spent together in Two Rock Bay. How we swam from the boat in the early summer sun, the glistening water forming droplets on wet, naked skin. The astounding revelation of who he really was...

Then I opened my eyes and came back to reality. As I crawled into consciousness, I could make out the now familiar sound of Greek being spoken outside the room. In amongst the rapid-fire words, I picked out my own name: *Tess Anderson*. The constant blip from the monitor by the bed became uncomfortably loud as I fought the pain and eased myself up on the pillows. Snatches of what had happened were seeping back. I looked out of the window, the only relief from the stark white walls of the hospital room, to see the beckoning blue sky and sense the rising heat of the Corfu sun.

Slowly, I eased myself up a little further. Every part of me seemed to hurt. I caught a glimpse of a stranger in the mirror above the sink: was that really me? There was dried blood on my cropped, newly blonde hair. When I raked my fingers through it, I saw my nails were broken, my wrists were bruised. I looked down at my legs, scarred by raised, red cuts. I clasped my hands together, wishing I was holding his.

I needed answers. I manoeuvred myself out of bed as carefully as I could and sat down on the side of it, trying to make sense of those last few days... Who were my betrayers and who were my friends? What had really happened last night? Had he died too? Did he mean it, when he said he loved me? Whatever the answers, I knew it wasn't over yet. I was still in danger.

There was a knock on the door. A doctor walked in, accompanied by a policewoman. Grave-faced, they stared at me as I waited, in silence, for them to tell me the news I was desperate to hear.

"What happened?" I mouthed. My last memory was looking at the moon after Jason and Jo had gone over the edge. The policewoman spoke.

"The English Inspector called us. We got the local police on Paxos to go by road, and to send their patrol boat round to the arch by sea." I didn't dare ask questions. I just waited for them to tell me what I feared, but had to know.

"We found you unconscious on the top of the arch. You were close to the edge; you're very lucky you didn't go over too."

I remembered Jason's beautiful blue eyes the day he rescued me. I could hear his music playing in my mind, as I recalled the precious memory of our making love on the boat in the bay. Without his sacrifice, it would have been me dead on those rocks in the waves. I'd never forget his last words. I knew now that I loved him too, but I'd never be able to tell him. The thought of that was agonising. The doctor spoke. I tried to focus on what she was saying.

"You are very lucky, Mrs Anderson. The effects of the poison have all but gone; you're just suffering from shock, and some olds cuts have been reopened by being dragged over the ground. You may have a bit of a headache for a while, and you could feel sick too."

"Have you told anyone where I am?" I asked.

"Yes," said the police officer. "Detective Chief Inspector Green knows, and he's told your friend Jane. She's on her way to collect you, to take you back to Paxos."

"We've ordered a water taxi for you; you need to rest," added the doctor, looking at the monitor by the bed.

"We've also told your husband, Mrs Anderson: he is your next of kin, according to your passport. He's flying to Corfu to see you tomorrow. He said to tell you he loves you and he wants to take you home."

"What?"

"That's the message he asked us to pass on to you."

What on earth was going on? Why did Sven want me back? Because Heffle was in trouble? Was he spinelessly crawling back to me, knowing he'd made a mistake?

"What's happened to Jo?" I asked. "The woman who poisoned me?"

"She died when she hit the rocks."

I shuddered. I wasn't sorry that Jo was dead—after everything she'd done to us—but the idea of Jason meeting the same fate was unbearably painful. An image came into my mind of him lying in a mortuary. I blinked away tears. "Did he suffer at all?"

"Did who suffer, Mrs Anderson?" the doctor said.

"Jason. The man I was with. Did he suffer at all?" I could only hope it had happened quickly. It was too much to think of Jason in pain.

The doctor hesitated. "You've been unconscious, so no one has told you, Mrs Anderson."

"Told me what?" I felt sick. I couldn't bear the thought of never seeing him again. All I'd have left were precious memories.

"About Mr Howard."

"Please don't say his body has drifted away to sea. Please say you've found him."

"Yes, we found him," she said softly. I could barely listen, my hands clasped together, my whole body trembling.

"We found him on the ledge. Jo, your attacker went over and died on the rocks below, but Mr Howard—he must have twisted round somehow and landed on the ledge."

"Landed on the ledge?"

"Yes, at the very end of the arch."

"Sorry." I shook my head, trying to take it in. "You're saying he didn't go over the edge?"

"He was unconscious too, which probably stopped him falling off, but we found him."

Did that mean what I thought it meant? "Are you—are you saying he's alive?" I burst out. I could barely believe it.

"I do hope so; he's in the room next door."

"Is he okay?"

"He has more bruises and cuts than you, but yes, he should make a full recovery."

Tears flooded my face, stinging the cuts on my cheek. I held my aching head. The doctor asked if I needed some painkillers, but I shook my head. I just needed Jason.

"Can I see him? Please," I said.

"Of course," said the doctor. "If he's up to seeing you. I'll go and see if he's awake and I'll ask him to come in."

*

Soon I heard a familiar voice.

"Hey you." He stood there in the doorway. Jason, my hero, my star.

"Hey," I replied, my eyes meeting his. He grinned when he looked at the monitor by my bed. "Your heart rate has shot up. You're obviously pleased to see me."

I looked up at him, dark bruises on his forehead and an angry, raised cut on his chin.

"My heart is pleased to see you. I think it would be broken if you hadn't survived."

The staff left the room to give us some peace. Jason's scratched and battered hands took mine. He gently squeezed my trembling fingers, leaned forward and kissed me on the lips.

"Saving your life is getting to be a bit of a habit, "he said.

271

"Can we ease off on the danger soon?"

"I'm not sure I could stand the boredom." I tried to smile. "Not having people after me: mad criminals and psychotic murderers."

"I don't think there are any left, are there?" he asked, his face close to mine, his eyes as bright and blue as ever.

"Well, I don't think Suzanna Heffle's too pleased with me."

"I think she's got enough to worry about. Besides, the nurse showed me a copy of the London evening paper online. There's the picture I took of her throwing coffee over you at Yan's Bar with the caption: *Heffle Loses It*. According to the report she's in custody in London."

So that explained Sven's sudden change of heart: he was just trying to distance himself from his lover, whose entire life was about to implode. It was unpleasant, realising what kind of man I'd been married to all these years, but nothing that Sven did could really hurt me anymore—not now that I knew Jason loved me. He loved me, and he'd risked his life to save me. Did I love him too? If I didn't already, I knew that I definitely could. "On that subject," I said lightly, "Sven's flying out to see me! I've just been told. Apparently he wants to take me home." I rolled my eyes, but Jason had turned away.

"Oh, I see." He let go of my hands and sat down in a chair near the bed. He looked exhausted. "That's an interesting development."

"Let's worry about that later," I said. "For now, I just want to say thank you."

"What for?" he said wearily.

"For saving my life. Again! I'm so sorry I keep putting you in danger."

"Hey, it's fine." He was trying to be brave, but I could see he was still in pain. "Listen, Tess. It feels like we've been on the run for ages. It's been fun—so much fun—it's been a blast, in fact. But maybe it's time for me to cast you adrift again. Go back to real life."

I stared at him. "What do you mean?"

"We've both got lives elsewhere… responsibilities. You're an ace reporter! You need to go where the stories are…"

I was too stunned to speak. All this time trying to decide how I felt about Jason—and he was the one rejecting me. I couldn't make sense of it. Had the Tripitos Arch been one close shave too many? I could hardly blame him for that. Or maybe I'd kept him at arm's length for too long; I couldn't blame him for that either. Then why had he said he loved me? Had it just been the heat of the moment? Unless—unless, no, had Jason had misunderstood me. Did he think I'd chosen Sven?

"I'm so glad I met you, Tess," he was saying, "and I don't regret it for a second—any of it. You're an extraordinary woman—"

"Jason," I broke in. "I hope you don't think—" But I couldn't get the words out. I felt myself swaying, the room spinning round. I was dizzy, too dizzy to talk. I could hardly think, let alone speak. "Sorry, Jason, I'm going to be…" And I was. I threw up all over my unflattering hospital gown. Jason called for help and left me with a nurse.

Once I was clean again, I was ordered back to bed, despite my protests. As soon as my head touched the pillow, exhaustion began to take over. I couldn't keep my eyes open for long. There'd be time to explain to Jason later. We'd got our wires crossed, that was all. I wanted him, not Sven. In spite of what he'd said, I was sure he wanted me too…

When I woke up, Jason had gone. He'd been discharged and returned to Paxos. He'd left me a note on the little stand by the bed.

'Hope you feel better soon. I'll be on *Sea Biscuit*. *Please come and say goodbye. Jason x'*. Goodbye? I felt sad. He really was going to sail out of my life forever.

*

After sleeping, I felt physically better, if not emotionally. The doctor said I could go, and I got the sea taxi to Gaios. On the way I turned on my phone and found a text from Sven.

'Tess, so sorry you were attacked but so relieved you're OK. I'm coming to take you home. Let's make it work. I'll do anything. S xxx'

Yeah, just because Heffle was no longer available. I turned my phone off again. I'd reply to him later. We'd have to meet, I decided. But not to get back together. The opposite, in fact. Whatever happened with Jason, I wanted to draw a line under that whole chapter of my life. It was time to put Sven behind me, once and for all.

I arrived to find Jane there, waiting for me with a taxi. She was devastated about what Jo had done—she kept apologising, saying over and over that she'd had no idea; she just couldn't believe it. "It wasn't your fault," I told her. "Jo fooled us all." We talked through the events on the arch. It was hard to believe in the glorious sunshine that it had all really happened.

Back at the villa, we sat in the garden. Dave came out with a pot of tea. He looked pale and shaky. He barely spoke, except for a brief "Hello", after which he went back into the house, leaving Jane and me alone.

"Is Dave okay?" I asked.

"No, is the short answer. He's on anti-depressants. He's barely talking. He's waking up in the night, sweating, having nightmares. He's got himself so wound up about all of this. I've seen him a little depressed before, but never this bad."

"Oh, Jane, I'm sorry, that's awful."

"I keep pushing him to have counselling." She turned around to check he was still inside the villa and not listening. "I'm pretty shaken up too, but I'm not reacting like him. We both need to be strong; the Leans are dead now." She sighed. "But let's talk about you and Sven for a minute." I'd told her he was flying over. "You're not going to take him back, are you? Please tell me you're not."

"God, no! My mum would have told me to work at it, fight to stay together—that's what she did, after all. It worked for her and Dad. But Sven's just gone too far. It's too little, too late."

"Well, that's a relief!" Jane poured the tea. "And Jason?" She passed me a cup.

"I wish I knew. When I spoke to him in the hospital… he sort of, went cold on me. He left me a note—said I should find him on the boat to say goodbye." I shook my head. "I really thought we had a chance. He obviously saw it differently."

"Are you sure?" Jane said. "You'd both been through a lot. Maybe you misunderstood him—or he misunderstood you. Did you tell him about Sven coming over?"

I nodded.

"Well, that could be it, then!" she said. "He probably thinks you're getting back with Sven, and he's no longer wanted *en voyage,* as they say."

"I thought that too, but… wouldn't he have at least asked me? Instead of just… giving up?"

"I don't know, Tess. You've given him mixed messages for ages." Jane sipped her tea. "You can hardly blame him for being confused. I'm sure you can work it out when you see him."

"It might be too late then. If he's already making plans to leave."

"Well, what have you said to Sven? That's one thing we can sort out, at least."

"I told him I'd meet him at Yan's Bar. Eleven o'clock tomorrow morning."

"I want to be there, Tess. To make sure he doesn't upset you."

"Thanks, Jane," I said. "But I need to do this alone."

Jane went into Lakka to buy some food. I sat in the sun in the peace of her garden for a little while longer, watching fluffy white clouds as they hurried by above me. I hadn't felt this relaxed—or safe—for a really long time, and yet I wasn't happy. Jason was slipping away from me, and I didn't know why. Was Jane right? Had he misunderstood about Sven, or had Jason and I just run our course? I thought of the Restless Lovers song: *Our Weekend, Our Affair.* Was that all it had been for him? A brief

275

affair? I grabbed my phone and dialled his number. Whatever the truth—no matter how hurtful—I had to know. If there was a chance of salvaging things, I couldn't just let him walk away. The call went to voicemail. I hung up and sent a text instead: *Jason, we must talk, Tess x*'

I went inside and took a very long, cool shower. My bruises and cuts were too sore for hot water. Then I sat outside again, drying my hair in the sun. Dave was nowhere to be seen. I moved a sunbed into the shade and fell asleep.

"Hey, sleepy head. Tea?" It was Jane. "How are you feeling?"

"Oh." I yawned. "Better than I was. What time is it?"

"6:30."

"Oh wow, is it really that late?" I sat up and groaned. "God, I feel stiff. These bruises are hurting."

"You look better than I thought you would." She squatted down beside me and took my hand. "So good to have you back here, Tess." I smiled. "Food will be ready in an hour if you're up to it. It's a recipe I got from Maria, her grandmother's"

"Yes, that sounds good. I'm pretty hungry actually. Where's Dave?"

"He went for a walk; don't ask, he's just not really here. I'm not sure what's going on in his head."

"He'll come out of it," I offered. "Give him time."

I helped Jane set a table but did a double take.

"Four places, Jane? Is there a guest?"

"Oh, just some travelling troubadour," she laughed. "And I think I can hear his taxi arriving now."

I put the last knives and forks down.

"Jane, what are you up to?"

"Just making sure you don't fuck it up!" And before I could answer, a taxi door slammed and Jason appeared, dressed in his finest, carrying an acoustic guitar.

"Jason! Hello, stranger." I wasn't hooked up to a monitor this time, but my heart reacted just as dramatically.

"Jane booked me for a gig," he said, looking sheepish. "It's just me, I'm afraid. The band can't make it."

"I always liked the singer best. Even though he was always a bloody poser! Bit of a small gig for you though, isn't it?" I laughed. There didn't seem to be any awkwardness between us at all. Surely Jane was right—it was just a misunderstanding. We'd be able to sort it all out.

"Well, our last proper gig was in Germany, in a football stadium, in front of twenty-four thousand people."

"Tonight there's an audience of… er… three! Well there will be when Dave gets back." I joked.

"And a cat," added Jane, as Mrs Boutari sauntered by and sat on the patio, no doubt hoping we'd drop some food.

"Hang on," I said, wanting to seize the moment. "I'm just going to change."

"Change?" Jane called after me, as I rushed into the house.

"Well, if I'm going to a wild rock gig with a star, I need to wear something more rock and roll," I shouted through the open door.

In the bedroom I took out the see-through white embroidered top Jason had bought me in Lakka. What the hell, I thought, as I took my bra off and put the top on. I slipped on my favourite little skirt and borrowed Jane's make-up. Brushing my hair and wishing it would grow more quickly, I went back outside where Jane was pouring wine. Dave had returned and was being introduced to Jason, who saw my outfit.

"Wow," he said. He looked sheepish again. "I'd better live up to this, hadn't I?"

"Let's hope my cooking lives up to it first!" said Jane, carrying out a serving dish.

"I hear Tess has become a bit of a fan of Briam after you two had your first meal together in Parga."

"And the other night in Lakka." I added.

"I got the recipe from Maria," said Jane. "It's her granny's, so it better be good."

"I think it depends what, or rather who, is served with it," I said, grinning, "and tonight's side orders are perfect."

We sat and ate slowly. The mood was relaxed, although Dave, who'd only just returned, was still sullen, quiet and nervous, picking at his food. He wouldn't look at any of us. I nudged Jane and nodded towards her husband, but she just shook her head and frowned. I stole a few glances at Jason: sometimes he looked back; sometimes he didn't. It was hard to gauge exactly what he was thinking, but the look on his face when he first saw my outfit had convinced me he wasn't quite over me yet.

The evening turned into night and the moon stood in for stage lights with citronella candles flickering around the patio. Jason sat on a single chair, strumming his guitar, as Jane and I sat on the ground in front of him on cushions. Dave excused himself and went inside, apologising for having a headache and needing to lie down.

Jason played three songs in a row—songs which Jane and I knew the words to by heart—including *Thanks, Janine*, which he'd played for me in Suffolk. We were singing along when Jane got up and grabbed my hands.

"You dancing?" she asked, or rather ordered, as she pulled me to my feet. It was wonderful, and we both fell apart laughing as Jason said in his best rock star voice.

"Hello, Lakka! And this is my new song, it's called *Show Me How to Love Again*, and it's for a good friend of mine who keeps getting me to save her life. This is for Tess Anderson, who, I think… is in the audience somewhere here tonight."

I laughed and waved, shouting, "Over here, in the mosh pit!"

He started singing. *"You said you could never love again, but I knew you had a vacant heart. The night in the bay, your lips meeting mine, two bodies together, our hands entwined…"*

As I listened to the lyrics, I felt the smile disappear from my face. I burst into tears. It was so beautiful. I couldn't believe someone could write something so wonderful just for me. Jane hugged me as Jason played on. When he ended, we clapped—but it all got too much for me, and I rushed inside. Locking myself in the bathroom, I sat on the floor, put a towel over my head and howled. It all flooded out—not just the last few days but all of it, every bit of emotional tension I'd been holding back. I cried for my mum and my dad; I cried for Jake. I sobbed with relief that I'd seen the end of the Leans and the madwoman, Jo.

I had to pull myself together, wipe the tears from my face and get out there to tell Jason I loved him. Tell him Sven was finished for good. If he rejected me, I'd just have to live with it, but I had to take that chance. Jason was too good to lose. I took some deep breaths, undid the bolt, turned off the light and walked into the garden. But he'd gone. I was too late.

"Where's Jason?" I asked looking around. Jane was alone, stacking plates.

"He left, walked back to Lakka."

"But why?"

"He wouldn't say. When you ran off like that... He thought you didn't like the song—or rather the sentiment behind it. I tried to explain, but he didn't believe me. He thought I was just trying not to hurt his feelings. Then Dave came in, wanting some painkillers, and Jason said he'd give us some space." She looked at me, her face full of concern. "Tess, he's leaving Paxos tomorrow. I think you've really blown it."

23. Plain Sailing?

Morning brought the sound of shouting. I lay in bed, listening to Jane and Dave arguing, wondering what was wrong. I heard Jane shriek and a door slam, the window in my room shook in its frame. I'd never heard them argue like that, nor had I heard Jane scream that way in all the years I'd known her. There was a sudden silence, then footsteps going to the gate. Someone had left. I knew it was Dave when Jane opened my door and climbed onto the bed beside me, crying. She hugged me, and whispered,

"Don't ask. Just don't ask. Sorry, Tess."

"Hey, what's going on?" I asked, cradling my friend. She looked at me, tears streaming down her face. She was trembling, and struggling for breath. "Hey love, calm down," I said. "Whatever it is, we can do this."

"I can't believe it. Why didn't he tell us, tell DCI Green?"

"Tell us what? Tell DCI Green what? Jane, what's happened?"

"It was Dave," she said quietly. "Dave told Crusher Lean where you were."

"What?" I couldn't believe what I was hearing. "Seriously? But..."

"I'm so sorry, Tess. He's admitted telling Lean's men you were here in the villa. Fucking stupid idiot! I can't believe it. He's already given a statement to the police; he just hadn't given one to me, until last night."

"I sat up and shook my head. Mrs Boutari wandered in, took one look and scooted out.

"Dave wouldn't do that," I said, unable to take it in. Jane held her head in her hands and sobbed.

"He bloody did. Crusher Lean sent his thugs to see Dave once they'd tracked me down. They got my car number when I drove you away from your house. They threatened him, said they'd kill me if he didn't tell them where you were."

"Oh, Jane, the absolute idiot."

"If only he'd told the DCI, they could have set a trap."

"So where does that leave you and Dave?"

"Not sure. Right now, nowhere. He was doing it to protect me, but come on, Tess—he should have gone to the police straightaway."

I got up and grabbed a box of tissues from the top of the drawer unit. I sat beside Jane. "Come on, head up, let's wipe those tears."

"Sorry."

"No need to be, and stop crying, the box is almost empty." She swallowed a sob and sat still while I gently wiped her tear-stained face.

"At least I now know why he's been so weird recently," she said.

"It's obviously been weighing very heavily on him," I replied softly. "Look, if it helps, I forgive him. He was trying to protect you. I don't want to see you two break up over this. He's been such a good partner to you."

"He nearly got you killed!" she spluttered.

"But he didn't. We won, and the Leans and Heffle lost. Dave won't be charged with anything, will he?"

"I doubt he'll face charges," she said, wiping her tears. "He was threatened with menaces. I think any jury would feel sorry for him. And anyway, what could they charge him with? Withholding information? I think there are enough other people to charge in connection with the Leans."

"Look, Jane, you two need to talk. I'm going to Lakka. When Dave gets back, I want you to sort it out. I don't want your marriage to end because of me."

I got dressed quickly and walked down the hill as the heat rose. I was on a mission to find Jason before Sven arrived. His phone was still off. It was hurtful that Dave had betrayed me, but he'd only done it to protect Jane. I understood that. It wasn't as if he'd tried to kill me himself for money, like Jo had done. It was completely different. If I could forgive him, then Jane could too, eventually.

I got to *Sea Biscuit,* but the yacht was empty. Jason wasn't there. Ben the flotilla skipper was on his boat moored next to Jason's.

"Hi, Ben. Jason about?"

"He's just gone to get some stuff. He's due to sail off soon. I'm taking the flotilla out this morning as well. I've asked him to tag along. He seems pretty low right now—I don't know why. I think I can cheer him up though. I've got two women on one boat who're big fans of his. They've bet me I can't get him to come to Emerald Bay with us so they can swim with him. I think he's in there!"

"Oh," I said, wishing Ben hadn't been in such a talkative mood. "Well, can you tell him I need to see him urgently, before he leaves? Please, it's important." Ben nodded and shrugged.

I walked into Yan's Bar just as Sven's water taxi came up to the quayside.

"He ought to get a season ticket, it's cheaper," said Maria. Jane had told me she'd filled her in yesterday when she came into town to get the recipe for *Briam.* I took a deep breath as Sven walked towards me. I started to wobble and held the table to steady myself when I saw a big bunch of flowers in his hand. On his face was that familiar warm, Sven smile. He was wearing a white open shirt and tight chinos. It made my heart leap a little to see him, taking me back to better times. Maria looked at me and gave a quick shake of her head. I remembered Jake's phrase. "Keep it framed and focused." I repeated it and told myself to keep a cool head. I looked across at *Sea Biscuit* where Jason was back, loading two bags of food into the cockpit. He looked sad, like a lost Labrador.

"Tess! How lovely to see you," said Sven. "I'm so pleased you're out of hospital and on the mend. Can I get coffees?" He kissed me on the cheek. Maria nodded then raised her eyebrows as she threw me a glance and went to the kitchen to get the drinks.

"These are for you," he said, offering me the flowers. I laid them on the table but didn't sit down.

"So, you and Suzanna?" I asked.

"Finished, totally and utterly finished. When I realised what she'd done—and Jo! Oh my god, I'm so sorry. I had no idea about any of this! I'm really sorry my actions put you in danger, Tess. Look, I love you. Please come home with me."

"Sven, you saw that email she sent you. You knew she was connected with the solicitor in the Lean case. How could you have kept it all from me? You've broken my heart and our marriage."

"Tess, hey, those emails, I never really read them, took it in you know. Look, Tess, I know you, and if we both try, we can make it work, we can go back to the way we were." He stood beside me. He touched my hand. I pulled it away. Maria hurried back with two white cups and saucers.

"Sven, you sat here at this very table while your then-girlfriend threatened to destroy my most precious, most treasured possessions unless I agreed to save her career and not publish those emails. She was asking me to withhold evidence. I didn't see you objecting. She paid Jo to kill us! Now Jo's dead."

"I really didn't know. That was unforgivable. I'm so sorry. Come home, let's start again."

Maria coughed as she put the cups down on the table between us. She tapped my shoulder and nodded towards the quayside. I looked across and saw Jason walking towards us. Sven turned to see what had taken my attention.

"Oh… is this your lover boy coming over?" asked Sven. His tone changed to a sneer. "Some faded, ageing rock star?"

"Sven! Jason's shown me more love and care in the last ten days than you have in ten years." I was furious. "Look, I don't believe you're capable of going back to your old self, the Sven I fell in love with, and frankly, I could never trust you again."

"Sorry to butt in, Tess," said Jason walking up to us, "but I didn't want to go without saying goodbye. Ben's invited me to join the flotilla, I could do with the company." He turned to Sven. "I just want to say, Sven, that you'd better take damn good care of her. She's very special, and if you don't treat her well, you'll have me to answer for."

Sven sneered.

Maria suddenly ran to the bar. A moment later, music started booming out. She must have plugged her phone into the music system. The track was *Our Weekend, Our Affair*. It was clear where her vote was going.

"Do you remember this, Sven?" I said to my husband. "The song we started out to.

The song we first held hands to? The song Jane played at our wedding. Well, it's now the song we're going to end to, because the person I love now is the man who wrote it, the man who sings it, this man right here."

I turned to Jason. His face crumpled; tears welled up in his eyes. He couldn't speak.

"You're not serious?" Sven said. "I've come all this fucking way to bring you home!"

"Then I'm sorry to say you've had a wasted trip," I said.

Sven pushed Jason out of the way and stormed off, picking up the flowers from the table and hurling them to the floor. "You'll be back, Tess," he yelled as he left. "And Jason, she's not the dream princess you think she is. She's needy and vulnerable."

Jason smiled, taking both of my hands. I looked up at him.

284

"I like 'needy and vulnerable'," he said. "It sums me up too."

"Jason," I said, "just shut up and kiss me." Everyone's eyes were on us, but we didn't care.

"My mother has a recipe for wedding cakes too!" said Maria, rushing over to hug me the moment we finished kissing. We laughed. I could see Sven boarding his water taxi. He motored out of the bay and out of my life. Maria waved as Jason and I walked hand in hand to *Sea Biscuit*. As we reached the yacht, Jane ran down the road and threw her arms around me.

"You got the right guy in the end!" She gave me a hug. "Thought I'd miss you! Here, I guessed you might be off for a night or two, so I've brought your clothes." She handed me my bag. "And," she whispered, "that little top's in there!"

"Jane!" I blushed. "Thank you. How's Dave?"

"Relieved you've forgiven him. We'll get there. But what about you? And this guy! Talk about a dreamboat."

"Does she mean me or *Sea Biscuit*?" Jason asked.

Jane laughed. "A little bit of both, maybe!"

I kissed Jane goodbye, and Jason and I climbed aboard the boat. Jason blew her a kiss.

"You take care of her, Jason."

"I've got quite a good track record so far," he said, grinning. We undid the mooring lines and motored slowly away from the quay to the sounds of Jason's music coming from the café.

"Two Rock Bay sound good?" he asked, as I waved goodbye to Jane.

"Only if we can swim under the stars," I said, "and make love under Selene." I squeezed his hand, not wanting to let go.

"Under who? I don't do threesomes, not anymore. Not after that gig in Bristol!"

"What? Jason! Honestly. Selene, the moon, you idiot." I nudged him in the ribs. "Remember the wish I made at the well in your garden?" I said.

"Did it come true?" he asked, his eyes sparkling in the sun, the remains of a tear just visible on top of his cheek. It certainly had. Jason had seemed so out of reach back then, but now he was mine. "It just has." I grinned as I reached out my hands for his. Our lips were about to meet, when my phone rang. I considered ignoring it, but the screen showed the caller was DCI Green.

"You'd better take it," Jason said.

"Everything okay, Ted?" I asked.

"Tess, I'm in a park. I needed to make this call in private…"

I clasped Jason's hand. "What now?"

"People are rushing to give evidence against Heffle," the DCI continued. "The Lean's empire collapsing into a black hole is sucking a lot of people into it—including your husband, I'm afraid. He may be charged, too. We're picking him up from the airport when he lands."

"My soon-to-be ex-husband," I said, with a glance at Jason.

"The way the evidence is building, it looks like we'll have a queue of guilty pleas in the hope of lower sentences. We can't pin anything on the prime minister yet, though."

"I'll be back in a few weeks, Ted. I'll sharpen my reporter's pencil."

"Oh, I nearly forgot. Milly the care home worker?"

"Yes?" I held my breath, ready to hear the worst.

"…She's come round."

"Wow, brilliant news!" I shrieked, grinning.

"She wants to thank you for your bravery, Tess."

"It should be me thanking her for her bravery! I'll go and see her as soon as I get back. That's the best possible news, Ted, thank you!" Jason gave me a quizzical look; I just smiled and gave him a big thumbs up. "Milly!" I mouthed and he smiled broadly.

"…Tess", Ted sounded uneasy. I heard the sounds of the park behind him: children's voices, a dog barking. "I may have a good story for you."

"Oh?"

"I'm sending you something from my private email. Ever heard of an island called Poros?"

"I'm sure Jason will have. Why?"

"You might want to head there… just an anonymous tip-off from me, Okay? Let me just say a celeb rehab clinic nearby may be worth investigating, it could be hiding a major worldwide scandal. Be careful though, these guys make the Leans look small fry.

"I've got to go Tess. Check your email."

"Will do," I said, as he ended the call.

Jason smiled at me. "I believe we were in the middle of something…"

"Jason, hang on. How long would it take to get to Poros?"

"Hmm. Maybe seven or eight days, comfortably, less if we rushed. Why?"

"I'm not sure yet. But there might be a story there…"

"Fine by me. So long as we can swing by Two Rock Bay first?"

"Please." I grinned. We headed out of the bay as Ben's flotilla motored in line either side of us.

Jason shouted across to them, "Nice formation, Ben!"

"Well, we want to make sure you don't hit the reef out there, word has it you got a bit too close last time!"

"You cheeky bas…!" Jason laughed as I squeezed his hand.

"You've lost your bet, Ben, about getting Jason to Emerald Bay!" I shouted.

"That was made up, just to make sure you didn't mess it up!" He waved as the flotilla drifted away.

I looked at Jason. "He really is a cheeky bastard. Unless …it was your idea?"

"I'm saying nothing. Had you better tell Steve you're not coming back for a while?"

"He offered me extended leave earlier, so I'm taking it. I guess I should give him a news story though."

"Oh?"

"Yeah, something like: *Award winning Television reporter Tess Anderson, credited with helping to bring down the Lean crime network and expose a corrupt government minister, has tonight*

287

confirmed she's madly in love with once and future rock star, the very posy Jason L'Amour, who's saved her life on numerous occasions. Ms Anderson said, 'I've never been so in love, and plan to wear a very special top when we get to Two Rock Bay'. In other news…"

Jason laughed and put an arm around me. We waved goodbye to Ben's flotilla as we turned to head for the open sea and Two Rock Bay. I looked behind us at the entrance of Lakka Bay and saw a speedboat coming towards us at high speed.

"Jason, I don't want to worry you, but we're being followed. Look."

He spun round. "Pass me the binoculars, Tess." I did, but as he looked through them, his shoulders relaxed, and he laughed. "I don't think it's a problem." I watched as the speedboat came alongside. It was Maria.

"Yassas! You two might be too busy to cook for a few days! Here." She passed me a big bag. "There's some *spanakopita*, pizza and *baklava*. From all of us at the bar. On the house. Now go, and…. make fun. Have love!" She waved and roared off. I clutched his hand.

"Shall we *make fun* and *have love* Jason?"

"Well, the auto pilot is on." He grinned. I kissed him, and went below to put on my special top.

The End

Did You Enjoy This Book?

If so, you can make a HUGE difference.

For any author, the single most important way we have of getting our books noticed is a really simple one—and one which you can help with.

Yes, you.

Us indie authors and publishers don't have the financial muscle of the big guys to take out full-page ads in the newspaper or put posters on the subway.

But we do have something much more powerful and effective than that, and it's something that those big publishers would kill to get their hands on.

A committed and loyal bunch of readers.

Honest reviews of our books help bring them to the attention of other readers.

If you've enjoyed this book I would be really grateful if you could spend just a couple of minutes leaving a review (it can be as short as you like) on this book's page on your favourite store and website.

Killer in the Crowd,
by P N Johnson

Live music is in her blood, but as the death threats arrive, she fears there's a killer in the crowd.

Cath Edgley is a normal schoolteacher at a normal high school... until she hears the shocking news that fading rock star Raven Rain has been murdered.

Because, to Cath, Raven Rain is more than just a picture on a magazine – he was also the ex-lover of her missing mother, Betzy Blac, lead singer of '80s punk girl band, Décolleté. A woman who went missing over 30 years ago.

Warned by a string of mystery text messages to "trust no one", Cath is inspired to solve the mystery of her mum's disappearance, once and for all.

Cath finds herself thrust into the sordid underbelly of the '80s music scene, when rock and roll played second fiddle to the sex and drugs.

Along the way, she also finds herself playing a new role: unwitting replacement lead singer for Décolleté on their first tour in over 30 years.

Can Cath find the killers before she becomes their next victim?

Are the superstars she encounters all that they seem?

And what exactly happened to the punk superstar, Betzy Blac?

If you love mystery thrillers with a musical twist, then you'll love Killer in the Crowd, the debut novel from P N Johnson.

"Utterly compelling. Mystery in the music world."
    – Steve Harley – Cockney Rebel – singer, songwriter

"A real escapist page-turner with plenty of plot twists, oodles of drama and a compelling cast. Terrific."
    – Nick Crane, author and broadcaster

Acknowledgements

Thanks to Pete and Simon at Burning Chair for their continued enthusiasm and support.

To my writing friends who've encouraged and inspired me - Andrew McDonnell, Sally Harris, Jonathan Blunkell, Bridget Kinsella, Catherine O'Hanlon, Mair Stratton, Linda Taylor, Jill Whitehouse, Delyth Atkins, K.A. Lillehei, Carla Burns, Delianne Forget, Linda Friesen, Hazel Stephens and Arun Debnath to name a few.

Special thanks to my brilliant editor Lynsey White.

To Fi for everything.

And to Tess for letting me tell her story, and to you for reading it. Thank you, x.

About the Author

Phil's career in TV and radio saw him doing everything from tracking down criminals in Spain and going on high-octane police chases, to interviewing pop stars, politicians and celebrities. He's met the rich and powerful and the most needy and humble, and his writing reflects this. As he told us: "I love fast moving action thrillers which offer escapism, entertainment and excitement. My stories are for rainy days and lonely nights, sunny beaches and poolside bars. They're for anyone who enjoys great locations and gripping tales, with jeopardy, tension and a fight for justice, love, hopes and dreams."

After leaving university, Phil joined the BBC and enjoyed various roles from presenting a local radio breakfast show to being a TV Newsreader, Reporter and Producer for both BBC East and ITV Anglia. He also worked on BBC Breakfast Time in London, and wrote scripts for a BBC TV comedy show. He even found himself playing football against Radio 1 in a premier league stadium! Phil produced and presented documentaries and feature programmes, as well as being the face and voice of Crimestoppers in the eastern region for many years. He also created the successful TV series: "999 Frontline".

Phil wrote The Little Blue Boat children's books set on the Norfolk Broads, which were produced as a play. He lives near

Norwich with his wife Fi, a former nurse turned silversmith, and has three grown up children. Phil loves music, travelling, walking, and sailing, which he's written about for numerous magazines; but his passion is writing, and bringing exciting new characters with amazing stories to the page.

Phil is a member of the Crime Writers' Association and the Romantic Novelists' Association.

About Burning Chair

Burning Chair is an independent publishing company based in the UK, but covering readers and authors around the globe. We are passionate about both writing and reading books and, at our core, we just want to get great books out to the world.

Our aim is to offer something exciting; something innovative; something that puts the author and their book first. From first class editing to cutting edge marketing and promotion, we provide the care and attention that makes sure every book fulfils its potential.

We are:
- Different
- Passionate
- Nimble and cutting edge
- Invested in our authors' success

If you're interested in hearing more about our books, being the first to hear about our new releases or great offers, or becoming a beta reader for us, again please visit:

www.burningchairpublishing.com

More From Burning Chair Publishing

Your next favourite new read is waiting for you…!

Killer in the Crowd, by P N Johnson:

The Great Big Demon Hunting Agency, by Peter Oxley

Push Back, by James Marx

The Blue Bird Series, by Trish Finnegan
    Blue Bird
    Blue Sky
    Baby Blues

The Casebook of Johnson & Boswell, by Andrew Neil Macleod
    The Fall of the House of Thomas Weir
    The Stone of Destiny

By Richard Ayre:
    Shadow of the Knife
    Point of Contact

Run to the Blue

P N JOHNSON

Printed in Great Britain
by Amazon

31122338R00169